PRAISE FOR THE JAYNE THORNE, CIA LIBRARIAN SERIES

"*The Book of Spirits* is a fast-paced fantasy with so many of my favorite things—grimoires, layered character relationships, and a dragon! If you haven't started the Jayne series yet, now is your moment!"

 —Alisha Klapheke, *USA Today* **Bestselling Author of the** ***Bound by Dragons*** **Series**

"...An adrenaline-fueled, action-packed adventure bursting with magic, love, friendship, and betrayal. Jayne Thorne and her merry band of allies are the best kind of found family, and I was on the edge of my seat hoping they'd all make it through their latest trials alive. As the penultimate book in the Jayne Thorne series, *The Book of Spirits* perfectly sets up the final installment, building to a thrilling conclusion that left me breathless."

 —Lauren Thoman, bestselling author of *You Shouldn't Be Here*

"Joss Walker's *The Book of Spirits* has everything you could ever want in an epic fantasy: a spunky heroine, deep worldbuilding, magical monsters, a dash of romance, and a sentient dragon. The stakes are high, and the pacing is fast, making this the perfect read to dive into for a break from reality."

—**Meredith R. Lyons, award-winning author of** *Ghost Tamer*

"Vivid world-building, a page-turning mystery, and a smart, adventurous heroine in the process of discovering her own power and learning from her mistakes makes for another great addition to an outstanding urban fantasy series."

— **Jayne Castle,** *New York Times* **bestselling author of the Harmony series, on** *Master of Shadows*

"Light-hearted books can get a bad rap, as though making readers smile is somehow a weakness on the author's part... Walker has a light touch with [her] prose, and the likable characters breeze through many of their interactions. Which isn't to say that *Tomb of the Queen* lacks gravitas. No, there's a good story here with real edge-of-the-seat moments... It's fun from start to finish, and I'm going to keep my eye out for more from this "new" author."

—**Charles de Lint,** *The Magazine of Mystery & Science Fiction* **on** *Tomb of the Queen*

"Writer Joss Walker brings the magic back! It will take a witch with heart, humor, and book smarts–plus some killer kickboxing skills–to save the world, and Jayne Thorne is the witch we need now. Hold on tight, you urban fantasy fans, because once you open *Tomb of the Queen*, the action doesn't stop until the last thrilling page."

— **Laura Benedict, bestselling author of the** *Bliss House* **trilogy, on** *Tomb of the Queen*

JOSS WALKER

the SCROLLS of TIME

JAYNE THORNE, CIA LIBRARIAN BOOK SIX

TWO TALES PRESS

The Scrolls of Time
© 2025 by J.T. Ellison

Digital ISBN: 978-1-948967-79-2
Trade ISBN: 978-1-948967-81-5
Hardcover ISBN: 978-1-948967-80-8

Cover design © The Killion Group, Inc.

For more, visit Two Tales Press.

"A librarian gets recruited by the CIA to help track down rare and magical books... Jayne Thorne has just discovered that magic is real, and the CIA needs her help. After a crash course in Magic 101, she's sent to Ireland to investigate a rare manuscript. The start of this series is everything I love about urban fantasy: a wise-cracking heroine who diffuses tense situations with a joke, plenty of adventure, and an interesting magical world that exists alongside our own. I can't wait for more adventures with Jayne!"

— **John McDougall, Murder by the Book,** on *Tomb of the Queen*

"Joss Walker's debut had me completely under her spell. Part cleverly plotted fantasy and part thriller, I was drawn in by her charming bookworm of a librarian with magical powers, dashing Irish rogue, and the complicated battle between 'good' and evil. Addictive and utterly delightful, this is a book to treasure."

— **Paige Crutcher, author of** *The Orphan Witch,* **on** *Tomb of the Queen*

"*Tomb of the Queen* is a relatable, fun romp of a thrill ride! The characters are lifelike and well-fleshed out, and the magic is done in a unique way that I have never seen before. I loved this book, and I'm sure that I will read it over and over again!"

— **Julie L. Kramer,** *USA Today* **bestselling author of** *Of Curses and Scandals,* **on** *Tomb of the Queen*

"This book was just my cup of tea! Or perhaps, my slice of pie? 🥧 Jayne Thorne, CIA Librarian, is a relatable, lovable, and smart heroine dead set on vanquishing evil. A genius mythology twist, swoony budding romance, and gorgeous library imagery, paired with non-stop action, makes *Tomb of the Queen* a winner for fans of urban fantasy. Stop everything and read this book!"

— **Ashley McLeo, author of the bestselling *Starseed Trilogy*, on *Tomb of the Queen***

ALSO BY JOSS WALKER

Jayne Thorne, CIA Librarian Series

The Scrolls of Time

The Book of Spirits

The Prophecy of Wind

The Keeper of Flames

Master of Shadows

Tomb of the Queen

Novellas

A Betrayal of Magic

The Eighth Road

The Guardians Mini-Series

Guardians of Power

Guardians of Fury

Guardians of Silence

Writing as J.T. Ellison

Standalone Suspense

Last Seen

A Very Bad Thing

It's One of Us

Her Dark Lies

Good Girls Lie

Tear Me Apart

Lie to Me

No One Knows

The Lt. Taylor Jackson Series

The Wolves Come at Night

Field of Graves

Where All the Dead Lie

So Close the Hand of Death

The Immortals

The Cold Room

Judas Kiss

14

All the Pretty Girls

The Dr. Samantha Owens Series

What Lies Behind

When Shadows Fall

Edge of Black

A Deeper Darkness

A Brit in the FBI Series,

Cowritten with Catherine Coulter

The Sixth Day

The Devil's Triangle

The End Game

The Lost Key

The Final Cut

My darling, dearest, and most appreciated readers:
This one is for you.
May your lives be blessed with magic.

PROLOGUE

The world was chaos and blood.

The Torrent had become a rushing river of obsidian, studded with something that couldn't really be rocks but felt like it. The lioness didn't have the capacity to find another name for it, though, nor could she identify the magical phenomenon that might account for the hard thing she now gripped tightly, digging in with both claws. Around her, bodies swarmed—the bodies of things like her, and the bodies of things not like her. Gray creatures with wings and horns and snarling mouths, with beaks and talons and pig snouts, lashed out against the creatures that tried to stand their ground within the Torrent. A weight pressed down on her mind, so heavy that she couldn't even think of what these creatures were. She couldn't even think what *she* was. *Rogue. Master.* Those words meant nothing now.

She couldn't even remember her own name.

Her body struggled against her mind. She shifted from lioness to hawk to mouse to lioness again. She had no control over her being. Her spine began to lengthen and her limbs retracted into her. She shrieked in agony. *Submit,* tolled a voice inside her mind. The same voice that had drawn her inexorably into the Torrent. *Submit to me.*

She lashed out in fury. Her serpent's fangs embedded in a scaly gray leg, and the Wraith in question shrieked, flinging her away. She hit the Torrent with a splash and fought to swim back to a rock, fighting against the flailing limbs and gnashing teeth of a dozen other Rogues and Wraiths.

You are mine, pressed the voice, and she felt herself changing again. Even forced to submit, she screamed her defiance.

She couldn't remember who she was, but she remembered that she belonged to no one. She would not yield.

Another Rogue in the form of a stag bellowed and flung up his head, catching a Wraith on his antlers. The Wraith snarled and wrestled free. It grabbed his antlers and lifted him bodily, tossing him into the raging river. He lowed, and the lioness-now-snake heard the snap of a leg. A moment later his head dipped beneath the surface of the Torrent. His body washed downriver and was gone.

Submit, the voice growled.

Another Rogue hissed at the command. She was a bat, trying gamely to flutter up amidst Wraiths a hundred times her size. One of them swatted her like she was no more than a fly, and she went tumbling. She hit the Torrent and it dragged at her wings, rushing her down toward the lioness-now-snake's rock.

A tail whipped out, coiled around the bat. Brought it to safety. A moment later, the lioness-now-snake wondered why she had done it. Why had she felt the need to save this pitiful creature, when she'd watched another of her kind die without much care?

Kin, a part of her mind struggled to say.

The Wraith that had swatted the bat fixed malicious black eyes on her. She fought against her snake form. Changing forms had always been so easy, the matter of a whim—now it was like pushing against sludge. She shoved, feeling her rage grow. She might not know who she was, but she knew *what* she was. She'd always been at home in her skin, and she'd never known a time when she couldn't change into whatever she wanted. Now the struggle enraged her. She would not be beholden to one form, not by any master. She was a Rogue, she was the best of the Rogues—

The Wraith swooped down, and something in her snapped like a band. Her snake form was gone and the lioness was back in an instant. She roared her defiance and fixed her teeth on his leg, ripping it from his measly body. She paid no mind to the way the Wraith's acid blood burned her mouth. The Wraith screamed and raked its claws across her skull.

Release him, boomed the voice in her mind, enveloping her so completely that her jaws began to loosen before the words had fully penetrated her brain. And then it floated to the surface, as if on a bubble of air. Her name. It flowed through her like lightning.

Release him!

But Gina Labelle had always been a contrarian.

At the last moment, she tightened her jaws. The Wraith screamed. Gina flipped over on top and brought her back claws up for a disemboweling move. *RELEASE HIM,* the voice in her mind howled. Pain lanced through her entire body, she was being crushed and shredded all at once, she couldn't stand it— she let the Wraith go and kicked him off her rock. She flopped over onto her belly, panting.

She would have no master. Rogues were the superior species. She roared. *We will have freedom,* she shouted to the rest of the bedraggled Rogues. *We will have no master!*

The Wraith she'd fought snarled. He'd gotten to his feet, or rather, one foot. His left leg stayed an inch off the ground and leaked rivers of black that hissed and spread like tar when they touched the Torrent.

We can prevail, she said, her voice strong in their minds.

Something landed in the Torrent behind her.

He was too large to comprehend, this Master who'd imposed his will upon her. His legs were tree trunks that stood firm against the rushing Torrent, and his body rose above them all. He had a thin, gray face slashed through in the middle by an eye patch. Horns curled Wraith-like from the top of his head. His one eye blazed, turning the naturally midnight blue even darker as a huge, furious Wraith advanced toward Gina from her other side.

Odin Allfather reached down and picked up the lioness as if she were a kitten. She shrank in his hands—or did he grow?—and he brought her up until they were face to snarling face.

You are full of rage, he said. He sounded amused.

Gina growled. Words between minds were too intimate for the likes of him. As a Rogue, she would speak only with other Rogues.

Soon enough, there will be space for that rage. Soon enough. But for now, you must keep it inside you. And you really must leave my favorite pet alone.

He gestured, and the Wraith who'd attacked her flapped toward him. The Allfather touched a hand to the Wraith's leg, and the river of black blood dried to a sticky tar. *You will serve me,* he told Gina, sending the Wraith away.

She could not resist answering that. *Never! I serve no man, master, or god.*

Odin laughed. His mouth gaped like the entrance to eternity, surrounded by teeth as clear as crystal, as sharp as knives. *You will serve me, because I will give you what you want in exchange. You and Alastor, my blunt instruments against the meddling humans, the Master who thinks she has the power of Gods.*

Gina bared her teeth. This was, perhaps, the moment she died. She'd prepared for such a moment countless times, and she would face it with grace. *And if I refuse?*

Odin's smile didn't falter. With an expression as gentle and beatific as a father's, he turned. Then he flung her into the Torrent.

She hit the dark magic and was sucked under immediately. It wasn't really water, but the liquid filled her, pressing against her mouth and nose and making it impossible to breathe. She fought and splashed her way to the surface to find that she was already many meters downstream. The writhing mass of Wraiths and Rogues continued to fight and change and snarl and scream. And barely visible, on her rock: her daughter, still in bat shape, watching her wash downstream with no apparent recognition whatsoever.

ODIN, still smiling, watched the river carry her away. He laughed again, a booming noise that frightened all the creatures under his control, near and far. He hadn't felt such delight in centuries, but watching the scared, confused faces of his new army of Rogues, his stone heart shuddered with something akin to joy, if he could feel such a thing.

The checklist was filling up.

Wraiths. Rogues.

Now he needed those infernal goddesses to bend to his will, and his war would come to an end. He would rule again, powerful and majestic, the rock against which all thought and fury crashed.

Yes, he'd lost the Wraith formerly known as Ruth Thorne; a pity. But what he gained by capturing the Rogues, and Gina Labelle, more than balanced the scales. With that woman leading an entire army of creatures, he could command... It had been unfathomable for so long, but now, thanks to the idiot Thorne girl, all things were possible. She had broken his choke-hold on the Torrent, yes, siphoned off parts of his power for herself, but in so doing, she was helping him remake the world.

It was time she understood who, exactly, she was fighting against.

Snarling animals swiped at one another, their loyalties forgotten. Their very humanity forgotten. The creatures swarmed the Torrent, confused and ready to fight anything that moved. Until the Allfather brought his hands together and sent out a command through the thousands of tethers that connected him to each Rogue. *Silence!*

They stopped. Some of them sat. Some of them cocked their heads in confusion as though they didn't understand why his word held such power over them. It was understandable: Odin had drunk the well at the base of the World Tree dry long before any of these pathetic shapeshifters had been born. It had blessed him with the ability to sort between the tethers binding these Rogues to him so he could control the movements of one particular Rogue or command them as a whole. It had allowed him to cast his Tether spell over the whole world, combing through the population of Earth's pitiful normal people and weak Adepts and calling only the Rogues to him.

Here in the Torrent, their magic would serve him and only him, strengthening this pocket of the vast river of dark stars and creating a well for Odin to draw on. Almost unlimited power—until he drank the magic dry, and the Rogues became husks of their former selves. But by then, he would have achieved his objective. By then, he would have the world in the palm of his hand.

He smiled. The pathetic so-called Torrent Control Organization had sent its best and brightest Masters to defeat him and had failed. Even their prizefighter, with all her Totems and the power of the goddesses behind her, had been no match for him. She'd fallen right into his trap and led an army of Rogues up to his door. Now, those very Rogues would be the TCO's undoing.

He cast his will over the silent Rogues. *Give me your power.*

As one, they opened themselves to the Torrent, and the dark magic began to flow.

Odin Allfather let his head fall back. Stars swirled in his vision, and magic filled him to the brim. He roared, and all over Earth, tiny pockets opened in the air, spitting out Wraiths to swoop down on the populace. *Nothing will stop me now.*

He did not notice the human form, tiny by comparison, crouched in his filthy shirt and camo pants next to a defeated tigress. The man watched and waited.

ONE

I n Nashville, Jayne Thorne, squashed on her couch next to her sister, Sofia, was staring at the kitten-sized dragon that preened on her lap. With some effort, she closed her mouth. "Hayden? You know how to turn back time? Not just pause it for a few moments, but actually go back to a certain point?"

"*What?*" Henry Thorne almost levitated out of his armchair.

The dragon dipped his snout in a little nod.

"That's not...possible." Henry pushed his spectacles up his nose and fixed Hayden with a severe look. "Stopping time, yes. But traveling through the space-time continuum isn't achievable with the technology we have. We can get into the Torrent, maybe reversing through a portal—"

Hayden snorted a tiny plume of smoke in irritation. *You say it is not possible because you have not done it,* he said in Jayne's mind. *Dragon magic is different. We have the ability to do whatever we want in time. No portals or Torrent needed. It lives within us.*

Jayne put a hand up to her temple. Magical theory had never been her strong suit. And since no one could hear Hayden except for her, she was left to interpret. She told her father, "He says dragon magic is different." Then, to Hayden: "What are you saying? Are you from another time?"

Are you? Hayden's round fire and cobalt eyes pierced through hers, seeming to reach down into her very soul. *You are blessed with powers that others do not have, Jayne. Is that not because you have gathered it from other times? Having totems makes you different. The goddesses you access do not exist in the now. They are trapped in their own time. You are the one that travels to them through space and time. This is not dreaming. You have engaged in this astral projection without thinking of what it is you do. And that is because of me.* He stretched then hopped off her lap with a pleased expression, his wings fluttering.

"What is he saying?" Sofia asked.

"That every time I talk to the goddesses I'm astral projecting. Traveling through space and time."

Jayne's fingers slid around to her forehead. She was pretty sure she was of the now. She hadn't tried talking to the goddesses since the abysmal failure at Kirkjufell. She couldn't bear the thought of facing their disappointment. What if they wanted to take their totems back? What if they wanted Jayne to find someone more deserving? She wouldn't blame them. Odin had set a pretty trap and they'd walked right into it. And now look where they were. Huddled in her apartment, Cillian in a cage going mad from Odin's siren call, Tristan and Vivienne lost in the Torrent. Could things get any worse?

A lone siren began to wail through the city. Jayne grimaced and reached for her now-cold tea. It was as if the Allfather had read her thoughts and sent a little greeting. Cities across the world had repurposed their emergency alert warning systems to calibrate for Wraith attacks, and it looked like the monsters were targeting Nashville again. A moment later, all of their cell phones blared with a text alert. *WRAITHS HAVE BEEN SPOTTED IN YOUR LOCATION. Stay inside, keep the lights off, and do not engage. You will be notified when the area is free of danger.*

Jayne ought to leap up. Rush out the door to meet the Wraiths head-on. But it wouldn't do any good now. And Amanda had ordered them to stay put. Odin was still trying to flush them out, and the relentless attacks were meant to be a beacon. Not reacting took all of her strength.

She shifted uncomfortably and tried to ignore the sirens. "Even if astral projection is a form of time travel, it's not like I can choose where I go and what time I return to. Most of the time I can't even trigger the astral projection myself. It seems a bit unreliable to make that a linchpin of whatever plan we come up with."

You would, naturally, need to learn the mechanics of time travel, Hayden agreed.

"How do I learn the mechanics of time travel?" she asked.

Henry leaned forward, his glasses slipping down his nose. "You don't. There's no one to teach you. And we're back to square one." He began to pace again. "The Time Stop I created was the work of decades. But now that we've cracked it, can we work on making it longer, maybe develop it into a Time Reverse? The relativity factor—"

It will not work, Hayden informed him. Jayne was rather glad her father couldn't hear that, and she opted not to relay it to him.

Instead, she said, "Hold your horses, Dad. How long would we need to make a Time Reverse work? Right now a Time Stop lasts for what, thirteen seconds? That doesn't give us much to work with."

"It's all we have," Henry countered. "And I know we can extend it. I *know* we can. And when we can, we can take it back to when Ruth..." He swallowed hard and stopped.

Jayne suspected she knew what he was going to say—he'd

been trying to turn back time ever since Ruth Thorne almost sacrificed Jayne in her wretched quest for power, back when Jayne was a kid. Sofia had rescued her and fled, but Henry and Ruth had supposedly perished in a fire and been declared dead. The two girls had lived as orphans for most of their lives, had only found out recently they'd been lied to for years. Now Ruth was dead, and Henry wasn't one hundred percent...there.

"That's a really long Time Reverse, Dad. If it can be achieved at all."

Not that way, Hayden said smugly.

"Dad." Sofia leaned forward. Her blonde hair was limp and unkempt, her face sallow. These days it was a struggle for her to just get out of bed, and she kept putting her hand to her belly when she thought no one was looking. Jayne mentally cursed herself and made a note to get takeout when the alarms subsided. Sofia couldn't neglect her body, not with the baby growing inside her. "This project is important to you. We know that. But what if Hayden has another way? Wouldn't it be worth exploring?" She extended her hand to Hayden. "You do have another way, don't you?"

Hayden sat up on his hind legs and nodded to her. He said to Jayne: *Your father has pursued time travel for years, and he has always failed.*

He blinked, waiting for her to convey the message. She shook her head, knowing there was more.

Time cannot be reversed. The way you speak of time—of traveling through time, going back, reversing time—it is not entirely correct. Time is not like a series of doors or interconnected rooms. It is more like a path. A road. Now, imagine that you have a map for this road.

"Like an old highway map?"

I suppose that will do. Yes. Now, imagine that you can fold the map. Hayden stared at her meaningfully, and an image formed in her mind. A large map spread out, then the center edges moved together, like a treasure map that folded together to create the X where the treasure was hidden.

"Folding time," Jayne breathed.

Sofia's brow wrinkled. "What? Folding time? How in the world do you do that?"

But Henry had that glint in his eye—the glint that meant he was cooking up something. "Folding time?" He pressed his hands together and put his fingers to his mouth. "Tell me more."

Jayne hurriedly explained what Hayden had shown her. Henry nodded along, then got up and started to pace again. "Folding time," he mused. "Which could be combined with a portal to *actually* travel to the place and time you need. But the mechanics—how would you do it? We don't have an effective Travel spell, just portals. Can a man portal to a different time?"

Hayden eyed Jayne. *He is getting ahead of himself.*

"You know my dad." Jayne offered her father a crooked smile. Something was stirring inside her—inside all of them. Hope. Sofia's dull eyes had taken on some of their fire again, and Henry had that faraway look he always got when he was conducting experiments and running numbers in his head.

But he will still not succeed alone, Hayden insisted. *For this sort of spell, you need the power of all the goddesses. You need their unique connection to time.*

"So you're saying that only I can do this? No one else?" Jayne asked him. Henry stopped midstride. His hands spasmed. It would have looked comical, except she knew that behind his shock was a grief at watching one of his long-held dreams crumble. Henry's quest to time travel had driven all of his research for his entire adult life.

She'd have to comfort him later. She got down from the couch and crouched before Hayden. "But if I've apparently time traveled whenever I've visited the goddesses, why didn't they give me the power before?"

Hayden nuzzled her hand, and she scratched him behind the ears. His eyes reduced to slits, and he made a noise that was almost a rumbling purr. *You cannot get the power of folding time from the goddesses you know. There are others. Goddesses who see the fate of every person on Earth before they are born. They can bestow a great power or take it away. They grant familiars to those who have the potential to raise them, and they snip the threads of fate as they are woven. They are Odin Allfather's greatest enemies, for they alone know how his time will come to an end and who will be responsible for it. These are the goddesses you must find...and free. In return, they will grant you the totem of Time.*

Jayne groaned aloud. "Not another totem."

Sofia and Henry were watching impatiently. "It's...sorry. Hayden says there are time goddesses we can go to for help. And if they grant me the Time totem, maybe I can learn how to fold time." She sighed.

"Another totem," Sofia echoed. "Is this the last one, Hayden?"

He nodded.

Sofia and Jayne exchanged a look. How far they'd come, these two powerful women, now charged with saving the world from a madman's diabolical grip. Jayne felt a thrill when her sister squared her shoulders and nodded. Her golden aura began to glow. Hope was a powerful thing. A drug as addictive as they come. Seeing it fill her sister, Jayne fiercely vowed to make it all worth it, for her, for her niece, for them all. Her totems flared in response, glowing on her forehead, and Sofia, seeing them, caught her hand.

"Well, it might be hard, but it's the first lead we've got on something that could help us. Maybe Jayne could fold time so that Odin never won the battle at Kirkjufell? So that the Rogues never came under his influence?" Tears swam unshed in her eyes.

Perhaps, Hayden replied. *There are rules to traveling in time. I do not pretend to know the details. But the Norns will reveal all, if Jayne Thorne is worthy.* He put a tiny, scaled paw on her wrist. *And you* are *worthy.*

"Thanks." Jayne smiled at him. "The Norns," she told Sofia and Henry. "We need to find out everything we can about the Norns."

TWO

A huge rhinoceros lowered his head and scraped his feet against the ground. All around him, the once lush grass of the meadow had been ripped up or stomped bare, and the air was thick with the musk of his rage. Shed antlers, feathers, and a broken tooth lay scattered around him, the remnants of many previous attempted shifts.

The rhinoceros trumpeted a bellow, then charged. Amanda Newport, head of the Torrent Control Organization, pushed her shoulders back and planted her feet, though all her instincts screamed for her to run. Next to her, Ruger Stern, her right-hand man and second in command of the TCO, actually flinched, and he was easily twice her size. But he didn't move either as the rhinoceros loped closer and closer.

Its horn sparked against the wards keeping it imprisoned, and it shrieked with rage. The wards had been carefully constructed so as not to harm the Rogue, Cillian Pine, while being strong enough to keep him from breaking out—no mean feat, as the headmaster of Aegis, Seo-Joon, had informed her when Amanda entered the magic school's Time Catch to ask for his help. The dome was large enough to keep Cillian comfortable, but he had no interest in comfort. He prowled away, and a moment later he was back to the griffin form he favored.

"No change, I see," Ruger said.

"None whatsoever." Amanda and Sofia had thrown every spell they could think of at Cillian in the hopes of pulling him back to himself. Amanda had left them to long, private conversations. Sofia had entreated him with words like *honor* and *duty* and *the right thing. Baby, future, love.* None of it mattered. It was like Cillian had been replaced by a wild thing. All they could think to do was reinforce the dome and hope that Odin's influence would wane over time. *But we don't have time,* Amanda reminded herself.

Cillian wheeled around and reared, slashing at the wards with clawed talons. He'd done this enough times that Amanda could almost say she was used to it. Ruger, on the other hand, leapt back with an oath.

"So he's really gone." Ruger rubbed at a three-day stubble. CIA dress code demanded that he shave regularly, but Amanda didn't have the heart to enforce petty rules. Her own suit was wrinkled; she wasn't sure when she'd last had a shower. Or gone home. Her office was strewn with draft after draft of letters to the bereaved. *We regret to inform you that your son/daughter/child was lost in action...*

"Yes, I fear the Cillian we know is gone," she said. "He might be buried in there somewhere, or his mind might be completely wiped. We have no idea. Quimby says it's a good sign that he tried to follow Odin's direction into the Torrent, because it means he has some sort of connection to his humanity that can be drawn on, but to be honest, I was tired when she started talking, and the Geniuses never won awards for making much sense." She eyed him. "Speaking of, I hope your report is more decipherable?"

Cillian-the-griffin screamed his frustrations into the sky, and Ruger shook his head. "Poor bastard."

Amanda wondered if he still fought to get to the Torrent at Kirkjufell, where Odin had lured all his Rogue brethren, or if he just wanted out of the enclosure. Maybe his brain was scrambled, and he was going mad. No telling—he hadn't been able to shift back to his human form for days now. They had no research on the effects of long-term shifting.

Ruger moved away from Cillian, and the Rogue's cries at their departure broke something inside of Amanda. She'd failed them all. She followed Ruger over the dirt path. The Aegis Battle Academy Time Catch was a remarkable place. To either side of them, grass and moss spread like an emerald sea. A low mountain, made to resemble Kirkjufell and the site of their last battle, rose off to one side, while water burbled on the other. A beautiful fantasy: This was a training ground for the battles to come.

"Since we're on the subject of Rogues, I can start there. They're all gone," Ruger said.

Amanda's stomach plummeted. "All?" she echoed. She'd hoped that whatever siren spell Odin Allfather had cast upon them hadn't affected anyone outside of Kirkjufell. Most spells worked only within a certain radius. He must be using some kind of spell she'd never even heard of before. "No other captive Rogues?" she asked.

Ruger shook his head. "Not that I could determine. A few were killed when they went mad trying to reach Odin. Most people were too surprised to do anything to stop it." They'd only managed to capture Cillian because Sofia, acting on impressive instinct, had fashioned a kind of golden lasso that had slowed him just enough for other TCO operatives to join in. All the same, it had taken half a dozen powerful Adepts and a Guardian to get him down.

Amanda sat on a smooth boulder. "How many Rogues were with us?"

"One hundred eighty-nine," Ruger said.

The sinking feeling persisted. *Try to find a positive spin.* Once she started in on a defeatist attitude, it would be all the harder to come up with a plan.

And they desperately needed a plan.

She took a deep breath of air that smelled like salt and brine and fresh grass. Some people liked the fresh air of the great outdoors; give Amanda the city any day. This space was too much open, with too many opportunities for the enemy to appear and surround them. The sounds of battle still rang in her ears. Visions of the fallen, students and soldiers alike, paraded in, followed by the Rogues rushing toward the wretched gap in the mountain that housed Odin's filthy lair. She wished, not for the first time, that they'd remolded this part of the Time Catch so it didn't resemble Kirkjufell anymore. She had Iceland PTSD. They all did.

"We can assume that the Rogues are still alive," she said.

"Why?" Ruger's shoulders came up.

"Cillian's still alive," she reasoned. "And Odin must have wanted the Rogues for something."

"But he's not in the Torrent, he's out here, with us. Going mad. No, I think they're too powerful and mercurial, and Odin wanted them out of his way." Ruger stuck his hands in the pocket of his big overcoat and kicked a pebble. "He might have drained them once they were in the Torrent or picked them off. Or let them kill each other. Or turned them into Wraiths. Just look at him. If they're all in there going bonkers..." Amanda noticed he did not look at Cillian as he said it.

"If he could drain life, he would have done it to all of us," Amanda decided.

"Agreed. He obviously only has power over the Rogues," Ruger said. "Otherwise we'd all be in the Torrent."

She couldn't argue with him on that one. "We must believe the Rogues are still in there, because we must believe our friends can be saved," she said.

Ruger's shoulders came up even more. "I always thought you were a realist."

"I'm a leader." Amanda's fingers brushed over the necklace her late husband, Karam, had given her. "I can't afford to fall to pessimism. Surrender is not an option. Odin will kill us and submit the rest of the world to a kind of subjugation that will make most of them wish they were dead. So until we get concrete proof otherwise, we're going to assume that our friends and operatives are alive—and we're going to find out how to save them."

She fixed Ruger with a hard stare. The big man met her gaze for a moment, then nodded, running a hand over the top of his bald head. The shiny scarred flesh on his dark cheek seemed more prominent. He'd lost weight.

"You aren't taking care of yourself," she said softly.

"Neither are you," he shot back. "You want to get out of the Time Catch, take a shower, get a meal?"

"No."

"I didn't think so."

He was in pain, too. She couldn't fix that, but damn it all, she wasn't going to let him—and the rest of her troops—down. "Tell me about the ones who didn't make it."

"We lost around twenty percent of our forces," Ruger told her. She hissed through her teeth. "Some of our best men died. Augustin of the Disciples of Gaia was killed in action, leaving the Disciples leaderless, and Isra has told me she doesn't know whether the rest will continue to ally with us. They want a meeting to determine our next moves."

Amanda stared across the field. They didn't have a next move. "This can't be the end," she murmured.

"It can't," Ruger agreed. She looked over at him in surprise. "You're right, old friend. We have no other options and nowhere else to go. You've never been able to let us lose, and it's always been to our benefit." He smiled at Amanda's snort. His stubble was gray, she realized with a small shock. When had Ruger started to go gray? She wondered, suddenly, what people saw now when they looked at her.

She shook her head to dislodge those petty distractions. The lucky ones got wrinkles and gray hair. She was lucky.

Amanda's phone buzzed. "Speaking of stubborn people unable to let us lose," she muttered, fighting a smile. She picked up the call. "Hello, Henry." Did she dare hope the Thornes were back in action?

She had to concentrate; Cillian's roars were very distracting. She stuffed a finger in one ear. Henry's voice was tinny, and he talked with more enthusiasm than clarity—which was only to be expected from any Thorne, really. "*Time,* a way to...find the goddesses and ask them..."

"You're breaking up. Why don't you come down to the office and we'll discuss it?" Reception was always bad in the Time Catch, anyway. Amanda listened for his affirmative, then hung up.

She turned to Ruger. "Henry Thorne thinks he knows what we're supposed to do next."

Ruger's eyebrows raised. "And you listened to him?" Amanda nodded. He inflated his cheeks and puffed out a stream of air. "We're all going to die."

"Come on, you." She didn't swat him—that wasn't the sort of relationship they had—but she did roll her eyes. "We might as well see what the Geniuses are up to. It will either get us out of our predicament..."

"Or it will cause untold destruction and alienate our allies." Ruger gave her a weak smile.

Amanda's phone buzzed again as they made their way toward the portal at the front of the academy. She sighed. When the Thornes got a bee in their collective bonnet... "What now?" she said into the phone.

"I hope better manners are on display when you meet the president," said the cold voice of Isaac Fitzgerald, Amanda's boss' boss and the head of the CIA.

Amanda nearly dropped the phone. *This is what you get for not checking the caller ID first,* she thought grimly before forcing out an apology.

"How goes saving the world? Do you have some wild trick up your sleeve? Because we're running out of ballistic missiles," Isaac told her.

"We're exploring options—"

Isaac snorted. "Don't try to corporate-speak me. You need a plan, or you need to suit up, because if you don't have anything better to do, you're going out on the front line."

Amanda swallowed her bitter reply. She'd already been on the front line, unlike Isaac. She doubted he'd been sprayed with Wraith blood or caught in a deadly magical battle. She imagined him snug in a CIA bunker, sitting in his leather chair with a glass of cognac while Wraiths swooped overhead and terrorized the rest of DC.

He was still talking. She forced her mind back to the conversation. "...and I meant what I said. President Eisner herself wants to tour your facility. She says it's past time to inspect the Torrent Control Organization, and I couldn't agree more. You can expect our visit tomorrow afternoon."

What? "That's not enough time," Amanda said.

"You're out of time," Fitzgerald said with relish and hung up.

Amanda held her phone very tightly and tried not to hurl it on the ground. Breaking her phone wouldn't get her a new boss. She took a deep breath, corralling her self-control. Then she began to walk toward the portal, at such a speed that Ruger, whose strides were normally twice as long as hers, had to trot to catch up. "What was that?" he said.

"We're moving up the timeline. Get the Thornes to my office ASAP. I want to know what they're planning and whether it can even be spun to sound like a decent idea. And then I want them out of the way. We have more pressing things to attend to."

"More pressing?" Ruger puffed from behind her. "What's more pressing than the end of the world?"

CHAPTER
THREE

Sofia Thorne cradled her belly and tried not to weep as the father of her child rampaged around his cage.

She couldn't feel Cillian's mind anymore. The connection between them was severed, and if she hadn't known every contour of his body and soul, every feather on his griffin form, if she hadn't known the exact way he tossed his beak or lashed out with his talons, she would never have recognized him. Any passing person would have thought him no more than an animal.

Would their daughter grow up thinking such a thing?

Someone had managed to find a deer for him to tear into, and its carcass lay in one corner of the meadow. There was a large tree for shade when—if—he wanted to sleep, and a rocky outcropping he could explore in a different form if he were so inclined. As a zoo enclosure, it had plenty of space and ways for him to entertain himself. But it was a prison.

"Do you think he'll ever come back to himself?" Matthew, her half-brother and an excellent Adept, stood next to her. He ran a hand through the blond hair he had inherited from his dead father, and worry crowded the gray eyes he'd inherited from their mother. Behind him stood Zia, Rebecca, Rufus, and Medina: the first graduating class of the Aegis Battle Academy. They'd signed on as operatives with the TCO, fought for it, nearly died for it. They'd injected themselves with the blood of powerful dead Adepts and experimented with magics and processes that had never been experimented with before. And through it all, Cillian had been with them. Leading them. He'd trained them for battle and he'd sat with them after, patiently going through every move. He'd talked to Matthew when the pressure of being Ruth Thorne's son had been too great, and to Rebecca when she clashed with her birth mother, Amanda. He'd tutored Zia on moves that capitalized on her short stature, and he'd counseled Medina on surviving in a combat situation with her religious and pacifist convictions. He'd been there for each and every one of them.

Now they were trying to be there for him, and he couldn't even comprehend it.

Rufus put a hand on the wards, fingers stretched. Cillian wheeled toward him and screamed, arcing down with one talon. The ward sparked and Rufus flinched, sending a burst of magic into strengthening the wall. He stepped back hastily.

Sofia swallowed her tears and forced herself to turn away. "I don't know," she admitted.

It was a hard thing to say. All the Rogue students had disappeared with Odin into his portal. These five had lost friends, and not knowing if they would ever see them again was its own kind of pain. How did you move on? How did you not give up? They were too young to have to learn these hard lessons.

Voices sounded from around the bend. Sofia recognized Amanda's and saw Rebecca stiffen. Rebecca and Amanda looked exactly the same and often acted the same as well. Sofia squeezed her shoulder, then nodded to all the cadets, who lined up at attention on the edge of the road.

Amanda came around the side of the hill. "—have an entire area devoted to battle tactics and war games. Of course, space is no trouble, so we have quite an advantage there."

Sofia was surprised by the dour face of Isaac Fitzgerald, his short gray hair plastered to his skull by liberal amounts of hair gel. He wore a black suit rumpled and dusty from the long walk. He'd eschewed anything to do with magic for so long that at first Sofia couldn't understand what would possibly have driven him to enter a portal.

Then she saw the woman behind him and broke out in a cold sweat.

President Elizabeth Eisner wore a pale blue pant suit, as though she were taking a walk around the reflecting pool and stopping for brunch, rather than touring a war-training field of a magic academy. She looked around with a great deal of interest, her sharp brown eyes taking in the flow of the landscape. Behind her two Secret Service agents roughly the size of the boulders in Cillian's enclosure walked with their hands on their weapons, heads on a swivel. Unease radiated from them, but Eisner herself seemed utterly fascinated.

"Madam President!" Sofia was seized by the ridiculous urge to curtsy. She tried saluting instead. "This is a great honor. We weren't prepared..."

Eisner came forward and shook her hand. Sofia's mind went peculiarly blank. "The honor is mine," the president replied. "I understand I'm in the presence of some great war heroes."

She went down the line, shaking every student's hand. Rebecca nodded and thanked her, just as professional as her mother. Rufus stuttered something at his shoes. Medina turned pale, and Zia blushed and muttered, "I didn't really do anything." Which was partly true; she'd been injured in a Wraith attack in Glasgow and kept out of the Battle of

Kirkjufell. Cillian had promised to help her rehabilitate her healing muscles, Sofia remembered with a fresh pang of grief.

Eisner then turned to the cage. Cillian seemed to recognize a big player, at least: He'd stopped shrieking and fighting, and now he stood with his head proud and his eye cocked at the president. One talon scratched in the dirt. Sofia recognized the look. He was sizing her up, determining which angle to attack from. "So this is...a Rogue?"

"The only Rogue in our custody," Amanda confirmed. "Odin Allfather's attack at Kirkjufell left the other Rogues enthralled, but we managed to keep hold of Cillian. We're researching ways to break the hold now."

"Why not just put them down?" Fitzgerald's lip curled with distaste. He stared at Cillian. "Animals have a purpose, and when they can't fulfill that purpose anymore—"

"He's *not* an animal," Sofia snapped before she could stop herself.

Isaac's head whipped around. Sofia pressed her lips together. Her throat constricted around all the insults she wanted to hurl at him. *Probably for the best.*

Amanda, thankfully, stepped in. She looked tired— exhausted from long days trying to put out fires and clearly finished with Isaac's nonsense. "Rogues are human beings," she said firmly. "A lot of people can go their whole lives without even knowing they're Rogues—or at least, they could before the Torrent started breaking open. The attitude that Rogues are in any way inferior has given many of our enemies a moral high ground against us. It even resulted in the death of my predecessor."

There was a short, awkward silence. Isaac's lip was still curled. Amanda looked as professional as ever, but Sofia could tell from the slight tightening of her fist that she wanted to punch him. On the road, the students bristled with resentment.

Amanda cleared her throat. "President Eisner, Sofia Thorne has been one of the prime masterminds in the development of this school. Perhaps she could give you a tour."

All the blood left Sofia's head. *Give a tour to the freaking president?* For a moment she thought she was about to faint. But then she saw Zia smiling at her, and Rufus bouncing on his toes, and she imagined them rushing back to the dorms. This was a chance she couldn't pass up. Judging by the steely glint in Amanda's eye, this was a chance she *wouldn't* pass up, not if she knew what was good for her.

And they needed all the support they could get. If President Eisner thought they did good work, they could ensure the prosperity of the school for years to come.

So she pushed aside thoughts like *There's no way I'm good enough* and *Why didn't she give me any time to prepare?* "I'd love to give you the tour," she said, smiling. "Why don't we start with the classrooms?"

EISNER ADMIRED EVERYTHING, from the sprawling manor and its classrooms to the small but neat dorm rooms and the dining hall, where a flustered cook apologized at least a dozen times for only having fresh quiche for lunch. The president peered at the magical textbooks in the library and smiled fondly at the fields where students could play tennis, soccer, volleyball, basketball, and more. Seo-Joon joined them and waxed poetic about the systems in place to keep the school independent and safe for young Adepts of all backgrounds. Sofia and her cadets showed Eisner how the land could be reshaped to make any terrain they required, whether it was a perfect replica of Kyoto or a grain field in the middle of Nebraska. The kids' magic was exceptional, and the president was clearly charmed.

"And this place, this...Time Catch." Eisner's brows came together. "It means we're frozen in time?"

"Not really. Here on this side of the portal, we're still moving through time. Aging and going gray..." *Gestating babies.* Sofia kept her hands away from her belly. "But out there, barely any time will have passed by the time you return to the TCO."

"I could use one of these in my office," Eisner muttered.

"Time Catches are terribly dangerous when used incorrectly, ma'am," Amanda said crisply, and Eisner laughed.

"How much does all this cost?" Fitzgerald butted in.

"The resources are allotted from the TCO's budget," Amanda replied.

"That wasn't my question. I have the right to know how you use funds provided to you by the CIA and, ultimately, the American taxpayer. Don't think I didn't notice that you don't have normal subjects in your library. Do you not include classes on social governing and politics? Do you let your children remain ignorant of American history? What happens if one of your magical cadets wishes to drop out? How will they meaningfully contribute to American society?"

"Our courses comply with American standard schools," Seo-Joon answered for them. "The magical library is, of course, quite comprehensive, but students take core classes as well. After all, military engineers will always be in style, no matter whether we fight magical or nonmagical wars."

The ground rumbled. Sofia frowned. Term was on a break for the moment as they recovered from the Battle of Kirkjufell, and students weren't supposed to work on reshaping the school grounds without adult supervision. She and Seo-Joon were the only ones who seemed to notice it, though. Isaac Fitzgerald was waving his arms about. "And why couldn't this, say, be incorporated into a military academy like West Point? Why keep these children a secret?"

"Not a secret, sir. Just safe. We believe that separate magical training will reduce the risk of civilian and nonmagical personnel being injured," Seo-Joon replied.

Fitzgerald didn't seem to like that they could answer his questions. He continued to grill Seo-Joon, barking orders. Sofia frowned at the grass beneath her feet. It rippled without a wind. The ground vibrated again. It was as though a wave of some sort was being sent through the Time Catch. But a wave of what? And to what purpose?

A sudden surge of power knocked them all off their feet. Eisner went over with a noise of surprise; one agent moved to catch her while the other one whipped out his weapon. A crack rippled through the air, and Sofia thought she heard a laugh—a deep, bone-chilling laugh. The laugh cut to her very soul. She exchanged an alarmed look with Amanda and Seo-Joon. They needed to get the president out of here, *now*—

There was a crash from across the field, something shattering. *The wards.*

FOUR

S ofia sprinted down the road. Part of her mind screamed objections, that she should be turning back to protect the students if the school was under attack—but she couldn't help herself.

Cillian burst from between the rocks surrounding his enclosure and took to the air. His golden griffin wings caught the light of the sun, dazzling against the blue air, and Sofia's heart broke all over again. For a moment, his flight was pure joy. For a moment, it was as though he was back.

Then he spotted the group of people along the road behind her. His black eyes showed no sign of intelligence or understanding. He screamed an ear-piercing, hateful call and dove.

No! Later, Sofia would wonder if she screamed it aloud or just in her mind. She spun around and threw out a wide Shield spell in an arc of golden light. Cillian crashed into it.

And crashed through it. He tumbled to the ground in a flurry of wings and beak, but it didn't stop him. He flipped over and zeroed in on the president.

"*Cillian,*" Sofia screamed. The Secret Service agents raised their weapons. Isaac Fitzgerald, who was carrying a gun as well, did the same. They fired off multiple quick shots, but as Sofia had learned fighting Wraiths on the battlefield, it wasn't easy to hit a moving target, and Cillian was fast. All the same, her heart plummeted at the reports.

Amanda and Seo-Joon stepped between Cillian and the president. Green wards rose over them all, glowing and flashing as the Shield spell grew stronger. Cillian hit that one, too, but it was stronger, and his talons raked across it with a shivering scrape.

He fell to the ground and hit his head, hard. Sofia ran toward him. "Cillian," she gasped. "I know you're in there. It's me. I'm here for you. Remember—" She stopped, choking on her own lack of breath and her grief. "Remember what we talked about." *The baby.* She wasn't going to reveal her pregnancy to her students, the president, and her boss' boss right here and now. "I know you're fighting. Keep fighting. We're all fighting for you."

The griffin blinked, dazed. It was hurt, confused, it didn't know where it was. For a moment Sofia saw real emotion in there, *human* emotion—

Then its eye darkened with rage.

The talon swept up so fast she barely had time to jump back. Sofia flung up her arms, one to protect her belly and one to protect her face, and it was the only thing that kept her from getting disemboweled and blinded. The skin of her forearms shredded in a bright lance of pain. She didn't realize she'd fallen to the ground until she blinked away stars and saw the azure sky above her.

Cillian's head came into view. She'd never noticed how sharp his beak was before.

"You can't," she tried to whisper. "Remember...what we talked about..."

He drew his head back to strike. Then he reared instead.

Zia stood over her, swiping two long magical daggers in front of herself. "You won't!" she shouted. "I know you don't want to do this!" Tears fell from her chin to make little craters in the dirt of the path. "This isn't you."

Cillian screamed his defiance and rallied for another attack. But the distraction was enough. Rufus, Medina, Matthew, and Rebecca threw a green-and-golden net over him and pulled with everything they had. Amanda drove the edges of the net into the ground with glowing magical stakes. Seo-Joon ran to Sofia.

"A little trip to the TCO, I think," he muttered, wiping at the blood with his T-shirt. "Tamara will get this fixed up in no time."

He helped her sit up, just in time to see Isaac Fitzgerald and the Secret Service agents leveling their guns at the struggling and prone Cillian. Point-blank range.

"No!" She staggered to her feet, seeing spots. A concussion, maybe; she'd hit the ground hard.

"This threat tried to kill the president," Fitzgerald snarled.

"This threat is a person. You can't just execute him." She swayed on her feet. *Don't faint yet,* she thought. If she fainted, Cillian would lose his fiercest advocate. Instead, she shuffled forward, trying to put herself between him and the guns.

"Put the guns away," Amanda said.

"You can't possibly take her side after seeing that. Putting this *thing's* life above the life of our own president?" Fitzgerald snarled.

"President Eisner is safe now," Amanda said. "Cillian will be taken away, and his enclosure will be strengthened.

"Unbelievable." He pointed at the main building. "This place is full of danger, and she refuses to take care of it! How can we expect this so-called school to train its students to do what needs to be done? This Rogue isn't your friend anymore.

It's a beast bent on destruction, and there's only one thing you can do with it. What happens the next time he escapes? Does he know how to get through the portal, back into the real world? Will he kill innocent people?"

"Cillian was subdued by newly minted cadets." Amanda came around in front of Cillian and took Sofia's upper arm, supporting her and standing with her. Sofia felt a rush of warmth, and her head swam. "They were able to take him down without killing him, working together quickly to protect the rest of the group without causing casualties. Personally, I would call that something of a victory. You should be impressed instead of threatened, sir. Our training program works. It creates soldiers who can act quickly and *morally*."

"It also created an army of highly trained Rogues who are now working for the enemy! You breed traitors and free agents with no loyalty to the country that supports their education."

"That's not true," Sofia began.

"And you." He rounded on her. "Your loyalties don't lie with the United States. They lie with him." He brandished his gun at Cillian again. If Sofia weren't on the verge of passing out, she'd kick it out of his hand. Instead, she tossed a Snatch spell at him, and the gun was in her hand moments later. Fitzgerald's face turned puce. If this wasn't so serious, she might laugh at his reaction. As it was, she handed it calmly to Amanda.

"Students from all over the world attend this school with the aim of protecting all life," Amanda argued, giving Sofia a stern look.

"That's not the point of the CIA, or its satellite missions!" frothed Fitzgerald. "If you want to run some hippy nongovernmental army, do it on your own money."

"And let other governments crush the United States?" Amanda shot back. "France has already allied with La Liberté. I shouldn't have to remind you that the CIA considers it a terrorist organization. We can't be left behind in this, or you'll end up with nonmagical armies that don't know how to engage with this new enemy."

"Enough," Eisner said, her tone brooking no argument. "Isaac, stow it. You've always been opposed to the TCO and its needs. Unfortunately, those needs are proving extremely important. We're in the middle of a war." She faced Sofia again. "What needs to happen right now?"

Sofia swayed. "I need Jayne," she mumbled, and went down.

❧

She woke in the familiar white-clad room of the TCO's hospital wing. Jayne was leaning over her, eyes closed, totems glowing on her forehead. Light flickered over her palms. She ran her hands up and down Sofia's arms. She felt warm and safe.

"You're not overdoing it, are you?" Sofia croaked. Healed, but parched.

Jayne's eyes flew open. She threw herself over Sofia and wrapped her arms around her sister's neck. She smelled of Tristan's lavender soap. She was wearing one of his shirts, Sofia realized.

"Whatever you did to yourself, I am absolutely furious with you," Jayne whispered into her hair. "After everyone else, I'm not losing you, too."

Sofia smiled weakly. "Don't worry about me, sis." She was the mother figure, after all.

Jayne pulled away to reveal Amanda, Ruger, and President Eisner at the foot of the bed. Sofia blinked. She didn't think the president had the time to sit around in a hospital.

"Impressive," Eisner said to Jayne. "And you're the only one with these healing abilities?"

"So far," Jayne said. "But as the Torrent opens and magic returns, more Adepts will have the capacity to become Masters. We hope this ability will become a little more common, but healing has always been rare."

"You were out for about thirty minutes," Amanda informed Sofia.

"Enough time to dismiss Isaac. That man gives me a headache," Eisner joked. Amanda's eyebrows rose. "Don't tell me it's not the same for you. I inherited him, and it's not easy to just fire the head of the CIA until they give you real cause." She sighed. "But I like the work you do. I like the school. I want to know more about it. What does it need?"

She had more questions, too. Sofia tried to concentrate on them, but she was feeling really woozy.

"You need food," Jayne announced.

There was a small kitchen near the room. Jayne brought back electrolyte water and some saltines. When Sofia tried to push the package away after a couple of bites, Jayne shoved it back toward her with a stony look that said, *Think of the baby.* Sofia's muscles were sore, and the skin on her arms was fresh and pink where Jayne had repaired it. She'd have some wicked-looking scars for a while.

Amanda and Seo-Joon answered what questions they could —curriculum, potential majors, the differences between Guardian magic, Rogue magic, and Adept magic. Where they envisioned their students working and contributing to world safety. How their numbers were growing daily, astronomically. Amanda surmised that when all was said and done, the magical world would be the predominant species on the planet, and nonmagical humans would be relatively rare. A total reversal in the population. Training these new Adepts was going to be vital, and it would be especially important to have them properly educated when they started having children of their own.

The president was agog at this but rallied with even more queries. *Smart woman,* Sofia thought.

"And your needs?" Eisner asked when she'd exhausted all these avenues.

"We need..." Amanda exchanged a glance with Seo-Joon. "We need Aegis to be neutral ground," she said at last. "This school is the first of its kind, and it has the potential to be the best. Other countries will ally with us in exchange for our magical protection if they think we won't interfere with their political or economic interests. We'll also get the best of the best in students. The training program in France that La Liberté has in mind will teach its students that magic users are always superior to the rest of the world, and there are plenty of other splinter groups that feel the same way. If we want to be unified and make sure our nonmagical citizens are protected, this project can't be an extension of the US Army."

Eisner tapped her chin with one finger. "That won't be easy to put through Congress," she said.

"You don't have to tell them that it's a military academy," Sofia said, dabbing at the corner of her mouth with her napkin. "After all, in times of peace, we'll still need it to teach our students how to use their magic responsibly."

"I can't lie to them, or they'll have me in front of the Armed Services committee answering questions for days." Eisner thought for a moment, tapping a nail against her front teeth. Then she looked around, ensuring no one else was in the room with them, and leaned in. "I need you to keep this to yourselves. My daughter is one of these people you'd call an Adept," she said in a low voice.

Sofia's heart stuttered. "Your daughter?" she echoed.

"Small things. She creates light when it's dark. She kicked a soccer ball wrong and managed to deflect it before it could break a window. We haven't told many people yet, and I don't want her to keep part of herself a secret. I don't want her to think that she has to hide who she is."

"With us, she won't," Sofia said. "She'll learn how to use her powers safely, and she'll be with other kids who know what she's going through."

"Send her to us, and we'll make sure she gets an assessment," Seo-Joon said warmly.

Eisner sighed and seemed to sit a little taller, as though a weight had been removed from her. "I'll tell her." Her brow wrinkled. "I have to sell this to the American people without them feeling threatened. Nonmagical humans are going to be confused and wary when they find out about Aegis. And if the Wraiths don't stop attacking, the entire magical community will be blamed."

Her finger tapped against her chin for a few moments more. "It is a school that should guide our children—all our children —on a better path of life. A path that protects and improves for everyone. One that allows for the differences between us and doesn't discriminate. Perhaps one day, the magical and nonmagical worlds will be able to coexist. Until that moment arrives, I charge you with training the troops who will create that path for us. Aegis Battle Academy will get all of the funding and resources I can provide. I swear it."

CHAPTER

FIVE

I t took some convincing for Jayne to leave Sofia's bed. In fact, she didn't leave until Sofia swung her legs out and proclaimed that she was going to take a shower and get cleaned up and go home, and Jayne couldn't mother-hen her on that. Her sister did look better—but Jayne couldn't close her eyes without seeing Sofia, pale as a corpse, staggering between Seo-Joon and Amanda, her clothes soaked near black with blood.

Jayne knew Sofia could take care of herself. The problem was, she wouldn't take care of herself *properly* until Cillian was in the picture. Healed. Himself again. Jayne didn't want to give up on him any more than her sister did, but she wasn't about to let Sofia risk herself like that. Not to mention her baby. Jayne shook her head vehemently. No, thank you, sir.

A thought floated through her head. Could she fix Cillian? Was the thrall of Odin something that could be healed?

No! Hayden shouted, startling her. He burst from her arm and landed in the hallway, shaking his head. *Do not even think of it, Jayne. It is too dangerous to try.*

"Chicken," she said, and he snorted in annoyance

There are limits. Stay the course. The Norns are your priority now.

"You moved fast," she said.

Practice makes perfect. He vanished with a pop, and she felt him snuggling down beneath her skin.

"Only I would manifest a smart-ass dragon familiar."

Hayden rumbled a laugh but didn't reply. Figured.

She was late for her date with her dad, so she set off toward the Genius Lab to pick him up. Henry had, with some help from Jayne, explained to Amanda their need to go searching for the Norns and the Time totem. Amanda had listened with her head in one hand. "How many more totems are out there that we don't know about?" she'd asked wearily.

"Hayden says it's the last, but I want to consult with Katie Bell," Jayne replied. "Despite Hayden's assurances to the contrary, for all we know, there's a totem for every goddess in every mythology in the world."

"Well, I sincerely hope you won't have to track down all of them to defeat the Allfather."

"Ditto," Jayne said. "We'll cross that bridge later, though."

Amanda had waved her away.

Jayne greeted Quimby, who barely looked up from her computer to acknowledge her and collected Henry. They set off together to the library, walking fast, as he always did.

"What's your new project?" she asked.

"Time travel, of course," Henry replied. "Your familiar might claim that only the Norns hold the secret to folding time, but if there's one way to do something, there's almost always another. Mythology is all well and good, but science shall prevail."

But do we want science and technology catching up to myth? Jayne thought. Everyone regretted things they'd done in the past—impulsive messages sent, breakups gone wrong, crushes never kissed. Fights that tore families apart or actions that resulted in someone getting hurt or worse. If anyone could go back in time, how much would they want to change? And how would tweaking one action make the rest of the world different? Chaos theory was real. The ripple effect of her father's discoveries could change the very fabric of the universe. She wasn't sure the world was ready.

Plus, Henry Thorne was the sort of man who would obsess over the situation so thoroughly that he might spend the rest of his life trying to find the perfect answers to his past. It could drive him mad.

The TCO library was cozy, but it took a moment for that reality to present itself. The room looked, at first, depressingly tiny, more of an abandoned office with dusty filing cabinets and a few books stacked on tables. The real magic of the library was the way it unfolded as you stepped through the door into the glorious haven Jayne so loved. Shelves formed, ladders appeared, squashy chairs and pots of tea set themselves in their path, beckoning for an occupant, and of course, there were the books. Anything and everything you needed. Make a request of the librarian, and a vast collection appeared, stack after stack, row after row, where you could do anything from finding the history of the world's most obscure spell to being taught a new language in a matter of moments.

A white-haired woman with leathery brown skin sat in one of the armchairs, leafing through a book with a flowing gold script on the cover—*The Definitive History and Background on the Disciples of Gaia*. She looked up as Henry and Jayne came in, and her deep brown eyes twinkled. Her mouth thinned in mock disapproval.

"Henry Thorne and the prodigal daughter," the Guardian named Xiomara grumbled. "You're disturbing my work."

"Well, it *is* our library," Jayne said, amused.

A moment later the TCO's librarian appeared. Katie Bell was a middle-aged woman with a cheerful round face, a penchant for the color pink and truly hideous Christmas sweaters, and a pearl-lined string for her glasses. "Two of my favorite people," she exclaimed with a smile when she saw them. "Henry, I was hoping to see you today."

Henry blinked. "Why?" he asked.

Katie turned the same shade as her cardigan. "Well...I...um. You always seem to have the most interesting things to talk about."

Xiomara shot her an affronted look. "And I'm just chopped liver, as you Americans like to say?"

Jayne tried to hide her smile behind a hand. Xiomara rolled her eyes and returned to her book. Katie stammered a bit more then gathered herself.

"Not that I meant—anyway, what can I do for you today?"

"We're looking for anything you have on the Norns," Jayne answered. "We need to learn how they deal with fate and time."

Katie paled. Xiomara looked up, delicately placing her book on the table. She was waiting for Katie's answer, too.

"I have...a bit. Are you looking for an overview, or—"

"The more in depth, the better," Jayne said.

Katie's frown deepened. "Come this way, then," she said, starting toward a stack that had appeared on their left. The rows went on forever, into a darkness Jayne hadn't seen in this space before. Henry followed, enraptured.

Jayne started after them, but a strong, liver-spotted hand closed around her wrist.

"Are you sure you know what you're doing?" Xiomara asked, staring down the stacks at Katie's and Henry's retreating backs.

Jayne felt a flash of exasperation. "How can I be? I don't know anything about the Norns yet."

She knew what she'd been taught in her Introduction to

World Mythology class back in college, but she suspected the truth—like the truth of all the goddesses so far—was far more complicated. The Norns were part of Viking mythology, three women who spun the threads of fate at the base of the World Tree. Some myths said they visited each child at birth, determining their ultimate fate. Beyond that, Jayne knew almost nothing. Too much of that class had been focused on dude gods anyway, not their more enigmatic female counterparts.

"Be careful, Jayne Thorne. Fate isn't something to mess with."

"Right," Jayne said. "I'd better go. I'll lose them if I don't."

Xiomara let go of her hand at last. Rubbing her wrist, Jayne headed toward the bookish darkness.

Katie led them past shelf after shelf of theory, history, mythology, language. They didn't stop at the expected shelf for DEITIES, L–P, nor a shelf Katie had recently created, marked simply TOTEMS. They walked for several long minutes, the hallway growing grimmer and darker and dustier as they went.

Finally, Katie stopped under a shelf labeled DANGEROUS KNOWLEDGE. The books were chained like the ones Jayne had seen in the Trinity Library in Dublin, which told her they dated from medieval times at least. Katie was pale but resolute.

"I'd have thought it was lack of knowledge that was dangerous," Jayne half-joked.

"In most cases, yes." Katie didn't smile. "But in some cases, you've got to be careful with the knowledge you find."

She ran her finger near the spines of the old, cracked books until she found a plain one in green leather. *The World Tree* was stamped in gold lettering down its spine. She whispered a spell, and the chains animated, unlocking themselves with a grating slowness.

"This is what you need," Katie said and put the book on a cart with a black foam cradle to hold the cover when it was opened, preventing the ancient leather from cracking. "Read it here, and whatever you do, don't take it out of the library."

As they walked back to the desk, she said, "Out of curiosity, Jayne, what do you need it for?"

Jayne explained what Hayden had told them about time travel and the Norns. "If we want to change the outcome of the battle, we have to find a way to fold time and rescue the Rogues, then defeat Odin once and for all."

"Time travel?" Xiomara raised her eyebrows, shifting in her chair. "You can't possibly believe in that old story. Besides, what goddesses used to do is hardly a concern of ours."

"Jayne's familiar says it's possible," Henry told her. "With the Time totem, which the Norns can bestow upon Jayne."

Xiomara paused. For a moment Jayne thought she was remembering something, or perhaps just lost in a different thought, caught up in her book. Finally she spoke, her voice soft, missing its usual fire. "The Time totem is a dangerous concept. The Norns themselves are dangerous." She nodded to the book in Jayne's hand. "Not everyone has access to that story. Nor should they."

Jayne resisted the urge to tell Xiomara she could handle it, because the old woman had probably forgotten more about the history of the Torrent than Jayne would ever know. She took a deep breath. "You seem like you know a lot about them anyway. Illuminate me."

"Some." Xiomara put her book down again and leaned forward, the ends of her silver braids swinging. "You are not the first person to seek out goddesses, and you would not be the first person to seek out the Norns."

Her gaze darted to Henry. For once, Jayne's father looked just as bewildered as she felt. "What do you mean?" Jayne said. "Did Ruth go looking for the Norns?"

Xiomara fingered the end of one long braid. "She did, though she did not find them, thank the Goddess."

"They never would have given her mastery over time," Jayne said. Goddesses were particular, and Ruth Thorne had always been too bent on turning the world toward her own ends. But thinking about her mother made her itchy. The light in her eyes, leaving for one last time...

Nope. Not going there.

"Does anyone need tea? I need tea." The TCO library boasted a small but well-stocked kitchen that, like the rest of the space, expanded to meet the needs of the person seeking a solution. Jayne opened a drawer that kept getting deeper and deeper until she found a vanilla chai blend that looked soothing. She held it up, and everyone's hands went in the air. She turned on the kettle and settled in to listen some more.

"Okay. Sorry. Please keep going."

"The Norns are not gentle goddesses," Xiomara said. "The tales that are told...when a Master stands before them and asks for the totem of Time, they give him a taste of what he seeks." She stood and folded her arms. "The Norns do not just guard the secret of traveling to the past. They can go to any point that was, is, shall be, or even *might* be. Do you understand, Jayne Thorne? All the possibilities contained therein? The Norns have driven Masters mad by showing them the full scope of the past, present, and futures. Do you comprehend at all what it would be to have a totem that did the same? In your head? All the time?"

The kettle beeped. Jayne poured out the steaming water into pot spelled like the rest of the library, growing larger until it had enough water for everyone to have a cup. She added the tea bags and then brought it and several cups to the table.

"I think I know more about having a totem in my head than you do," she said. The words came out harsher than she intended, but her momentary chagrin was overridden by frustration. She'd been through so much. She wasn't a little girl anymore, shielded by her sister's protection spells and unaware of the magical world at her fingertips. She wasn't even a wide-eyed Adept still learning to sling spells. She was the foremost and most powerful weapon of the CIA's Torrent Control Organization, and she should have a say in how she was wielded.

"The Norns *are* powerful," Katie put in. She put on her glasses and gestured for the book. Jayne slid the cart her way. Katie flipped through page after page with that soft *shirring* sound that Jayne liked best; only now, the sound seemed ominous in the silence of the library. Finally, Katie found what she was looking for. She cleared her throat, licked her lips, and read:

"'The Norns have the capability to see every possible future for every possible person. This has made them enemies among their pantheon, as they have, with one look, with one touch, seen the precise time and circumstance of a god's death. Such knowledge was considered an ill omen in the past, a sign of bad luck, as any mortal unlucky enough to discover the way to kill a god or goddess would become their sworn enemy.'"

Xiomara collapsed back into the chair with a wave of her hand. "As I said."

Jayne couldn't decide whether Xiomara sounded smug or irritated. Both, really.

"But that must be why the Allfather shut them away," Katie argued. "They know how to create a future that will destroy him. At the same time, they also understand a future that would destroy his enemies, so he doesn't want to kill them outright."

"If he even could," Xiomara agreed.

Katie nodded. "Right. So, what if we sent an expedition to the World Tree?"

"Sounds cool. What is, and where is, the World Tree?" Jayne asked, sipping her gloriously yummy tea.

Henry chimed in. "The World Tree is a different sort of pocket. It was created before the Torrent was locked away, and it was not a point at which magic leaked into this world. It's a little more like a Time Catch—it's a point removed from Earth. A pocket created from within the Torrent, rather than from without."

"I'm not sure I like the sound of that," Jayne said. "How do we get there?"

"No idea," Katie said. "Maybe it's in the book." She handed it over.

"You are going to leap without looking and catch a case of madness, my girl," Xiomara proclaimed. Her mouth was a thin line.

"Jayne has already traveled in time," Henry reminded Xiomara. "Jayne has been blessed with a familiar who holds this specific knowledge—so the Disciples of Gaia say—and her ability to meet the other goddesses is a form of time travel in itself."

"Astral projection and traveling in your own timeline are two very different things," Xiomara shot back. "Can we afford for our last best hope to risk losing her mind?"

"Can we afford not to?" Jayne asked quietly.

Her question cut through Henry's sputtering arguments and Katie's *hmm*. They all stopped and looked at her as one. Jayne took a deep breath and tried not to let the pain choke her. "I've *failed*. I was supposed to defeat Odin, and instead he walked away with people I love in thrall to him. He's won. For now, at least. If I'm the last best hope, I have to get better. I'm not good enough to defeat him, and the Norns can help me. I need all the power I can get." She crooked a smile at Xiomara. "I promise I won't go mad." She held up the pot. "Tea?"

Xiomara was not amused. "Don't make promises you can't keep," she said.

Well, if she wouldn't take it as a joke... "If it will make you feel better, we can run this by Amanda. It's not like we're swimming in options. She's got a cool head. She'll assess the risks and decide if it's too much."

Xiomara flipped her braids over her shoulder, her dark mouth twisting in contempt. "Amanda is desperate. Don't act like she's a neutral party in this. She'll never say no to your plan, no matter how half-baked it is." She breathed out hard through her nose. "Keep your book," she told Katie shortly. She turned on her heel and stormed out.

They watched her go. Katie's eyes were as wide as teacups. "Did she just...insult my books?" she whispered. She looked like she was going to cry.

"Don't listen to her." Jayne patted Katie's arm. "Your books are marvelous."

But she didn't like the way Xiomara had left, either. They needed to be unified, now more than ever, and watching one of her oldest, staunchest allies turn against her made her feel that perhaps—just perhaps—Xiomara had a point.

CHAPTER

SIX

If Jayne had expected to feel tingles of forbidden power upon finishing the Norn book, she was disappointed. On her third cup of vanilla chai, she sat in the library and drummed her fingers on the book's cover absently until it emitted a tiny meep of protest that made her realize what she was doing. "Oops. Sorry."

Of course, the knowledge within was dangerous. The Norns were slippery creatures, according to this manuscript, who would easily give a supplicant what they asked for...even though most of the time, it wasn't what the supplicant truly desired. "A girl will have to be careful," she said aloud and rubbed at the scaly patch on her arm. "I'm counting on you to help me with that."

Hayden sleepily rustled affirmatives in her mind; he was half-napping. "Yes, I know. Being a dragon is a hard job."

Okay. She needed a plan.

The Norns had first appeared in literature in the *Poetic Edda*, so Jayne returned the Norn book and grabbed a dictionary of Old Norse from the Languages shelf. She didn't speak Old Norse, but Katie Bell took care of the needs of the TCO with an ingenious Translation spell that allowed an Adept seeking a new language to be immediately fluent, like a mental dictionary download. Jayne loved it. She didn't think she'd ever get over how new knowledge could simply bloom in her mind as though it had always been there, latent, waiting for its chance to stretch and show off. She spoke so many languages now that she could be a translator for the UN. Which, if she screwed this up, could be the only job she'd ever be able to get again.

Focus, she told herself, delighted when the Viking word for that slipped into her mind. *Berserk:* a heightened state of focus during battle. Fitting. Old Norse gave her a stranger translation for focus—*arin-elde*: hearth fire, and *bak*: to bake. Maybe the spell was wonky after all. Latin to Old Norse could be a challenge, even for Katie. Then again, the hearthstone was sacred throughout many cultures, the heart of the home, the one place that, even when the walls collapsed, would stay *in situ*, possibly cracked but not vanquished. Steadfast. Maybe it wasn't off after all.

She tested out another thought, directed at Odin himself: *Ha deg vekk, fordømte rasshøl! Get lost, damn asshole!* That cheered her immensely.

Smiling now, Jayne checked out a copy of the *Poetic Edda* and retreated to her Nashville apartment to read with a cup of tea that didn't come prepacked in a bag.

She came through the front door and her breath stuttered. The momentary joy and peace she'd felt in the library fled. The apartment smelled wrong without Tristan in it. She could wear his shirts and use his soap and it still wouldn't make a difference. It was like she was trying to inhabit a ghost in the hopes it could replace the real thing. The empty spot on the key holder by the door, the lack of the bitter, soil smell of coffee grounds. The silence.

Maybe sitting here with a book wasn't such a good idea.

Berserk, Thorne. If she could make this work, if she could meet the Norns and convince them to give her the Time totem, she could get Tristan back. She could get it all back. *And you know you're going to succeed, because you're going to have a daughter and she's going to get stuck in the Torrent and she needs your help too, by the way. And it's Tristan's daughter as well. We think. So he has to be returned in one piece at some point.*

"Yeah, because I'm gonna turn back time. It didn't work for Cher, but I'm Jayne Thorne, damn it. Also, you're talking to yourself. Loser. Get to work."

She took a deep breath of air that completely and utterly lacked Tristan Labelle, then went into the kitchen, humming. A quick raid of the fridge turned up no pie, so she settled for some box cookies (completely inferior) and sat in Tristan's armchair. Soon the *Poetic Edda* flowed through her brain in lilting alliterative syllables that she couldn't help but read aloud. She forgot, as was typical with a good book, everything about food and contact with the outside world, taking breaks only to sip her tea and soothe her throat as the stories of Grimnir and Loki and Thrym flowed through her.

Night had fallen by the time she heard a key turn in the lock. Her heart soared for a fraction of a second with a stupid, useless hope. By the time the door had creaked open and Sofia said, "Hello?" into the dark hall, Jayne had managed to tame her feelings.

"In here." She blinked and looked around. At some point she'd turned on the light; she wasn't sure when.

Sofia came in and wrinkled her nose. "It smells a bit stale in here," she said, and set about opening windows. "You haven't been answering your phone."

Jayne stretched. When had her neck started to ache? "I was reading. Did we lose the war? Is it the end of the world?" She hadn't heard any Wraith sirens, at least.

Sofia rolled her eyes. "Maybe you just have a father and sister who want to get in touch with you."

Right. That. Jayne worked her shoulders up and down to loosen the stiff muscles, then said, "Listen to this. According to *Fáfnismál,* there are countless Norns. Maybe one for each future!"

Sofia looked unimpressed. "And *Fáfnismál* is..."

"A poem." Jayne brandished the *Poetic Edda.* "But in the *Völuspá*—that's another poem—they number just three. And they don't just travel in time. They *construct the content of time.*"

Sofia sat on the couch and put a hand to her head. "Let's pretend that it's been a long day and I just got mauled almost to death by the father of my child, and I'd like you to explain this all to me like I'm five years old."

Jayne set the book aside. Sofia's eyes were bleary from lack of sleep and grief, and she looked seconds away from passing out. "When did you last eat?"

Sofia waved a hand. "Baby doesn't feel like eating."

"Baby doesn't get to say." Jayne sighed and went into the kitchen to peruse the takeout menus.

She found a place that would deliver dim sum and ordered dumplings, congee, egg tarts, and an assortment of stir-fries. Then she ordered a rhubarb-vanilla-clementine pie, checked the freezer for ice cream, and went back to the living room.

"You *are* going to eat," she told Sofia. "And while we wait, I can try to explain about the Norns."

"Norn away."

"Okay. The Norn named Urd has the knowledge of the past, down to the most minuscule detail." Jayne tried not to squirm with envy at that. "Verdandi knows everything that is happening *right now,* in the short and the long term—the split-second decisions and the long-held dreams of every person on the planet, and how they weave to form a dense and confusing tapestry that only she can read. And Skuld sees the future, all that will and all that can be."

Sofia whistled. Jayne explained the rest.

The dangerous book in the TCO library had confirmed the Disciples of Gaia's belief that the Norns visited each person the day they were born. Urd saw the circumstances that had brought them into the world, Verdandi saw the world around them in completion, and Skuld saw all the paths they might take through it. And together they wove a person's fate.

The fate could be changed, but it was not easy.

"So my first task—at least, in my mind—is to understand whether it's my fate to take control of the Time totem and defeat Odin once and for all. And if it isn't, well, my second task is to find out how to *make* it my fate."

"No wonder Xiomara warned against this," Sofia said. "How do we even get to the Norns? Since Odin was the one who locked them away, it's not like you can hop a plane or a portal to them, right?"

Jayne shrugged.

"You're not trying to put together some sneaky mission through the Torrent, are you? Because that would be stupid."

"Every other goddess has been accessible through a manuscript," Jayne said. The doorbell rang and she stood. "Why not the Norns?" she tossed out, going to retrieve their food.

She gave the delivery driver a handsome tip and brought their food into the living room. They didn't bother going over to the table—Jayne fetched bowls for each of them, brewed a fragrant jasmine tea, and filled Sofia's bowl with congee and prawn dumplings.

"Has it been bad?" she asked, feeling a stab of guilt.

"What?" Sofia looked at her like there were too many ways to answer that question. "I mean, yes, but what exactly?"

"Pregnancy."

"Ah." Sofia nodded. "I get morning sickness most days. Sometimes I'm too tired to do anything but sit at my desk, and since I'm not supposed to go back to Aegis very often, I end up dozing off in the TCO canteen a lot."

No one really knew what a Time Catch did to a fetus in development, so Sofia was supposed to stay out as much as possible. "You know you don't have to do this alone, right?" Jayne said.

Sofia was silent for a moment, staring at her congee. When Jayne didn't even hear her breathe, she knew her sister was crying.

She slid onto the couch next to Sofia just as the other woman let out a great sob. Sofia nestled her head on Jayne's shoulder and shuddered with such pain that tears sprang into her eyes, too. She'd felt so isolated in her grief that she hadn't seen her sister was suffering the same. "It's okay," she murmured, even though she had no idea whether it could ever be okay again. "We'll get him back."

"You didn't see the look in his eyes." Sofia hiccupped. "He didn't even know me. He was so excited to become a father, and then he tried to kill—" Her words dissolved into a fresh spate of tears.

"We *will* get him back." They'd get them all back, every last Rogue that had disappeared through the portal. Even their enemies. "And even if we don't, you'll never go through this alone, Sofia. I'm always here for you."

Sofia cried for a long time. When her sniffling subsided enough, she said, "I don't even know who I am anymore without Cillian."

Jayne fished a tissue out of the box on the side table and held it up for her sister to blow her nose. Sofia let out a little laugh. She'd always been the motherly sister. Jayne reminded her, "You are who you have always been, strong and smart and a natural caretaker. You'll give your child a good life, and Cillian *will* be in it."

Sofia took another tissue and wiped her face, staring out the window at the Nashville skyline. "I can't help thinking that of the two of us, I'm the monster," she said quietly at last. "I can't help thinking that if one of us should have lost their minds, it should have been me. I killed my own mother, after all."

Jayne took her by the shoulders. "You are a hero," she said firmly. "You did something that so many people would never be able to do, and it hurt like hell, and I'm here for you. And I'm only here for you because you were *there* for me. Just think what might have happened if Ruth had killed me and taken the totems. There'd be no hope for Cillian. There'd be no hope for anyone."

She picked up the cup of jasmine tea and pressed it into Sofia's hands. "Now, drink. Eat. I promise you'll feel better."

They demolished the dim sum, and even though Jayne's belly was groaning by the end of it, she got the ice cream out of the freezer and cut Sofia a generous slice of pie, reserving a smaller one for herself. They took a moment together to relish the tangy rhubarb-clementine and the creamy vanilla ice cream. Then Sofia sat back.

"What about you?" she asked softly. "How bad has it been?"

"It's...hard," Jayne admitted, thankful she didn't have to keep up her sarcastic cheer around her sister. "Okay, it's awful. I wake up and expect him to be there. I go to the gym, or the canteen, or home, and I just...I can't get used to the feeling that he's gone." She palmed at her eyes and set her face. She was finished with tears for tonight. "But I also know that I'm going to get him back. *We'll* get them back. Together."

"Starting with the Norns? You never told me how you were going to find them," Sofia said.

"The Codex Regius," Jayne said. "It's the original *Prose Edda*. The *Völuspá* was first recorded in it, and I bet that if the Norns are bound to any book, it's that one. It's in Reykjavik."

"And you have a plan?" Sofia said.

"More or less," Jayne said, shrugging. "Pose as a worker in the institute where the codex is kept, sneak into the vault where it's held, pay a visit to the Norns. We've done this five times, Sof. We can do it again. Grimoires 'R' Us, right?"

"As long as we're not rushing into things," Sofia said with a grimace. "I know we want to save Cillian and Tristan and all the others as quickly as possible, but we still have to think of our safety—your safety. After all, if you die getting shot by some squirrely security guard, what happens to them?" A line creased her brow. "Come to think of it, why not just ask the institute to help us out? It's not like we're trying to keep magic a secret anymore."

"Katie says the chances of their cooperation are low," Jayne admitted. She'd put her favorite librarian on the case of manuscript research the moment she'd realized where the Norns could be found.

Her phone rang. "Speaking of..." she said. "Katie! What can you do for me?"

Katie's posh voice was tinny over the long distance. "I've got news," she said.

Jayne noticed she didn't say whether it was good news or bad news. "Okay?"

"The Codex Regius isn't at the Arní Magnússon Institute for Icelandic Studies anymore. It's been removed. It's possible that one of our other magical friends got wind of what was happening and made the same bet we made."

"That sounds..." *Unlikely,* Jayne wanted to say. But was it more unlikely than someone taking a random interest in the manuscript right at a time when Jayne would need to access it? "Do we know where it is?"

"Thanks to Isra, we do." Katie sounded pleased. "There's an increase in interesting activity at the Royal Library in Copenhagen. The codex was there before, you know."

"I know." Jayne laughed. "I read that book, too. The entire collection of Icelandic myths and great works was housed in Copenhagen until 1971. So it's back?"

"We suspect so. But if it's been moved on account of you, you can expect resistance. This will call for careful planning, Jayne."

"Why does everyone remind me of that?" Jayne thanked Katie and hung up. It seemed her impulsive reputation was coming back to bite her.

She took a forkful of pie and grinned at her sister. "So, Copenhagen. Ever wanted to go?"

SEVEN

Henry Thorne was sitting on another failure of his Time Reverse when he got what might be his most audacious, his worst, his most brilliant idea yet. His heart gave a tremendous thump, and every hair on his body stood on end. He felt like he'd been struck by lightning.

"What's wrong?" Quimby asked. "You look like you've seen a ghost."

"Perhaps I have." He blew out a huge breath and straightened his glasses. "The problem with totems is someone has to give them to you," he told her. She was fiddling with the receptor field on their Time Stop but paused to look at him, nonplussed.

"Ookay..."

"What if one could *make* a totem?" he said.

Quimby frowned at him. Her frizzy mane of strawberry blonde hair stuck up around her welding goggles. "Make a totem? I've never heard of anyone doing that. Where would we even start? I suppose they're elemental—"

Henry waved away her doubt. He was in the business of doing things other people didn't do.

"You'd start with a sacred object. Totems sit on the forehead, but is that because they need access to the mind, or is it because we've only ever seen them on Jayne, and that's where her goddesses choose to put them? Imagine if we had a totem that could be carried, exchanged, even given away."

"Then it wouldn't be a totem so much as a...gadget. Like the one we're trying to make now," Quimby pointed out.

Henry shook his head. He wasn't explaining this right. "Totems draw on a Master's power and meld to their character —otherwise anyone would be able to use them, and the goddesses wouldn't be so precise about who gets to have them. And with the clue Hayden gave us about folding time, rather than spinning it back like a dial on a machine—"

The door to the Genius Lab opened, and his daughters came in. They looked like they'd had naps, each of them, and a bit to eat. Sofia had regained some of her luminous glow. Some.

"You've been crying," he said, noticing their red-rimmed eyes.

"Thanks, Dad." Jayne rolled hers in response.

"Yeah, wonder what we'd have to cry about," Sofia grumped to Quimby. "I thought you were supposed to teach him the finer points of etiquette."

Quimby shrugged and picked up her welding torch. "I'm afraid in the Genius Lab, it's Henry who's teaching me. Could you move, please? You're blocking the light."

Henry couldn't contain himself. "Jayne. Sofia. What if *both* of you had access to the Time totem? What if *both* of you could fold time?"

The sisters exchanged glances. "We'd be conjoined twins?" Jayne guessed.

"We'd have *two* Time totems," Henry replied.

"A cool idea, but not sure the goddesses would go for it," Jayne said.

"True. But what if I could create the totem? Myself."

"You want to...make one?" Sofia looked around, as if a goddess might jump out of a test tube and shout "Surprise!"

"That's pretty ambitious, even for you, Dad," Jayne said.

"On the other hand, it would keep you focused on something other than leaping into the Torrent at the worst possible moment," Sofia added. "So, by all means."

"Everyone quiet," said Quimby. She straightened. "Don't move."

She twisted the dial on the Time Stop. Henry felt a strange lurch in his stomach...then Quimby said again, "Everyone quiet. Don't move."

She twisted the dial on the Time Stop. Something *dinged*. Henry blinked.

It worked!

He scrambled for his stopwatch and a piece of paper. His mouth was dry and his mind was spinning. "How long? How long was that?" He grabbed Quimby by the shoulder and nearly threw her to the ground with a hug. "You *reversed time*."

Quimby was laughing wildly. "I don't know. Two seconds?" she guessed. She was breathless with victory.

Jayne looked at Sofia doubtfully. "Dad, Hayden already said this wouldn't do the trick..."

But Henry didn't need to listen to the opinion of a know-it-all dragon familiar who was, in all likelihood, stuck sometime in the past. The Time Reverse worked. He could make it work better. They'd adapt the Time Stop and the Time Reverse together, increasing the range and time span.

Another thought struck him. Had anyone been affected outside of this room? Had the whole world gone back in time a couple of seconds? Or had they frozen for those moments, waiting for Henry to catch up? Or was he now *two seconds behind* everyone else?

There was so much to research, and so little time.

So much research, so little time, his mother, Alexandra, had said, with something approaching fondness. The last time he'd seen her, when he'd slipped through a back door of the Torrent during the battle in Iceland, she'd looked just the same as when she'd disappeared into the Torrent thirty years ago. Her hair was longer, her clothes threadbare, and there were worries in her eyes that had not been there when she'd disappeared. But it had been her.

There is one thing you must research. One victory you and your kin must take. You must free me from this place. One hand gestured to the enormous rotting tree around her, to the bars as wide as trunks, that Henry could never have cut through on his own.

Every time he thought he was being foolish, or dreaming too deep, he remembered his mother's voice and face. The way her eyes had pierced his through the bars of her prison. *You cannot defeat the Allfather without me,* she'd hissed.

And, well, in the moment she'd looked a little mad. But when had Henry not flirted with madness? And his mother knew things that he could only dream of knowing. If she said she was the key to defeating the Allfather, he believed her. And so he mused on the creation of a machine that could reverse time, take him back to before she was thrown in her prison—or a machine that could speed up time, rot the tree around her until they stood in a pile of sawdust.

"Do you think you can help?" Jayne asked, and he realized he'd been ignoring the whole room during a conversation he was supposed to be part of.

"Of course." He coughed. "Let me see what I can do."

He thought he'd gotten away with it for a moment until Sofia put a hand on his arm. "Do you need a break, Dad? The canteen's serving chicken soup."

He liked a good bowl of chicken soup. But he didn't have

time. They needed to capitalize immediately on Quimby's success. "You girls run along. I'll join you in a little while."

Sofia and Jayne exchanged a look. "We will be back to drag you to dinner," Jayne informed him. "Don't even try to get out of it."

When they left Quimby looked at him. "Do you even know what you agreed to?"

He shrugged, and she laughed. "I tend to tune everyone else out when I'm deep in thought." Then they went back to what was really important: the Time Reverse and all the beautiful things it might be able to bring them.

They were attempting to adjust the temporal field when the door to the laboratory opened again. "It can't possibly be dinnertime," Henry protested, looking at his watch.

But it wasn't the girls in the doorway. It was Xiomara, in a teal dress accented with a wide ribbon belt embroidered with birds and flowers. Very cheerful, considering the dour look on her face.

"Ah..." Had they had an appointment? Verbal agreements seemed to slip out of Henry's mind the way magic and physics formulas never did. "I'm working on something."

"You're always working on something." Xiomara sounded bitter.

Henry stiffened. What had he done to earn her ire this time?

She moved farther into the room, braids swaying. "That's been your excuse for years. Decades, even. You were always working on something. Working too hard to corral your wife. Working too hard to look after your children. Working too hard to see the bigger picture." She picked up a vial of blood from the on-hold magical doping experiment, curled her lip at it, then set it back down.

Henry's fingers spasmed into a fist. He took a deep breath

and forced them to relax. "I think you're being unfair," he said in the mildest, most even voice he could manage.

"Am I?" She spun toward him. "You've always been so obsessed with your work that you didn't notice your world crumbling around you. Isn't that true? Blinded by love, and by the fact that Ruth let you do whatever you want without worrying about the consequences?"

"I...no," Henry protested, but it sounded weak.

Quimby folded her arms. "Is there something we can help you with?" she asked coldly.

"You need to stop Jayne before she does something that turns this world on its head," Xiomara said.

Henry's throat closed around his words. He swallowed, then said carefully, "We've seen no other way. If you know of an alternative to seeking out the Norns—"

"Accept your fate," she bit out, so fiercely that Henry recoiled. "What's done is done and cannot be done again. We gambled, and now we face the consequences. Better to make the best world we can out of it than to succumb to madness trying for a different outcome to what's already passed."

"Jayne will never accept that." Henry shook his head. His daughter was stubborn, strong-willed, and willing to do almost anything to save the people she'd lost. And didn't he know she'd succeed? Did he not already know she had a daughter of her own?

Unless she's already pregnant, came the thought unbidden. *Unless Trinity is the remnant of an alternate universe.* He didn't know enough about time travel, after all. Not really. And his scientific mind had to accept the possibility that he was deceiving himself.

"Jayne will do what she thinks is right," he said again, gently. Xiomara tossed her head. "Whether or not we endorse it, she will. If I tell her not to go to the Norns, she'll find her own way to the World Tree and possibly get herself killed along the way. The best course of action is to support her, and make sure she doesn't do anything rash."

Xiomara trembled. A moment later a spell spun from her hand and smashed into a pile of papers, sending them coasting around the room. "Hey!" Quimby shouted, hurrying around the side of the table. Henry's hands were up, ready to defend, before he noticed they were moving. With some effort, he lowered them. He didn't want to look like a threat.

"Jayne Thorne is already doing something rash. You cannot interfere with the timeline! You are aware of the butterfly effect, the branching timelines effect. The Torrent Decomposition Effect."

"Those are all theories," Henry pointed out. Because no one, as far as he knew, had ever actually succeeded at time travel before.

"What's the Torrent Decomposition Effect?" Quimby asked.

Katie Bell and Henry had come up with the Torrent Decomposition Effect one rainy day at the TCO when they'd been stuck in a long canteen line together. "It is a theory that when a timeline branches, following a big event that has two greater outcomes, the Torrent diverges to support both timelines, thus becoming weaker in each world. It's a possible explanation as to why it was possible to lock off the Torrent years ago. If time travel creates alternate universes, and the Torrent has to divide itself between each one..."

"Holy cow," Quimby said. "That's astonishing. Why didn't you tell me? That changes everything."

Xiomara wasn't finished. "Henry Thorne, your blood-sworn duty as a Guardian is to protect the Torrent. It is *not* to bow down to the whims of the women in your life, no matter how powerful. You already abandoned the Guardians, abandoned your pocket, and left everything worth protecting behind, all so you could follow Ruth on her insane quest for power. Then you hid when all your poor decisions blew up in your face." Xiomara stomped toward him, fists clenched as though she were getting ready to punch him. Henry couldn't help taking a step back. "Well, not all of us are willing to go hide in a Time Catch. I've had enough of you laying your troubles at our door."

"Jayne is *not* Ruth," Henry snapped back. He wasn't sure what he'd expected to say, but that wasn't it. He took a deep breath and said again, more gently, "Jayne is not Ruth. She's not doing this for the power. She's doing this to save people we care about. And yes, I've made mistakes. But this is not one, and I will stand by my daughter's side, and fix all of the messes I've made. Nothing, and no one, will stop me from that."

Xiomara stared at him for a long moment. Her lined brown face was flushed, and her chest rose and fell with emotion. "You still don't understand." Her disappointment stung. "It doesn't matter *why* Jayne is doing this. Do you think anyone will care why the world has been destroyed, or forgive her for it when the time comes? Will anyone look back with reason, knowing that she went mad, but it was for a good cause?"

Her hands came up. And Henry must have been on edge, for a Shield spell spread over him and Quimby before he saw that Xiomara had made no spell of her own. Her hands were outstretched, yes, but her palms were facing him, a gesture of peace. They looked at each other through threads of shimmering gold.

"The Guardians must protect the Torrent, even from people we once called our friends and allies. If you don't do something about her, we will," Xiomara said softly. Then she turned on her heel and left.

EIGHT

The portal spit them out into a tiny apartment overlooking Købmagergade, one of Copenhagen's pedestrian streets. From there it was a twenty-minute walk to the Royal Library, where the Codex Regius currently resided. It was a dreary day in Copenhagen, which wasn't abnormal. Jayne zipped her raincoat all the way up to her chin and eyed her sleeves with some doubt. Nothing for it—she was going to get damp.

As long as the manuscript can be put in a Carry spell, it will stay dry, and nothing else matters. What was a little discomfort when saving the world? You'd think the flat would have an umbrella, but of course, it didn't. Maybe she could conjure up a Dry spell. Except two women walking down the street in the rain with an invisible umbrella floating above their heads, keeping them dry while others were drenched, would be rather suspicious. They needed to keep the magic to a minimum so they didn't attract any Wraiths.

"Are you ready?" Jayne asked.

She must have sounded anxious because Sofia rolled her eyes and patted her belly. "Come on, Jayne. It's not like the baby's going to get wet."

"That's not what I'm worried about," Jayne muttered, pulling up her hood. Although she could catastrophize about Sofia getting wet, and then getting sick...

But Jayne could always heal her, even if the worst happened. Far more likely was the possibility that they'd run into some kind of trouble at the library, and Sofia would get hurt. They still didn't know who'd taken the manuscript out of Reykjavik, or why.

It wasn't the Disciples, at least: Isra had briefed the TCO team before they left, with Ruger presiding.

"I found a Disciple with access to the Royal Library's annex, where the rare manuscripts are kept," she'd said in her mellifluous voice. "That ID will get Jayne and Sofia through the locked door. The Royal Library staff is quite small, though, especially those who work with medieval manuscripts, so Jayne and Sofia will need to stay out of sight as much as possible. They can pose as Danes, thanks to Katie's expansive translation dictionary collection.

"There are security guards, but if you walk like you know where you're going, you can probably get past them without much trouble. Just keep your ID visible so they don't have to ask for it," Isra said. "Other than that...if the fire alarm goes off, they don't use sprinklers."

"Thank the Goddess for that. All those books...," said Jayne.

"As if they would." Sofia chuckled.

"Thornes," Ruger warned.

Isra was unbothered. "In lieu of water, it's a museum-grade fire suppression system. Fires are extinguished by depriving them of oxygen. If you hear the fire alarm, you have thirty seconds to exit the annex before shields come down over the doors and all the oxygen is sucked out of the room through the ventilation system."

Sofia and Jayne exchanged meaningful glances. "Right, then," Jayne said.

And off they went.

If anything did go wrong, they had a Time Stop primed with exactly one use. Other than that, they were flying by the seat of their pants. There hadn't been time to prepare more.

Brushing rain from her forehead, Jayne pocketed the safe-house key and followed Sofia out onto the cramped stairwell. They had a ticket for a tour of the new part of the Royal Library —the Black Diamond annex—and plenty of time to get there.

The streets were quiet. No one strolled or browsed; the few other people on the street walked at a quick pace with their heads down. They had someplace to be, and they weren't inter-ested in dawdling. Jayne wondered whether it was the rain or the Wraiths that created this attitude. She could not help glancing up at the skies. No sign of Wraiths, happily. No siren, either.

They walked to a square adorned with a statue of a medieval knight on a rearing horse, then past the parliamentary palace of Christiansborg and the ruins of the Old Stock Exchange, which had caught fire during a Wraith attack a few months before. Jayne felt a pang as they passed the crumbling brick and sandstone walls, held up by scaffolding and taped off. How much culture and history would be destroyed by this war?

They went down to the edge of the water and turned. The Black Diamond was a large square building of polished black marble and glass that leaned out over the canal. It sparkled even in the dreary light of the rain. Jayne's heart quickened, though she wasn't sure whether it was from the sight of one of the world's greatest libraries, or the job ahead of them.

"Focus," murmured Sofia, taking her hand.

"Berserk," Jayne said.

"Huh?"

"It's Old Norse for 'focus.' Probably not a literal translation."

"Jayne? Are you demented?"

"Demented and sad. But social," she replied with a grin.

Sofia laughed. "God, I miss that movie."

"I miss movies, period. I need a long weekend and some popcorn." *And Tristan,* she couldn't help but think. That did it. "All right, sister. Thornes, activate."

Jayne took a deep breath. They were here to borrow the manuscript. And they really were here to *borrow* it—after she'd spoken to the Norns, Ruger would bring it back.

The walk went quickly, and they weren't too drenched when they found the doors. They hung their coats in the cloakroom and headed out into a wide-open hall with a warm wood floor. The wall by the canal was one enormous window, affording them a view of the gray-green water and the charming old warehouses-turned-apartments on the other side. Escalators took visitors upstairs to reading rooms, halls, and auditoriums, while a café served coffee and buns that smelled of sugar and cinnamon and cardamom. Jayne's mouth watered. *Focus.* Sweets later, codex now.

Sofia checked her phone. "We've got twenty minutes until the tour starts," she said. "Reconnaissance?"

Jayne nodded. "Reconnaissance." She took her sister's arm and they began to stroll around the room together.

"One lovely thing about this job," she said. "I'm traveling as much as I always wanted to."

Sofia laughed. "That's you. Either you want to be deep in some historical building, or at home deep in a book."

"The hours are strange, though." At home it was nine in the morning, but here it was three p.m. Jayne had thought that traveling by portal would help with jet lag, but it just meant she sometimes had to get up in the middle of the night instead. Even now, she found it hard to reconcile the sandwiches and salads people were eating at the café with the breakfast she'd hastily gobbled down an hour ago.

Sofia's mouth drew into a thin line. She leaned against Jayne and whispered, "Don't look, but we're being followed."

Jayne forced herself not to react and whirl around immediately. "Who is it?"

"He's dressed like security, but I think we can agree he's not. The uniform looks genuine, though. We won't know who he's with until we engage."

Jayne nodded and wiggled her fingers, warming them up. *Ready for action?* she asked her totems. They stirred, as did Hayden. "Options?"

"Cancel the mission," Sofia began.

Jayne shook her head. "Nope."

"I knew you'd say that." They wound around a cluster of comfy-looking chairs and pretended to admire the view over the canal. The water was peaceful, little drops of rain dimpling its surface. "Try to lose him?"

"How?" Jayne pointed at the lamps far above their heads and pretended to gawk like a proper tourist would.

"I create a distraction, you run for the book?" Sofia said.

Jayne snorted. "Like I'd leave you to fend for yourself."

"I can hold my own in a fight," Sofia snapped. "Who taught you how to kickbox, hmm?" Then she plastered a smile on her face. Just another happy tourist. "Jayne, you have to stop treating me like I'm made of glass."

"But we weren't sent here to have an overt conflict," Jayne argued in a whisper. Which was true, even if her real motives were to protect Sofia and the baby. "It's not smart to split us up so there's only one of us on each front."

"Well, we can try to distract them some other way..." Sofia frowned, thinking.

"Ladies?" said the security guard who was definitely not a security guard.

"Too late," Jayne muttered from the side of her mouth. She turned. "Yes, sir?" she said in perfect Danish.

He was a tall, bald white man whom Jayne only vaguely recognized—maybe she'd seen him at the Battle of Kirkjufell? Or perhaps he was a member of La Liberté? She scanned his hands and hip, but he carried no weapons. Of course, if he used magic, his hands were the weapons.

"May I look inside your bag, please?" His voice echoed and carried in the space, causing people to turn their heads. He was attracting attention intentionally.

Jayne slung her purse off her shoulder and handed it over with a relaxed attitude. "Sure," she told him with a brittle smile. "I have nothing to hide."

He unzipped the bag and removed her wallet, checking its contents before handing it to Sofia. A packet of tissues, a box of mints, a pen, and a tiny notebook. Jayne's phone. He inspected them all with an air of high suspicion, as if he knew one of them was a disguise for something else.

Then he came to the little Zippo lighter at the bottom of her bag. "You don't look like you smoke," he said, a suspicious glint in his eye.

"I burn a lot of incense," Jayne explained. "Must have forgotten to take it out of my bag."

"Lighters are, of course, prohibited in the Royal Library." He moved to put it in his pocket.

"Wait." Sofia's hand shot out. Jayne saw her stop and mentally curse herself. Now the guard could be certain that the lighter was no lighter at all. "We'll go put it in the pocket of our coats," she said.

The guard flicked the lid of the Zippo open. His thumb came

down on the sparker, and just as Jayne clamped her hand around his wrist, time stopped.

The man froze. Sofia too was frozen midlunge for the lighter. Sound had dropped away to nothing, leaving the Royal Library in eerie silence. Jayne had thirteen seconds and no plan.

She sucker-punched him in the jaw, layering it with a spell that would knock him off his feet when time started again. Then she ran for it.

Sofia was right—she wasn't made of glass. She could handle the guard. Jayne needed a head start on getting to the codex, and in the heat of the moment, she couldn't think of anything better than Sofia's plan B. Besides, if the man had wanted to kill them, he'd have hung about until they were distracted and assassinated them from a distance. He wouldn't have played security guard and tried to disarm them first.

She nearly slammed into the door leading to the rare manuscripts annex. Jayne flashed her badge and with shaking fingers punched in the code Isra had given her. Behind her, the guard was getting to his feet. "Stop," he shouted. She had a feeling he wouldn't have bothered with that either if he were trying to kill her.

She whipped through the door and heaved it closed behind her, hoping to delay his entry. She pounded down a neat hall with a marble floor and white doors to either side.

For a few more seconds, it would be just the two of them. Then he might be joined by his allies, and she had no idea how many there were.

Jayne stopped running and closed her eyes. *I need you,* she called to the goddesses. Then she sketched a hasty Find spell in the air.

She felt the presence of Amaterasu, the goddess who had given her the Spirit totem. A thin golden strand of light emanated from Jayne's outstretched hand like a thread, tugging it down the hall. Jayne took off again.

She followed the thread to a room with a closed door. It didn't respond to her badge, so an Unlock spell forced it open—

And set off the alarm as well.

Jayne cursed. It seemed the Time Stop was finished. No time to waste now.

She barreled into the room, which was cool and low-lit to protect the books. Each book lay in a vitrine case, neatly labeled. A box of latex gloves sat on a table in the center, and a safe off to the side held loose sheets between glass.

Shoot. Which one was it?

Amaterasu's golden thread landed on the vitrine farthest from her, and Jayne hopped over the case and hurried down to the correct one.

Jayne sent a silent apology to the gods of old books and grabbed the vitrine with the Codex Regius with her bare hands and wrenched it from its stand. She heard a noise and whirled around to see two Adepts in the doorway. Also strangers. How many were there?

"Whoever you are, you don't know what's at stake," she said.

"We know exactly what's at stake, Jayne Thorne," said the Adept on the left. She was a little shorter than Jayne, but stocky, with muscles that suggested a weight-training regimen. She also looked like she chewed concrete for breakfast.

Jayne started to slip the book into the Carry spell she'd prepared for this moment. A Lance spell smashed into her hand, breaking her wrist and making her drop the book. She clutched her wrist with a hiss of pain and felt Hayden curl into a protective ball.

You okay? she asked him.

Anger was the only response. Great. No dragon to help. They threw that spell on purpose.

Okay, hang tight. I got this.

"You idiot," Jayne snarled, advancing. "Do you have any idea how priceless this book is?" Then common sense took over. The Lance spell had been gold, not green. These were no ordinary Adepts.

They were Guardians. That's why Hayden had been stunned. Jayne was, too.

She stared at them. "What are you doing here? We're on the same side." At least, she hoped they were. But the woman had happily decommissioned Jayne with one blow. Could they be part of the Kingdom? Had Hans and Ruth succeeded in turning more Guardians to their side?

The male Guardian scowled at his partner. He was Asian, with a long face and a black ponytail. "We weren't supposed to use our magic." He came forward and scooped up the codex. "We are sorry for this," he told Jayne. "But we are Guardians of the Torrent, and we cannot let you put it in danger. We are all agreed."

He nodded to his associate, and they began to back away. If they left the annex with this book, Jayne knew she could say goodbye to it forever.

She used her good hand to push to her feet. If these fools thought a broken wrist would keep her out of action—well, they had another think coming. But she couldn't use her magic, not without risking the book. They must know that; it was probably why they didn't put the book in a Carry spell of their own.

So she charged them.

NINE

Jayne tackled the man, head-butting him right in the solar plexus. He went down with a gurgle that would have been amusing on the mat, but she was too focused to think about it now. The woman shouted and grabbed Jayne by the arm with the broken wrist. Jayne yelped with pain. She was injured and battling two-on-one; she wouldn't get out of this without fighting dirty.

"Give up. There are almost a dozen of us and only two of you," the woman said.

How does she know that? Jayne thought.

"Admit this is a mistake," the man gasped, blood pouring down his chin.

"And then what?" Jayne twisted around and tried to throw a punch, but the woman blocked her fist easily, twisting Jayne's arm and forcing her to the ground with a cry. "Ow!"

The woman pinned Jayne's good arm next to her head and put her knee on Jayne's chest. She dug around in a back pocket until she came up with a zip tie. "You don't win every match you fight. A lesson you could probably learn right about now."

"So what? We give up? Let Odin win? Is that what you really want?"

Jayne could either lose and learn—or cheat. She chose cheat. If Hayden couldn't help, she had other weapons. She closed her eyes, as if capitulating—and called upon the goddesses.

A moment later, fire roared from her hand. The female Guardian yelped and leaped up, shaking out her fingers. The skin on her palm was already red and blistering.

"Sorry, not sorry," Jayne said, smirking. She leaped to her feet and, with a much more fervent apology to the book gods, kicked the Codex Regius behind her.

It's in the case, it will be fine, she prayed, sending a flicker of flame up to the ceiling.

"What are you—" The man's face paled as the fire alarm began to sound, low and urgent.

Jayne moved so that she was between them and the book. "You've got thirty seconds," she said. "I'll fight you, but do you want to risk the suffocation?"

"You wouldn't," the woman snarled. "You need to survive yourself."

"Never underestimate the power of a smart woman with a stupid idea," Jayne said.

The alarm blared. They stared at each other. A good ten seconds passed.

After another five, the man jerked his head at his companion. "Come on," he said. "It's not like she can set up a portal in fifteen seconds."

They bolted for the door, and Jayne took off in the opposite direction, going for the book. She scooped up the Codex Regius with relief. How much more time now? She could hear people out in the main hall, shouting as they directed tourists toward the exits. She slung the book into the Carry spell, surprised by its weight, and started to run.

Her wrist throbbed. She wasn't going to make it. She pushed her legs faster. There was no choice, she was going to do this, she was going to succeed—

She slammed on the door to the main hall and flew through just as the shield thumped down behind her, grazing her calf and heel. The main hall was chaos. She looked for the security guard and Sofia, and almost missed the Knockout spell aimed right at her face.

Jayne dropped to the ground, rolled, and came up with a Shield spell on her bad arm. She could hold that, at least, while she looked around for her enemies.

"Give it up." The Asian guy was back. "You're surrounded and you have nowhere to go."

Jayne pressed against the door to the annex, looking for an escape. And ah, yes, there was the security guard, too, trying to flank her from the other side.

The Asian looked plenty intimidating, in a fighting stance with two wicked knives of golden light, while his companions prepared spells of protection. Too bad he didn't look down.

A long rune-covered staff whipped under his feet. He fell onto his backside with an "Oof!" Sofia brought the staff back and spun it around in time to shatter the Stun spell that the guard fired her way. "Never take your eyes off a Thorne sister," she snarled.

"You don't get it." The security guard's face was resolute. He reached into the Torrent and brought out a staff of his own— no, Jayne realized. A glaive, a long polearm with a broad-headed blade at its tip. The edge of the glaive sparkled with golden magic. "We can't give up. We won't give up. Your sister wants to turn herself into a weapon that will only help this world descend into chaos. She's going to help the Allfather win."

"You are so wrong." Sofia lunged and they exchanged a loud patter of blows. "And we don't give up on the people we love. You're Guardians. Shouldn't you care about the world you're guarding?"

"Our job is to preserve the Torrent," the security guard said, spinning the glaive in a move even Jayne thought impressive. "As long as the Torrent endures uncorrupted, life will persevere here."

In Jayne's opinion, they were a little past that. As was evidenced by the crash of a Wraith through the enormous observatory window.

She should have known to expect them. It should have been part of the plan. Jayne dashed away from the Guardian and called her own staff to her, whirling it through the air and slamming it into the Wraith's leg just before it could come down hard on a civilian and her child. "Get out of here," Jayne growled. The scared woman didn't need to be told twice.

The Wraith swiped at her and she leapt back. She parried another blow—then dropped her staff as the impact jarred her broken wrist. How possible was it for her to heal herself while she was fighting?

That was a question for any time, but now. The Wraith kicked her staff away, and Jayne was on her own. The Wraith leapt forward, and she threw up a hasty Shield spell. It sank its claws into the shield and slowly pushed down. Jayne felt the spell cracking and gritted her teeth, shoving back with everything she could muster. Her forehead started to glow, and she felt the Wraith begin to pull back. But her wrist throbbed, and she didn't know where Sofia was, and every moment she got distracted, her panic ratcheted a little higher.

Hayden? Little help here?

She could feel his frustration, but he didn't answer. Damn it.

The Wraith's claws broke through the shield. They sliced the leather of Jayne's satchel strap and bit into her shoulder. She screamed.

Then the female Guardian was there, slashing up with a long sword. The Wraith's arm severed from the rest of its body. That was enough. It unfurled its nasty wings and flew away, screaming.

"Why did you do that?" Jayne gasped from where she lay on the floor.

"You are our enemy in this, Jayne Thorne," the woman said. "But we do not want you to die."

"Well, you should have thought of that before you tried to interfere with the mission—"

"I will not argue with you now." The blonde frowned, then reached into the Torrent and brought out—

"A net gun?" Jayne would laugh if she wasn't about to pass out.

The Guardian leveled it against her shoulder and aimed toward another Wraith that swooped through the glass hole three stories above them. She fired. A glittering net of magic unfurled as it spun through the air and hit the Wraith full-on.

The woman put the gun back in the Torrent and retrieved her sword. "You have a problem with that?" she said.

Jayne guessed she didn't.

Two hands appeared under her arms and began to haul her up. Jayne screamed and tried to punch up. For her trouble she got a searing pain in her shoulder as her fist grazed a stubbled cheek.

"Good grief," said Ruger. "This is what I get for dropping everything and coming to save your sorry self?"

Tamara appeared next to Jayne, in black tactical gear and

with a sniper's rifle on her shoulder, sight against her eye. She took out a Wraith with a neat shot, and it tumbled to the canal with an almighty splash.

"Sofia called for backup and explained it all," Ruger said, hastily bandaging her shoulder. "Do you know how much trouble we're going to be in with the Danish government?"

Jayne held her wrist. "What're they going to do, pelt us with Legos?"

Ruger wasn't amused. "This was a covert operation, Jayne."

"Yeah, well." She wasn't smiling, was she? "Maybe you should ask your boyfriend about that. His people made this mess."

The last of the Wraiths was flying away, just as the Wraith siren kicked in. A harried voice came on over the intercom. "The fire alarm is still active. Please proceed to Christiansborg Palace, where a basement room has been made available as a Wraith bunker."

"We're not finished here." Jayne turned on the remaining Guardians. "You're coming with us, back to the TCO. And you're going to tell us who sent you on this mission, and what you're trying to do."

They exchanged glances, and the blonde smiled. "No, we're not."

She leaned back, and a spell began to unfurl above her head. Too late, Jayne realized she was no ordinary Guardian. She was a Master. One of the women whose magic had bloomed when the Torrent started escaping from the spell that had contained it for so many years.

The woman made a complicated motion with her hand, and thunder crashed above them, drowning out the wail of the Wraith siren and leaving Jayne's ears ringing. On the ceiling of the Royal Library, black clouds swirled and lightning flashed.

Jayne felt a raindrop on her forehead. Then two. Then the rain started coming down in buckets.

"You jerks!" Sofia screamed, trying in vain to make some kind of Dry spell of her own. "You're making it rain on *books*?"

Jayne helped her, lending her strength, creating a sort of Canopy spell that could deflect the rain and extending it over the bookshelves around and above them. "The codex," Jayne gasped. It had been in the satchel Carry spell—

Which now swung by a broken strap from the Asian Guardian's hands. With a flourish and a wave, he and the other two disappeared through a golden portal.

"Thornes." Ruger sighed and grabbed Jayne's good arm. "Let's get out of here, before the real police come."

TEN

They slunk back to their safe house and through the portal. Jayne was shivering by the time they were back at the TCO, in front of the wall of stars that commemorated their fallen comrades. Dozens of new stars had appeared at the end of the wall, some inscribed with the names of those who fell at the Battle of Kirkjufell. Others sat ready to be etched with the names of all the Rogues lost in combat, the ones who Odin had called. Amanda hadn't given the final order for that, though. She, like Jayne, thought that felt too much like giving up.

Jayne needed a splint for her wrist, dry clothes, and a cup of tea, and a chat with her familiar as to what had happened to their connection. But first, she needed answers.

Danilo was the first Guardian she saw, waiting unhappily for them at the portal. He started toward Ruger, brown eyes full of concern, but Jayne got to him first. He was a big Māori man with biceps the size of her head, but she was too angry to think about whether he could crush her in a fight or not. "What. The. Hell," she snarled. "You guys said you were with us! You almost killed people with your little stunt back there. You made it *rain on books*. What gives?"

A huge brown hand landed on her shoulder and shoved her back. Then Ruger was between Danilo and her. "You watch yourself," he said.

Jayne stopped, more out of shock than anything. She'd never seen Ruger look like this before. Serious, angry. Dangerous, with all that danger directed at her, and not at whoever was threatening her.

She squared her shoulders. Danilo should answer for himself, just as she and Tristan had to answer for themselves in a debriefing. "I want answers. The mission was compromised by Guardians who were supposed to be on our side."

"And I want you to show some respect, or you're going to learn how easy I've been going on you in sparring lessons," Ruger warned her.

"Oh, right," she said, but she didn't try to push past him again. Ruger was a wall of a man, and they both knew he had the skill to take her out. So she spat out her words past him. "We all know how to talk. We can even speak each other's languages. So why was it easier to sabotage this mission than to talk about it?"

"Because you would not talk about it," said a severe female voice. Jayne, Ruger, and Danilo turned. Xiomara strode toward them, braids swinging. She was dressed in a black combat suit that was kitted out to kill Wraiths, with sheaths for almost a dozen magical weapons. Her hair was soaked.

"You were there," Jayne realized. A fist of ice formed in her belly, fury roaring with it. "You disabled Hayden."

"We were supposed to be on your side, is that what you said? But are you on *our* side? We are not equal partners with the Torrent Control Organization. The great Jayne Thorne and the TCO decide what is best for the world, and all the seasoned Adepts and fighters that the Guardians and the Disciples of Gaia have to offer are seen as lesser. Consultants at best. Soldiers for you to bend to your will."

Jayne set her jaw, even though it hurt to look at an old friend this way. "You didn't want to join the TCO. That means that some things are out of your control. Like whether the TCO decides to go after the codex."

"And some things are out of *your* control," Xiomara returned smoothly. "Like whether we try to stop you."

"But why?" The pain came out real and raw, and Jayne couldn't hide it. "You know what's at stake."

Xiomara stalked forward until she could poke Jayne in the chest. "You will go *mad*, Jayne Thorne. Or did your father not tell you? The Norns will drive you insane, and then what will be done with the power of the goddesses inside you? What destruction will *you* wreak when you are no longer you?"

Jayne's eyes flicked to Henry's. He stood off to the side, pale and furious. He didn't believe she would go mad. He wasn't hiding anything from her. "I've heard the risks of madness," she told Xiomara. She'd been warned of it from her very first lessons with Ruger. "I can handle it."

"Everyone who thought they could handle this power sounded just like you." Xiomara whirled from Jayne to target Henry. "And you. Trying to destroy the fabric of time with your little experiments? We will not stand for it."

"If the Norns agree to it, then it can be done." Henry folded his arms. Jayne caught a glint of golden anger in his eyes, but he did not back down as Xiomara approached.

"The Norns have more power than you'll ever know, yet you seek to bring yourself to their level!" She threw up her hands. "You understand nothing, any of you! Seeking the limits of your science will destroy you. And I'm sorry to say, I think you'll deserve it."

A door opened down the hall, and they heard the brisk tap

of Amanda's footsteps. She strode into view—a fast walker for such a short woman—smoothing a lock of red hair behind her ear.

"What's going on?" she asked. "Did the mission succeed?"

"That depends on who you ask," Jayne sneered. "We had the codex, but Xiomara's Guardian goons stole it."

"I warned you not to do this," Xiomara said to Amanda, who folded her arms and narrowed her gaze. "I told you of the risks. But my experience means nothing to you, eh? The Guardians, the Disciples—we're just tools for the TCO to use and discard when it no longer suits you."

"I don't have time for your hurt feelings," Amanda snapped. Jayne cheered silently. Her boss wasn't playing around. "You advised me on the situation, and I made a decision with that advice in mind. I understand it wasn't the decision you wanted, but I'm not in the business of making everyone happy. Right now, I'm in the business of saving the world. I have complete faith in Jayne Thorne, and you should, too."

Jayne felt an unexpected blossom of warmth at that. It wasn't often that she received praise from Amanda—usually, she stood on the other side of her boss's desk and got a litany of all the ways she'd breached mission protocol. She tried to smile at Amanda, but the other woman was locked in a staring contest with Xiomara.

A contest that Xiomara lost when the soft voice of Isra piped up: "We have faith in Jayne, too."

Xiomara turned, jaw going slack in astonishment. Isra, a tall Egyptian woman who represented the Disciples of Gaia and acted as their liaison to the TCO, came to stand beside Jayne. She radiated a calm certainty. "The Disciples believe that the goddesses bestow their power upon the worthy. The goddesses have said, unmistakably, that Jayne Thorne is the one in whom we should place our hope."

"You're living in the past," Xiomara shouted. "Your world has always been too simple. You of all people know worshiping a person over the Torrent leads to disaster. And as for you—" She turned back to Amanda. "How far will you go to get what you want? Who will you kill?"

"I take all life seriously," Amanda began, cheeks heating.

"Did you...know about this?" Ruger asked Danilo. Danilo muttered something and looked at the ground.

"Xiomara, where is the codex?" Jayne asked.

Xiomara's eyes darted to the side. "As if I would tell you."

"You *will* tell us." Amanda stepped forward.

Xiomara laughed. "Or what? Will you start another war? I think you should try to finish your first one."

Everyone started talking at once.

Jayne's shoulder and wrist pulsed with pain. Her mind buzzed with too much to parse—anger, confusion, betrayal. Xiomara had always been supportive of her and Sofia. A mentor who could steer them in the right direction. She'd never exactly been motherly, but she'd helped them make sense of a confusing world at a time when the people who should have helped them were gone. Now she was turning her back on Jayne.

"Come on," said a soft voice, and Sofia put her arm around Jayne's ribs. "Let's get you to Tamara. You need a patch-up."

"Not yet," Jayne murmured. She tried to push her swirl of feelings aside and focus on what was more important: the codex. She might have started this fight about loyalties and alliances, but what she really needed was to find the damn book. She thought of the way Xiomara had glanced sideways when asked about it. She'd put on a brave face, but Jayne knew a lie when she saw one. Yet her scoffed *As if I would tell you* had given nothing away.

Her body language, on the other hand...

Jayne reached up to adjust her hair and her wrist twinged. *Okay,* she thought, trying to push through the pain. Xiomara hadn't exactly been *lying* when she had refused to tell Jayne where the codex was.

But she was afraid Jayne would find it anyway. Which meant it had to be possible to find.

The satchel, Hayden said, still groggy.

Bingo.

The codex had been in the leather satchel. The Asian Guardian had taken it from Jayne and disappeared. Jayne didn't see her here—indeed, it would be foolish for her to come.

But if Xiomara had been at the Royal Library, there would have been time for a hand-off after, while Jayne and the others were staggering back to the safe house. Would Xiomara have trusted the codex with anyone else? Or would she want to keep it on her person?

Or in a Carry spell? Jayne thought.

Exactly, Hayden answered, sounding more like himself.

It would be just like Xiomara to have it stashed on her person when confronting the TCO. Convinced with all of her Guardian power she couldn't be detected, and a control freak in her own right. But if she had it in a Carry spell, it wasn't like Jayne could tackle her and root around in her pockets. *Or could I?* What sorts of spells could she layer together to pull something out of a Carry spell?

A Carry spell was a bit like a pocket version of a Time Stop, wasn't it? If she made a portal just large enough for, say, her hand and a book, could she reach into someone else's Carry spell? Of course, she'd have to locate the spell...

"What are you doing?" Sofia whispered. Jayne had started to move her hand. It inched through the air, shaking, and she sketched out a Finding spell. *All the healing later,* she promised it. She layered it, the Find with a spell for Rending, a sort of way to rip a hole in the magic as though it were a purse and she was a pickpocket.

Something flashed just at Xiomara's hip. The woman looked down for a moment, distracted. By the time she looked up again, understanding dawning on her face, Jayne had already started to run.

She tackled Xiomara and took them both down, screaming through gritted teeth when her wounded arm hit the floor with a thump. Xiomara was too shocked to do anything for a good moment—enough time for Jayne to shove her good hand into the Guardian's Carry spell and grope around for the book. Her fingers brushed leather, but before she could pull the book out, Xiomara kicked her hard in the chest. Jayne went flying. Hayden burst from her arm, all teeth and growls.

The codex sprang into the air as if it had wings of its own.

It was mayhem instantly. Danilo leapt for the codex but missed. Isra shoved another Guardian to the side. Amanda darted in and grabbed Xiomara by one arm, then the other, forcing them both behind her back. Jayne hit the floor and saw stars.

When her vision cleared, Ruger and Henry knelt over her. Ruger was trying to prop her up. Henry cupped her cheek with one hand. The other held the codex.

"Good job," he whispered.

"This is a mistake," Xiomara spat. "You're all making a huge mistake."

A growl sounded deep in Hayden's throat. Xiomara said something in a tongue Jayne didn't understand and Hayden was instantly back inside her arm with a sound like a snap.

"What the hell? How *dare* you command my familiar." She sat up, spells rising from her palms, but Amanda yanked her back.

"Enough!" Amanda dropped Jayne's arm and jerked

Xiomara to her feet. "You will be escorted off the premises and banned from the TCO offices, immediately. Because you have been of such great help to the TCO in the past, I won't press charges against you for endangering the lives of our operatives. Don't expect me to be so generous in the future."

"Do you think I care about your generosity—" Xiomara raged.

A high-pitched beeping, completely unlike the Wraith alarms, started up. A light above the permanent portal to Aegis Battle Academy was flashing.

Sofia's face drained of color.

Amanda let go of Xiomara. She spoke into her watch, and a moment later, her voice boomed out of every speaker around them. "Code black, code black. All available combat hands assemble in the portal room."

Sofia grabbed Ruger. "Advance team," she said. Her eyes were wide, her jaw tight. Ruger nodded and pulled Jayne to his side. Her wrist burned in reply. *Heal,* she shouted at it mentally, but nothing happened.

Around her, everyone had started to run. Some were off to get tactical gear, while others made knots of groups that could go through the portal one by one. Amanda flagged down a couple of security guards as Tamara thundered in from the hospital, slinging her rifle over her back. "You two, escort any Guardian not directly employed by the TCO off the premises," she said.

"Don't be foolish," Xiomara told her as the guards hauled her up. "Let me help."

"I think you've helped enough," Amanda told her.

Xiomara shook her head. "We're not finished discussing the codex, or the Norns. But I will not leave magical children to die. Regardless of my allegiances."

Amanda looked at her for a long moment, then she seemed

to come back to herself. "Fine," she said, moving behind Xiomara to undo the handcuffs she'd placed on the older woman. "We appreciate the help."

"You'd better," Xiomara grumbled. Rubbing her wrists, she set off at a brisk pace toward the portal.

Jayne looked around. She couldn't take the codex into battle, but she couldn't just leave it behind, either. The library, maybe? Or could she put it in a Carry spell herself?"

"Jayne," Henry said softly from beside her.

Right. "Here." She nodded at the codex. "You take it to Katie Bell. Keep it safe until we're back."

Henry blinked at the book, then shook his head. "You're in no condition to fight, Jayne."

"Even with a broken wrist, I'm still more powerful than half those guys out there," she argued. "You can't tell me to stay behind when literal *kids* are in danger."

"With a broken wrist and a wounded shoulder, you are a liability," Henry told her gently. He pushed his glasses up on his nose. "We will spend all our time trying to keep you safe, Jayne."

"I'm not going to lounge around in a hospital bed while the rest of you are risking your lives—" she began hotly.

But Henry was smiling. "I wouldn't dream of it, my dear." He took her hand, the unwounded one. "But you need to do this. For the good of us all."

He flipped open the codex and pressed her hand to its pages.

CHAPTER
ELEVEN

The world was dark, a deep mossy green against rich black earth and silvery bark. Jayne looked up out of habit, to a canopy of dark leaves and, beyond them, a sky scattered with stars like diamonds over deep velvet.

Her wrist and shoulder didn't hurt anymore. She tested them out, pressing gently against the spot where the Wraith's claws had punctured her shoulder, turning her wrist in circles. In the astral projection, at least, she didn't have to worry about her injuries.

Small blessings, she thought.

She felt Hayden begin to stir on her arm.

You okay?

I am fine, little one.

He woke up slowly as she looked at the tree. It was larger than any living thing she'd ever seen. It was easily the size of a skyscraper, shooting into the sky, with its branches twisting up and around in limbs as thick as a car. The bark was a ripple of gray-speckled brown, with divots large enough for her fingers to fit inside them. The leaves stretched from the tips of her fingers to her elbow.

Ah, Hayden said, fully detaching from her arm and dropping to the ground. He grew until he came up to her shoulder. *Greetings, Yggdrasil.*

"The World Tree," Jayne whispered Yggdrasil was a sacred tree in Norse mythology, said to hold nine worlds in its branches. And the Norns were supposed to sit at the base. Jayne looked around for evidence of habitation and saw nothing but roots rippling over the ground, creating a treacherous terrain for anyone who might try to go around the tree.

The Norns once lived at the base, next to Mímisbrunnr—Mímir's wellspring beneath the tree. When Odin drank from the well, gaining knowledge in exchange for his eye, he used his new powers to imprison them at the top of the tree. Let us find what is left of the well, and we will know where to start looking for the Norns, Hayden suggested.

"All right." Jayne took a deep breath. She started to walk.

It was slow going. The moss was slippery, the roots treacherous. Things darted beneath them—snakes, mostly, many of them intent on twisting around the roots of the tree and making it unstable to walk upon. Jayne thought she saw a squirrel stop to chitter angrily at them. She tried to keep one hand on the trunk while she walked, for stability, but when a gaping hole opened in the earth between one root and the next, she had to pick her way to safer ground and go around it.

The great ash tree of Yggdrasil was far from the only tree around them. They were in a tightly packed forest of birch and ash and oak, trees that whispered and creaked in the wind. After a while, Jayne noticed that she heard no animals, except for the snakes and the lone squirrel: It was as though no birds lived in this forest, no deer or rabbits or foxes or even crickets.

It might just be that astral projection didn't lend itself to animals. Or it might be suspicious.

At last, they came to a divot in the tree where a toppled pile of stones lay. They had clearly been cut, for they were all of the same general shape and size. Jayne picked up a gray stone that had tumbled down over the roots to rest near her feet.

The well, Hayden said.

Jayne made her way to the stones. Drawing closer to the well, an acrid stench invaded her nose. She coughed and covered her face with one hand, but it was too late. The smell had invaded her and she couldn't shake it now. She tried not to gag. Holding her nose, she approached the well and pushed a few stones aside to look within.

At the bottom of the well, she could see something that glittered blackly by the faint light of the stars. It lapped at the sides of the well, but it did not move like water. More like...sludge. Sewer sludge.

"You're telling me that Odin drank from this well?" she said, toeing a brick over the side. It landed in the fluid with less of a splash and more of a *gloop* before sinking slowly beneath the surface. "Gross. No wonder he lost his mind."

The well was probably corrupted by the Allfather, Hayden said. *Let us ascend.*

Jayne looked up. And up. "I was never a champion tree climber," she admitted. She'd usually climbed high enough in P.E. to take out her book and read where she'd be hidden from the teacher.

Who said anything about climbing? Hayden stretched and rustled his wings, and a moment later, he was twice as long and twice as tall. The look he gave her was entirely too smug.

"I didn't want to assume." Jayne clambered up one leg. *You've had a rough day.*

A very human thing, Hayden scoffed and tossed his head. When Jayne was settled he beat his wings once, twice, then pushed away from the vast roots and began to flap up.

It took them a little effort to get through the forest canopy.

Hayden's wing almost got tangled in a branch and he had to pull an inelegant maneuver in which he pushed from limb to limb until they could clear the canopy, with leaves and twigs sticking wildly to Jayne's hair. In the open air Jayne's nose finally seemed to clear of the stink of the well, and she looked up at the wide, deep sky and let herself smile. It was hardly a carefree smile—back at home, her friends and family were battling for the survival of the school, and what she accomplished here could save or sink them. But she couldn't fly without smiling. This was what magic was made for—to do the impossible, and to help people.

Her smile slipped as Hayden jerked suddenly to the side. "What the—" she gasped.

Then she heard it. A second wingbeat in the air. Wind brushed across her back. She twisted around to see a gray shape streaking away from them. "A Wraith!" she cried.

More than one, Hayden replied grimly, and then there was no more time to talk. He twisted and dove, narrowly avoiding the swipe of a claw. Another Wraith swooped at them from the side, and Hayden tucked them into a barrel roll. Jayne slipped loose but managed to clench her thighs around his shoulders, clutching him tight until they'd righted themselves.

"Get us up there," she gasped. Hayden folded himself tightly, shooting upward until he was forced to snap open his wings or fall out of the sky. The top of the tree was still stories and stories away.

Yet more Wraiths were swooping in on their position. The sky darkened as one shape after another filled it, and soon it was hard to see. Hayden gasped as a Wraith got too close, and he couldn't turn in time to avoid the slash of its front claws. Jayne felt something soak into the side of her pants—blood.

I can't. Hayden sounded pained in her mind. If he was vanquished up here, he wouldn't die. He would just disappear back into Jayne's arm, and then she would have a long fall to the forest floor.

Too many people depended on her for this.

"Take us back down," she ordered. "We'll have to find another way."

They crashed through the crown of trees and hit the ground hard. Jayne rolled off Hayden and he reduced to the size of a cat, trembling. Jayne picked him up and stroked the soft leathery skin under his neck. His rumbling purr sounded pained.

"Are you okay?"

I will be fine.

"I don't like seeing you hurt."

Do not become emotional. That will not serve us well.

"Fine. All right, what do we know? The tree is surrounded by Wraiths," Jayne muttered. "So we can't exactly fly to the top."

And there were more, the farther up we went, Hayden added. *Odin is guarding the Norns well. He knew, perhaps, that we would come.*

"And we couldn't see the Wraiths from the forest floor because of all the trees in the way."

Jayne bit her lip. Of course, that had probably kept the Wraiths from seeing them, too. She looked up the long trunk of the tree again. Those limbs truly were enormous, not like climbing the spindly apple trees in the park as a kid. She didn't have to fear the branches would break. If she fell, it would be her own fault. "All right. If we stick close to the trunk, maybe they won't see us."

Hayden looked up. *And if they do?*

Jayne swallowed, then put on her brave voice. "I've got a dragon. I think I can figure something out." She smiled down at him. He licked her cheek in solidarity.

I am your familiar. My thoughts are your thoughts, he reminded her. *You do not benefit from false bravado with me.*

"Maybe the false bravado was for me," Jayne muttered, and started climbing.

Hayden had to give her a boost to the first branch by growing almost as large as a tow truck so that she could scramble up. Then he turned back to cat size and scampered after her. He was still bleeding, though the wound looked shallow on Jayne's inspection. "Maybe you should rest," she said.

That is not possible, he told her shortly. *I will not abandon you now.*

Jayne began, slowly, to climb. Her palms scraped against the hard bark, and her shoes irritated her so much that she ended up kicking them off and sitting on a branch to peel off her socks. "I'm getting my workout, at least," she told Hayden.

Climbing higher, she was again struck by the eerie lack of life on the tree. A tree like this should be full of birds and squirrels and beetles and spiders. But there was nothing. As they climbed above the other trees, she began to see signs of the Wraiths—shadows that passed across the moon, the soft growls of a searching predator. They knew she was here. But they didn't seem to want to search the tree itself. Jayne supposed it must be difficult to use as terrain. If she stayed quiet, perhaps she could get all the way to the top of Yggdrasil without provoking their ire again.

She looked up. The top was so vastly far away that she couldn't even see it. She almost muttered, "How long is this supposed to take?" to Hayden, but remembered at the last second to keep her mouth shut. She'd once vowed to go out with a sarcastic quip on her lips, but she didn't want to prove Ruger right and have her own sarcasm be the death of her.

Your thoughts, my thoughts. Keep moving.

She settled into a pattern: Reach for the next limb, pull herself up, pause. Listen for any change. A fight broke out between a couple of Wraiths, making the tree rustle and rattle at its outer branches. She used the distraction to scale even farther. Now she knew what climbing to the top of the Empire State Building must feel like. Her arms and legs began to ache, then to burn. Eventually, she couldn't even think about anything except her breath: *In, out. Stop, listen. In, out.*

We're nearly there, Hayden told her.

Jayne chanced a look up again. She could barely make out the glimmer of something—the edge of a golden circle. A cold wind blew through the top of the tree, plastering her shirt to her sweaty skin and making her shiver. The circle swayed and swung, and Jayne realized what she was looking at.

The circle was the bottom of a hanging cage. And within that cage sat a wrinkled old woman.

CHAPTER

TWELVE

Sofia, Ruger, and Danilo were the first ones through the portal. They came out onto the wide green lawn of Aegis to see the school, up on a hill, beset by Wraiths. They screamed and raked at the roof, sending up sparks as their claws hit the slate tiles.

Sofia dug her fingernails into her arm until she stopped hearing the phantom screams of children dying. Then she worked a quick Walkie-Talkie spell—she and Seo-Joon hadn't come up with a better name for it yet—and turned to Ruger and Danilo. "First objective: Make some magic. Draw the Wraiths away from the school and give them a real fight. Danilo, can we trust you?"

Ruger started to object, but Sofia held up a hand in her bossiest way, and he bit his tongue. She had to know. Danilo was a Guardian, and while he might be nice, it seemed as though most of the Guardians had loyalties that lay elsewhere.

He seemed to take it the right way. "I'm not going to let any of our people die today if I can help it," he replied.

"Good. The two of you can oversee the rest of them." More

people were coming through the portal in teams of four, reaching into the Torrent for their Wraith-killing weapons.

She set the Walkie-Talkie to a universal frequency, which meant anyone who'd done the second half of the spell—which every student and faculty member at Aegis did at the beginning of the year—could hear her. "Good day, everyone. Except I guess it's not much of a good day. Everyone who's taken War Games 2.0 or higher, listen to me now. It's time to put your training into practice. Wraiths and Rogues are attacking Aegis, so treat this as the Red Scenario with a small twist: Instead of human combatants to disarm and capture, you must disarm and capture the Rogues." The Red Scenario imagined a full-scale invasion of Aegis by Wraiths and humans. The kids had never done well with a mix of killing and capturing enemy combatants, so Sofia added, "Remember that these Rogues are lost in their own minds, and some of them were your friends. We are trying to bring them back to themselves, and we want them alive. That being said, if it's the Rogue's life or yours, choose yours. Everyone currently enrolled in War Games 4.0, you're in charge of making teams. Your objective is to protect the school itself and to organize a safe escape route toward our portal. We will coordinate a safe corridor from our side. Game leaders, check in with me when you have your teams. Over and out."

A spell *whooshed* overhead like a firework. "Farther away!" Sofia shouted to the Adept who was in charge of making magical noise. He started to run over the lawn.

Where did the Wraiths come from? How did they get in here? Sofia wondered wildly. Could Odin just...open any pocket he wished?

Focus. Battle now, difficult questions later. She turned to the people pouring out of the portal. Aegis didn't have any tunnels, but the cellars did have an alternate door at the bottom of the hill for trucks to drive food directly into the school. The kids would probably be coming out of that, and they'd need protection as they fled.

The Wraiths were winging toward them now, filling the sky with their gray and black wings, their screams and shrieks. And from across the hills—

"He means to utterly destroy us," Xiomara said, coming up to stand beside Sofia. Henry put a hand on Sofia's other shoulder.

"Not today," Sofia said, and felt anger blaze in her, giving her new energy. If Odin thought to demoralize them by coming for her kids, he was making a huge mistake. Aegis had made sure that no one was unprepared for a scenario like this. They'd kick his old, smug ass, and then they'd figure out how he'd managed to get in here, and they'd patch up the security breach.

Amanda was directing teams with long-range Wraith weapons to set them up. They had more magical net guns, harpoon guns, and good old-fashioned sniper rifles. A long line of armed Adepts moved in concert toward the cellar, just as Sofia received confirmation from Zia that it was uncompromised and ready for the evacuation. "We're not ready yet," she replied. "Give us a few minutes."

"Great," Zia said. "I've got an idea."

"Uh, what?" Sofia asked. Zia didn't reply.

Sofia tried not to grimace. Zia seemed to have gone to the Jayne Thorne school of planning battles, which was some variation on "Wing it, sling spells, break stuff."

Speaking of... "Where's Jayne?" she asked, looking around. Her sister would be right on the front line if she were here.

"Jayne's taking care of something," said Henry. On Sofia's other side, Xiomara bristled.

Sofia could guess what he meant. "Let's hope she takes care of it in time," she said.

And then the Wraiths were upon them.

Xiomara pulled a long, gleaming ax almost the length of her body from the Torrent. She swung it with a roar that shocked Sofia. The old lady's tiny frame and pinched propriety had never led her to expect something like this. Sofia pulled her weapon from the Torrent, selecting a spear with a long range. Henry's own weapon was a bow and arrow. Sofia raised an eyebrow.

"I figured it was time to contribute. I've been putting in some practice," he said.

Today was just full of surprises.

Not all of them were good. The Rogues sped over the ground, and Amanda hastily mobilized ground forces to meet them and protect the people operating the net guns. But the Rogues were ready to kill, shifting from shape to shape, snapping and tearing, while the Adepts were afraid to hurt someone who might be a friend.

Seo-Joon's voice sounded in Sofia's ear. "We're in place. I'm helping form the protective corridor."

Sofia looked out over the green. Two lines of soldiers had made a path for the kids, spinning shields to cover it. It didn't look like the Wraiths had realized what it was for yet. "Zia?"

"Give me a minute." She heard Zia shuffling around, then a couple of curses. Then a strange rumbling sound. "All right."

"Oh, crap—" said Seo-Joon.

But Sofia didn't hear what he said next. A giant tail slammed into her, knocking her backward.

She hit the ground, and black dotted over her vision. It hurt to breathe. She groped around for her spear; she was dead if she didn't get it up to block in time and in the right way—

"*No,*" shouted a voice. Sofia blinked. Her vision cleared, and she managed to raise her pounding head. Xiomara was standing over her, eyes flashing murder. Black blood soaked the head of her ax. She stared down the gigantic Wraith. Blood dripped from a gash in its ruined knee.

"I've had enough of you," Xiomara said.

Henry stepped up next to her and pulled back the string on his bow. He loosed an arrow that hit the Wraith right between the eyes. It dropped like a stone.

Xiomara turned and shifted the ax to her other hand so she could help Sofia up. "Thanks," Sofia said. One rib still twinged when she breathed, but she wouldn't even have to go to the hospital. Xiomara had saved her life.

Saved her life, and still tried to steal the codex.

Xiomara seemed to read her thoughts. "Life is complicated, Sofia Thorne," she said softly. "You didn't already know that?"

"I guess I did." Sofia massaged the back of her head. "In any case, thanks for—"

A blur hit Xiomara and took her down.

Cillian was in his wolf form. He howled. His front paws were on Xiomara's shoulders, keeping her pinned to the ground, and his teeth gleamed sharp.

Sofia did the only thing she could think of. She hit him forcefully with the metal-capped blunt end of her spear.

He snarled. "That's right," Sofia said. "Focus on me."

She backed away. He stalked after. "Focus on the baby, Cillian," she said, hoping that she sounded strong and not pleading. "You think we're going to have a boy, but we're going to have a girl. I feel it in my bones. The most perfect little girl you ever saw. You're going to hold her when she comes out, and you're going to sing to her every night, and you're going to teach her how to become a griffin like you. You're not going to hurt me."

He snarled low in his throat.

Or maybe you are, Sofia thought, and moved her spear into a defensive stance.

She could have let Cillian kill her, if it was only her he was killing. But it wasn't. And she'd do anything to protect her daughter.

Anything.

She brought the spear up and lunged for his chest. Whether it was her nerves or bad luck or a last-minute change of mind, the spear missed his chest and went into his fur, catching and tangling. Sofia dropped the spear and put up a Shield. He howled again. Behind her, a chorus of screams sounded as the Wraiths started attacking the corridor they'd made for the kids. It was all coming apart, and she couldn't concentrate on putting any of it back together. Her Shield smashed against a passing Wraith's tail, and Cillian had her on the ground next, golden eyes staring into her green ones. His nose was wrinkled in a soundless snarl. His musk was overpowering, both Cillian and something not-Cillian at the same time.

This was the part where he went for her throat. No Xiomara to help her now, no one helpfully standing by with nothing to do but protect her. *Man,* she thought. *Jayne's going to be so pissed.*

As final thoughts went, it could have been better.

I love you, she told him. *So much. Come back to me.*

There was a screech and a crash and the blaring of a horn. Cillian looked up. Sofia twisted her head, almost without meaning to. Her brain struggled to make sense of what it was seeing upside-down.

It was a truck. A large transport truck. Aegis owned a few of them and used them for food deliveries. This one had been used to haul apples.

Now Zia sat in the driver's seat, and a Wraith was stuck to the grill like a bug. She pumped her fist. Then she saw Sofia, and her eyes widened. She threw herself toward the door of the truck.

And Cillian stepped off Sofia.

She jerked away from him and stumbled to her feet. For a wild moment she thought he was going to go for the children, but...she almost *recognized* him now. He pawed at his nose and whined. Then he looked at her piteously. Sniffed deeply at the air in front of her belly.

"Cillian?" Sofia whispered.

He began to back away. He shook his head violently.

"Cillian, it's me." She started forward.

Zia appeared, breathless, beside her. "Stay away from her," she shouted at Cillian.

Sofia grabbed her and turned her around. "Zia, take care of the kids," she said.

Something hard hit her in the back, and she tumbled to the ground again. Pain ripped across her shoulders. A moment later it was echoed in her heart as Cillian screamed in an unmistakable way. Hot blood spattered over her, and he hit the ground with a solid thump. She rolled over as the light faded from his eyes.

His lips were curled to the last, teeth bared. He died hating her.

The world went white.

Sofia didn't know how long she screamed. She knew only that her throat was raw, and her entire front was covered in blood and hair when she lifted herself from Cillian's form. She looked around, seeing but unable to comprehend.

The back of the truck had opened and children were spilling out, running the last few yards toward the evacuation portals. The Wraiths dove for them, screaming their fury, and the Adepts threw up Shield after Shield. Their attempts were futile. Rogues attacked the Shield-wielders, bringing them down and creating holes in the protection. Two kids were swept up and carried away in a Wraith's claws. Zia's face was bloody, her eyes wide.

A few feet away, Ruger lay on the ground. Danilo was frantically applying a tourniquet to his elbow. The rest of his arm was gone. The grass around him had disappeared in what looked like a lake of blood. A Wraith dropped on Danilo like a stone, and they rolled, fighting furiously. Tamara's gun jammed and a Wraith picked her up with its tail, flinging her too far and too high for her to possibly survive.

They were all going to die. "Retreat," Sofia whispered in a broken voice, but nobody heard her. "Retreat..."

Something soft thumped on the ground behind her. She barely mustered the energy to turn, but she did it for her daughter. She had to try to survive.

The lioness looked at her with a hunger that seemed all too personal. It opened its mouth, and Sofia could swear the Rogue was smiling in anticipation.

She groped for a spell, a Shield, anything that could buy her another moment. But her mind wouldn't connect. *Cillian.* She'd failed everything and everyone. She hadn't protected the Aegis students, she hadn't fixed Cillian. She hadn't even protected her own baby.

Someone was shouting her name. Sofia turned toward the voice, barely seeing the shape of her sister. *You're too late,* she thought numbly.

The world shimmered...and she was gone.

CHAPTER
THIRTEEN

J ayne felt something spark in her heart. She was nearly there. She forced herself up the last few branches until she came to the cage.

"Agnes Jayne Thorne," said the Norn before her. Her voice was like sandpaper.

"Shh. I'm going to get you out of here," Jayne whispered. "But it's just Jayne, if you please."

The Norn laughed. "There's no need to shush me. The Wraiths don't come this far up." She waved a gnarled hand, and Jayne followed it to squint between the thinning leaves. It had been some time, she realized, since she'd heard the wingbeats of a Wraith, or the growls and screams of some squabble or other.

"They despise us, you see," said a voice from behind. Jayne craned her head—though not too far, acutely aware of her trembling legs and how far it was to the ground—and saw a younger woman, perhaps forty or fifty, in another golden cage. "We know what they once were, and they can't stand it."

"I'm guessing you'd like to get out?" Jayne said.

"Can it be called a guess?" said the oldest Norn.

"An educated one," said the middle-aged one.

"A turn of phrase, more like," said a younger voice, this one off to the right of Jayne. "Miss Thorne has come to rescue us."

Jayne examined the lock. Or rather, the space where the lock should be. Instead of a keyhole there was nothing, just a smooth panel of gold. Runes had been etched into the gold. She ran her fingers over them. She should have expected a spell. "The question is, how am I going to get you all out of here without the Allfather noticing?"

"You won't," came the youngest Norn's voice. "The Allfather is all-seeing, thanks to the drink he took from Mímir's well."

"He has placed wards on these cages," said the first one. "He will know the moment they open."

"What sorts of wards?" Jayne asked. If it were a matter of replacing the Norns with something that could resemble them, she was certain Henry and Quimby could whip up something…

But Henry, at least, was fighting to save Aegis. The Geniuses didn't have time to mess around with a riddle.

"How bad would it be if he did know?" Jayne said.

"A good question, Jayne Thorne," replied the oldest Norn. "He desires you dead either way. But knowing you have slipped us loose will sharpen the edge of his anger."

"I feel like I could use that to my advantage," Jayne murmured. Angry people made mistakes. Then again, an angry Allfather could just destroy the world as she knew it.

It's not like we have the time to choose, Hayden reminded her.

"All right, all right. So if we don't care how to break open the cages, how can we get them out?" Jayne stared at the bars. They couldn't be bent out of shape, and a few experimental spells bounced off them, one nearly severing Jayne's little finger in the process as it ricocheted away.

"Jayne Thorne glows with the power of the goddesses, yet she thinks like a mere mortal," *tsked* the middle-aged Norn.

"We expected better," the old Norn cackled.

"Enough with the negging," Jayne muttered. These old ladies sounded like a combination of Ruth from her early years, musty and self-satisfied professors, and a couple of men Jayne had tried to date. Was she really sure she wanted to free them?

Save the world, she reminded herself. She took a deep breath and closed her eyes.

Here in the astral world it wasn't difficult to get ahold of the other goddesses—except for Medb, who'd given Jayne the Earth totem and pretty much disappeared. But Jayne didn't think she needed the Earth totem anyway. She respectfully greeted the goddesses who would respond and set her focus on Amaterasu, the sun goddess, who had bestowed the Spirit totem. *Lend me your power,* she thought.

Amaterasu appeared and sank into what might have been a curtsy or perhaps simply an exaggerated nod of assent. "The totem is yours to use, Jayne Thorne," she said softly. "You know what to do."

Jayne opened her eyes. "I have an idea."

The Spirit totem carried the power of the sun, something so hot it could melt any spell. If Odin was attacking Aegis—and who else could it be, really?—then perhaps he would be so focused that the destruction of the cages would slip through his notice, just for an instant. Just long enough to do what Jayne needed to do. She set her hand on the gold plate and let the sun shine forth from her palm.

The box glowed. Her arm itched, then burned. The cage began to warp.

Moving quickly, she pulled on the bars of the cages until they were large enough for someone to step through. The old Norn got to her feet. Taking Jayne's offered hand, she put one sandaled foot down on the tree trunk, then the other. She wore rags in the general shape of a dress, belted in the middle with a crusty piece of rope. She was bent with age, but her eyes were lively. She pushed a tangle of white hair out of her eyes and looked out over the forest.

Jayne leaned past her and touched the cage again. This time she did not need the power of the sun, but the power of memory, and of true nature. *Remember what you were,* she thought, and the golden bars began to twist and straighten. For millennia, maybe, they'd been in the same shape. The golden box unmelted, runes blazing over its surface once again.

That might fool Odin for a little while, at least. She looked to the next cage.

Clambering over the branches was almost more difficult than climbing them. She had to pick her way carefully, balancing on her bare feet. The middle-aged Norn sat cross-legged, calm but for the hunger in her eyes. How long had it been since she'd tasted freedom?

Jayne called the totem forth and melted the bars, putting them back in place after the Norn had staggered free. The Norn stretched, wincing as stiff muscles woke up again.

Too close, Jayne heard a scream of rage. The Wraiths had scented her magic. She needed to work quickly before they overcame their fear of the Norns and attacked. "Keep me steady," she said to Hayden. He grew to the size of a Great Dane, curling his claws over the branches and providing her with a solid mass to lean on. Bolstered, she set out toward the final cage.

The youngest Norn had her fingers wrapped around the bars, face pressed against it. Her eyes were luminous as they rested on Jayne. Behind her, the leaves of the great ash tree shook as a Wraith swiped at them, trying to get through the dense canopy. Jayne tried to swallow her fear and focus. Her hand trembled. *You are mutable,* she told the bars of the cage. *You bow to the powers of the goddess.*

The bars softened a little but did not pull.

A branch cracked. A Wraith screamed. Jayne jumped, startled.

The youngest Norn's hand closed around her wrist. "I have seen all possible futures, and in none of them do I die today, Jayne Thorne," she said in a voice like a honeyed knife.

Jayne focused on that hand, pale and slim-fingered, with calluses at the fingertips from wielding swords and weaving the tapestry of fate. She could do this. She closed her eyes, and the lock melted away as the fury of the Wraiths grew louder.

The Norn darted through, and Jayne called upon the totem one last time. *Remember what you were,* she thought. Then she was yanked away as a Wraith finally crashed through the crown of the tree.

When Jayne saw its face, she realized why the Wraiths didn't like to come here. Wherever the leaves touched it, an open wound appeared on its skin, leaching blood and magic in a sticky, poisonous combination. Jayne was grateful for her Master abilities, which kept her from succumbing to the Wraith-borne illness that sometimes came with a wound. Its twisted face was filled with pain, but it snarled at them, lashing out with a whip-like weapon. The weapon curled around Jayne's arm. She braced herself against a branch and pulled hard with all her strength.

To her surprise, the Wraith let her pull it forward. It sailed toward them, its empty hand open, claws out. Next to Jayne, the young Norn screamed.

"Hayden!" Jayne cried.

He appeared between them in an instant. His jaws fastened around the Wraith's throat, and his tail curled around the whip. The whip wrenched from Jayne's hand, leaving a scarlet welt behind. The young Norn grabbed her arm and began to pull her toward the trunk of Yggdrasil, where the other two waited.

Jayne thought of her scream. "Did you really know you weren't going to die today?" she asked. "Or was that a lie to keep me from freaking out?"

The youngest Norn laughed. "There was no need to lie, Jayne Thorne. I am hard to kill; impossible, perhaps. My chances of dying in the Wraith's attack were nothing. Yours, on the other hand, were around fifty percent."

"Lovely," Jayne muttered. That would teach her to ask questions.

Jayne and the youngest Norn approached as the older one, who'd broken a branch to use as a cane, jabbed at a knot in the tree. A crack appeared in the bark, darker than everything else. "In," she said, jerking her head impatiently.

"At last, I get to relive a scene from *The Princess Bride*." Jayne rubbed her hands together and ducked into the cool darkness of the trunk. *You going to be all right out there?* she asked Hayden.

It is better for me to stay here, he replied, which wasn't exactly an answer. But seeing as he and Jayne were technically the same person, she shouldn't have been surprised by it.

Someone spoke a word, and light flickered around the inside of the tree. Within it was built a snug home: A hearth sat in one corner, with a hollow branch acted as a chimney. A table held bright fruits and bread, fresh and steaming as if it had been taken from the oven just moments ago. In the opposite corner of the room sat the loom, a huge frame of ash at least seven feet long, strung with threads so fine they looked like hair plucked from a giant's head. The Norns went to the loom one by one, lovingly running their fingers through the thread, letting the weights at the bottom click and clack against each other.

The cloth was weaving itself, dozens of tiny shuttles burrowing in and out of the warp like fleas, leaving a riot of color behind. From afar it was beautiful, the whole world somehow trapped in the loom, with larger patterns swirling over and around each other. But when Jayne approached, it got messier and more confusing. Little threads balled up and bunched and refused to lie flat. They tangled with each other and sometimes split into a new, third color or thickness.

She reached out to touch the loom. A gnarled hand swatted her away.

"This is not to be touched by any mortal hand. Even yours, Master of Totems," said the oldest Norn.

Now that she saw them together, it was obvious: They were the same woman, three times in her life. They shared the same sharp face with its arrow nose, though the youngest had unlined, smooth skin, a full mouth, the figure of a fertility goddess. They shared the same hard blue eyes, though the middle-aged Norn's were full of wisdom and patience and understanding that the others had either not yet gained or long ago shed. They shared the same body movements, even, though the oldest Norn's were slower and stiffer than those of her younger selves.

The oldest spoke again. "I am Urd, the past. I know everything that was."

The middle-aged Norn came forward and put a hand on her older self's arm. "I am Verdandi, the present, the now."

The youngest tossed her golden head. "I am Skuld, what shall be and what may be."

As one they said, "We are Fate."

They came away from the loom and bade Jayne sit, which she did. They broke the bread into four pieces and shared it out. It was soft and fresh, and Jayne had to wonder at how it had come into being. It had to be a spell. Maybe they'd teach her, and she could use it to conjure pies from the air.

"Maybe not," Urd said.

Great, Fate could read her mind.

The three women approached the table and filled their

plates. Skuld let out a throaty moan at the taste, which made Urd cackle and Verdandi swat them both.

Verdandi fixed her softened eyes on Jayne. "We are indebted to you," she said. "You freed us from an eternal cage. No mortal has ever succeeded in this task. Many have tried and failed."

"Um." Jayne wasn't sure how to respond to that. "You're welcome?"

"We do not like being indebted," said Skuld, tilting her head as if contemplating. "It makes things complicated."

"And it's not as if anyone has ever come to speak with us out of the goodness of their hearts," snorted Urd.

"So out with it," said Verdandi, though not unkindly. "What boon is it you would have of us, Jayne Thorne?"

These were not women who suffered fools, Jayne reminded herself. She swallowed again. She wished Hayden were here. He seemed to know more about the Norns than anyone, as though he were some locked-away part of herself that understood them. "You're right. I do need something," she said. "I need the power to travel in time."

They were silent for a moment. Then Skuld reached over and took an apple. The crunch of her bite was loud in the quiet isolation of the tree.

"For what purpose?" Urd said at last.

"To defeat Odin Allfather. To save the Rogues."

Urd's eyelids fluttered. "Your love is among them," she murmured.

Jayne's throat squeezed suddenly. She nodded, unable to speak.

"He suffers. He is confused, constantly at war with himself. He seeks to protect his friends, but they do not recognize him," whispered Verdandi. Her eyes had rolled up into her head, as if she could see the interior of the Torrent in the back of her mind.

Skuld let her head fall back. "Odin will use the Rogues to

subjugate the world. Those who ally with him will be his lieu-tenants, safe so long as they are obedient. Those who refuse will die painfully. In no future do I see Tristan Labelle bargaining for his life."

Jayne clenched her fists until she found her voice. "I have to save him," she said hoarsely.

The Norns opened their eyes. They looked at one another. Then at her, and their mouths opened. They spoke with one voice.

"No."

CHAPTER
FOURTEEN

The shock of it stole Jayne's breath. *No?* They couldn't possibly think to refuse her. Odin would destroy the world. Why would he imprison them if they had no intention to interfere with his plans? Did they have some sort of ancient mythological Stockholm syndrome?

"You..." She was gasping. "You can't." She couldn't find the breath to continue. The Rogues would die. Aegis would fall. Everyone she loved would die.

A sinuous shape threaded between her ankles. *Breathe,* Hayden reminded her.

They watched her squirm for a few moments. Then Verdandi came to her aid. She spoke gently, as to a daughter. "The power to manipulate time is dangerous, and it is not to be used by the selfish. Indeed, those who would use it for selfish ends do not deserve to have it and cannot control it. They drive themselves mad. Sometimes, their actions even bring about the end of the world."

Was that what had happened to the Allfather? Had he gone mad searching for answers through time?

"I'm not—" Jayne stopped. Urd's lips were pursed like she

was ready to burst out laughing. Verdandi's eyebrow was raised in warning. Skuld's eyes held a challenge—*Not what, Jayne Thorne?*

She was about to say, "I'm not selfish." But that was a lie, and if she knew it, the goddesses surely did as well. "I'm not the Allfather," she said, softer than she meant to.

"There was a time when he wasn't the Allfather, either," Urd said drily.

"I *am* selfish." Jayne stood. "The love of my life was taken from me. Friends were taken from me, and I'd do anything to get them back."

"And that's why—" Verdandi began.

Jayne spun. "But I'm selfish for so much more than them. I'm selfish for the whole world. I want everyone to have the power I have, to feel what I feel when I'm in the Torrent. I want the Torrent to flow freely again. I want to bring the world back to what it was before Odin invaded, and I want it to be as perfect as it can be because it's my world, and I love it as deeply as I've ever loved anything. The nature in it, the history in it, the rich cultures I never got to explore. The books. Oh, the books are magnificent. I want it...no. I *need* for it all to be there again, so I can see it for myself. So my children can see it. So yes, I'm selfish. I'm selfish for this entire Earth, and I'll give up anything to save it."

She stopped. She'd talked so fast she'd forgotten to breathe and now gulped air and tried to calm the trembling in her limbs. The Norns, still seated at the table, glanced between themselves.

Urd said, "Would you give up your past?"

Skuld said, "Would you give up your future?"

Verdandi said, "Would you give up your life, here and now?"

"Yes," Jayne replied. "Anything."

Jayne, Hayden cried, shocked.

Trust me, she told him.

The Norns looked at each other again. Then they stood.

Skuld put her hand on Jayne's right shoulder. "The ability to fold time will lead to disaster for you. Even if you save the world, you will never be the same. There is no future where you will be who you are now when this is done. Can you accept that?"

Jayne let a small, bittersweet smile tug at the corner of her mouth. "Can I accept who I would be if I let the world burn, just to save myself?"

Urd laid a hand on her left shoulder. "The other goddesses were right about you, Jayne." She sounded pleased.

Verdandi stood in front of her. "You will be the first to fold time in many years," she said. She was smiling, but her eyes were grave. "Do not waste this power. And do not let Odin take it from you, or this world will end."

The goddesses leaned in and touched their heads to Jayne's. A sharp burning filled her skin, and she sensed a circle being etched around the glyphs that made up the other totems. Connecting one to another, then another, then another, until they were all touching the thin golden light. Contained within the circle, unending power.

Jayne's forehead smarted when they pulled away again. Then, in her mind, something began to unroll, like a creamy bolt of cloth. Only this cloth held a map.

It took Jayne a second to realize it wasn't a map of any one place. It was the map of time.

It looked like a cross between a three-dimensional topographical chart and an intricate family tree. Possibilities grew smaller and smaller until they reached a point, and branches led from decisions down to little pocket timelines, some with maps of their own that could be unfolded and examined. Jayne spotted the big, complicated mountain that was the Battle of

Kirkjufell, as well as the smaller decision to ascend Yggdrasil instead of fighting for Aegis.

"So, um. How do I navigate this?" she said.

"You have the map of time in your mind. You can recall it when in the world of the living." Two hands appeared in Jayne's mind—Verdandi's, closing over Jayne's own hands. "You stand at one point on the map. To get to another, you must take the point on which you stand and fold it until the point where you are matches with the point where you wish to go."

"Anyone who is touching you during the spell will travel with you," Skuld added.

"And Jayne—if you adapt this spell, you can move back in time in other ways as well. Turn back time on one place only, or on one person. Or on one mind." Urd's eyes bore into her.

Jayne felt her own eyes widen. She could turn back whole minds? "Like the minds of the Rogues?" she whispered.

"Do you see now why this power is so dangerous?" Urd asked.

Jayne could find Ruth somewhere in the past and turn her mind back to a time when it was uncorrupted. She could right every wrong, erase the bad things that had happened to all of them. She could save person after person after person—

And now she truly understood just how dangerous this power was. She couldn't possibly save every person on Earth, and so who was most important to save? And what gave her the right to decide whether one little girl's life was less important than the next? And if one was saved, but went on to do something horrible... Oh, the possibilities were almost too much to consider. And this was her power to control now.

This is why you are worthy, Hayden said with irrepressible fondness.

"No, this is why everyone just goes back in time to kill Hitler," she muttered.

"Agnes Jayne Thorne," said Verdandi in the voice of all mothers everywhere.

"It's a joke, it's a joke," Jayne protested. "I promise I won't destroy the timeline by trying to stop World War II."

"Don't you think World War III is enough?" Urd quipped.

Jayne squeezed their hands. They would be with her; she wouldn't be facing this new magic alone. "Didn't you hear how selfish I am?" She smiled.

Urd cocked her head. The Norns drew together as one, then split apart into their individual forms again. "No more joking. We are running out of time."

She pressed a finger to Jayne's forehead, and a jolt went through her, like touching a live wire. A brief pop and burn and she was back in the hallway, watching the last of her team disappear through the portal to Aegis, to fend off the attack.

"We went back in time?" she asked Hayden.

You have to start somewhere, he replied.

"Well, here goes nothing." With a deep breath, Jayne stepped toward the portal.

CHAPTER
FIFTEEN

Mayhem. Blood. Screams.

Jayne stepped through a few moments after she'd left, and a full-blown battle was taking place. It took a moment to get her bearings. Wraiths dove at a long line of soldiers who were trying to protect a corridor between the school and the portal. Sofia, Xiomara, and Henry stood fighting against the largest Wraith Jayne had ever seen—Huginn, one of Odin's special lieutenants, one of the first Wraiths ever created. He must have been sent to spearhead the attack on Aegis.

She watched Xiomara deal Huginn a punishing blow that shattered his knee. In the distance, Cillian, in his wolf form, was running from his breached enclosure to join the fray.

Jayne closed her eyes on the horror that was Aegis in the now and folded the map in her mind—and opened her eyes on the Aegis that had existed twenty minutes before.

Sofia's mouth fell open, and Xiomara looked around, confounded. Jayne strode forward, pulling her staff from the Torrent and spinning it into Huginn's head. He was trying to take advantage of their distraction. He roared and flapped away.

"I did it," she said to Sofia.

"I..." Her sister's mouth was slightly agape. "I can tell."

Jayne looked down at her fingers. She was glowing bright gold with the use of the totem, light shimmering off her like heat, but the edges of the golden light faded to green, like flashing sunlight in a rainforest.

Sofia's awed look turned to horror. "The kids," she said. Then she looked out over the field. Cillian was loping closer, looking half-crazed with rage. Amanda had rallied her troops and was calling orders in a quick pattern. Tamara tossed her sniper rifle and reached for another weapon.

"You know what needs to happen to protect the children." Jayne put a hand on Sofia's arm. "I'll take care of Cillian."

Sofia nodded and started to turn away. Then she gripped Jayne's arm. "Help him," she whispered. Jayne knew what she really meant: *Don't kill him.*

Jayne squeezed her arm back. "I promise," she said.

Sofia ran. Jayne stepped up beside Xiomara and swung her staff at a Wraith trying to sneak up behind. "Still think this is folly?" she said.

The older woman's face was set and pinched. Sweat dripped from her temple, and she shifted her grip on the huge double-headed ax. "Yes," she said shortly, and swung.

Jayne laughed, incredulous. "Be stubborn, then. Keep the Wraiths off my back while I deal with our friend here."

"Jayne, be careful," Henry Thorne warned from behind her. Jayne shaped a small Shield spell and laid it over her arm, just as though she were facing a medieval foe. The problem was, she had to get close enough to Cillian to touch him without getting her arm ripped out of her socket. And from the way his nose wrinkled, from the way his golden eyes flashed—that was going to be a problem.

More Rogues were flowing toward them, all with the intent

to kill. But Amanda had learned from her mistakes: She barked orders with cold precision. "Fight to immobilize. But if it comes down to their life or yours, fight to kill. Fight to survive." Ruger and Danilo stood shoulder to shoulder. Ruger kept wiggling his left arm like he couldn't believe it was still there.

Jayne breathed deep, reaching into the Torrent, pulling at the earth to breathe with her. As usual, her Earth totem was reluctant to help, but she spun up a violent windstorm and sketched a quick boomerang-style spell that sent the wind out like a blade, sweeping the feet out from under every Rogue on the ground. Cillian leaped for her, and she brought her staff up just in time to block the swipe of his lethal claws.

He was still two hundred pounds of enraged predator coming at her at speed. He hit the staff, and his snarl became a puppyish whine as they went down. Jayne used their momentum to flip him over, and he landed hard on his side. She rolled without bothering to get up and seized a clump of his fur. No time to think about what would happen if this didn't work or wonder how much of her hand he could bite off at once. She cast herself into the spell.

The Fold spell treated time like a map. The trick was to take Cillian back to the final moments of the Battle of Kirkjufell, before Odin had cast his spell on the Rogues, without trying to physically move both of them to Iceland. Jayne thought of the Cillian she'd known then, wiser and older than she was, with battles under his belt and experience taking care of an entire school of remarkable children. The Cillian who knew who he was: a considerate, good man who was about to be a father.

She took the angry, mindless Rogue in front of her, and she folded the spell like a sheet of paper until he aligned with his own self. It didn't want to take: The spell squirmed angrily, as though Cillian's mind were rebelling, and Jayne felt the creeping pain of the spell. She fought to control it. Agony raked across her arm. She refused to open her eyes. If she saw what Cillian was doing to her, she might not have the courage to keep going.

Then the spell moved into place with a snap. Cillian went slack. Jayne opened her eyes.

He lay on the ground in a daze. His eyes were green again, blinking in confusion. Jayne still had all her fingers, and the pain on her arm, as it turned out, was Hayden pulling free. He leapt into the air to intercept a Wraith coming down on them.

Cillian got to his feet slowly, clearly hurting. He looked at Jayne, and her whole body sagged in relief. It was unmistakably him.

He dipped his head in thanks. Then he took off at a loping run, in the same direction Sofia had gone.

Jayne couldn't find the strength to stand. Her mind spun and her eyes refused to focus. Maybe she shouldn't have tried that spell in the middle of battle, she thought. Now she was just going to lie here until a Wraith spotted her and put her out of her misery.

"Come on," said Henry Thorne, and dug an arm under her shoulders. Her arm throbbed but had healed enough during her time with the Norns that she didn't gasp in pain. "Let's get you home."

"There's still a battle going on," Jayne protested.

"And you can't participate, and you're endangering those of us who want to protect you," Henry told her. "You've done enough for us, Jayne. Things are going much better than the last time." Ah. It seemed that people retained memories of the past even when it had been folded away. Good to know.

Rogues were being dragged in nets both magical and mundane toward the portal to the TCO. They seemed to have the Wraiths on the retreat, though they still fought. Huginn, the enormous Wraith with the shattered knee, was trying to pull

Wraiths and Rogues toward the corridor protecting the kids. They bombarded the Shield spells with an array of magic that sparked and sizzled. More than one Adept went down under a direct attack.

Cillian leapt for Huginn. His jaws fastened around the Wraith's good leg, and Huginn howled, shaking and flailing. Cillian was thrown free. He hit the ground with a thump but came up growling.

For a moment, Rogue and Wraith stared at each other. Cillian's ears flattened against his head. Huginn clenched a fist. Cillian whined. He seemed unable to attack—indeed, it looked as though he was resisting something. His paws dug into the ground and he pulled backward.

A shout came from farther up the corridor, and Jayne heard the sound of an engine. Spells sparked as the Wraiths and Rogues redoubled their attack. Huginn glared at Cillian one last time, then snarled. He turned away—

And dove toward the Adepts holding the corridor nearest Jayne.

"No," she gasped, reaching for any spell that could help them. But the Torrent felt far away, and its magic slipped through her fingers. Her mind couldn't make sense of the patterns. Everything was an exhausting blur. "No!" If she didn't concentrate, they'd die—the children would be caught, and turned into Wraiths—

Huginn broke through and landed heavily in the road, right between the oncoming truck and the portal. He bellowed in pain as his legs hit the ground, but he didn't fall. He swept his wings, and Adepts fell away.

Jayne could see Zia at the wheel of the huge apple truck. Her eyes were wide, wild, and she flinched when she realized Huginn wasn't going to move.

Then her jaw set. The engine roared. The truck tore down

the makeshift road, tearing up clumps of grass. Zia's mouth opened in a snarl, then a scream.

Too late, Huginn realized his bluff had been called. He tried to launch, but when he flapped his wings to get off the ground, Zia hit him square in the torso.

She pumped the brakes. The truck skid sideways and Huginn slumped from the hood. A Disciple of Gaia swung his katana, and Jayne looked away before Huginn's head detached from his body. She had no need to see more death today.

Adepts swarmed the back of the truck, handing down kids. Jayne recognized the president's daughter, surrounded by heavily armed Secret Service agents, hustled from the truck and toward the portal. Shield spells burst into being like fireworks as Adepts surrounded the knot of students.

Zia counted them off as they passed, then turned to Sofia when the woman came running up to the truck. Then Sofia spun a quick Whip spell and flicked it at the air over Jayne. A Wraith she hadn't even noticed recoiled with a howl.

"Thanks for that," Jayne said. Sofia wasn't listening. She was staring at Zia, gasping for breath. "You, girl...you need a driver's license."

Zia's whole face lit up in a grin. "Can I?"

"We're getting you enrolled in driving lessons ASAP." Sofia turned as Cillian trotted up to her. She fell to her knees and threw her arms around his shoulders. Her whole body was racked by sobs.

"Let's give your sister some privacy," Henry advised and started to turn Jayne around. It wasn't as though she could really argue with him, she thought with some chagrin.

With the children through the portal, the battle was starting to break up. It seemed that Odin's chief objective had failed. *Victory at last,* thought Jayne. She could go home and sleep, and tomorrow she could take a look at all the Rogues they'd captured and see if she could turn back their minds.

A Wraith, smaller than Huginn and with the crafty face of a jackal, had taken it upon himself to organize the retreat. He howled, and the Wraiths dipped away from their targets, flapping over the sky of the Time Catch to wherever they'd invaded from.

He howled again. This time, the Rogues turned from their fights and began to run, slither, and fly away. A few Adepts shot net guns after them, but none took. That meant something important for later, Jayne was certain, but for now she could barely think.

Sofia still clung to Cillian. "Stay with me," she said, still weeping. "Stay."

Cillian had dug his paws in again, resisting the call to the Rogues. A rumble started up deep in his throat, and for a moment Jayne was certain he was losing himself again. But his eyes were green and clear and tender. He lay his canine head against Sofia.

Sofia, on the other hand, was pulling away. "I can't..." She was panting. Sweat beaded on her forehead. She put one hand to her belly. "It's like the baby wants to go."

Cillian's eyes grew wide. "I know," Sofia said. The wolf got to his feet—then stumbled. His whole body was trying to turn toward the retreating Rogues.

Sofia stumbled. "Get him out of here," she said to the nearby Adepts. And then, to Cillian, "I'm right behind you."

Adepts gathered around Cillian to usher him forward to the portal. Soon Jayne and Henry were caught up in the press, and Jayne couldn't do a thing to fight it. She craned her head, looking for Sofia.

Her sister was speaking in a low voice to Seo-Joon via their

Walkie-Talkie spell. She winced like she was having a bad cramp.

Her feet started to leave the ground.

"Sofia." Jayne struggled. "Dad, Sofia!"

Henry turned and all but dropped Jayne. "Sofia!" he shouted.

Sofia's face was twisting with confusion and fear. She kept drifting. Her mouth formed the word *Cillian,* the word *Jayne.*

A lone winged form circled around in the sky, and an eagle Rogue the size of a car glided toward them. "No!" Jayne screamed. Cillian howled.

The eagle's talons closed around Sofia's shoulders and pulled her away.

CHAPTER
SIXTEEN

S ofia crouched on a rock that was not a rock, watching a
sickly black Torrent rush by. She'd been dropped here by
the eagle Rogue, right before she'd violently thrown up. The
battle, the fear, the horror, all combined with shaking up a
pregnant lady, were too much for her. Hopefully vomiting into a
river of magic didn't do any lasting damage to the river.

Rogues lay all around her in various states of despair and
exhaustion. Some of them let the Torrent carry them far downstream. Others found space on the rocks, sometimes by pushing
off smaller Rogues.

No one had bothered her yet. She hadn't stopped panicking
enough to figure out why. She pulled her knees up to her chest
and shivered. When she looked up, the space above her was
black, a night sky without stars. She wasn't even sure how she
could see.

The lioness who'd had her place taken stalked around the
rock, looking for a place to lie down. Her golden eyes alighted
on Sofia, and Sofia thought she spotted some recognition there.
The lioness growled low in her throat. Sofia felt her baby stir in
response and had to choke back another wave of nausea.

The lioness started toward her lithely, moving in a way that showed she saw Sofia as prey. Sofia drew her legs in farther. She reached for her magic, wondering exactly what sort of spell a person could pull out of the Torrent when it looked like this—

A large form stepped in front of her. An entirely human form.

"Non, Maman," said Tristan Labelle.

The lioness snarled at him. He folded his arms and stood his ground. "You will not attack me. You remember that much," he said. "Find someone else to go bully."

She growled. He hurled several words in French that seemed to rile her up even more.

Around them, the other Rogues paused in the licking of their wounds or their petty bickering to enjoy the show. Gina Labelle watched Tristan for a long moment as if wondering whether she should kill him or not. He picked up a rock, turning it over in his hands, ready to hurl it at her.

She tossed her head as if to say he wasn't worth her time anyway. She made her way down the rocks and shoved a hawk off the end of one so she could flop down.

Tristan turned back to where Sofia stared at him, wide-eyed and open-mouthed.

He looked more than a little the worse for wear. His jeans were scuffed and torn, as was his shirt. A soft beard had grown over his chin and jaw, and his normally impeccable dark hair stuck up in all directions, untamed and wild. His blue eyes looked a little wild, too, and when he gripped Sofia by the arms she almost gasped at the force of his fingers. He pulled her into a tight hug.

"I will not lie, it is good to see another human, even though I wish you were not here, for your sake," he said in English, speaking fast and low, his French accent broad from days of disuse. Still gripping her by the elbow, he led her behind a little

129

outcropping, ousting a few small Rogues who didn't want to bother with an argument. "What are you doing here?"

"I don't know," Sofia confessed in a whisper. "We were at the school—Aegis was under attack—and we won, and then I felt myself being...*pulled* and I couldn't stop it."

"Aegis," Tristan muttered. "So that's where they all went. I can resist the Allfather's call, likely because he cannot see me amongst the Rogues. I have enough genetic Rogue in me to be part of the masses, but not enough to fall entirely under his spell. I felt the summons but was able to stay behind."

"But why did you want to?" Sofia asked. "Jayne..." She didn't know what to say. Jayne looked hollower every day that Tristan and Vivienne were gone. She'd made a family for herself, and Tristan had walked away from it. In her heart, Sofia understood his reasons. She'd have done the same, if her choices were to follow Jayne into the mouth of the beast or stay behind, wondering if her sister was lost forever.

"Until I know how to save Vivienne, I cannot leave her," Tristan said somberly. "I didn't know whether I'd be able to get back into this place once I left it, and I did not want to draw attention to myself. You must realize, we are only safe because Odin does not know we are here. But it would be easy for him to find out. We cause a disturbance, we get caught. We must sit tight, as it were." He smiled at her belly. "How's the baby?"

Sofia's stomach flipped over again, and she barely avoided being sick all over Tristan's shoes. "I think this place disagrees with her," she said. She tried not to think about what being trapped in a sickening pocket of the Torrent might do to an unborn child.

Tristan was giving her a calculating look. "She must be the reason you're here," he said at last. "She's a Rogue, and she's responding to Odin's call."

Lovely. So Sofia had a little Odin beacon inside her.

"Do you think Jayne understands?" Tristan asked abruptly. "Why I'm here?"

Sofia scratched at the ground, thinking. "She does," she said finally. "That's why she'll only kick your ass, instead of completely wiping the floor with you when you get back. And she knows you didn't abandon her by choice. She's working to find us. She's working to get us out of here. Every last Rogue."

Tristan started to nod. Then he stiffened. His eyes grew wide, his hands spasmed into claws. He began to tremble. "Tristan?" Sofia whispered. All around them, the noise of Rogues grumbling and fighting had fallen to nothing. In her own belly, she felt her daughter curl up like a fist.

She risked a peek over the rocks. Everywhere she looked the Rogues were immobile. Their eyes bulged in their sockets, their limbs trembled. They struggled to draw breath. As one, they were in a deep agony. Sweat broke out on Tristan's brow, beading and sliding down to his beard.

Sofia put a hand on his arm. He didn't notice. She wasn't sure what else to do. For a full minute, the air around her was still as the Rogues struggled.

Then everyone seemed to exhale at once. Tristan slumped forward and Sofia caught him by the shoulders. A Rogue screamed, and another Rogue snapped at it.

"Gods, my head," Tristan mumbled. "That was...difficult." He blinked away tears of pain. "Odin is displeased. The battle did not go the way he wished, and he feels the Rogues could have done...better."

"We *are* going to get out of this," Sofia said, taking his hand and giving it a reassuring squeeze. "Jayne will find us."

Tristan looked at her with uncustomary bleakness. "We will get out of this," he agreed. "The question is, are we going to get out of this alive?"

CHAPTER
SEVENTEEN

J ayne woke up in the TCO hospital, the sense of loss overwhelming.

Yes, she'd managed to turn back time and alter the course of the battle. But she'd lost her sister this time. She had work to do. She needed to refine the spells, figure out how to swoop in moments before the action, and remove the person being attacked. And that was going to take practice.

I'll save you, sis. Promise.

It was relatively quick work to get Tamara to discharge her. She was fine, and Tamara could use the space and breathing room. "You Thornes always seem to bounce back anyway," Tamara said with a quick smile. "But I want you to pop over to the neurological unit and get a brain scan done."

Jayne frowned. "Why?"

"Boss's orders. Something about timelines and insanity? Ask a Genius."

"I swear to God, if my dad's the one insisting I get a brain scan, he's going to have to get one first," Jayne said under her breath.

Tamara laughed. "If you manage that, send it over. I'd love to see what a Genius brain looks like."

Jayne stomped down to neurology, where she waited for the doctor to be available. Someone had kindly left behind a battered copy of a thick novel called *Fourth Wing*, but Jayne couldn't even get past the first page. Sofia. Sofia was gone.

Was she destined to lose them all? Is that what the Norns meant when they said she wouldn't come out of this the same person?

Amanda, Henry, and Xiomara joined her as the doctor, a bald and cheerful man named Preston, called them in. "What's with the honor guard?" Jayne asked, standing. Henry offered his arm, but she waved it off. She was feeling much better now that she'd had a rest and a drink of the TCO's special electrolyte water.

"Henry wants to talk to Doctor Preston about the potential effect of time travel on the brain. I'm here to make sure my best operative hasn't done something irreparably harmful to herself." Amanda sighed. "And Xiomara's here because she insisted. And after her performance in the battle, I felt it wise to rescind her previous banishment."

Jayne glared at Xiomara. The woman came through for them at Aegis, but Jayne hadn't forgotten her attempt to steal the codex. "Not convinced of my sanity? I guess you wouldn't be the first. But I'm just regular crazy Jayne Thorne, original flavor. No new madness detected."

"We shall see," Xiomara said frostily.

Half an hour later they were grouped around a set of computer screens, looking at cross-sections of Jayne's brain. Preston had given them a complicated monologue on the Torrent, magic use, and potential neurological effects, interrupted frequently by Henry's questions. But at last, they got to the crux of the matter. "All in all, it looks good," Preston told her with a smile. "Entirely healthy."

"So traveling in time hasn't resulted in any sort of mental issues?" Jayne pressed.

"Nothing that shows up on a physiological scan. You realize I'm a doctor of the brain, and not a doctor of the mind?" Preston told her.

"Great." Jayne stood. "If that's all, I'm going to figure out how to rescue my sister." A bout of dizziness kicked in, forcing her to lean over the table.

"First, you're going to have lunch." Henry pushed his glasses up his nose and took his daughter's arm. "Doctor Preston, a pleasure to meet you. I'm sure we'll be consulting again regarding magic and its effects on the human brain."

"Nothing would please me more," Preston said, shaking his hand with enthusiasm.

Jayne was pretty sure she heard Amanda mutter, "Nerds," as they walked out.

"How's Cillian?" Jayne asked on the way to the canteen. "Is he...?"

"He's back," Henry said with a tight smile. "He was examined as soon as he arrived and he seems to be his old self. He both remembers and doesn't remember his time as a...rogue Rogue, as it were."

"What do you mean?" Jayne frowned.

The canteen smelled of lasagna and burned coffee and donuts. Jayne suddenly realized how ravenous she was. She piled her plate high with pasta and salad and followed Henry to an empty table. Amanda sat with her, tucking into a small side salad. Xiomara ate nothing. She still looked like someone had forced her to bite into a lemon.

"You've changed our timeline, but time is delicate," Henry said. "It can split and splinter, like a tree. For example, everyone in this room remembers two outcomes of the battle at Aegis. Some of them even remember dying once." He grimaced. "You turned back time, but you did not keep us from experiencing what we experienced. You just...created an alternate reality. A new timeline for us."

"Which means what, exactly?" Jayne said around a mouthful of lasagna. "Did Odin win in that other timeline?"

"Perhaps. I'm not sure what happened after you showed up to turn back time. Odin might lose that war, too."

"Could we go back and check somehow?" Jayne asked.

"*No!*" Xiomara said fiercely.

Henry raised a brow at her. "I'm not certain how one would go about it, admittedly. Hopping between realities is possible, but one runs into difficulties regarding meeting oneself, making choices without understanding their full significance in context, and, of course, returning to one's original reality should one so choose."

Even for Henry, that was a bit of an obtuse explanation. "So how does time travel work? Every time I do it, I create a new reality?"

"Probably not." Henry rubbed his face and took a distracted bite of his chocolate cake donut. "Let's say you want to turn back time later today and have something different for lunch. Unless you, say, had a lunch of poisonous mushrooms, how you fed yourself today wouldn't greatly impact the course of your life. But let's say you go back in time to..." He cast about for something.

"To prevent Ruth from turning evil?" Jayne suggested, thinking about her conversation with the Norns.

Henry nodded. "That's an excellent example. If Ruth could be turned away from her darker impulses, our family would never have been torn apart. You would have been raised knowing about the Torrent, the Kingdom would have been a minor and unimportant faction in magical geopolitics, and the Allfather might even still reside in his prison. The timeline would have branched into a new reality for the world that you created."

"An alternate reality that splits the Torrent, according to some," Xiomara butted in.

"According to some," Henry agreed mildly. "Now, let's say you create an alternate reality for a short time. You go back in time to change the outcome of a battle, but we still lose the war. There will likely be some things that are different: people who would have died but are now alive, places that would have been destroyed but are still preserved. That sort of thing. The timeline can reintegrate if the deaths aren't too significant. But no matter what, *you'll* always remember the things you've done."

"So, no way to erase my memory of that embarrassing haircut I got when I was seventeen?" Jayne joked.

"That is enough, Jayne Thorne," Xiomara said loud enough for half the canteen to turn and fall silent.

Xiomara stood. She hadn't changed out of the clothes she'd been in for the battle, Jayne realized. Her face was streaked with dirt and mud, and probably blood. Wisps of hair escaped from her braids, and the hem of her dress was torn and scorched. "Rearranging the fabric of reality is not a joke," she spat.

Jayne stood, too. She was tired of being treated like a child by everyone who had a single gray hair. "Believe me, I know," she replied. "I met the goddesses who gave it to me. They were convinced that I could use it responsibly. Why aren't you?"

"Because you are a Thorne! You act first and think later, and if this power will save someone you love, you don't care if it destroys the entire world. You'll use it."

"It won't destroy the world, though," Jayne said. She sounded pleading; she stopped and took a breath. She didn't need to beg for Xiomara's approval. "You heard my dad. If I have to create an alternate reality in which Odin doesn't win, I will. It's better than only one reality where he does."

"It will harm the Torrent," Xiomara said.

"You don't know that. Dad says it's just a theory."

"I *do* know that. It has happened before. Time travel has destroyed the Torrent, and you will let it happen again." Xiomara stood back and raised her voice to the room. "I shed blood and risked my life for the Torrent Control Organization," she declared. "I will do it no more. The power you have is too great, Jayne Thorne, and if possessing it does not drive you mad, using it will. One way or the other."

Jayne snorted. *Fine by me,* she opened her mouth to say, but Amanda leaned over and put her hand on her arm. Amanda stood and straightened her suit, and Jayne recognized her diplomat expression, the one she put on when she had to talk to someone politely, like her boss' boss.

She went around the table toward Xiomara but stopped short of trying to touch the woman. "We value your expertise and leadership. Knowing what you now know, is there any way we can talk about this, to try and mend fences?"

Around the room, Guardians were standing up. They'd planned this, Jayne realized. A confrontation. A demonstration, perhaps. Ruger, sitting next to Danilo with a cup of coffee, looked stricken.

"Will you swear not to travel in time? Will you swear not to use the powers of these goddesses?" Xiomara asked Jayne.

"Uh. No. Using them saved all your butts, and I'm going to have to use them again if we—"

"Then I have nothing more to say on the subject. Except that *true* Guardians"—her eyes cut to Henry—"protect the Torrent. And it seems that now the time has come to protect the Torrent from *you.*"

She turned on her heel and strode out of the canteen. The

Guardians who'd stood, followed. Danilo turned his head to give Ruger one last glance, eyes blazing with anguish and something more. Some kind of promise. He walked away, and Ruger looked like a wounded puppy, coffee forgotten in one trembling hand.

Amanda sighed and got out her phone. "Have a security team meet to escort the Guardians off the premises," she said to whoever was on the other line. Then she sat and rubbed at her forehead with one hand. "Just once, I'd like people to be less dramatic when making their grand declarative statements."

"Grand declarative statements are fun," Jayne said. But she'd lost her appetite. Xiomara had always been stalwart in her guidance. She'd known right from wrong. Breaking with her made Jayne feel like she was on the wrong side.

And she'd been awake for almost two hours, and she still didn't know what she was going to do about her sister.

"If it makes you feel any better, the Disciples of Gaia support Jayne more than ever," said Isra, coming over with two cups of tea. She handed one to Jayne, who moved her swiftly up the favorite-persons list. "We have long held a prophecy about the one who wields all the totems."

"As someone who saves the world and her sister?" Jayne quipped.

Isra leveled a look at her. "As someone we will follow into death."

Charming.

EIGHTEEN

"We'll find her," Henry said. He sat with Jayne and Cillian in the Nashville apartment, sipping a cup of green tea. Half a slice of blueberry pie congealed on a plate in front of him, forgotten. Jayne couldn't blame him. Even she didn't have an appetite for pie. It felt wrong to eat it without Sofia.

Cillian had taken Tristan's armchair, his big frame filling it in a way that seemed cramped, not cozy. His shoulders were rounded, and his elbows rested on his knees. His shaggy blond hair fell over his eyes, obscuring his expression, but Jayne knew what it was: kicked puppy. He'd looked that way from the moment he'd snapped out of his mindless state and realized Sofia was gone.

"It's been a week, Dad," she said quietly. "She's—"

"Scientific advancements don't happen overnight," he reminded her softly and pressed his teacup against his lips.

That was the problem. Everything in Jayne screamed that she had to find Sofia now or risk her being lost forever. Who knew where the Rogues were being kept or what they might do to her sister? The longer they waited to rescue her, the worse things seemed.

"And you can't feel anything anymore?" Jayne said to Cillian.

He paused, then shook his head. "The voice is gone." He snorted softly and added, "Just when it might have been useful."

Jayne reached over the coffee table and put a hand on his knee. It was the only thing she could reach, and barely—and her touch startled him, making him tense up. "It's not your fault. It's going to be all right," she said. The very words she couldn't say to herself.

"I almost..." He swallowed and said thickly, "I almost killed her. I almost destroyed our baby..."

"But you didn't." Jayne pushed some steel into her voice. "You knew, in the end, that it wasn't what you wanted to do. And you came back to us, and I know that Sofia would tell you to stop dwelling on the past and start thinking about baby names."

"Aye, but Sofia's not here." Cillian lifted his head and closed his eyes, letting a tear slip from the corner of one.

Jayne pressed her lips together. She gingerly got up from the couch and went around to the chair. Kneeling, she wrapped her arms around Cillian. For a moment it felt strange, putting her arms around her former lover. Then Cillian's enormous arms came around her chest and he squeezed her so hard her ribs protested. He smelled different than he had when they'd been together, she realized, and was a little embarrassed to know it. His scent was muskier, more like the wolf. He'd spent the equivalent of more than five years in the Aegis Time Catch with Sofia, living an extra life. Now all of that was gone. Jayne couldn't imagine how he felt.

"It's going to be okay," she said again.

Though she had no idea *how* it was going to be okay.

W HILE HIS DAUGHTER believed that all answers could be found in books, Henry Thorne believed, wholeheartedly, that any problem could be solved through good logical thinking. If you had a problem with a spell, you could dive into the theory of it, tweaking its form or motion. If the technology was failing, an analysis of your hypothesis, materials, and methods was necessary. And many problems were just opportunities in disguise: How could he get a different result by changing a few different elements?

At the moment Henry had two opportunities: the opportunity to pull Alexandra and Trinity from where they were trapped in the Torrent, and the opportunity to save Sofia. And when it came to choosing between his mother and his daughter, well, there was no choice at all in terms of priority.

"Still trying to tweak the Find spell?" Quimby asked, looking over the diagram on his desk. Henry was back at the table with the Time Reverse. It was disassembled, its parts scattered over the table, and he was contemplating how Jayne's Fold spell could be added to it to widen the Reverse capabilities.

"The Find spell isn't going to work," Henry said with a sigh. "It's designed to search for anything on this plane, this world. It could potentially be adjusted to search other planes, but we'd have to locate them one by one and map out an exception for each, and that wouldn't actually tell us if we had the correct plane or Torrent pocket in which the Rogues are trapped."

"You never give up on a problem." Quimby sounded suspicious.

"I said the spell wasn't going to work, not that I've given up." Henry groped for his cup of tea without taking his eyes off the part he was scrutinizing. "I'm going to go back in time to save her."

There was a long silence. Henry was just getting lost in the mechanics again when Quimby said, "You know Amanda's put limits on how Jayne's allowed to use that Fold spell."

"And?"

He looked up. Quimby was biting her lip, tugging on one curly lock of hair that had escaped from her ponytail. Behind her cat-eye readers, her eyes darted from side to side. "Um. We're not allowed to use it if the TCO's primary objectives have been achieved in an incident."

"You sound like a corporate email," Henry told her, going back to the disassembled Time Reverse. If they could etch the spell on a metal plate and fix it somewhere in the Reverse...

"It *was* the corporate email," Quimby said. She came forward tentatively. "I sort of memorized it. In case..."

In case she had to quote it at him. Henry rubbed at his forehead and stood up. "What is science for?" he asked her.

She blinked and took a breath. "It's to make people's lives better. At least, that's what I think."

"I couldn't agree more. That's why I intend to use the Time Reverse to go back for Sofia. I intend to make her life better."

"But what if you make a whole lot of other people's lives worse?" Quimby asked.

"I won't," Henry said. "I know how to be careful."

Quimby didn't have anything to say to that.

It took a couple of days to scale down the Fold spell into something that could be etched onto a nanoplate and attached to the Time Reverse. Then it took some hours to reassemble the tiny bits of machinery. Cillian wandered into the Genius Lab and Henry let him help, mostly out of a sense of duty to his son-in-law-to-be and a feeling of pity. "Maybe we should both go," he suggested.

Cillian's eyes lit with a hunger that made Henry suddenly doubt himself. "Could we? I mean, I think I could help..."

"We don't know that the new Time Reverse is going to work," Quimby said. Her mouth was tight, and she stared at Henry in warning.

Henry pushed up his glasses. "I'm redesigning the interface to a touchscreen that can take us between significant points and allow us to calibrate for specificity. We should be fine."

Cillian blinked at him, then looked at Quimby. She sighed. "He means he's put a screen on it that should help you find a specific point to Fold to. Simplifying the spell, which isn't always a good idea." She said this last bit to Henry in a slow, clear voice, as though he were a child.

Henry wasn't sure what Quimby thought she could teach him about spell theory. She wasn't exactly magical herself. He knew what he was doing, and Cillian was better in a fight than he was.

Besides, he could see in the big man's frame, in his eyes, in the set of his mouth: He had to do something. He had to redeem himself. Henry understood that feeling more than he would have liked.

The day Henry was ready to retrieve his daughter was stormy. He woke early that morning and slipped down to the lab, letting himself in and snagging the revamped Time Reverse before Quimby came in with her morning coffee. It didn't take a genius to see she didn't approve of this mission, and he didn't want her trying to talk him out of it—or worse, tattling to Amanda. She hadn't yet, but if she knew it was happening? They'd all forgive him when he came back with Sofia and a proven piece of valuable tech. Jayne would be so happy and so proud. He focused on that and sent a quick text to Cillian.

Ready?

Cillian met him in the canteen. He'd been out for a run, and his hair was plastered to his head. His T-shirt was soaked. "It's pissing down," he explained, but when Henry suggested waiting for him to change, he shook his head. "I want to get moving," he said. "And soon enough, I won't need shirts, if you know what I mean."

Henry did know. Wolves didn't exactly wear clothes.

They walked together to the portal to Aegis. Another benefit of having Cillian along, Henry realized, while the big man talked to the security guard on duty and signed them both out. Cillian was one of the co-founders of the school, and it wasn't at all odd that he was taking an early-morning trip there with his father-in-law. For someone who was admittedly bad at duplicity, Henry thought, this was all going rather well so far.

They stepped into the portal, and out onto the site of the battle. Henry needed to be as close as possible to the action; he hadn't managed to work in any sort of transport spells and wasn't sure how they'd interact with the Reverser.

"All right," he murmured.

The day here was just beginning, as well, but much finer than outside the Time Catch, with the pink of sunrise tinting the clouds above. Cillian stretched, closing his eyes. A soft wind blew, carrying with it the smell of fresh grass and the forest behind the manor. Henry turned on the Reverser and flicked through options on the interface until he got to a dial. He ran his finger in a counterclockwise motion until he found the date he wanted. Then he zeroed in on the time.

"Come here," Henry said. "I've set the inclusion zone to about three feet in diameter."

"Inclusion zone?" Cillian sounded bemused, but he did as

Henry asked. His hands clenched and his nostrils flared. His breathing was uneven. "Are we sure this is the right move?" he asked. "Are we sure we're not...I don't know, mucking it all up?"

"You want her back, don't you?" Henry said shortly.

Cillian's fists squeezed again. "Of course I do. I also know what she'd say if we ruined everything and lost the battle. If the Wraiths took the kids..."

"We'll only need to do the one trip," Henry promised him. "It will all be worth it."

"It will all be worth it," Cillian echoed. He nodded once.

Henry was feeling a little short of breath himself. "Well," he said. "Here goes nothing."

He pushed the button. The world shimmered...

...and filled with bodies. The battle was raging. Chaos slammed into him like a wave, and he stumbled, nearly dropping the Time Reverse. He hastily put together a Carry spell and tucked it away. "All right," he said to Cillian. "We find Sofia first—"

Cillian wasn't there.

Henry turned, first in one direction, then another. The big man was rather hard to miss; if he wasn't on the battlefield, it meant something was wrong with the Time Reverse's inclusion zone. Well. There was an...opportunity.

Henry had chosen to ignore Amanda's mandates about time travel and restrictions on the new power in their midst. But he wasn't exactly ignorant to the *theory* of time travel, and he knew that the more time was adjusted, the more complicated things got. He couldn't go back for Cillian now.

Jayne and Xiomara stood side by side, fighting Wraiths. Sofia had taken off at a run toward the corridor to strengthen it. Henry reached into the Torrent and withdrew his magical bow and arrow, then grabbed the nearest Adept. Hopefully whoever this was had strong magic—strong enough to take Sofia's place on the corridor. "Come with me," he said, and was proud at how authoritative he sounded.

The Adept turned at once, and they set off toward Sofia at a run.

They raced up the corridor, with the green light of the Shield spells glowing around and above them. A Wraith's claws scraped on the Shield like chalk on a blackboard. "What's the objective, sir?" panted the Adept as their boots pounded on the trampled grass.

Henry spotted Sofia's blonde ponytail up ahead. "You'll be taking over for her." He skidded to a stop and grabbed his daughter by the shoulder.

She spun, one hand already shaping a Knockout spell. She let it fizzle out when she saw who it was. "Goddess, Dad. Are you *trying* to get yourself a new scar?"

"Shield spell," Henry told the Adept. He shifted his grip to Sofia's arm and began to pull her along. "We need to get you to safety."

"Uh." She stopped resisting and they started to trot back down the corridor. "What's going on?"

"I have reason to believe that you're being targeted by the Wraiths, specifically," he said.

"Me? Why?" But Sofia put a hand on her belly, and Henry had to wonder if he was right.

They reached the portal just as the apple truck came screeching toward them. It slammed into the big Wraith, and Zia hopped out. Sofia started to pull away from Henry. "She's fine," he said sharply—

Then Sofia screamed, "Jayne!"

A Wraith was headed straight for Jayne. And this time, there was no Sofia to crack her whip and stop it.

The Wraith hit Jayne in the shoulders. Henry watched, felt the ghost of the pull, as though his muscles were committing it to memory. Jayne was dragged through the dirt as the Wraith fought to gain ground, her staff long dropped. Sparks of a spell flicked between her fingers, but she couldn't summon the strength to follow it through.

The Wraith dodged an attack, then another. It flapped up and up, with one talon around Jayne's legs and one around her middle.

Then it wrenched her body in half with an unmistakable crack.

Sofia's scream rang in his ears, his heart. Henry's fingers trembled. He pulled the Time Reverse from his Carry spell. *Time is a cruel mistress indeed,* he thought, spinning the dial.

He landed hard on Aegis ground. He'd gone back a little too far—just a little. Darkness flickered at the edge of his vision, but he shook out his shoulders and looked at the interface again. In about two hours, the attack on Aegis would begin. He'd just have to stop himself from retrieving Sofia until *after* the Wraith attack; there wouldn't be much time but he could do it. If only Cillian were here—

He could go back for Cillian, of course. But he thought of what he'd said to the man: *We'll only need to do the one trip.* Things were looking to be more complicated than that.

But it would all be worth it. He could make everything work out. This setback was hardly a setback, after all—

Every problem was an opportunity.

CHAPTER
NINETEEN

J ayne woke to something nosing at her face. "Go away," she mumbled, flopping over in her bed.

No. Hayden's claws scrabbled at her sheets, dragging them backward, off her body. *You must get up. Something's wrong.*

Jayne sat bolt upright, holding her breath. She listened, hard. Her apartment was still, silent. No rustle of someone trying the door handle or messing with the lock. And her apartment was on the second floor, so it wasn't exactly easy for an intruder to get through the windows, even if she hadn't put protection spells on them.

She looked at the clock. Six a.m. She deflated. If Tristan were here, he'd be brewing coffee in a little moka pot on the stove for him and Vivienne, getting ready to go down to their local bakery since he sneered at any bread from the TCO canteen. He'd promised to make Jayne croissants sometime; it seemed like it took forever when he did, but he was always moaning about the lack of decent ones in Nashville.

Now it was just her, and her fancy teakettle that could boil water to the perfect temperature for green tea, and leftover pie for breakfast. No snarky Vivienne, no warm-eyed, warm-armed Tristan. Just a cold, dark apartment with rain lashing against the window. "Yeah," she murmured. "Something's wrong, all right."

Enough of that. Hayden was obviously channeling the part of herself that hated moping. *Something is wrong. How often are you using the Fold spell?*

"Shouldn't you know?" Jayne swung her feet out of bed and wiped a thin sheen of sweat from her arms. She must have been having a nightmare before she woke up; happened often enough. "I haven't used it since the Battle of Aegis."

Well, someone is. Hayden stopped to scratch behind one ear with his hind foot. *I am feeling thin and time-stretched. Tossed about. Yesterday when I woke up you were an old woman! It took me hours to find out where I belonged!*

Jayne thought of Xiomara and her insistence that this power was dangerous. Had Jayne done something to unravel time? Or was she going mad, just as Xiomara had feared, and she was time-traveling without knowing it?

Hurry!

"I'm up, I'm up. Do I have time for a shower?" She could feel Hayden's panicked head shaking, so she pulled on the first clothes she could find: exercise leggings and a T-shirt that mashed up *Star Wars* and Miyazaki movies. Not exactly CIA-level dress code, but what were they going to do—fire her?

When she burst through the portal into the TCO, the first thing she noticed was that the room seemed...dim. The lamps flickered, as though something had taken up residence in the bulbs. The wall of stars across from the portal seemed to shift every time Jayne looked at it—from polished to dusty to mottled, with letters appearing and disappearing at the end. She got closer slowly, holding Hayden in one arm like a cat.

A bronze star before her was blank. Then it shimmered, as if through a heat haze, and letters fuzzed into view. RUGER STERN. "Oh no," breathed Jayne.

The letters disappeared, only to be replaced with SOFIA THORNE. Jayne's throat closed around a pained cry. Then the name disappeared. The star shimmered again.

JAYNE THORNE. TRINITY THORNE.

Jayne's grip on Hayden tightened and he squirmed. "All right, what's happening?" she said. "How do we fix it?" She closed her eyes and cast about for the Norns, but felt only sensations, the impressions of emotions: Contempt, from Urd. Intrigue, from Skuld. Waiting to see what she'd do. Patience, from Verdande. As if they'd known this would happen. The answers had to be here, in the TCO, ready for her to find.

Goddesses. They never helped when you needed it. So who else knew what was going on?

Katie Bell. Isra. Henry. One of them might know.

"Okay, Jayne," she mumbled. "Try not to feel dead." Keeping her eyes resolutely fixed on any point but the wall of stars, she turned and made her way down the hall toward the TCO library.

The library was darker than usual. No one sat in the reading chair, and the nook for tea and coffee was still, smelling of stale grounds. "Katie?" Jayne called.

A shadow darted from one bookshelf to another.

Jayne summoned some sunlight from her totem and leaned between the stacks, letting her light illumine row upon row of books. More shadows seemed to slip back between the covers and around corners.

She finally heard voices. A few moments later Katie and Isra came into view, conferring. "There you are," she said, relieved.

Katie did not look happy to see her. Isra was flat-out frown-ing, and she hurried forward. "What day is it?" she snapped.

"Uh. Thursday." Jayne looked around. "How long have you guys been back there?" she joked feebly.

Isra did not smile. "What time is it?"

Jayne shrugged. "Seven? Ish?"

"What did you last eat?"

"Um, pie. Dinner of champions. What's going on?"

Isra looked at Katie. "She does love pie. It's feasible," Katie said, taking her glasses off and polishing them on her pale-pink sweater.

"Would someone care to tell me what's going on?" Jayne said. "What's with the invasion of the shadow moths?"

"Time Wraiths," Isra corrected. She adjusted her hijab, looking pinch-lipped. Behind the anger in her expression, Jayne realized she saw fear. "Something has been interfering with the timeline in ways it shouldn't."

"Was it the Battle of Aegis?"

Isra thought, tapping her fingers against her wrist. "It started last night, so I want to say no. But since Katie and I can't figure out the source, we have to infer that it may well be."

"How bad are the Time Wraiths?" Jayne asked. Hayden stretched up and tried to swipe at one with a gray claw. It fluttered out of his reach.

"They're attracted to the destabilization of the timeline," Isra explained. "They...feed off it, if you will. This makes it destabilize faster. If it destabilizes completely, the timeline will unravel and we will be taken back to the alternate branch of the last stable point. Probably the Battle of Aegis."

"And at the alternate branch?" Jayne asked, heart sinking. She had a feeling she knew the answer.

Isra's eyes were wide and serious. "We lose. The Norns refuse to grant you the Time totem."

"Right." Jayne took a deep breath and settled Hayden

around her shoulders. "Not an option, then. Any ideas on how to find what's causing these Wraiths to appear?"

Katie and Isra looked at each other. Katie had deep bags under her eyes; she was a night owl and had probably been rudely awakened in her rooms next to the library. "That's what we were trying to find out."

Hayden's tail flicked against Jayne's collarbone. *The Wraiths feed on destabilization,* he reasoned. *That means they will feast where the destabilization point is highest. Where the problem is stemming from.*

"Do you think so?" Jayne asked.

Do you doubt me? Hayden replied.

"I mean, you're me. So we both know the answer to that question. And now my friends are looking at me like I'm talking to myself, so let's go." Ears only slightly burning, she turned and led the way out of the library, with Isra hot on her heels.

"I'm going to stay," Katie called after them. "I've already caught a couple of the buggers trying to eat the books."

Oh, the Time Wraiths went after books, too? Jayne prepared a quick Knockback spell. This was getting personal.

There weren't too many Time Wraiths in the canteen, nor down the corridor that housed Amanda and Ruger's offices. The mausoleum was free of them, silent but for the soft snoring of its attendant, a seventy-year-old Adept named Gerry.

"Do you think it could be concentrated at Aegis itself?" Jayne asked.

"That...would be difficult." Isra chewed on her lip. "But it is a strong possibility. We must check."

They went to the portal together and popped through. Jayne looked out over the green landscape, searching for any sign of shadows that shouldn't be here. Post-battle, the grass was still flattened, and much of the ground had been churned to mud.

"I don't see anything," she admitted.

"I do." Isra pointed. "Not a Wraith, but evidence."

The manor on the hill was shimmering in a way that meant it was temporarily adrift in time. A moment later half the roof was gone. It shimmered again, and the roof was there, but a long low outbuilding on the right side of the house was charred and reduced to rubble. Then it changed again. Jayne's stomach convulsed. "So it *is* the battle," she said softly. She'd had a chance to talk to Ruger afterward; if they had to turn back time, he'd be dead. As would Cillian, and probably Sofia, and a whole host of people.

"But the Wraiths are not here." Isra gasped, then clapped her hands together. "It is not the battle that is causing the problem. Someone is *interfering* with the battle."

Jayne almost said, "Yeah, me." But then she realized—Isra meant someone else.

She groaned. Who had looked into the details of the Fold spell? Who had insisted it could help him in his research? She should have seen it before. "I don't know where, but I think I know who," she said. "We should have checked the lab first. Let's go back."

They returned through the portal, and Jayne stopped by the security guard's desk to look at his sign-in roster, just in case. The desk was empty, but the roster was not. Any last hope she had evaporated in a mist of fury when she read the names of the last two people to go through the portal.

"I think it's my dad's interference," she said. Isra looked understandably alarmed.

Sure enough, the shadows were thickest at the door of the Genius Lab. Mothlike Time Wraiths crawled over the handle, slipped between the cracks of the door and the frame, wiggling in and out of the keyhole. Jayne swiped her identification card and wrenched on the door, ignoring the unpleasant tickle of the creatures that brushed against her hand as they scattered.

Henry was in the lab, gray hair in disarray, with a three-day beard and a wild look in his eye like he hadn't slept since the battle. He flicked through paper notes with an urgency, muttering: "Slight internal delay upon arrival, combine perhaps with a dampening effect?" He looked up. "Ah, Jayne." He sounded relieved. "Come help me with this."

She folded her arms. "How many times, Dad?" Henry blinked at her. His glasses were smudged and sooty. *"How many times?"*

"Oh, the Reverser? She's working beautifully, you know." He held up his Time Reverse, battered and with a cracked screen. "I think I've almost got it now. See, the first time, I saved Sofia, but that killed you. Then I tried to stop me from doing that, and I made a marvelous discovery." He started tearing through papers, voice rising in pitch, the words tumbling out. "See, I can't actually interact with my own self. It's like trying to push a ghost. He doesn't see or hear me. But I missed my window to act, so I had to go back a third time, and while I was doing that the second me got himself killed, so I had to travel back in time to save *him* so that I could travel back in time to save *her* but I had to make sure I didn't kill *you*..."

"How. Many. Times?" Jayne demanded.

Henry rubbed at the corner of his mouth. There was a stain there like old blood. "Fifty? Fifty-two? Uncertain." Then he turned back to his table, muttering.

Isra was trembling next to Jayne. Her face was pale, her nostrils flared. "This," she said through clenched teeth. "This is exactly what Xiomara warned us against! Time travel is not for the weak of heart and mind!"

"I—I—" Henry shook a finger. Then he paused. "I had a full doctor's examination last year. My heart is in peak physical condition. As for my mind—" He thumped the Reverser down on the table and grabbed a screwdriver. "I can crack any code, and every problem is an opportunity. I'm going to do this."

"You can't." Isra pulled her phone out of her bag and tapped on the screen. "I've called for backup. You're going to be stopped."

"Jayne, do something," he said in a mild voice. As if he were saying, *Jayne, take out the trash.*

Jayne sighed and closed her eyes. She could feel tears brimming beneath the lids, of fatigue and frustration and above all the grief that threatened to swallow her every day. She'd lost her love, her Rogue, and now her sister. And her father was losing himself. Again. "No," she said softly.

Henry paused, screwdriver poised over the bottom of the Reverser. "Don't you want your sister back?"

"Of course I do," she snapped. Hayden growled softly in her defense. "But we're supposed to *talk* about this, Dad! Amanda put limits on the Fold spell precisely because of this! You're destroying our only chance to save our world, when you should be talking with me. We can put a plan together, a better plan than this."

Henry's mouth set in a stubborn way she knew all too well. Jayne schooled her anger and came forward to put a hand on his arm. "Let's make a plan, Dad. A real plan. We know Sofia was taken alive, so Odin must have wanted her for something specific."

"That doesn't mean she's alive now." Henry threw the screwdriver on the table, chipping the ceramic bowl holding his mismatched bolts and screws. "There is absolutely *no* guarantee that she's still with us."

"If your father won't listen to reason, he will have to be subdued," Isra told Jayne, a spell sparking on her fingertips.

"No, no." Jayne found herself talking faster. "He will listen to reason, he will. He's upset, he got carried away. He's trying to save his daughter—would you really do anything different?"

Footsteps thundered in the hall. Isra's backup was arriving.

"It does not matter what I would do," Isra said, folding her arms. "What matters is that your father is trying to do the impossible. Some things cannot be changed. He is destroying reality in the attempt to disprove that."

Henry's finger was shaking again, in Isra's direction. His lip curled at the insult. "There's no, there's absolutely *no* evidence to prove that. I believe that any moment in time can be changed—"

"Dad," Jayne whispered. She took him by the shoulders and turned him so that he was looking at her, only her. "You have to stop."

And he did stop—talking, anyway. His mouth hung open, and he sagged against her hands a little, staring at her like a lost child. Behind him, Isra moved quietly toward the table. If she could snag the Reverser, they could at least control the situation for now. It seemed no one else could really hold the Fold spell in their minds in all its complicatedness. "I know it's hard," Jayne said, and her voice trembled. "I'd do anything to get her back. But you have to hold on to your hope, and you have to think of the bigger picture."

Henry's face hardened. "I don't care about the bigger picture."

"You can't be that selfish, Dad!" Jayne said, giving his shoulders a little shake. "You can't save your own little corner of the world, at the expense of saving the world entirely."

But he could. He'd done it before, retreating into what he knew and loved best and letting his wife wreak havoc across the Torrent and the Earth.

Henry swallowed. "It's all I know," he murmured. "It's all I care about. The world is a cruel place, Jayne. Trying to save it all just leads to madness and ruin anyway."

"Please come with me, Dad," Jayne whispered. "I'm not going to go mad, and I am going to save the world, and you're going to help me. We can do it." She risked a glance at Isra. The woman was reaching out for the Time Reverse—

Henry's eyes narrowed. He spun around, and faster than Jayne could blink, he flung a golden Knockback spell at Isra. She slid back and hit the table on the other side of the room with a cry of pain, just as three Disciples of Gaia burst in. Henry grabbed the Reverser and clutched it to his chest.

"You," snarled a Slovak man in a cloak and long leather boots. "You will regret that."

Isra stood, rubbing at her lower back. "You can come with us peacefully, or you can resist, Thorne, but you will come either way," she said. "Your daughter will not help you."

Henry looked at her. "I can't, Dad," Jayne breathed.

"But it will work." His voice broke. "Jayne, I promise. Here, I can prove it to you—"

He spun the dial and grabbed her wrist. Everyone shouted at once. "No!" Jayne cried, trying to wrench away from him as a spear cut through the air between them...

...and the world shimmered again.

CHAPTER

TWENTY

The lab turned to mist around them, and Jayne's breath was stolen from her body. Before she could think to miss it, the mist dissolved, and she found herself on the grounds of Aegis Academy.

"Excellent." Henry sounded excessively pleased with himself. "Found a workaround for taking a companion. Of course, I suspected it would work, since I've already seen you in there... And you'll notice I was able to fit a portal into the device, though it only works about half the time." He subsided, muttering.

Jayne stared around her, open-mouthed. *"Dad."*

The battlefield was overrun with Henry Thornes.

He was everywhere: helping Jayne, helping Sofia, fighting Cillian, wrapping a wounded Tamara, arguing with Amanda. More than one Henry lay glassy-eyed and bloody on the field, and every time she saw one, her heart stopped, then started painfully again. There was a Henry by the portal, a Henry by the apple truck, ushering kids—"How many times did you say you did this?" Her eyes were watering. Her brain was having a hard time keeping track.

"Hm." Henry scanned the field. "I'm not actually sure."

"Amanda's going to *kill* us—"

"No, no." He drew himself up. Blood trickled from the corner of his mouth, and the look in his eyes was wilder than ever. Jayne swallowed. Something about it reminded her of her mother. "We have three objectives: Win the battle, keep you from being killed, and keep Sofia from being drawn in with the Wraiths."

"*No,* Dad," Jayne said. The words came out forceful and angry, and Henry flinched. For a moment she felt sorry, but only a moment. If he hadn't been able to make those three things happen in over fifty attempts, there was no way to make them all happen in the same battle.

"We've got to keep the kids safe. That's priority number one." She reached into the Torrent for her staff, only to find herself groping after nothing. It was a weird sensation to reach for a magical item that refused to materialize.

"Your staff is already here," Henry explained. "Inanimate objects can't be in the same place twice unless they're fitted with a shield, like the Reverser." He patted the Reverser as though it were a dog.

Jayne snatched it from him. "Stop, Dad," she snapped over his protests. "You brought me here, and now you get to deal with me being here."

Without waiting for him to answer, she ran toward the corridor and the stalled truck full of kids, cursing him under her breath. She'd worked spells into her staff with love and intention. She knew exactly what she wanted out of it. Now she had to borrow some other weapon and learn to use it while saving the world from her father's insanity. Never a dull moment in the Thorne household.

Wraiths had managed to punch a hole in the defending line on the corridor and had surrounded the truck. Zia and Henry stood in front of it: Zia had a Shield spell up that was taking a beating while Henry frantically tried to get the truck working again. "Hayden, now," Jayne said and set her teeth against the pain. Her familiar pulled from her arm. They'd need air support.

On it. Her dragon landed neatly on the ground and swelled to the size of an eagle. Then he launched himself at the nearest Wraith just before it raked its claws across Zia's shield. The two of them tumbled end over end, snarling. Jayne reached into the Torrent for whatever weapon she could grasp. What she really wanted was something that could hit, and hit hard, channel all her anger at her father and mother and Odin and everyone who'd contrived to put her in this stupid situation in the first place—

Her fingers slotted into something heavy, and when she drew back her hand a band of steel had fit itself over the skin, ending in a knifepoint on one side. Brass knuckles. Nice. Knuckles for her other hand fell in the dirt. She scooped them up. *And I could probably even wear them while wielding the staff,* she thought. Too bad she didn't have time to layer spells over them. She grabbed the nearest Wraith's tail and punched it hard in the side, digging the knife tip into its tough leathery skin.

"The kids," she shouted to Zia as the girl rose from her crouch. Dirt and blood smudged her face, and her eyes were wide. "Get the kids out."

A Wraith was trying to tear off the back of the apple truck. Hayden swooped in and bit its shoulder, then launched again. The Wraith snarled and leapt into the air after him. Jayne closed her eyes and pressed her hand to her forehead. *Vesta,* she thought. *I need you right now.*

A moment later fire erupted all around the truck. Jayne corralled it into a controlled line, urging it higher and hotter, using a Breeze spell to push the heat out as the Adepts still in the corridor stumbled out of the way. Vesta's pain was a sharp stab just below her heart. Jayne wondered if the goddess might recognize her adopted daughter Vivienne among the Rogues engaged in the battle, if there was some way to save her—

The kids came first. She helped Zia usher the last ones out and toward the portal. Then she found her father. "Status?" she panted. Sweat dripped down her back.

"Jayne?" Henry gaped at her. "But you—I thought—ah. I must have found a way to do it."

"You can act smug later," Jayne snapped, and Henry deflated like a balloon. Jayne refused to feel bad about that. If it wasn't for Henry, she could be thinking up real ways to get Sofia back instead of cleaning up his messes. "Can we get this thing going?"

Henry worked on the truck, and she scanned the battlefield. All was chaos, but she spotted a second Hayden darting in and out of the fray. He had a strange aura about him, an orange glow. The same orange glow enveloped a figure with a whirling staff—herself. She was facing off against Cillian, and Jayne could only hope that in this timeline, she managed to give Cillian his mind back.

Henry pulled a Surge spell out of the Torrent and pressed it into the truck. It rumbled to life, and the last of the children disappeared through the portal. A ragged cheer went up. Jayne sagged and let her Fire spell drop. She smelled burning hair and charred grass and other sickly-sweet things that she didn't really want to contemplate.

She had to end this. She shoved on the door to the truck and stumbled away. "You stay here," she told Henry. "I'll take care of the rest."

His eyes were so full of hope that it felt like a lie to turn away from him.

Jayne staggered over the field. The mud beneath her feet

burned her even through her soles. She made her way toward Sofia just as the Wraiths began to flap up and away. She might as well try to keep Sofia safe—

And what if you can *save her?* whispered a part of her mind. *What if this is finally the right combination?*

"Jayne?" Sofia shifted her grip on the golden knives in her hands. "Where's Cillian?"

She thought Jayne was the *other* Jayne. "He'll be all right," Jayne told her gently. "It's going to be okay, Sofia. I promise."

She reached for her sister's hand. "The kids are safe. Let's go—"

The ground trembled, nearly throwing Jayne off her feet. Before them, one of the largest Wraiths Jayne had ever seen slowly unfurled his wings and stood, then looked down on them haughtily. His mouth split into something that might have passed for a smile were it not so terrifying.

Most Wraiths didn't seem to have much sentience—they were taken over, wholly, by Odin Allfather, unable to do much more than his will. Ruth Thorne had been an exception to that rule and battled to her last breath for her autonomy. Most Wraiths, it seemed, didn't have her stubbornness or strength of will. This one, though, seemed aware and perceptive.

Jayne pretended she was addressing Odin himself. "You've lost," she called to it. "The kids are gone. Don't even—"

A tail slammed into the side of her head and she went flying.

"Jayne!" Sofia screamed.

Jayne's ribs pounded with pain, but she was smart enough to roll over and keep rolling as the Wraith's huge claw slammed into the space where her head had been.

Sofia leapt for it. She stabbed it hard in the shoulder, releasing a gout of black blood and scrambling for its neck. The Wraith wrapped its hand around her torso and pulled her off its back. It held her up, talons squeezing, and plucked the knives from her hands one by one.

Jayne lay frozen on the ground. *Get up,* her brain screamed, but she couldn't move, she couldn't bear it. The Wraith's tongue flicked out and touched Sofia's belly.

Then it cocked its head as if listening to something.

The world became dark. It took Jayne's disoriented brain a moment to realize what was happening: The Wraiths had lifted from the field as one, blotting out the sun as they took to the sky. They flapped toward the horizon, bristling with arrows and harpoons, dropping blood over the field as they flew. Beneath them, the Rogues flowed toward that same horizon.

Jayne's body finally responded to her brain's panicked commands. Surely she could still do this. She climbed to her feet and rushed at the Wraith, pummeling everything she could reach with her brass knuckles. If she could get him to drop Sofia, maybe she could put a protective cocoon around them both and keep Sofia grounded.

The Wraith launched into the air with Sofia in his grasp.

Too late, Jayne flung a Lasso spell after him. If she could just tether him—but the Lasso missed, and then he was too far to aim for. She didn't realize she was crying until the tears blurred her eyes and she couldn't see anything at all.

Henry's arm slipped about her shoulder. "I thought we'd do it," he said hoarsely. "I really did."

She looked at him. This was the Henry from her timeline. The half-crazy one. He rubbed his palm along the rough stubble of his cheek and sat in the mud next to her, holding his Time Reverser in his lap. He must have lifted it off of her in another timeline. "I really thought..." His eyes glazed over for a moment, settled on the distance where the Wraiths were fast becoming specks. Then he shook himself. "No matter. We're doing this together now, and next time we can—"

"We're done, Dad." Now that the battle was mopping up, she could see the Time Wraiths everywhere, flitting shadows that clung to backs and crawled over the apple truck. She shivered, imagining them inching under her clothes or crawling over the nape of her neck.

Henry's eyes grew frantic. "But I've already set the coordinates. Sofia is within reach. What if you stood on the other side, ready with the Lasso spell the moment the Wraith lands in front of us? We could subdue him and run back to the portal together. We can win."

Jayne knew when a cause was lost. She pressed her hand against the Time Reverse, and before she could give herself the chance to change her own mind, ran a Surge spell through the console. She heard the pop of receptors within the machine as they overloaded and broke.

"What did you do?" Henry snatched the Reverser from her. "Jayne, how could you—you've doomed your sister!"

"Dad." Jayne was too tired, too heartbroken to talk about this. "I told you before, things needed to happen the way they did."

"Why?" Henry exploded. "You changed the outcome of the battle once. It can happen again! We just haven't found the right angle yet."

"Dad, stop," Jayne tried.

"You think I need the Reverser to fold time? I've folded hundreds of times, Jayne. I'm much better at it than you!" Spittle was flying from Henry's mouth now. His bloody hands shook, and his mouth warped in the first snarl Jayne had ever seen from her mild-mannered father. "I'm going to go back, and you're going to help me save your sister, if you ever loved her at all!"

"No, you're not," Jayne said softly and grabbed his hand.

"We're going to get you out of here so you can think properly." *I hate it when Xiomara's right and I'm wrong.*

Henry might have more experience with folding time, but he'd never had to hold an entire map of it in his head. Jayne gathered up their timeline and folded it haphazardly. They had to get as far away from this place as they could.

THEY LANDED SOMEWHERE outside of the Time Catch, in an open field that stank of pigs. The sun was bright and pricked at Jayne's eyes. She stood on a dirt road with a stable to one side—little more than a shack, in fact—and a fence made of woven branches.

A hissing sound made her twist around. A woman in a long wool skirt and apron stared at them from where she stood, a yoke and two water buckets balanced on her shoulders. Her bonnet had come half undone to hang about her neck, and her mouth was open in astonishment.

"Devil's children," she breathed.

"Colonial Virginia," Jayne guessed. "Maybe not."

Before they could be hauled before a magistrate and accused of witchcraft—or just stabbed by someone with a pitchfork—Jayne folded again. This time she could feel the Norns in the back of her mind, watching. They seemed to be amused. That was good, right? Better to be amused than concerned.

The day that appeared was much darker, with the most thunderous cloud Jayne had ever seen blotting out the sky. A spell whizzed overhead, and Jayne ducked, pulling Henry with her. "Give it up, Aaró!" shouted a familiar voice. "You and your... associates." And then, lower: "Where the hell did they come from?"

A red-haired woman stepped into view, holding a spell ready to launch. She was fifteen or twenty years younger than she'd been when Jayne last saw her, but it was undeniably Amanda Newport.

Amanda narrowed her eyes at Henry. "You look familiar."

"Don't mind us." Jayne grabbed her father's hand and folded one last time.

She didn't have much time to focus on the specifics of the when, but she wanted somewhere safe, somewhere she could sit for a minute. And when the world resolved around them into Langley, Virginia, and the Kryptos statue shone in the sun, Jayne allowed herself to breathe out. It was a lovely day, with no one to call them a witch or try to shoot them with magic, and no Wraiths to appear out of nowhere.

"Jayne, do you realize what you've done?" Henry raged. "You have to take us back to the Time Catch. If we go back in time far enough, maybe we can put in the right security systems—"

"Enough, Dad." Jayne took his hand. "The only place I'm going right now is a diner, and we're going to sit down and talk about this properly. Portal, now."

She whipped one together out of thin air and pushed him through.

The diner near her apartment served breakfast all day, so Jayne ordered a skillet meal for each of them and got them settled in a booth by the window.

Henry stared at the table. Half a dozen things ran through Jayne's mind—*I had to, it was the right call, we can't use magic that way*—but in the end, all she said was "Dad, she's not gone forever."

"How do you know that?" He sounded angry, of course, but beneath that anger was a heartbroken sort of hope. He wanted her to be right, so badly.

"I just know." Sofia had always been there. She always would be. Jayne's faith in her sister was unshakable and had never been misplaced. "I have faith, Dad. You have to have faith, too. We managed to capture a lot of Rogues, you know. I folded time back on Cillian's mind. Maybe if I do the same for the others, they can help us find the Catch where Odin was keeping the rest of the Rogues. And when we find them, we'll find Sofia. I promise."

"They can't be in a Time Catch," Henry said. He'd finally dug into his meal, but his first bite of egg and cheddar and potato was suspended halfway between the skillet and his mouth. "You can't move from a Time Catch to a Time Catch. You have to come back to the real world. Besides, we already know that Odin doesn't really use Time Catches as his prisons..." His eyes got that glazed look again, and for a moment Jayne was afraid she'd lost him to his ranting. "He uses pockets. He used a pocket to trap Alexandra and Trinity. He used a pocket to seal off the Norns. So he must be using a pocket to store the Rogues, too."

"Well, we've broken into one pocket," Jayne said, thinking of the great World Tree.

"Two," Henry corrected her absentmindedly. "I broke into the pocket with your grandmother during the Battle of Kirkjufell. It was a stealth mission, but still."

"See? Thinking it through helps. So we can get in. But how do we know where to go? Odin could have countless pockets around the world, stuffed with things he wants to imprison or keep for later." Jayne took a gulp of extremely inferior tea, appreciating the hit of caffeine even in a lower form of beverage.

Henry tapped his fork on the skillet. He didn't seem to care that he was spattering ketchup everywhere. "We don't know where it is," he agreed. "But we do know where it was..."

Because Odin had opened the pocket at Kirkjufell and pulled them all in.

Jayne's heart began to warm. Her own fingers tapped on the table. She smiled at Henry. *Now* they were coming up with something.

"Y'all need anything?" asked the waitress, a pitcher of water in her left hand.

"Just the check," Jayne said. "And a slice of strawberry rhubarb to go."

CHAPTER
TWENTY-ONE

G ina Labelle was starting to remember, slowly, who she was.

The details did not please her. She had been powerful; now she was powerless. She had been a free woman and Rogue; now she was in thrall to a powerful Master.

She had sworn that she would answer to no Master nor Adept. She would not be chained the way her silly children were. Rogues would run free in whatever form they chose, take their place as the superior beings in the world.

Her plan had failed.

She looked around the pocket, stuffed with Rogues who had forgotten themselves, who were barely more than base animals licking their wounds, and she was filled with rage. So when one huge Wraith swept down and wrapped its tail around her, she welcomed the chance to disembowel it.

She turned into a mouse, first, to slip free of its tail. But one talon scooped down to catch her. She turned into a venomous snake next, but her fangs scraped off the skin of its leg. It let out a peculiar huffing sound; when she realized it was laughing she grew even angrier.

They were rising in the air. No matter how she twisted and lashed, she couldn't get it to let her go. It wasn't until they'd emerged from the pocket and landed on the boggy ground of an Icelandic field that she realized the Wraith hadn't been tasked with killing her.

It had been tasked with bringing her to its master. Their master.

Odin Allfather had constructed a throne for himself out of the bones of Wraiths and Adepts that had been collected on the battlefield. It suited his massive frame, his cruel face, his horns. He sat stroking his iron-colored beard and watched in interest as Gina became the largest lioness she could. Odin's smile was terrible. She faced off with him, determined not to falter without giving him the fight of his wretched life.

Instead, he spoke into her mind, booming and oddly cajoling.

Speak with me, great Rogue.

Gina snarled.

Odin laughed. *You are spirited, and that is a blessing. I have need of spirited ones.*

I will do nothing for you.

Gina had said nothing aloud—could say nothing as a lioness—and had no Rogue-Master connection. Yet at this pronouncement, Odin laughed harder than before.

You already do so much for me, he told her softly. *The other Rogues fear you, do they not? You can control them.*

I thought you controlled them, Gina replied, hoping that her mocking tone came through in her thoughts.

Oh, I do. Odin flexed a hand, then turned it into a fist. *But I have many things to think of, and my powers are better directed else-where. That's why I had Alastor bring you to me.* He waved a hand at the Wraith, and the Wraith—Alastor—took a few steps back, like a lieutenant attending its commander. *I'd like to offer you a deal, Gina Labelle. How would you like to have the ultimate power over your Rogue brethren? An army of fighters, and the ability to do whatever you wanted to any Adept in the world?*

Rogues should be free, Gina said again, trying to ignore the hunger that gnawed at her. So much power...

And you will lead them to their freedom. Serve me willingly, and I will release you—and them—from the hold I have on your minds. You will be able to live without prejudice and destroy anyone who opposes you, without retaliation. More than that, I can give you power... He leaned forward and fixed Gina with his lone, piercing midnight blue eye. *Why is it that a Master carries the power of the goddesses? Isn't that something you deserve? What would you do if I said you could have it? The world has never had a Rogue goddess before. Isn't it time?*

Gina could feel the seductive pull of what he was saying. But she'd been on this Earth long enough to be wary of tricks. *I'd say, what will it cost me?*

Nothing. Odin looked away, bored already. *One or two small favors for me. One of which is ripping the totems from the head of one very irritating Adept that we'd both like to see dead.*

Kill Jayne Thorne?

Oh, yes. And all of her ridiculous brethren, too.

Gina broke his gaze. Trapped in his pocket, she'd seen both her son and her daughter for the children they were to her, not as the combatants they'd turned into. Vivienne and Tristan had chosen their sides, openly and defiantly, turning their backs on La Liberté and everything it stood for. An hour ago, she would have thought they had a point. Odin's stranglehold on the minds of the Rogues spoke of slavery and subjugation, not the sort of benevolent dictatorship he was promising Gina now. And if she wanted to have her freedom, she would have to kill

Jayne Thorne, the bonded partner of her daughter, the partner to her son...they cared about Jayne. And she cared about them, didn't she?

Didn't she?

Odin leaned forward and steepled his fingers. *Well?*

CHAPTER

TWENTY-TWO

J ayne and Henry emerged from their unauthorized portal onto the silent field at the base of Kirkjufell Mountain. "Are you ready?" Jayne asked.

"I'm ready." Henry smiled at her. A little bit of food and a few cups of tea had turned him slightly saner, but what they both needed was a week of sleep. But Jayne hadn't wanted to return to the TCO just yet—if Isra was smart, she'd already alerted Amanda what had happened, and Henry would be detained the moment they went back. And now that she'd done plenty of unnecessary folding of her own, Jayne was a little afraid to face her boss. *We didn't change anything,* she reminded herself, thinking of Colonial Virginia and the early-days battle of the TCO. The most they'd done was order a couple of extra meals.

"Remember, Dad, we're here to do one thing. We're not going to try to save everyone," she said.

Henry looked around. The air was full of birdsong and buzzed with midges. Water burbled as a stream made its way toward the fjord over moss-covered rocks. Such a peaceful place. So different from their last encounter here.

Finally, he said, "I think we'd both best remember that."

Jayne's grin was more of a grimace. The Thornes didn't want to save anyone unless they could save everyone. Stupid hero complexes, all of them.

"Stay with me," she said, taking his hand. She closed her eyes and brought up the map of time in her head. And this time, carefully, delicately, as if she were a doctor in an operating theater, she found the moment she wanted and, imagining her fingers pressing their timeline gently down, folded.

The world turned to mist around them. And then to carnage.

Wraiths tore into Adepts, slashing through their Shield spells as though they were made of tissue paper. Adepts clustered together, holding weapons they barely knew how to use as they tried to protect themselves from the onslaught from above.

Jayne looked up. She could see herself by virtue of the orange aura. Up there, she'd had no idea how it looked from the ground. "I think we're going to need some help," she murmured, and a moment later Hayden slithered out of her arm. "Are you sure you know what you're doing?" she asked Henry.

Henry was already heading toward the mountain and the enormous pocket at its base. "No," he said when she caught up to him. "But I'm going to give it my best shot. Between my magic and yours—mostly yours—we should be powerful enough to create a pocket of our own. And we're close enough to this pocket that Odin shouldn't notice the power displacement."

They made their way toward the rend in the Torrent. Jayne remembered being so frustrated when Odin hadn't emerged, but now that was to their benefit.

They started with a Net spell, combined with elements of a

Carry spell. Except this Carry, in addition to carrying things like Rogues, was going to carry part of the Torrent as well. Jayne lay a Shield spell over it for good measure, just in case Odin had a way to attack pockets.

Then she took a deep breath and dove into the Torrent itself.

She let her fingers trail in the river of stars, pulling against the weight of the spells she'd made, fighting the fatigue. *Break free,* she tried to tell the river. *Follow me.*

It did not want to. Understandably, the Torrent was most attracted to itself and liked to stick together. Jayne had to pull on bits of it as thin as threads, directing them into the spell to create a sort of proto pocket. But it wasn't enough magic. If she couldn't do this any faster, she'd be here not just until the end of the battle, but the end of the world.

She got an idea.

She began to wind the Torrent not toward the pocket, but around her body—an easier proposition because she was in the Torrent, and pieces of it were sticking to her already. It rose around her, surrounding her. She wound until the Torrent was as tight as a shroud and she was starting to gasp for breath.

Then she let herself fall into her own Carry spell.

The Torrent stretched. It tried to pull her back. Jayne resisted. Then, with a sound like a *snap,* she was through.

Her own pocket.

The Torrent here flowed slower, and the stars sparkled not so brightly. It was peaceful. Jayne took another deep breath. She spun a little spell between her fingers and watched it drift on the current.

Hayden? she called.

An image flashed behind her eyes, of Wraiths circling and snapping in the night. Hayden was flying full pelt, diving and weaving and snapping his tail at any unlucky Wraiths who got too close. He seemed to be enjoying himself.

Tell Dad I'm ready, she said.

You do not wish to come out? Hayden asked.

What's the point? I'm in here, and soon the Rogues will be in here. And I'm supposed to cure them, aren't I?

Your father will dislike this plan immensely, Hayden warned her. Jayne sent him the mental equivalent of a shrug. Henry didn't get to criticize her plans these days.

You will need some way to hide, Hayden said. *The Rogues attack anyone not on Odin's side.*

Right. Jayne thought. She needed something like the invisibility cloak from *Harry Potter*. Or maybe a Camouflage spell? Was there a way she could make herself look like some other part of the Torrent?

While she contemplated, she started to bring the pocket to life. She created flat black rocks for the Rogues to rest on, out of the Torrent, and a few more jagged ones that might work as convenient hiding spots for her and Sofia, when she got here. She created a bank to either side, verdant with moss.

She started getting flashes from Hayden as he winged down to Henry. Hayden butting Henry with his snout when he tried to step in between a Wraith and a fallen Adept, pushing him away from interfering in the battle and back toward the pocket. Henry shaking his head emphatically, mouthing her name. Henry realizing what Hayden meant and shaking his head even more emphatically. Hayden releasing a small, angry burst of flame from his jaws.

Your father argues, and he cannot even hear my words.

Convince him, she replied.

They were running out of time. Hayden cast his gaze over the battlefield. Through his eyes, Jayne saw Tristan pleading with Vivienne. Her heart broke and soared at once. That had been one of the worst days of her life, and yet—and yet, she might be getting him back so soon.

Light appeared at one end of the pocket. The Torrent began to flow faster around her. It seemed angry, its current cold and stinging. Henry was grafting the end of their pocket to Odin's. Jayne sighed. *Good work, Dad.*

Then the first Rogue came through.

He was huge, an elephant bellowing in pain, swinging his head from side to side. A tusk caught a Rogue in fox form that leaped in after him and sent it flying. The Rogue snarled when it hit the bank, a small patch of earth that resembled the bog they'd used as their battlefield. It got to its feet, eyes locked on Jayne.

Too late, Jayne remembered her camouflage.

She pulled on her images of the moss and the water and the twinkling, dim light, and drew it over herself like a cloak. She hurried backward. The Rogue stalked toward the place she'd been, confused.

She placed a hand over her mouth and nose. She didn't even want to breathe. She brought in another layer to the spell, trying to mask her scent with the smell of stagnant water and wet earth.

The fox Rogue sniffed at where she'd been. His intelligent eyes narrowed, but he darted away as more Rogues tore into the pocket, snarling and crying and shaking their heads.

They kept coming and coming. Almost a hundred Rogues poured into the pocket before Jayne saw the light behind them flare again. *It is done,* Hayden said in her mind. *Henry says he hopes you know what you're doing—and that you can get yourself out of there.*

"Me too," Jayne breathed, reaching within for her totems.

It was easier to fold time back—or perhaps unfold time?— to where she'd come from. Maybe her body knew it was supposed to be there, or the tethers she had there were stronger. All the same, she was relieved when the mist resolved around her and the shapes of the Rogues changed.

The Rogues looked exhausted after the Battle of Aegis. *Good.* Maybe Jayne had some kind of fighting chance. They bickered and slept and snapped and lounged in the Torrent. Jayne began to creep along the rocks, moving slowly so that she wouldn't slip on stones slick with magic. Surely Sofia would be hiding out in one of the outcroppings she had created...

She checked the first one. No luck: A lion slept there and raised his head as one foot scattered pebbles over the stones. Jayne held her breath, but he was evidently too tired to fight her and simply lay his head down. She crept on.

She had to check a few more before she spotted the little ridge on the bank. She approached, slowly realizing it was more of a hollow built up with small stones to create a manmade shelter. The Rogues seemed to prefer to stay close to the Torrent itself; none of them prowled around here.

All the same, Jayne kept her footfalls light.

She heard Sofia's voice first. "...can't be certain, but you have to have faith."

Tristan replied, matching her tone for softness, "I always have faith in your sister."

Jayne came around the side of the hollow and before she could stop herself, said, "Are you sure? I don't think you have faith in my cooking."

Sofia's and Tristan's heads whipped up. They stared right at her—and through her. "Oops." Jayne let the Camouflage drop.

Tristan wore the same tactical gear he'd put on for the Battle of Kirkjufell. He'd stripped off his jacket and outer shirt and was down to a T-shirt that was crusted in dirt and dried blood. His beard was a fine cover on his face, and his dark eyes were hollow, his cheeks sunken. When had he last had something to eat? His hair stuck together in little greasy clumps; Jayne could see tracks where he'd run his hand through it. It had to have been more than a week since he'd bathed. Yet when he leapt up and threw himself at her, taking them both to the ground, his musk was like a magnet to her. *Home,* she thought as their lips crashed together. *My home. My heart.*

"What are you doing here?" he gasped when they finally came up for air.

"Um." Jayne wrinkled her nose at him. "Rescuing you? And Sofia."

"Yeah. Do you mind?" Sofia held a hand to her belly and rose from her crouch. "What's going on? I tried to fill in Tristan, but I don't know what happened after the battle..."

"So good to see you alive," she whispered to Sofia, pulling her in close.

"You can thank Tristan for that," Sofia replied.

And I will, Jayne thought. *If we manage to make it out of here.* "Well, the good news is that we have a way to bring the Rogues back," Jayne said. She looked around and swallowed. "The bad news is..."

The bad news was that the Rogues had heard the commotion. They began to appear out of the dark, growling.

"Okay," Jayne said. She reached one hand out for Tristan and one for Sofia. "Any ideas how we handle this?"

"Are you not the one who came to rescue us?" Tristan murmured.

"I didn't think this far ahead," Jayne whispered back.

"Jayne Thorne, you never change." His smile was a little feral. It thrilled Jayne, though she wondered what he'd had to do to survive here.

He spun a Block spell and an Attack, holding them neatly in his hands, and addressed the Rogues. "Shall we do this again? You'll have to get through me if you want her."

Jayne stepped up beside him. "And I'm not easy to kill," she warned them. "I think a lot of you know that, deep down."

The Rogues continued to fan out. Jayne pulled a Shield spell around them in a little dome.

They were completely encircled. A bad start to Jayne's rescue operation. But the Rogues didn't come closer. They growled, they howled, they stomped their feet and shrieked. But they didn't attack. And with a strange whisper, they fell silent, menace in their eyes.

A huge lioness landed in front of the Rogue army, fangs exposed.

"*Maman,*" Tristan whispered, horrified.

CHAPTER

TWENTY-THREE

Henry Thorne was not caught up in the Fold spell that took Jayne away. And since she'd destroyed his Time Reverse, he had to travel in time the old-fashioned way.

Well. He could work with that. It gave him plenty of time to think.

It gave him plenty of time to obsess over his two daughters, trapped in a pocket with a hundred Rogues that were out of their minds and eager for blood.

It gave him plenty of time to plan.

Jayne's pocket into the Torrent had activated and chosen a Guardian—which Guardian, he didn't yet know, but he was praying for it to be someone on the TCO's side. Sofia, maybe. The fact that it had activated meant that Odin couldn't move it around, and it couldn't be hidden from the TCO. But they had to allow Odin access to it or risk him understanding that something had gone awry. Which put Henry's children in constant peril.

And as proud as he was of the girls and their formidable magic, Henry would do anything to keep his children safe. Since his Time Reverse hadn't gone so well, he needed to move on to plan B. It was time to bargain with some goddesses.

Jayne's adventures in the Codex Regius had helped Henry locate the specific pocket of the Torrent in which the World Tree had been sequestered and the Norns imprisoned. So he put some dried meat and a bottle of mead into a Carry spell and, using his new knowledge and Guardian magic, took himself to Yggdrasil, the World Tree, in search of the Norns and a favor.

Yggdrasil was disgusting. Jayne hadn't described it as being anything like this. The tree was bowed, its roots rotting and soft beneath his feet. Each limb of the giant ash dripped with something dark and viscous, and Henry knew instinctively not to touch it. Beneath his feet, something flashed—a gray Wraith that looked like a serpent, forty or fifty feet long, wrapping itself around the roots of the tree and squeezing as though the tree itself were prey. Around him, no birds sang. No foxes trilled and screamed in the underbrush. Life had fled this place.

All life except for three parts of the same soul.

Henry found Mímir's well, or what was left of it, crumbling in front of a dark opening in the trunk of the ash. Beyond it, he thought he saw a glimmer of light, the curve of a staircase.

He glanced up through the dripping and slick branches. Then he took a deep breath, steeled himself, and went into the tree.

"HONORED ONES." Henry bowed as low as his old hips would let him. He was proud to be only slightly out of breath from the long climb up the stairs to the admittedly cozy home of the Norns. The carved-out ash trunk had been turned into a wooden house with a fire, a loom, and three chairs. Skuld sat at the loom. Henry was almost too afraid to look at it. If he looked at it, he'd want to touch it. Seek out spells. See how it worked.

"Henry Thorne." Verdandi crossed her legs and tilted her head. She was, to his mind, the most beautiful of the Norns: enough gray in her hair to impart maturity, but a seductive curve to her smile that said she still knew what love was—and perhaps that she knew how to get under a man's skin.

"You have never trifled with the goddesses before," said Urd. "That was your wife's domain."

"You are desperate in the now," Verdandi added.

"Your attempts to change the past ended in disaster—" Urd began.

"And so you turn to the future. To me." Skuld stood up and stretched, showing off the curve of her back and breasts.

"I need to know how to get them both back," Henry said. "What course of action will return Jayne and Sofia to me, unharmed?"

The Norns shared a look. Skuld tossed her golden hair over her shoulder. "What makes you think there is such a future?" she asked.

Henry's heart sank. "You have seen every future there is. Are you telling me that *none* of them lead to Jayne and Sofia's survival?"

Skuld consulted the loom. The tangle of threads begged to be made orderly, Henry thought. But that wasn't his job—life was messy. He could find order and patterns in other places.

He should probably leave this place before getting any *more* ideas.

"Knowing the future changes the future," Skuld said at last. "It will take a strict hand of fate to keep it on track. The future is its own beast, you see. It desires, it grows." She wound a shimmering thread around one finger. "It changes its mind."

"And we do not ordinarily interfere," Urd said.

Henry remembered his gifts and reached into the Carry spell. He put the mead on the table, along with the dried meat. "What would it take for you to interfere?" he asked.

"What are you willing to give?" Verdandi smiled as though she already knew the answer.

"You support Jayne. You want her to succeed; you've given her the tools she needs. You don't want Odin to destroy the world, actually. So you want to help me."

"We did not ask you what *we* want," Urd said sharply. Her blue eyes cut into him. "We asked what you would give."

Henry had never been much of a negotiator. He struggled at times to think of what other people wanted, what they valued. "You can have your pick of my technology from the laboratory," he began.

"We do not need any tool but the loom," said Skuld, plucking at a bit of the warp like an instrument.

"The TCO would value your input on matters of magical policy—" Henry said.

Verdandi actually laughed. "You wish for us to interfere in the petty lives of man, and your payment is allowing us to interfere in the petty lives of man?"

"I'll give anything," Henry burst out before he could stop himself. The moment he spoke the words, he knew they were foolish but right. Exactly what the Norns wanted to hear. "I'll give you my life. I'll give you my soul. They're my children, and I'll do what it takes."

The Norns looked at each other. "This you swear?" they said as one.

Henry swallowed. He pushed his glasses up his nose and remembered all the times he hadn't been there for his children. "This I swear."

Hastily, the Norns assembled around the table. Skuld

fetched four cups while Verdandi opened the bottle of mead. "Then let us discuss your fate, Henry Thorne."

CHAPTER
TWENTY-FOUR

Jayne took one step closer to Tristan, whether to reassure him or herself, she didn't know. *Gina Labelle*. This was...not good.

The lioness's amber eyes lit on Jayne, and her mouth opened in a half-smile, half-growl. Jayne shivered. Any Rogue could take on a lion form, but Gina wore it differently. The lioness was *her* animal. Also— "Is it just me, or does your mom not look as mindless as the rest of them?" she whispered to Tristan.

"I do not know," he said. "I do not know what that would mean."

It would mean she wanted to kill Jayne more than she wanted to defeat Odin, but Jayne didn't say that to Tristan. He'd understand himself in his own time.

"Vivienne?" she whispered. Tristan shook his head. He didn't know. Jayne cast out with her mind, seeking her Rogue. *Vivienne?*

No response.

Gina's growl grew more sinister. Tristan stepped around so that he could put himself between Jayne and his mother. "You are not doing this of your own volition," he said. "Fight, *Maman!*"

Vivienne, Jayne tried again. *I know this isn't you. You were trapped for so long, and now you have the chance to fight back against your captor. I can help you.*

"Anything?" breathed Sofia from beside Jayne. Jayne shook her head.

Gina sprang. Tristan released his Block and his Attack in quick succession, managing to sweep her feet from under her and send her tumbling. She rolled to her feet and looked around. The rest of the Rogues had backed up and were looking between Gina and Tristan.

"Tristan's been fighting Gina a lot lately," Sofia said. "When I came, she almost...well, I'm grateful for your boyfriend, Jayne." She gave a high, nervous laugh. "I think the other Rogues see this as something of a leadership challenge."

"Should we improve the odds?" Jayne said.

Sofia took a deep breath. She was thinking about the baby. Of course. Jayne pulled her staff—her glorious staff—into her hand and said, "Stay safe." Then she stepped out from behind the Shield.

Gina and Tristan were circling each other. "I know you're in there," Tristan said. "I know you don't want to be a mindless slave. You never did. You can fight back, *Maman.* You must."

Gina stopped. Her tawny fur twitched as his words sank in.

Something fluttered to the ground next to Tristan. A hawk. "Vivienne!" Jayne said.

"Jayne?" The hawk let out a heartbreaking cry. "I can't—I can barely—"

She screamed again as Gina Labelle pounced.

Jayne let out a feral cry of rage and swung forward with her staff. Tristan's face twisted in agony. He spun a spell of his own, and Sofia's Knockback spell hit Gina full in the chest. Both the lioness and the bird went flying.

Both Jayne and Tristan leapt for Gina. Tristan got there first. His eyes were even wilder than before, torn by grief. *"How could you?"* he cried, staring at the motionless hawk.

Gina got to her feet and swatted him easily with her paw. It slapped him across the side of the face, drawing three long scratches that barely missed his eye and tore the skin around his nose and mouth. He slammed into a rock and rolled to the ground, where he lay motionless.

Jayne felt a scream building in her throat. She let it out with an Attack that hit Gina's shoulder with a *crack* and spun her around. Gina howled and limped toward her. Jayne's staff flew toward the lioness, hitting her in the other shoulder. Gina staggered but kept moving forward.

"You don't care about anything." Jayne could barely breathe; everything came in quick gasps. She blinked away her tears. "Your own children are nothing to you."

Gina cocked her head. Then she growled softly, as if to say, *That's right,* and pounced again. Jayne brought up her staff and reinforced it with a Strength spell. It hit Gina on the underbelly and sent her crashing into the Shield around Sofia. Gina bounced off the Shield, shattering it in a burst of magic, and thumped to the ground.

Now Gina was between Jayne and Sofia. And Jayne wasn't about to let her attack anyone else.

She leaped and landed on Gina's back. Gina yowled in surprise. A second later, Jayne was thrown free, hitting the ground back-first. She gasped for air, and Gina's head appeared above her. One paw came down on her chest, pinning her with the full weight of the lioness. The other front paw lifted over her head. Claws emerged with a soft *schnick,* gleaming in the starlight. One claw came down to rest on Jayne's forehead. *The totems,* Jayne thought.

Then Gina collapsed.

She fell right on top of Jayne. "Oof," Jayne coughed, and tried to shove her off. But three hundred pounds of furry dead-weight was a lot to lift, and the best Jayne could do was wiggle her shoulders.

Gina's eyes were closed. *What gives?* Jayne thought.

Then her ears caught up to the rest of her. Rogues howled and screeched, and in the pandemonium, she heard human voices speaking English: "One target secured."

"Copy, one target secured," came Tamara's voice from a few feet away. "In need of immediate medical assistance. I'm running low on tranqs."

A figure stood over her. Jayne blinked against the shadow, but a moment later, Henry Thorne knelt and put a hand on her shoulder. "One target secured," he said in a shaking voice. "Whoever shot the lioness, well done."

"Dad?"

Henry looked grayer than the last time she'd seen him, somehow. There was a sorrow etched on his face, but he put his hand on her cheek and smiled at her in a way that brought tears to her eyes again. "I'm here, Jayne. I'm still here."

He called a few Adepts over, and together they Levitated Gina Labelle onto a gurney and out of the pocket. Jayne sat up as the pressure on her chest gave way to relief. "It worked." She grinned at Henry.

"Now the real work begins," he said. He glanced up at the pocket, eyes full of worry. But when he smiled down at Jayne, he'd carefully wiped any trace of concern from his face.

TWENTY-FIVE

Everything is warm. And smells sterile. Those were the first thoughts in Tristan's mind before his eyelids fluttered open. He'd always hated the smell of hospitals, but he had to admit a certain relief that he wasn't stewing in his own stale sweat and blood and dirt anymore.

His face felt stiff. He put a hand up to it and felt around the edge of a bandage. He also had a killer headache, and when he spotted the glass of blue water by his bed, he realized he was parched—and famished. He pushed himself up.

His headache started to clear with the electrolytes on board. In fact, his whole head felt clearer than it had in ages. Odin had been a constant barrage on the defenses of his mind for so long that, even though he was no Rogue, he'd spent most of his mental energy fighting the onslaught. He'd barely been able to focus on how to survive.

He pulled the privacy curtain away from his bed. In the next bed over, Vivienne lay in human form. Her dark hair was tangled, her skin covered with dirt. She was going to want a five-hour bath when she got up. Tristan grinned. And a coffee.

"Mon soeur," he whispered.

A medical Adept was changing her IV bag. "Let her sleep," he urged Tristan. "She's got a lot to process. You all do."

"Vivienne, we're back," he said.

"Honestly. Don't wake her." The Adept gave him a stern look, as if that would stop him, and continued on his rounds.

Tristan slid out of his bed and managed the two steps to Vivienne's before leaning on the bed rail. He was still weak from surviving the pocket. Still, he shook his sister's shoulder. "Vivienne."

She shifted a little. He shook her again. *"Arête,"* she mumbled in French. "Stop."

"Vivienne, we are in the TCO. It's over."

Her eyes fluttered open. "What?" she mumbled.

"We are free," Tristan whispered. He grinned, feeling his chapped lips crack. He realized now that he needed to see his sister's eyes before he could really believe she was herself again.

If he was in any doubt, the haughty frown she bestowed upon him convinced him. As did her "Then free me of your presence so I can sleep."

"Come. You are hungry, no?"

Tamara bustled in. "You're up," she said, and Tristan couldn't tell whether she was pleased or annoyed by the fact. "You might want to put on some clothes before you go roaming around the TCO."

He looked down. He wore a classic operating gown, one that was open in the back. Vivienne snorted.

"Thank you. Where is Jayne?" he asked, noticing clean jeans, boxers, and a shirt on a chair on the other side of the little room. Jayne had obviously prepared for this moment.

"She's working on the other Rogues." Tamara made a face. "And being very Jayne about it."

"What does that mean?" Tristan laughed. He almost

couldn't stop laughing. It was a beautiful sound, and life was beautiful, and he was finally free.

Vivienne sat up, putting a hand to her head. "Ugh. It means whatever she did to heal us, she is trying to do it to everyone, as fast as possible."

She grabbed her own glass of water and chugged it down.

"As a doctor, I have to advise you to stay in bed," Tamara warned them, flicking her short hair out of her eyes. "Vivienne's been under a terrible mental strain and so have you. You also received a nasty head wound that took some Healing power. You should spend time on your recovery."

"You can consider your advice received," Tristan assured her.

"And ignored." Vivienne pulled the privacy curtains around her bed. Tristan did the same. He wished for a moment that he had time for a shower before seeing Jayne again; he'd obviously been washed in the bed, but it wasn't the same.

Dressed and ignoring Tamara's continued clucking, Tristan and Vivienne followed the voices down the sterile marble hallway until they came to a small reception room. Two men sat there, with no sign of Jayne.

One of the men looked up—Cillian. He nodded to Tristan with a relieved smile. "Good to see *you*, mate." He gestured toward the Aegis portal. "She's in there. It's the only place we could think to put almost a hundred feral Rogues."

"Thank you," Tristan replied. "I am glad to see you recovered."

"I got lucky. I was the first Rogue healed." Cillian's expression darkened, as though a thought had passed like a cloud across his mind. "Erm, Tristan? She's also in the hospital. Your... mum."

"Not in some interrogation room awaiting justice?" Tristan's eyebrows rose.

"Still healing up, I reckon. But just so you know." Cillian's shoulders hunched.

Tristan wanted to ask, *Why are you telling me this?* Instead he said, "Thank you."

He didn't want to see Gina Labelle. Not after what she'd done. He couldn't trust himself not to cut her in two with a Scimitar spell. He took his sister's arm, and together they stepped through the portal.

The Aegis Time Catch had been set up like a field hospital. A lovely pasture spread out around them, sunny and warm, and blockaded in each pasture were the Rogues, held behind strong green-golden Shields. Tristan watched two Adepts fire a net over a Rogue that had taken the form of a buck and slowly force it to the ground. The buck bleated and tossed his head. Jayne moved around to his rear. She looked almost gray from fatigue but flicked her dark hair out of her eyes and steadied herself before placing a hand on the Rogue's hind leg. She closed her eyes. For a long moment, nothing happened, then something seemed to flash around her and the buck. A moment later a man lay shivering in the mud. An Adept hurried forward with a blanket.

Jayne stood and stumbled a little. Henry was sitting nearby with a laptop and charting their progress. "It's faster, certainly," he was saying. "I think we're about a quarter of the way there—oh! Hello." This he directed at Tristan and Vivienne.

Jayne's tired face lit up. She hurried toward them and nearly collapsed against Tristan. Her body was like ice. He rubbed his hands up and down her arms, and she almost purred against him, nestling her face in his chest.

Tristan had a wild momentary fantasy of tossing her on the grass and getting on with their reunion, but Henry and Vivienne were there, and Vivienne was curling her lip at him like she knew exactly what he was thinking. Jayne certainly looked in no way capable of anything demanding energy. "What have you done to my girlfriend?" he demanded.

"Me?" Henry sounded outraged. "I've done nothing, nothing but calibrate the Fold spell to account for minute-and-second accuracy and ease of spell use. Jayne has been diligently ensuring that we see to all the Rogues before we have any more breakout incidents and trouble."

"...*more* breakout incidents?" Vivienne said.

"Cillian got out once. It was a whole thing." Jayne shrugged and tried to pull away from Tristan. She lost her balance again, and he grabbed her by the elbow. "Oops. Thanks. Anyway, we're making good progress here. I think I should get back to it. Want to help?"

"Yes, I want to help." Tristan slid his arm from Jayne's elbow to around her chest. "I want to help *you*. You need rest, Jayne."

"I'm fine." She tried to wave him off, but he caught her fingers in his and pressed them gently. "I'll be fine," she protested, more softly this time.

Tristan leaned down and brushed his lips to hers, drawing a shiver out of her that made him wholly regret what he knew he should do next. "No, you're not," he whispered. "Come on, let's get you to bed. For a nap."

"Agreed," said a new, all-business voice. Amanda Newport was approaching from around the side of a Shielded paddock. She looked more pleased than Tristan had ever seen her. "You've done a lot of missions back-to-back—a lot of *unauthorized* missions, I might add. And you will be getting into trouble for that, Thornes. But for now, you need to rest. The Rogues will still be here when you wake up."

"They'll still be here, and in hell," Jayne said. She turned from Tristan and drew herself up to her full height—a good six inches taller than Amanda. "It's my duty to bring them back."

"And if you fry your brain, you can't do that duty, can you?" Amanda pursed her lips and arched a brow. Now it was Jayne who looked small. Tristan stifled a chuckle. No one should ever try to intimidate Amanda Newport.

"Come on." He steered Jayne away from the paddock and toward the portal. "Nap, then breakfast. I'll get you whatever you want."

"Shouldn't we get you whatever you want? When's the last time you ate?" Jayne asked.

Tristan shrugged and was about to reassure her when a beeping interrupted them. They turned their heads. The beeping was coming from Amanda's watch.

She blanched when she examined it. "Wraith breach," she said and started to run.

They followed, Jayne stumbling after Tristan, clutching his hand as though it were the only thing holding her up. "They must be after the Rogues," she puffed.

They burst through the portal and into the waiting room, where Cillian was explaining matters to the former buck Rogue. When he spotted them, Cillian didn't even ask what was wrong. He leapt up. "What can I do?"

Tristan heard the crash of glass. Before he had time to think a Shield spell was in his hands, ready to protect Jayne. Amanda was over by the wide glass window; she broke the glass with a Shatter spell and without stopping hurled a Net spell at the huge Wraith that was using its claws to tear into a window in the isolation ward.

Tristan recognized him with a thrill of fear. Alastor. "Whose room is that?" he said. He had the feeling he already knew.

"Your mother's," Amanda confirmed.

"Stay here." Tristan kissed Jayne gently on the cheek, then let her go just in time for her to drop into a chair. He tore down the hallway, ignoring her shouted protests as they faded behind him. A thunder of paws heralded Vivienne, bounding ahead of him as a tigress. They ran into the isolation ward, past Adepts and doctors rushing the other way. On the move, Tristan called up a Lasso spell.

Vivienne knocked a door open with her paw. The room was empty. With a growled curse, Tristan took the next one. Also empty. The third, however, held a bed and a monitor and Gina's restrained form.

And now Alastor, as well.

The Wraith was busy slicing through Gina's restraints, using his hideous gray-black claws on the thick cloth straps. Gina's eyes were open but glazed over, from magic or morphine or pain.

Tristan drew his broadsword from the Torrent. "I think I have had enough of you," he said. Vivienne growled in agreement.

Alastor's black eyes flickered with hatred. His bat-like snout split to reveal razor-sharp teeth as long as Tristan's finger. He put one heavy foot down, cracking the floor and tearing into the tile. Vivienne coiled her muscles, ready to spring. Tristan swallowed and layered an extra Slice spell down the side of his sword. He had the feeling it wouldn't do any good. Alastor was looking at him like he'd make a particularly tasty meal, and at ten feet tall and counting, the Wraith was even more impressive than Tristan's sister.

Alastor cocked his head. One foot scraped along the floor, making the tile scream. He was receiving orders from Odin, Tristan realized.

Tristan brought up his sword. He hadn't survived Odin's Rogue pocket and come all the way back to Virginia to die.

Alastor roared. Vivienne leapt for him, fastening her jaws around his knee. He lifted her by the scruff of her neck and tossed her into a cart of medical tools, which tumbled over with a crash and a clatter. Tristan rushed forward and swept his sword around—

And barely kept himself from slicing his own mother in half.

Alastor had drawn Gina Labelle against his body as a human shield. Tristan's arm trembled. His mother had fought to kill in the pocket, and the look in her eye had told him that it wasn't wholly Odin's influence that had made her do it. If he killed her and Alastor at the same time, would it be worth it? The big Wraith was bloody-minded and all too eager to act as Odin's hand of retribution. If Tristan let him go, he might be killing an untold number of Adepts later.

Gina hung from Alastor's grip like a rag doll. Tristan knew, suddenly, that if their positions were reversed and he was held hostage by an enemy, she wouldn't hesitate.

And in that same moment, he knew he couldn't be like her.

Alastor scrambled back over the floor, scattering shards of glass like jagged diamonds. His vast wings opened, smashing more windows to either side with the horn at their tips. Tristan fumbled to hold the Lasso spell and the sword at once, cursing his slow thinking. The Lasso whipped out and hit empty space where Alastor's foot had once been. The Wraith tilted backward into empty space.

Tristan heard the *pop-pop-pop* of gunfire. He ran to the window. Below, TCO agents had their firearms out and were unloading their magazines into Alastor's back. Tristan's heart squeezed painfully. If a bullet hit Gina... But they bounced off Alastor's hard hide instead, *plinking* to the concrete below. With some effort, the Wraith flapped his great wings, gaining height until he could turn and fly away, with Gina hanging limply in his talons.

TWENTY-SIX

"She's gone," Tristan reported when he returned. Vivienne walked beside him in her human form.

Jayne knew his words were seriously bad news but her heart couldn't help lifting at the sight of them both. It was impossible to conceive that they'd only been gone...well, she really had no idea, considering how many folds she'd done; every moment had felt like days. Jayne had convinced herself that keeping busy would help distract her, that working on a solution would feel like accomplishing something. Now that Tristan was back, she could truly breathe again, and she understood that everything she'd told herself was a lie to help her make it through. His absence had been a gaping hole, a loss of gravity, and now she was on solid ground again.

She loved him too much. And she wouldn't stop. Ever. No matter the fight, no matter the situation, she couldn't function without him by her side. She had strength from the goddesses, yes, but Tristan made her whole.

"What are you thinking, *mon amour*?" he asked, his voice low as a lover's.

"Ick," Vivienne spat. "Later for the mushy stuff. There is

work to do. Can we track the Wraith that took her? Do you think Odin's going to target Rogues one by one now?"

Jayne stood and tried not to sway as a fresh wave of dizziness swept over her.

Vivienne narrowed her eyes. "You are going to faint again."

Tristan was next to her in an instant. He slipped an arm around her waist and drew her close, and while the feeling was comfort and warmth and giddiness all wrapped up in one, Jayne stuck her tongue out at Vivienne anyway. "Tattletale."

"I do not know what Odin has in store for my mother," Tristan said. "But what can we do for her now? Alastor will either be downed by one of your American fighter jets, or he will escape, and we will have no idea where to."

The second was a far more likely outcome. Wraiths were hard to detect on radar, like most magic when mixing with the mundane, and Alastor was the third largest Wraith Jayne had ever seen—outsized only by Huginn and Munnin, Odin's direct lieutenants.

Amanda marched into the room. "Well, that was unfortunate. We don't have the resources to locate and fight for Gina Labelle," she said to them. "I know you want to save everyone, and if we weren't in a war situation, I'd agree. I'd rather Gina face her crimes in a human court than suffer...whatever fate it is she'll suffer at the hands of Odin. But we must first be loyal to the people who are loyal to us. Speaking of..." She scowled at Jayne. "How many unauthorized time-travel missions did you go on?"

"Um." Jayne tried to think. "Just the one."

Amanda snorted. "Try again."

"Look, we got the result we wanted, didn't we? Sofia's back, the Rogues are back. We've got a fighting chance now."

Amanda shook her head. "Ruger will get the report out of

Henry. You'll both be facing an inquiry for the improper use of magic, Jayne, and I can't stop it."

Improper use of magic. How very Hogwarts. Jayne giggled and looked around for Sofia, who would have shared in the joke. But Sofia was, presumably, still sleeping off her ordeal in the hospital while a team checked to make sure the baby was all right.

"You *can* stop it, though," Jayne pointed out. "You're in charge."

"The reason I'm in charge is because I know not to abuse my power," Amanda told her. "Just a thought, in case *you'd* ever like to be in charge."

"Gods no. Not me. Please, no promotions." Being in charge sounded stuffy and boring and like Jayne would have to sit in an office all day looking at reports. If she was going to spend all her time in a chair, she'd be investigating *interesting* written things with covers and characters, thank you very much.

"But the inquiry can wait, no?" Tristan said, drawing her in just a little more. His chest rose and fell evenly against her back, and she relaxed against it. "Jayne needs rest."

"We all do," Amanda grumbled, but she nodded. "Very well. Go home, get a full eight hours, report back when you're well rested. Tristan, Vivienne—I know eight measly hours of rest isn't going to be enough for you. Check in with Tamara when you come back to the TCO, and if she clears you for light duty, we'll see what we can do."

"We are fine." Vivienne sounded insulted.

"Tamara reports directly to me," Amanda said severely, pulling her hair from its bun and starting to redo it. "So I'll know if you don't follow orders. You want to be standing beside Jayne trying to explain why you're flouting my authority?"

Vivienne rolled her eyes. Tristan grinned. Jayne felt the warmth spread over her entire body. They really were back.

THE NASHVILLE APARTMENT waited for them, just the way they'd left it. Vivienne let out a gasp of delight at the sight of her bed but visibly kept herself from flopping against it.

"I am going to shower," she declared. "Until the warm water runs out, I think. Be quiet so I don't have to think about what you are doing."

She grabbed fresh clothes and a fluffy pink towel and disappeared into Jayne's bathroom.

"A shower would be nice." Tristan sounded wistful.

Jayne wound her arms around his neck and stared deep into his blue eyes. They were still as intense as the sea, but there was a new layer to them, a hollowness that she wanted to wipe away when she caressed his brow. "I can think of a few things that would be nicer," she said with a coy smile.

Tristan's hands circled her waist, and a moment later her legs were wrapped around his hips. Their lips met, softly at first, remembering where they'd left off, exploring. Jayne's fatigue fell away as a fire kindled in her belly and began to spread. It felt like so long since Tristan had touched her; now she needed him to touch her everywhere, to make up for lost time.

He seemed to agree. His tongue, so gentle as it had eased between her lips, began to stroke the inside of her mouth with increased urgency. His fingers dug into her thighs. He stumbled toward the bedroom, muttering, *"Merde,"* when they clipped the doorframe. Jayne giggled against his mouth, then gasped when he broke away to lavish her neck in kisses.

They landed on the bed in a soft thump. His hands slid down her thighs, dragging her pants and underwear with them. Jayne ripped off her shirt, then grabbed Tristan by the collar of his, hauling him up the bed so she could get to work on the buttons. When she got them open, she slid her hand over his skin, reveling in the way his breath hitched, running her fingers over his ribs, recalling the place of each scar. She still knew him, and the thought was a comfort.

He caught her arm and kissed the inside crook just above her elbow. Then he crawled up to her, putting one hand next to her head, hovering just over her mouth. "There was not one moment where I did not dream of you in some way," he murmured, dipping down to press little kisses against the corner of her mouth.

"I thought of you always," Jayne whispered back. The world blurred suddenly as tears sprang to her eyes. "Everything I did was to get you back." Him and everyone else she loved. "Gods, Tristan. I would have ended them all if it meant having you again."

His kisses moved lower, over her neck and chest, and all thought became a scramble of incoherent desire. She let herself drift on little eddies of pleasure that shivered brighter and brighter. He made his way down to her belly button, then her hips. Then the inside of her thighs.

He stopped, breath hot on her skin. With some effort, Jayne lifted her head. His blue eyes were luminous in the light of dusk. "Jayne?" he whispered. "I never wish to be parted again."

"Never," Jayne gasped as his mouth came down.

TWENTY-SEVEN

Henry unlocked the door to his private apartment and went into the kitchen to make himself a matcha latte. Jayne had introduced him to the joys of matcha; the making of it was meditative, in a way, requiring enough concentration that he couldn't wander off and forget about it, but he could still ruminate over a particular problem. Also, matcha had twice as much caffeine in it as coffee did, which made it ideal for gearing up for a late-night working session.

Jayne and Tristan, Sofia and Cillian. His daughters were back with their loves, and they'd done a damn sight better at choosing who to love than Henry had himself. He was happy for them. Their work was finished, for now.

But his wasn't. He still had people trapped in the Torrent, and he would do whatever it took to get them out.

Henry Thorne had learned long ago that you never take the only copy of a device into the field. His original Time Reverse 1.0 sat on the counter in front of him, disassembled.

He had shown Jayne the advertised capabilities of the Time Reverse: an etched spell to fold time, a miniature portal that had limited activation, a nice touchscreen interface. But the truth of the Time Reverse was not that it was supposed to be a handy Fold spell in a machine.

No, the Reverser was supposed to be a totem.

The Norns had given him some assistance: a tiny piece of the World Tree. That meant he didn't have to try to get in through the Codex Regius again, decreasing the risk of overloading his power and burning. And he assumed that through the World Tree, folding time would be a lot easier. He suspected that each limb represented a branch of time—but this hypothesis was highly literary and had no basis in scientific research. Yet.

Something twinged in the back of his mind, some ancient instinct. He stopped with his cup halfway to his mouth. There was a sound like a creak and a click.

He peered out of the living room and into the hall. The door to his apartment was slightly ajar; he opened it and checked the bright hallway before closing and locking it. *Must not have latched all the way,* he thought, but checked the bedroom and bathroom for safety's sake first. Everywhere was empty. And as there were only so many places for a thief to hide in a place like this, he pushed the thought out of his mind with his next sip. He had too much to think about.

A chip of the tree would anchor his fake totem and give him leave to visit the World Tree whenever it suited him. However, traveling to such a place was still a problem. Adepts traditionally used portals to travel, because going anywhere through other magical means was a surefire way to immolate. The big exception was Masters, like Jayne, committing an astral projection that temporarily removed their spirit from this world. Henry was nowhere near a powerful enough magician to do what his younger daughter could do. Thankfully, he was not averse to cheating.

Something scuttled behind him. Henry whirled around.

Then he sighed irritably. After spending twenty years in a Time Catch, his credit wasn't great, and he didn't have many options when it came to renting apartments. But did every single place he rented *have* to have a problem with mice and rats and cockroaches?

He carefully set the piece of World Tree into a tiny container at the back of the Reverser and screwed the panel in place. He'd run the last few diagnostics tonight, and tomorrow he could officially test it. And the best thing was, Amanda and the Disciples of Gaia couldn't get on his case for using time travel, because technically he wasn't.

Henry Thorne was many things, but observant wasn't one of them. He didn't notice the way all the birds had gone silent or the way the light behind him dimmed slightly. He didn't realize anything at all was wrong until the vase came down on his head.

Sheer luck saved him: He had bent his ear to hear the satisfying *click* of the panel above the screw, and his skull was no longer where it had been. The corner of the vase merely clipped him, smashing his head into the table.

He cried out and turned only to see Gina Labelle raise the vase for another try.

Henry couldn't think of anything to do. So he sucker punched her in the stomach.

She doubled over. "Oh, shut up," she gasped, staggering back. Henry was confused; she must be speaking to someone in her mind. "If you think you can do better, get in here."

A huge gray arm crashed through the kitchen window, tearing the screen and pulling the entire frame out. The huge, hideous head of Alastor poked through.

Henry had never been one for direct conflict. He grabbed the Time Reverse and made to run—only to find that Gina had turned into a lioness and blocked his escape. Her golden eyes flashed. A long tongue slipped from her mouth, and from behind Henry, Alastor chortled, a rumbling sound that made everything on the kitchen counter rattle.

A strange sort of calm came over Henry. *You're not going to die today,* he told himself. *This much you know.*

He'd simply have to skip diagnostics. He activated the Time Reverse 1.0 and spun the dial. *You know where you want to go,* he thought and activated it.

Henry's first Time Reverse had been a prototype with a few flaws. One of them was that when it pulled him in time, it truly pulled—wrenching at his body so hard that he spun around. His stomach heaved and his ribs seemed to jerk out of alignment. This time, when he landed at the base of the World Tree, he dropped to all fours, gasping and fighting nausea as his mouth flooded with saliva. He smelled the charred scent of burning hair and cloth. Maybe it didn't work as well as he thought.

"Henry Thorne," said an exasperated voice. "Will you *stop trying to kill yourself?*"

Joy tumbled through his body. Still, Henry waited until he was certain he wouldn't throw up all over the base of the tree before getting to his feet with care. The cuffs of his pants were singed, and there was no hair left on his arms.

"Hello, Mother," he said.

The tree looked much better than it had the last time he'd seen it—he must be visiting in a different time. The bark was a deep, healthy brown, the leaves bright yellows and greens. Alexandra Thorne sat next to the ruins of Mímir's well, on a small carved wooden chair with no back. She wore a plain linen dress not unlike the one Urd had been wearing, with a pinafore apron on the front. Next to her, in another chair, swinging long, coltish legs, sat a girl of twelve or so, with lightly curling blonde hair held back by a kerchief and piercing green eyes. She'd been practicing some sort of spell; Henry could see the Torrent fizzling between her fingers.

"Hello, Trinity." He smiled at his granddaughter. She smiled back, a mischievous smile that was all Jayne and pierced his heart. "You figure out that castle move I taught you last time I saw you?"

"Hi, Grandpa," she said. "I tried, but Grandmama Alexandra won't play with me. She doesn't like chess."

"Not now, Trinity. And Henry, do not change the subject." Alexandra stood. "You think I don't recognize a cheap trick when I see one?" She gestured imperiously toward the Time Reverse in his hand. It smelled faintly like melting plastic. "Only Masters can visit the astral plane."

Henry turned the Reverse over. "Well, I did it." He sounded more sulky and less satisfied than he'd have liked.

Alexandria stomped over to him and plucked the Reverser from his hands. She fiddled with the dial for a moment, frowning. "As I suspected. You've introduced a feedback loop to the Fold spell. You're borrowing extra magic *from yourself*. Henry, you fool, you can't borrow magic from another you! You're going to kill yourself. You must turn back."

"That I will do." Henry put his hands on her shoulders. "I promise, Mother. But I also promised I would set you and Trinity free. So I won't turn back time without you."

"Of course you won't. Trinity," called Alexandra, sounding for all the world like a queen. Trinity let her spells dissipate in a tiny shower of emerald fireworks and hurried over, stepping lightly on the roots of the tree. "But you know I don't mean you should turn back in a physical sense. You must stop with the endless experimentation. You must accept that there are limits to magic."

Henry opened his mouth to say, *Never*. Some things were worth dying for, and he happened to think that scientific advancement was one of them. He managed to stop himself, though. Alexandra had never stood for hearing *no* from her progeny. "Yes, Mother," he said, and bowed his head in what he hoped smacked of acquiescence.

"Lying child," she huffed with fondness. "All right, let's go. But this is the last time you use that Time Reverse, do you hear me?"

"Of course, Mother," said Henry, and this time he didn't even care that his lie was obvious. "But, erm, maybe prepare your best defensive spells. I left my apartment in rather a hurry…"

TWENTY-EIGHT

"Dad!" Jayne burst into her father's apartment with Sofia, Tristan, Vivienne, and Cillian hot on her heels. A TCO strike team was already there, headed up by Ruger. First, he'd told Sofia, who'd just been released from observation, and she'd called Jayne, waking her from the first decent rest she'd had in weeks.

All the lights in the apartment were on. Glass was strewn about the floor from a broken vase, mug, and kitchen window, and Jayne recognized the jagged scrapes of Wraith claws over the windowsill. There was blood on the floor—not life's blood, but enough to indicate someone had been hurt. The bedroom was empty, the bed made, and papers were scattered across the floor of the kitchen-living room space. Henry had obviously been working on something when he'd been taken.

"He's got my dad." Jayne's heart thundered in her chest. She clutched Tristan's arm so hard he made a strangled sound of protest. She'd *just* gotten everyone back, and now Odin struck again. "That ancient wacko has my father." Her forehead warmed, and she fought to keep the surge of power in check.

"Calm down, Jayne." Ruger stood in front of her and put a

large hand on her shoulder. Jayne looked up into his strong face. He took a deep breath, and she followed, sucking in air raggedly. Ruger was right, of course. If she wasn't calm, she couldn't put together much of a rescue plan.

When Ruger was satisfied, he patted her shoulder and stepped back so he could address them all. "Here's what we know: Henry came into his apartment at 10:59 p.m. At 11:06, the door opened again. Our wards didn't recognize the entrant, and Henry didn't say any of the codes to deactivate the alarms, so we were alerted. By the time an investigative team got here, he was gone. We're going to presume he's alive until we're proven otherwise," he said, glancing askance at the blood on the floor."

"This is *it*." Jayne's fist curled. "I am going to Iceland right now to kick that family-stealer's ass."

"We're going to make a plan, Jayne," Ruger said patiently.

"I have six totems and my team back together. *That's* my plan."

"We all want your father back, Jayne—"

"Don't act like this is equally meaningful to you!" she burst out. Her eyes stung with all the unshed tears she'd tried so long to push down. She just wanted to stop focusing on saving the next person and—and *breathe,* then find a way to get back on the offensive. "He's my dad, and it took us so long to get him back in the first place and now he's gone again—"

"Heavens, what a commotion," said a woman's voice that was at once foreign and familiar to Jayne. She'd never heard it before in her life, yet it was lodged somewhere deep in her memory. "Calm down, all of you. I can't hear myself think."

A woman in a blue linen dress emerged from the bedroom. She had deep brown eyes and long curly gray hair, the pointed chin of Henry and the full mouth of Sofia. She surveyed the kitchen and living room with disapproval. "Gracious, Henry, you *live* like this?"

"I *did* just survive a fight with a Wraith," Henry said, sounding more like a sulky teenager than Jayne had ever heard him.

"Dad!" She rushed forward, Sofia hot on her heels. She threw her arms around Henry; he stumbled back but his arms folded tight around her. "What happened? Tell us everything."

"What are you all doing here?" Henry asked, utterly bemused.

"The wards were triggered," Ruger explained. "We came immediately, as protocol dictates. Now you can fill us in."

"You put up wards on my apartment?" He sounded slightly scandalized.

"You're a Thorne," Ruger replied, a smile quirking the edge of his lips, twisting the shiny burned skin by his jaw.

"As am I," the old woman said. "Jayne, Sofia, I am your grandmother, Alexandra. Your father has succeeded in retrieving us from the Torrent."

Jayne was about ten seconds from imploding, so she sent a quiet thought toward the totems, which shined a greeting. She felt suddenly shy under the gaze of this woman. "It's good to meet you, ma'am. Grandma'am. Grandmother."

Sofia started cracking up. "Don't mind her, Grandmom. She's got a lot of magical adrenaline coursing through her system right now. We're thrilled to meet you."

"And I am thrilled to make your acquaintance as well, you lovely creatures."

"But how—" Jayne started, but Henry held up a hand.

"I'll just jump ahead to the good part," he said. He was brief in the telling of the story, describing Gina's attack with a curled lip but skipping straight over the part where he'd somehow miraculously retrieved his mother from the Torrent, which Jayne found somewhat suspicious. Usually her father liked to wax poetic when a certain contraption of his had worked. But he barely mentioned the Time Reverse, and not to her satisfaction at all. The Reverser had been about folding time, not astral projection. He was up to something.

But before she could ask what that something might be, she caught sight of a small, delicate hand holding on to her grandmother's skirts. A moon-pale face peeked out from behind Henry and Alexandra. Her nose was proud, her vibrant green eyes curious. The impish expression on her face made it impossible to mistake her.

Jayne's hand found Tristan's and squeezed. "Look," she whispered.

She locked eyes with her daughter, and her knees gave out.

Alexandra broke away from where she stood, lecturing the TCO on stomping all over the apartment with their shoes on, and looked between them. "Oh, yes. Jayne, meet Trinity. Yes, she's your daughter. No, you won't break the space-time continuum if you touch her."

"May I..." Jayne's voice was hoarse, and speaking felt like forcing words out around a stone. "May I give you a hug?" she said.

Trinity paused for a moment before slowly nodding.

Jayne managed to make it over to her. She ran an arm down Trinity's shoulder, decorated in the fine-spun linen of the Norns. It was odd—she'd known for a while now that she'd have a daughter named Trinity. But it hadn't seemed real until *now*. She was beautiful, with a lively intelligence in her eyes, but shy. Jayne leaned forward slowly so she wasn't startled, gathering the girl in her arms, feeling the solidity of her. Trinity's arms felt much surer when she wrapped them around Jayne's neck, squeezing between her shoulder blades and burrowing her head between Jayne's shirt and jacket. To Trinity, this was the Jayne she'd always known, surely.

"Hi, Mama. I've missed you."

Jayne absolutely could not breathe. This was...wild.

"Right." Alexandra pushed past them. "That should do it for introductions. Anyone who's *not* a member of my family may cease leaving scuff marks and mud on the floor. I'm sure that between us we can fight off any further attacks on my son."

"Uh." Ruger looked off balance. It was a rare moment for him. "I think the head of the TCO would like to meet you—"

"We'll be sure to drop in when we have a moment." Alexandra took his arm and led him briskly to the door. Jayne ignored the shuffle of agents heading out into the night and breathed in the leaves-and-earth scent of Trinity's hair. Tristan knelt carefully on their other side, putting one arm around Jayne and the other around his daughter.

"*Mon père. Bonsoir. Tu m'as manqué.*" Trinity shifted her head to his shoulder. Jayne locked eyes with him over their girl's golden curls. His were suspiciously bright. The tears flowed over as his mouth split in a smile.

And Jayne thought with a sudden, fierce stab in her heart: *I never wish to be parted again.*

"Hm." Alexandra came back into the living room and put her hands on her hips. "I thought I said everyone who wasn't a member of this family should leave."

Jayne gave Trinity one more gentle squeeze, then released her. She stood. Sofia held Cillian's hand so tightly their knuckles were white from the effort. Vivienne lingered by the kitchen counter, looking uncertain. "This *is* the family," Jayne said firmly. "Everyone here."

Cillian and Vivienne both threw her grateful looks.

"Well, I suppose with this many cousins and the like, there are plenty of bodies to make themselves useful. You look like a fellow who can handle himself." She pointed at Cillian. "You can go out in this Wraith-laden world and get me something to eat. It's been over twenty years since I've had anything sweet."

"Let me guess: pie?" he said with a self-conscious grin.

"Any fruit type will do, as long as it's strawberry. You." Tristan was next. "You've got the stink of a Master about you, so I'm sure you can put together some sort of Repair spell for that window. And remake the wards on this place."

Tristan shot a sly look at Jayne. *She's a Thorne,* he mouthed. Jayne narrowed her eyes at him. But he bowed to Alexandra as though she were some sort of court lady and went over to the window.

"Trinity, you can clean up the glass," Alexandra said.

Jayne squeezed her daughter's shoulder. "I know where the dustpan is; I'll clean it," she said. "Why don't you find a spot on the couch?"

"Eh...what should I do?" asked Vivienne.

Alexandra looked her up and down, taking in the measure of her. "You can make coffee," she pronounced.

By the time Cillian returned with two strawberry-balsamic pies, the apartment looked more or less the way it had before the attack. Everyone sat on couches and fold-out chairs around the coffee table, and Sofia found plates and forks and cups.

For a good ten minutes, nobody said anything. Jayne sat on her folding chair, inches away from Tristan but unable, some-how, to even take his hand. She couldn't tear her eyes away from Trinity. The girl sat primly, straight-backed with her knees slanted slightly to the side, as though she were some kind of royalty. She ate her pie in delicate bites, and her gaze darted around the room, trying to take in everything. She seemed particularly awed by Vivienne, who slouched in Henry's armchair and responded to Alexandra's sharp "Sit up, girl, you're not a gorilla," with a laconically raised eyebrow.

Alexandra finished her pie with a happy sigh and looked at Cillian expectantly. He stared at her for a moment before realizing what she wanted, then leaned forward and cut her another slice.

She took a bite and closed her eyes, savoring. Then she reached for her tea. *She even drinks it with her little finger extended,* Jayne thought. She didn't know anyone who did that unironically. "So." Alexandra set down the teacup. "Odin Allfather."

The room held its breath.

"Odin has one weakness: fire. Not just any fire—volcanic fire and magma. If you can bring him into the heart of that fire, you can destroy him once and for all," Alexandra declared.

A short silence followed. Then Jayne said, "That's it?" A strange feeling was curdling the pie in her stomach. It felt oddly like disappointment. After all they'd been through against Odin, it turned out they just had to chuck him in a volcano? They could borrow a military helicopter and end this war in five minutes?

"If Odin's susceptible to volcanic fire, why did he build his portal in Iceland?" Sofia asked.

Alexandra gave her a thin smile of approval. "Because the power of the volcano is a double-edged sword for him. It lends him nearly unbeatable strength of magic and mind and body, but it's also the only way in which he is vulnerable. We must trigger the sort of eruption he can't harness for his own use, the sort of eruption from which he cannot escape. You see that it is a delicate balance. But it is one through which I can guide you, I hope."

Jayne touched her forehead. Fire shouldn't be a problem, at least. "How do you know all of this? We couldn't find anything about stopping or hurting Odin at the TCO library."

"That is deliberate," Alexandra told her. "Odin had any and all knowledge of his personal history, including his weaknesses, destroyed, to the extent that he could. I only found out because

I have spent a long time in the Torrent. Far too long. Enough time to observe Odin and his Wraiths and understand them as well as any human Adept can."

Jayne looked at Trinity. "How did *you* end up in the Torrent? Did we...mess up somehow?"

Trinity's eyes flicked from side to side, and the ghost of a guilty smile played around her mouth. "I went looking for the books. The destroyed books."

Vivienne snorted. Cillian hid his chuckle behind his hand. Tristan closed his eyes and worked his jaw. "Thorne women," he muttered.

Alexandra clapped her hands together, as intense as any general facing her troops. "We are the only ones with solid knowledge of Odin's weaknesses. He will know by now that we have disappeared from the Torrent. The Norns were able to arrange for our removal, but even they could not unravel some of the more complicated spells. He will be angry and looking for us. We should move."

CHAPTER

TWENTY-NINE

A manda Newport sat with one elbow propped on the desk and her phone up to her ear, trying, and failing, to rub the headache away that had taken hold in her temple. President Eisner was on the other end of the line, speaking crisply as though it weren't two in the morning. Hopefully, she hadn't been up for the past twenty hours like Amanda had, though she probably had. Eisner was dedicated and smart. Amanda liked her.

She swirled the remains of a cup of coffee before downing it with a grimace. A half-full carafe sat on the desk beside her phone. Against the rules—she wasn't supposed to do lesser magics in her office—she threw a Boil spell at it under her breath. She was too damn tired to take a cup down to the canteen microwave. She poured another cup, this one searing hot, and took a sip. Better.

She tuned back in to the president, who was saying, "Thanks to your security footage, Interpol has issued an Orange Notice for Gina Labelle—she's back on the imminent threat list. She's back on the wanted list. We're working on official NATO support, but individual countries have been calling to pledge.

I've got papers here from Australia, New Zealand, India, South Africa, and Argentina, with more coming in by the minute. Some of them are happy to export their Adepts, while others want to keep them close. A lot..." She sighed. "A lot of them want promises for their magic-users. A free spot at Aegis for the kids, green cards for the adults. That sort of thing."

"With respect, the TCO has always had a liberal policy with green cards for Adepts," Amanda pointed out.

"You've never had this many Adepts to contend with, though, have you?" Eisner replied.

"Surely we can negotiate temporary contracts," Amanda said.

"We can...and the adults aren't really who I'm calling to talk about."

Eisner sounded tired. Amanda swallowed a sudden lump in her throat and reached for Karam's necklace. "How's your daughter?"

"Marie is fine. Shaken, but fine. Be straight with me, Newport. Does Aegis still exist?" Eisner said.

"It does." Amanda scratched at a waxy stain on her desk. "We're strengthening the Time Catch so that it's harder to get in. The wards on the school itself helped keep the Wraiths at bay, and our Aegis team is setting up emergency portal evacuation points in the school in case students ever need to get out in a hurry again."

There was a long pause on the other end of the line. "Aegis will recover," Amanda pressed, hating how desperate she sounded.

"We can't risk training students who will become more powerful Wraiths, or shelter Rogues, simply for them to be taken." Eisner's voice was flat.

"We won't." Amanda was talking too fast now but couldn't stop herself. "We won't. We're coming up with a plan for Odin, a way to beat him. And—look. If he *does* win, there won't be any safe place on Earth for those kids. Except Aegis, where they can learn to use their powers and become stronger and maybe, someday, take our world back."

It was a thought she hadn't admitted to anyone. She felt like crying as soon as the words emerged from her mouth. But it was her job to think of the worst-case scenario, to plan for it. "And you're right. Aegis had some unexpected operational weaknesses. For a Time Catch to be breached in such a manner...none of us knew it was possible. It has to be tied to the strengthening of the Torrent around us, and we're studying why it happened. This is a new world, Madame President. We're still learning."

"An awfully big lesson, General."

"Yes. But it doesn't change the fact that our mission is spot on. The right thing to do is train the world's Adepts, then send them out to create their own pockets with their own schools. So that if one gets attacked, we still have others. Backups. He can't attack them all."

"A training program." Eisner was silent for a while. Amanda thought she could hear the tap of a pen on a desk. "Now *that's* an interesting offer for the world. Something that might solidify a NATO-style deal. Well, I won't keep you. Lord knows we both have enough to do."

She hung up and left Amanda in her empty office.

A soft knock on her door roused her. She sat up, straightened her jacket. "Come."

Ruger stepped inside. Rumpled and exhausted, but standing tall, he took up so much space in her office that she was instantly cheered.

"Everything okay?" she asked.

"If you call having Alexandra Thorne back in the world okay. Sure. All good."

"Excuse me?"

"Henry did it. He managed to go into the Torrent and release both his mother and his granddaughter."

"Jayne's daughter? Trinity?"

"Yep. Jayne and Tristan's, so at least we know that for sure now." He gestured toward the couch. "May I?"

"Be my guest."

He sat heavily. The fine lines of exhaustion were clear in his posture and on his scarred face. Amanda joined him in the seating area.

"You need a vacation."

He laughed, humorless. "The Thornes are on the prowl, Odin has ruined many of the Rogues, half the magical world is being turned Wraith, all of the rules of magic that are known are being rewritten by the second...but yeah, I need to go drink something fruity on a windswept beach."

"We could reactivate the Tahiti Time Catch."

"Amanda," he scoffed. "That hasn't worked for two decades. Not since you—"

She held up a hand. "Don't remind me. It's not like I planned to swamp it with a tsunami."

He laughed. "The look on your face...it was priceless."

"It's good to hear you laugh, friend."

He smiled, but quieted.

"Want to tell me what's really on your mind?"

He narrowed his eyes at her, then sighed.

"I'm worried about Jayne. She's moved mountains, literally. But that much power in one person... I'm afraid for her. I don't know where this is headed, and I'll admit, I've grown fond of the little fool. I kind of miss the fool in her, actually. She's carrying the weight of the world on her shoulders. It's starting to show."

"She had to grow up sometime, Ruger. She knows the risks."

"Does she, though? Do you really think she understands where this is heading?"

Amanda poured him a cup of coffee. "Drink that. You need caffeine."

"Thanks."

While he sipped, she appraised him.

"Do you want out?" she asked finally.

"Out? Of the TCO? Of course not."

"Out of her command structure."

"It wouldn't matter," he said, staring in the cup. "Not like she listens to half of what I say anyway."

"You've lost officers before."

"None like her. And Amanda, if we lose her, it's *over*. All of this. The TCO, the CIA, the world as we know it. We'll be an army of Wraiths, bending to Odin's will, and everything we hold dear will be gone."

"Then we need to make sure we don't lose her."

"She won't let us protect her," he roared. "That stubborn, idiotic child thinks she knows better than everyone. And her father, my God, that man... Now add in the whole freaking family of them? I am overrun with Thornes, and each is as pigheaded as the next. Alexandra has a reputation, you know. Between her and Xiomara..."

"Xiomara is a problem," Amanda agreed lightly. "But she'll come around. When she sees Alexandra back from the dead, she will get in line. I know it."

"We need everyone on our side to work together if we have any hope here."

"Yes."

He threw up his hands. "Screw it. Let's go repair the portal. I need fruity drinks."

"I will absolutely make that happen if you're serious. You

could use a break. Take that Guardian friend of yours. Scoot for a week."

"Pah. I wouldn't be able to rest. All I'd be doing is hatching plans and fretting about the Thornes."

"All right then. I'm open to suggestions."

At the look on his face, she braced herself. Now the real issue was coming out.

"Jayne found a solution. We need magma to kill Odin."

"Like, volcano magma?"

"Yes."

"Let me guess: The Geniuses are going to try to manufacture that here, in our world, in the lab."

"Pretty much."

"That's just wonderful. 'Here lies the TCO, felled by the Geniuses trying to make a volcano inside.'" She laughed softly.

"I have to ask you a question." Ruger sat straight. "You're not going to like it."

"I don't like much these days. Ask away."

"Your necklace. Karam had it forged from the Torrent, right? From one of the original pockets?"

She reflexively touched the pendant, three triangles molded together, the symbol of the Guardians, heard her husband's dying voice: *"It has its...own magic that...I pray you will never... need."* She never took it off. It held Guardian magic, that she knew. But what kind? Something more than the golden energy their magic manifested?

"What are you saying?" But she already knew the answer.

Ruger nodded. "Exactly what you think I am. You told me once it was special. You're the only non-Guardian in the world who can touch that magic without burning. I think there's a reason why."

THIRTY

S ofia and Cillian stepped through the portal, immediately happy to be back on Aegis grounds. The grass had been smoothed out, and the roof of the school had been replaced. A real road now ran from the portal to the storage unit of the warehouse where their food was kept. Teams were finalizing the escape portals around the school—they would act like fire alarms, activating when the first students went through and sending a notice to the TCO. "And wherever else we get our Adepts from," Amanda had told them. It looked as though their planetary initiative was bearing fruit; the president had secured agreements with several allied countries already.

Trinity fizzed with excitement next to Sofia. She had begged to come with them. "Why not?" Jayne said, looking at Sofia for approval. Her little sister had wiggled an eyebrow and nodded toward her boyfriend, and Sofia took that to mean she'd really like some alone time to sort through the complications of seeing their preteen daughter in the flesh before she was even born.

"Please, Aunt Sofia?"

"All right. But you have to promise to behave."

"Thanks, sis," Jayne had whispered. "Send her back if she gets into trouble. Let her test one of the emergency portals."

"Mama," she whined, and Jayne's face had drained of color, making Sofia bite back a laugh. This was utterly surreal for them all.

"Come on, niece." Sofia tugged her by the arm. "Let's get you to school."

Trinity's face had practically glowed when they stepped through the portal. "I haven't seen this place in *so long*," she declared. "May I go to the library?"

"Hold on, niece. Let's get a report from Seo-Joon first." The headmaster was striding toward them, a hand up in greeting.

"Everything looks good," Sofia said when he stopped. He eyed Trinity with wonder and Sofia said, "Later. Is everything secure?"

"Tight as a drum. Who is this?"

"I'm Trinity, obviously. Hi, Headmaster." And to her aunt: "Can I go now?" She turned her vivid green puppy eyes to her aunt, and Sofia couldn't help but laugh. "All right." Trinity took off for the Aegis library at a run.

"Niece?" Seo-Joon asked incredulously. "Something you forgot to tell me?"

"My dad broke into the Torrent and brought out my grandmom and my niece. Trinity is Jayne and Tristan's girl. Only...not yet."

"Are they mad with joy?"

"Shell-shocked," Cillian replied. "Both of them. It would be hysterical if it wasn't so weird."

"I assume she has magic, and she's a student in a future class, and that's why she knows exactly where she's headed?"

"All of the above." Sofia laughed.

"Huh. She is going to be absolutely impossible when she's a student here," Seo-Joon mused, watching Trinity's linen dress flap in the breeze as she tore up the road to the manor house.

"And you'll have to deal with her. Can't have her aunt being accused of special treatment." Sofia stuck out her tongue.

"That she remembers it is good," Cillian said. "It means Aegis survives."

"Maybe. Or maybe she came from a different timeline altogether," Sofia mused.

The air turned still, charged. Seo-Joon bobbed from foot to foot. "So, if it's okay—I mean, we're trying to prep the dorms for new students, and I know you need to practice, and I left Zia and Rufus in charge of cleaning, which means they've probably tried some spell and turned the entire first floor into a slip 'n' slide..."

"Yeah. You go." Sofia nodded to him. Seo-Joon took off with a palpable look of relief.

"Hasn't forgiven me, huh?" Cillian murmured.

"It's just some PTSD. Don't worry. We're all going through it."

Things hadn't been right between them since the battle. When Cillian had rushed into her hospital room, her heart rate had gone through the roof. She couldn't get the image of him out of her head: a wolf, prowling. Ready to tear out her throat.

But he was *her* wolf, and the father of her child, and she was determined to get through this phase and find their deep connection again. It wasn't his fault.

"Now's our chance to fix all this." She took his hand and ignored the warning prickle of her skin. "There's still a Kirkjufell setup over the ridge. We can practice."

Henry and Quimby were adapting their glass magic boosters to latch on to a specific Fire spell that Jayne was perfecting. Sofia and Cillian would be responsible for dropping a larger version of the booster into a volcano near Kirkjufell.

Jayne would be responsible for luring Odin there and ultimately killing him.

Simple. Elegant.

Probably a disaster in the making.

Sofia opened her satchel, which held three baubles that looked a bit like glass floats for them to practice with. "All right." She closed her eyes and breathed in. She felt Cillian change, shifting. Her whole body screamed at her to *run,* so loudly that she took two steps backward before she could convince it that Cillian was himself, here to help, here to work with them.

She planted her feet and forced her eyes open. Cillian's magnificent bronze-and-white griffin stood before her, wings twitching. His sky-blue eyes settled on her. Calm, trusting. She could be trusting, too.

She came forward. Stroking his neck helped, as did swinging her leg over his back when he knelt. But there was a tenseness in her belly that didn't go away as they lifted off, and when she squeezed his sides with her thighs it was more out of panic than ridership.

Easy, he said.

Sofia huffed a laugh. "Yeah," she said, voice cracking. "Sorry."

They did an air lap to get used to things, and when she finally relaxed, Cillian led her toward the mountain. In a real simulation, they'd have more Rogues acting as Wraiths, but for now, they did the regular fly-by. Cillian took them to a cruising altitude a few hundred feet above the top of the volcano, and Sofia fumbled at the satchel.

She had to grab hold of his neck whenever they hit light turbulence or an updraft. She fumbled the first float and watched it tumble through the sky, smashing on the moss-like stars in a green sky.

No matter. Cillian's voice was calm, smooth in her head. *We'll try again.*

The next float bounced off a rock and smashed down the side of the mountain. The third missed as well. And then they were out.

We're not thinking on the same wavelength, Cillian said as Sofia muttered a curse. *Why don't we try to take some of the pressure off, eh?*

He brought them down to the ground and transformed back to human. He'd trimmed his blond hair after getting his mind back, and bits of it stuck out at odd angles. His eyes were compassionate and loving—but Sofia saw anguish behind them.

"It's not your fault," she said.

"It's not? You flinch from me because I never hurt you?" He got into a defensive stance, brought his arms up. Then he nodded. Sofia could attack at her leisure.

"You weren't in your own mind; you can't blame yourself." She got into a stance herself and calmed her breath. Then she darted forward, trying to tap him on the shoulder. He batted her arm away and she tried not to flinch at the contact. Teeth flashed in her mind.

Cillian didn't move. He was as patient as the mountain. She feinted right, then left, brought her feet around to trip him, then elbowed him in the chest. He dodged her feints, caught her elbow, and braced against her foot.

She was pressed against his chest. She could feel the pounding of his heart, the hitch of his breath. She risked looking up.

His face was etched with pain. "Don't—" She reached up to cup his cheek as the first tears fell.

"I tried to kill you, Sof. And the baby. How do I—" Then he was falling, and she with him. He collapsed on the ground, face twisted with grief. "How do we even explain it to her? How will she ever forgive me?" He looked at her, and his expression pierced her heart. "How will *you* ever forgive me?" he whispered.

Sofia realized she was crying when the first tears dripped from the tip of her nose to land on his cheek. "My heart already forgives you," she replied, kissing the spot where their tears mingled. "My mind forgives you, too. My body...just needs to remember."

Cillian drew a shaky breath. "How?"

Sofia lay her head on his chest and looked out over the verdant plain, the sweep of the blue water as it flowed out toward the sea. Somewhere far away a bird called—a Rogue, maybe. "We will find our way back to each other," she said, breathing deep of his scent. The scent of her partner, her lover. "Our bodies will find a way."

CHAPTER

THIRTY-ONE

Trinity closed her eyes and inhaled the intoxicating scent of old books. *This* was what she'd been missing for so long. There were other things, of course—she missed her parents and the whole family. She missed her Aegis friends, some of whom hadn't been born yet, who wouldn't be walking these halls for twelve years at least. She missed conversation with people besides her great-grandmother, who, though wise and full of knowledge, had never let Trinity climb the World Tree or try out spells to let them escape. And didn't care for chess. But she'd really, *really* missed the Aegis library. And life was never better than when the library was empty and all hers, just like now.

Now she just had to hope that the book she needed was already in here.

She'd convinced Mama and Père that bringing her to Aegis while it was being reinforced was the best way to keep her out of trouble. She was out of her time, and who knew what would happen if she disrupted this timeline? But the library was the very spot she wanted to be. After all, she was a Thorne, and she had to continue her research.

The books were shelved haphazardly in a way that made her click her tongue. Her mother mustn't have spent any time here. Whoever was currently in charge of these books had no respect for the Dewey Decimal System. Also, it made it a little more difficult for her to locate a book without her Find spell—and she knew from experience that unauthorized spells in the library brought adults running.

She ran her fingers down each volume, plucking out whatever looked interesting to her. If she had time after her research, she could come back for some light reading. Who knew how long Aunt Sofia and Uncle Cillian would be doing their battle preparations?

There! She pulled the green-bound book away from its companions and flipped it open. *An Adept's Unauthorized Guide to Practical Magic,* it read, and in gold embossed letters below the title: *A.T.*

"There we are, Grandmama." Trinity half-skipped to the tables at the far end of the library. "Such a rebel in your young days." She flipped open the only known copy of Alexandra's book and picked up her place.

Alexandra had always preferred false modesty over the real thing, Trinity had learned. For example, she called herself an Adept when she was nearly as powerful a Master as Mama with all her totems. When she'd been in her prime, she'd been glorious to behold, according to the books and journals of her contemporaries. Her unauthorized guide had ended up in the Aegis library by mistake, Trinity was certain—most books of this sort were catalogued in the TCO's main library, where only Adepts with special dispensation were allowed to look at them.

Either that or no one had actually *read* Grandmama's book.

For Grandmama Alexandra had quite a radical notion printed on these typewritten and hand-bound pages: the notion that pieces of the Torrent could be sequestered, cut off.

Bits that had been corrupted or flowed through parts of the world where powerful and dangerous Masters worked counter to the needs of humanity. Alexandra described, in detail, how one might cut off the Torrent's flow to those places.

And a smart girl could infer, from her reading and from her grandmama's stories, that Alexandra, in her attempt to do good, had once met with the Norns and bartered for the secret of time travel. And in her ensuing madness, she'd managed to cut off the Torrent from *everywhere*. And *everyone*. For decades.

Her great-grandmother was the one who'd cursed the Torrent. And Trinity was sure no one knew that yet.

At the end of the first chapter was a little-known theory on time reversal. Trinity narrowed her eyes and found a notepad in the messenger bag she'd borrowed from Mama.

She was going to bring the Torrent entirely back to Earth. For good.

THIRTY-TWO

"A little more, I think." Henry examined the levels in their magic-enhancement float as Quimby carefully poured in more oil. "Yes, that's good." The oil would act as a reagent with the magma and hopefully give the Eruption spell a little extra boost. Now, he just needed Jayne to put a bit of her spell into a magical suspension that he could lower like a net into the float before bottling it up. Their very own magma nuke, sure to take out any and all of Odin's physical being.

"It's going to be heavy." Quimby wrinkled her nose. "I know Sofia's strong, but are we sure she can carry three of these?"

"We can't send her without backups." Henry scratched his chin and frowned. "We'll have to see. Maybe we can fit Cillian with saddlebags." Cillian didn't usually train with a harness or saddle, because he needed to shift so often, but they might have to lock him into his griffin form for the battle.

The door to the lab opened, and Alexandra swept in. She'd changed her linen dress for a smart suit that looked straight out of the fifties—which, knowing her, it probably was. "Well?" she said without preamble.

"Hello, milady, my ma'am, umm, Ms. Thorne." Quimby bobbed her head in a little bow.

Alexandra Thorne was a fearsome creature. Even worse than Xiomara. No matter how many times Alexandra told her, Quimby couldn't seem to grasp that she wasn't talking to the queen. It probably pleased his mother, Henry thought, hiding his smile. He continued tinkering with the glass.

"The enhancer should be ready to go as soon as Jayne is," Quimby said, still blushing.

"Good. And for the rest of the battle?" Alexandra knew, as did they all, that no battle plan survived contact with the enemy.

Quimby showed her the shock sticks and other devices they'd used on the Wraiths at the first Battle of Kirkjufell. There was no doubt they'd helped, even if Odin had won the day.

"And I've been working on this." Henry hurried around to his side of the table, where the Time Reverse 1.0 sat. "No longer a long-range folder of time. You are looking at the new and improved Time Stop. It freezes time, flips it around, loops it, all on an interval of under thirty seconds. It could give us the crucial edge we need to land a blow right after it's landed wrong, freeze an enemy before he changes the course of the battle for good—"

"Henry Thorne." Henry withered. He'd forgotten how much scorn his mother could put into his name. Alexandra fixed him with her piercing stare. "Haven't you had enough of time-destroying magic?"

"This is different," he said, but his protestations felt weak even to him.

"It *will* destroy you, Henry. Don't think you know better than I do about this." Her nostrils flared. Her hands, folded in front of her, squeezed together so tightly the tendons stood out.

"Haven't you had enough of that? Don't you want to live to see your grandchild born?"

Henry looked at the gadget in his hands. He thought of Trinity's mischievous glance. That was a Thorne glance if ever there was one. He could see them spending long afternoons in the lab, tinkering with all sorts of interesting magics. Yet—

"Jayne is hell-bent on saving the world, no matter what it may do to her," he said. "And I? I'm hell-bent on saving Jayne." He patted the Reverser. "If one second can make the difference in her life or death, so be it. Just in case, Mother."

"Last resorts too often become first resorts," Alexandra replied, icy-eyed.

RUGER ENTERED Amanda's office with two fresh cups of coffee. He stopped at the door, taking in her frizzy hair half-fallen from its bun, her wrinkled collar. Her eyes were red-rimmed and she kept blinking slowly, like a sleepy owl. "When was the last time you rested?" he said.

"I napped on the couch," she replied without looking up. She was poring over another agreement—an attempt to get as many Adept children into Aegis as possible before they risked the world. "I'll have another nap after dinner."

"You'll have another nap after our meeting," Ruger corrected. "Let's get to it, so you can get some sleep."

Amanda made a face—a face that brightened when she spotted the second cup in his hand. When he moved to pull it back, she said, "Recall that I'm your superior officer and can charge you with insubordination."

He set it down on the desk. "I'm only trying to look out for you."

She opened her mouth to retort, then stopped. Then she

smiled. Even with eyes dull with fatigue, and new wrinkles in her forehead and around her mouth, she was still fierce. "So we have a plan."

"We have a plan," Ruger agreed. A small strike team would return to the Battle of Kirkjufell and use Alexandra to draw Odin out of his portal. Jayne would attack him and lure him toward the nearest active volcano and use the Earth totem to trigger the eruption. Sofia and Cillian would drop the magical enhancers to prevent Odin from escaping the blast, and while Jayne stayed to make sure he actually died, the rest of the team would help mop up the Wraith problem.

Amanda folded her hands and looked at him frankly. "This is a bad plan."

He studied her office. The former heads of the TCO seemed to glare down on him, as though their legacy lay in his hands. "It's not the best plan," he agreed, speaking more to them than his boss. "But we've learned a lot from the last battle. Jayne's more powerful than ever. She can do it."

"Yes. *She* can do it." Amanda picked the hair tie from her hair, grimacing as it pulled at her curls. "If we have to rely on one Adept to win or lose our battle, our plan's a bad plan. No matter how powerful Jayne is."

"She has an important part to play, but she's not the only one. We have a new class from Aegis ready to take to the field, even with the disruptions at the school. We'll have Adepts from other countries, Adepts who know how to fight Rogues and recognize Odin for the threat he is. We have Henry, and his genius hasn't exactly failed us." At her raised eyebrow, he amended his statement. "Gotten us into some trouble." This time she flat out snorted. "Okay, maybe I'm being naive. I want to believe he can figure this out."

"Don't even talk to me about Henry." Amanda scrubbed at her face. "Haven't you been lectured by that mother of his?

When has he ever brought us a solution that didn't lead to a more difficult problem? He's too fixated on what his gadgets can do for him and not fixated enough on what the penalty is for the rest of us. You saw him destabilize the entire timeline in his quest to save Sofia. I know Jayne got a note on her record, but if it hadn't been for her...we might not exist right now. What if he does the same thing again? What if he tries to 'save' Ruth?"

She let out a sigh and sagged back in her chair. Their eyes met, and Ruger recognized the particular gleam in hers. He didn't like it. "Henry Thorne might be someone we have to take care of."

A chill washed over Ruger's back. In CIA language, *take care of* meant one thing. And the TCO might say a lot of things about independence and freedom, but at the end of the day it was a CIA branch.

Amanda caught his wince. "Not like that, you idiot. Retired to a stable Time Catch for his own safety. My God, those girls would have my head. He is a liability, yes, but not one I would remove from the Earth."

"Well, our little liability says everything's ready," he said, trying to stay lighthearted, but Amanda's eyes narrowed. "Jayne also says she'll be good to go by tomorrow. Sofia and Cillian are practicing their part." He leaned forward and did a rare thing: He took Amanda's hand in his. "We're coming up on the end."

He didn't know whether it was a comfort or a warning. Amanda squeezed his hand tight. "We're coming up on the end," she repeated softly, fingering the necklace. "Goddess preserve us."

Ruger's pocket chimed. He checked it and felt his frown clear. "Got a message from our contact. Anything else we need?"

"No. Go ahead. And have fun." Amanda smiled slyly at him.

But when Ruger stood up, he pulled her with him. "You're taking a nap, remember?" he said. "Imagine thinking you should lead us into a world-saving battle when you haven't slept in two days."

Despite her protestations, he frog-marched her down to the portal hall and virtually unlocked her door for her. "If I see that you've clocked in before a full eight hours have elapsed…" he threatened.

Amanda rolled her eyes. "You'll do what, report me to your boss?"

She shut the door on Ruger's smile. "Something like that," he murmured. Then he headed a few doors down, to his own place.

When he stepped through and opened the door, he was assailed with the delicious smell of roasting vegetables. He came in and hung his keys on the peg by the door, chuckling a little. "Only you," he said.

"I don't get much time for cooking when we're on the run," said Danilo, turning around. He put his knife down and leaned in for a kiss. Ruger put his arms around Danilo's shoulders, locking his fingers together at the back, enjoying the solid form against him.

Danilo smiled against his mouth. "So. Business first, or pleasure?"

"Why not both?" Ruger found his stomach was growling.

Danilo served the sweet potatoes up with an egg each and a side of tomatoes, lime, and coriander. He added a liberal dash of chicken salt—a staple in New Zealand and Australia—and settled in to give his report. "The Guardians know you're planning to turn back time on the Battle of Kirkjufell. Because Jayne's going to do it, and because she's got the backing of the goddesses, they don't think it's necessary to interfere. Mostly." He grimaced.

"Xiomara's still angry," Ruger guessed. He shouldn't be surprised. After her decades of cooperation with the TCO, he could understand why she felt betrayed. He couldn't agree, but he could understand.

"The truth is, Jayne's got the power of time travel whether we like it or not. The Guardians don't want to kill her as long as they think she's a force for good in the world. Her father is another matter. A lot of Guardians think he's deranged, or worse. I've managed to convince them that if we steal the time-travel technology from him, we can stop him. Especially if your lot jump in and do your part. So, while you're at the battle, we'll be at your lab. You might want some good Adepts on security that day."

Amanda's words flashed through Ruger's head. *Henry Thorne might be someone we have to take care of.* "Or maybe..." He tapped his fork on his plate. "Maybe we just make sure Quimby's out for the day, and you take care of it."

Danilo's eyebrows rose. "That's how you want to play it?"

"Let's just say Jayne's earned my confidence. Her father, not so much. We would have the TCO's support if he was removed from the premises and put in a nice safe Time Catch for a while."

Ruger pushed his chair back and put their plates in the dishwasher. Danilo came to help, and they cleaned the kitchen together. It surprised him how easily they fit in this space; Ruger had always lived alone and had thought he always would. Sometimes a man became too used to the way things were done.

Maybe that was why Danilo was good for him. "Let's leave the rest of it, yeah?" he said, catching Ruger's hand. Ruger let Danilo lead him over to the sofa, where they sat down in their usual spots—Ruger up on one side, with Danilo sprawled half across him. He let his fingers trace the tattoos on Danilo's arm, up to where they disappeared into his shirt sleeves.

"Don't go back." The words slipped out of him before he had time to think.

Danilo was still for a moment. "That would probably break my sacred oath," he said. "That smart?"

"I'm tired of being smart." Tired of thinking of what was best for the world. Ruger wanted to be selfish. He wanted to take Danilo somewhere with no battles, no bosses, not even cell reception. A place where they could just—be. He couldn't remember the last time he'd just *been himself.* Did he even know who that person was?

"You know," Danilo said, mock casual, with his head pressed against Ruger's chest and his eye fixed somewhere on the floor, "I lived next to my pocket for fifteen years. Went practically nowhere. I've got a lot of catching up to do if I want to see the world. And I'd say America's a good base for that. If there's anyone you know who's got space for an old Māori."

Ruger chuckled. "Come off it, you're not old."

Danilo twisted to look at him. "I'm older than you."

"Three months. Doesn't count at our age."

Their eyes locked. Danilo's were soft, brown, and vulnerable somehow.

"It's funny," Ruger said at last, in a voice just above a whisper. "I was just thinking how little time I spent in the Southern Hemisphere, and how much it might suit me."

"Well, I guess when this is all over, we've got options," Danilo remarked with a smile.

Ruger bent to kiss him again. *When this is all over.* He held the dream tightly.

CHAPTER
THIRTY-THREE

"Again."

The Disciples of Gaia fanned out around Jayne, rolling their shoulders and twirling their weapons. Jayne took a deep breath and gave Vivienne what she hoped was an encouraging smile. Things had been going well for them since the Rogues' return. Much better than they had between Sofia and Cillian, Sofia had confessed in a private moment. She'd seemed near tears, and Jayne wasn't sure what would make her feel better. Her sister was supposed to be the one who had everything under control: the steady partner, the baby, the job that wasn't possibly going to kill her. Jayne couldn't even reassure her that everything would get back to normal, because what if it didn't? What if Sofia and Cillian never were the same?

The difference became even starker now. A dark-skinned Disciple named Jeremy darted forward, quick as a whip. Before Jayne could even react, Vivienne was in front of him. She turned into a kangaroo in time to kick him five feet in the air, then twisted, shrinking and becoming a black snake that tangled around the feet of another Disciple named Anju. Jayne spun in time to deflect an attack from a third Disciple, and Hayden picked up a fourth, carrying him a good two hundred feet before gently depositing him on a hill. All around them, new Adepts and Aegis students watched what they were doing. Seo-Joon was taking notes on their performance.

"You can see how a Rogue and a Master who are truly in tune with each other work like two halves of the same body. Even Jayne's familiar is keeping out of the way." The admiration in his voice was warming—and a little embarrassing. Jayne was thrown off-kilter enough that she nearly got hit by a dulled arrow, but Vivienne dove in front of her and snatched it out of the air in hawk form.

"When did we get this good?" Jayne panted.

"We have always been this good," Vivienne replied simply, and her tone shocked Jayne again. Nothing smug or self-righteous about her now. She said it as though it were a known truth. "We have always been this good, but now our minds are truly devoted to the same purpose, and you've been bestowed with all of the totems, and that strengthens me as well. We're unstoppable."

As long as we can keep our thoughts straight, Hayden put in, wings flapping.

Enough out of you, Jayne told him. She dropped to the ground just in time to see someone throw a dummy grenade to surprise them. She opened her mouth to say *hound,* but Vivienne was already changing. A cheetah streaked across the field, ducking her head to snatch up the grenade before turning into her tigress form in order to swat the explosive as far from them as physically possible.

Jayne drew them back to the spot she'd marked in her mind. "Now," she murmured, and Vivienne charged back toward her. Her Fire totem blazed and blue flames burst from the ground, surrounding her like a wall. The Disciples pulled up short.

"Of course, we don't have anyone like Odin here," Isra said, giving the motion to stand down. "But I think we all did good work. Jayne, is that...the extent of your fire abilities?"

"Of course not," Jayne said, trying not to scoff. She didn't really want to use the full extent of her Fire totem, either. It wouldn't be fair, and she didn't want to hurt anyone before the battle.

Then Seo-Joon came trotting up to her. "How about a little demonstration?"

"Of the other totems?"

"It would be good practice," Vivienne told her, which only made her brow wrinkle more. The Vivienne who'd gone into Odin's portal would have sneered at the idea of Jayne showing off. Now she was...encouraging it?

"Fine. Practice run. Everybody stand back," Jayne said.

She closed her eyes, breathing in, connecting first to the earth, grounding herself. She called for Queen Medb and predictably heard no reply. That was a bit worrisome; she would need all the power of the Earth totem to make the volcano erupt. Vesta was next, and in answer Jayne felt a warm swirl of fire. A cold breeze and a few drops of rain lashed against Jayne's face when she called the storm, and she felt Freya's greeting. A moment later the warmth of the sun flickered against her eyelids, the blessing of Amaterasu.

And beneath that, she felt things growing and ungrowing, spooling and unspooling, warping and weaving, and heard the laughter of the maiden, the mother, and the crone.

Jayne opened her eyes. Around her the battlefield was frozen—no, not frozen, but moving so slowly that she could see the wingbeats of a dragonfly, the slow blink of Isra, moving in tiny increments, across the field away from Jayne. It was like her very own slo-mo Time Stop.

She called for the fire first. There was no volcanic base here, but it roared to life around her anyway. With another call she summoned the wind, and the flames were whipped into a fire spout that created a circle of charred grass around her. She leaned into the spirit of the fire, coaxing it brighter, hotter, angrier, then sending it spinning over the field in a dozen little fiery whips. She watched as everyone's eyes widened in slow motion, as the Disciples fought to change position and get out of the fire's path. But they were so slow it was nothing at all to divert the flames around them.

It wasn't easy work, though. Jayne estimated that she held the inferno for six or seven seconds of real time before a throbbing pain stabbed through her temple and she dropped her arms. The flames likewise dropped, scattering across the grass and starting little fires that the Disciples of Gaia hastened to stamp out.

The children stared at her. So did the adults. More than one mouth hung open.

"Well done," said Vivienne, dropping to the ground from her hawk form and turning into a human again. She favored Jayne with a smile that seemed completely genuine.

Now it was Jayne's turn to be open-mouthed.

The Adepts around her roared. Seo-Joon came forward, eyes shining, and clapped her on the shoulder. "I honestly don't think Odin will know what hit him," he said. "If you can do that—"

"We'll see." They'd underestimated Odin once before, and the results hadn't exactly been pleasing.

"We believe in you," Isra told her. "The Disciples have faith. And I will personally follow you into the field of battle as part of your team." Her wide, dark eyes shone with a fervor that made Jayne squirm. "You are blessed by the goddesses, Jayne Thorne. And you are worthy."

"I wouldn't know about that." Jayne glanced at Vivienne, but again, saw nothing but actual admiration.

She paused to get a drink, and her muscles chose that moment to quit working. She sat hard on the side of the hill and upended the rest of her water bottle over her head.

Vivienne was watching her, dark eyes sharp. Like Cillian, she'd cut her hair after coming out of the pocket, as if the experience had been a bad relationship she was eager to get behind her. Now she said, "I am tired. Would you like to have breakfast?"

Vivienne had never been the first to admit defeat. "Where did you have in mind?" Jayne asked.

"I wish—for canteen waffles." Vivienne's smile was self-conscious, uncertain. All the things Vivienne herself never was.

"Help an old lady up." Jayne stuck out her hand.

"You and I are in the same decade, Jayne." And *there* was that eye roll. Jayne never imagined she would miss it. She grinned.

Food was just what they needed before a long battle, and they portaled back and loaded their canteen plates with a little of everything. Jayne got waffles, bacon, a soft-boiled egg, and a stack of toast with yogurt and fruit in a separate bowl. Vivienne matched her, grabbing two rolls as well. She even poured herself a cup of coffee from the drip pot.

"You *must* be tired," Jayne joked. It was common knowledge that Vivienne Labelle was banned from every café in the area for criticizing their roasting and brewing capabilities and now had to use the Nashville portal when she wanted a cup of coffee that didn't, in her words, taste like "burnt sour socks."

"Mm." Vivienne took a drink, closing her eyes briefly. Then she smiled and reached for a few creamers and a pile of sugar sachets.

Jayne got herself a nearly serviceable cup of Earl Grey and they sat, tucking in. She took a few minutes to revel in the salty, crunchy bacon and the pillowy waffles, covered in maple syrup.

Then Vivienne took a long drink of coffee, set it down, and looked Jayne over frankly. *Here it comes,* Jayne thought.

"I like your scarf," Vivienne said, gesturing to the soft cotton-and-wool blend that ran in an ombre from white to silver to black. "Where did you get it?"

"That's it," said Jayne, a little too loudly. The few other diners in the canteen glanced at them. Vivienne blushed. Jayne tempered her volume. "What's wrong?"

"Why does anything have to be wrong?" Vivienne picked at her waffle.

"You compliment me on my fighting forms, and we're working together better than ever. You said something nice about my fashion sense. You're *drinking canteen coffee.* Something's wrong."

Vivienne opened her mouth to deny it again—then shut it again. Her eyes were suddenly wet. Oh no. Jayne reached across the table to take her arm. "I'm sorry," she said. "I didn't mean to make you cry."

"You can't imagine what it was like," Vivienne whispered.

"No, I can't," Jayne agreed, rubbing up and down her arms.

"I couldn't resist. Most days, I couldn't even think. Then I woke up and I remembered everything I'd done. People I tried to kill."

"Everyone knows you weren't acting under your own volition," Jayne tried.

Vivienne brushed it off. She took a moment to put her finger up to one perfect set of eyelashes at a time, flicking her tears away. She took another drink of coffee. In a voice somewhat less shaky she said, "When I woke up, the first thing I feared was that Tristan was dead. The second thing I feared was that he hated me. I realized...if I do not have Tristan, I do not have anyone. I am not very good at making friends, Jayne Thorne."

"I'm your friend," Jayne said, squeezing Vivienne's shoulder lightly. "And if I'm your friend, that means all my friends are your friends, too. In fact, I'm something better than your friend. I'm your sister. And that means that you can be as obnoxious about American coffee and American bread and American dress sense as you like, and I will always see you for the capable, intelligent, and powerful woman you are."

Vivienne's face broke into a smile, and for a moment it looked like the spirit of Amaterasu shone from her face. She didn't try to blink away her tears this time.

"And when we've gotten our revenge on Odin for putting you through hell, we are going to sit on my couch for a week and watch all the films that formed me as a kid. And we can give each other highlights and argue about magical theory and drive your brother crazy."

"I—thank you, Jayne." Vivienne sniffed and wiped her eyes. She didn't seem to care that she was messing up her mascara.

Jayne's phone beeped. When she saw Amanda's name on the screen, her stomach gave a funny sideways jolt, like it was trying to time-travel away from her breakfast. "It's time," she said.

THIRTY-FOUR

I t took some hours for the team to assemble from the Time Catches and pockets and crannies of the TCO. Eventually, the crack team was ready: Jayne stood with Tristan and Vivienne, Cillian and Sofia, Isra, Ruger, and Quimby. Behind them, Henry and Amanda were getting their tactical gear on. Amanda was trying to tell her TCO assistant how the armor was supposed to go, and Jayne could hear the assistant gritting her teeth from where she stood.

Her amusement at the situation didn't last long. "What are you doing in here? And wearing that?" she asked Trinity. Wow. Less than a week and she sounded like *that* sort of mom. But the sight of her twelve-year-old in tactical gear was different than a thin crop top or too short shorts.

"I have to come, Mama." Trinity was doing up her hair in a ponytail. "Grandmama and I are the lures."

"The what now?" Jayne exchanged a panicked glance with Tristan. His eyes blazed. He stepped forward.

Alexandra met him, hand up. "It is not up for debate," she said in her most imperious voice. "Odin wants *us*. There was a reason he kept the two of us trapped in the Torrent, you know.

He might not emerge from his pocket to deal with you, but he will absolutely come out if he sees me."

"Stuff you and your debates," Tristan said, and Alexandra reeled back like she'd been slapped. "This is my daughter, and you will *not* determine whether she leaps into danger."

"*Père.*" Trinity put a hand on his arm. She held a bow and arrow so confidently, Jayne thought. When had that happened? *How* had it happened? "Grandmama's right. I need to be there."

"You don't understand." Tristan knelt to look her in the eye. His gaze softened. He kept looking at her with wonder as if he couldn't really believe she was here. "If you are out there, your *maman* and I will not be focused on the mission. Our only job in the world will be protecting you."

"Correction." Alexandra poked him with the edge of a staff. His nostrils flared. "Jayne's mission remains the same, for if she kills Odin, Trinity and I will be protected for all time. It will be *your* job to ensure your daughter comes to no harm while the battle is ongoing."

"This is a bad idea," Tristan said. He rounded on Amanda. "Did you authorize this?"

"This plan is full of bad ideas," Amanda replied. "But Alexandra has a point. Plus, Trinity has more skill and practice than many of our adult Adepts. She's been battle-trained at Aegis for years."

"That doesn't matter, she is still a *child*," Tristan began hotly.

"As are all the young ones from Aegis."

Henry's watch beeped. He sucked in a breath. "We'd better go. The window has opened."

Tristan stood, shoulders rigid with fury. "No. You're not coming," he said to Trinity.

His daughter gave him a pitying look that resembled Jayne so much, Jayne was caught between laughter and horror.

"Sorry, *Père*. This has to happen. And you can't actually stop me."

Tristan stared at her for a moment, frustration and loss and fear playing across his face. Behind him, Isra was the first through the portal, directed by Henry. Cillian and Sofia went next. Then Alexandra, her steel-tipped staff tapping on the ground like a cane.

"Are you going to risk the world?" Amanda told Tristan sharply. Trinity raised a brow. Now *she* looked more like Jayne than ever.

Jayne put her hand on his arm. "They're right, my love. We need every weapon we can utilize to beat him. My grandmother and Trinity have knowledge that can help stop him. They must come with us."

Tristan groaned under his breath and looked heavenward. "She gets this from your side of the family," he told Jayne darkly before stalking away, his hand on Trinity's shoulder, firing instructions at her. "You will stay behind me at all times. You will follow my lead and obey every order. You will—" Whatever he said next was lost as they went through the portal together.

"We'll have some fun family discussions if we get through this," Jayne said.

Vivienne put a hand on her arm. "We will make sure she is protected," she said, squeezing. "We think as one."

And with that, Jayne took a huge, steadying breath and went back to Kirkjufell for the third time.

They emerged on an empty field. Jayne located the nearest active volcano, a few miles away, and thought at Hayden, *Remember the view.* He stirred in her mind, ready to be drawn forth. Then she took a breath. "Link hands, everyone."

Amanda had stressed that their objective must not be to change the outcome of the battle, no matter how the Rogues had suffered. No one knew how all their carefully laid plans might change with even one tiny adjustment to the timeline. Jayne closed her eyes and let the Norns take her through the tangled tapestry of the past, selecting a spot toward the end of the battle, moments before Odin had put his Command spell on the Rogues. She held the spot in her mind, folded it—

The sounds of battle roared through the air. Jayne instinctively threw herself to the earth and felt the *whoosh* of a Wraith flying overhead.

"Civilians, behind me," Amanda snapped, stepping in front of Alexandra. Ruger and Tristan made a wall between Alexandra and Trinity and Henry and the battle. Jayne swallowed her heart as she watched an Adept get slashed from naval to nose by a nearby Wraith. She knew, she *knew* she could not save everyone. But she so wanted to.

"We will not have to wait for long," Alexandra called. "Odin will have felt us."

As if called by her words, there was a shimmering in the air, and two forms dropped to the ground.

Neither of them were Odin.

Gina Labelle straightened. She was in her human form, her wild hair swinging and her eyes nearly black with hatred and the gloom of the battle. Behind her, Alastor the Wraith stretched to his full height, snapping his wings open.

"You..." Jayne stopped. Alastor hadn't been at the Battle of Kirkjufell, surely. And Gina—she chanced a quick look at the battlefield, but that was no help. It was a mass of bodies, and even a lioness would be hard to distinguish.

"Me." Gina's eyes slipped past Jayne and she smiled cruelly at Henry. "We did not manage to kill you. A pity. But we did get something out of all this."

"Time travel," Henry whispered. "You stole my notes."

"And we will bring your head back to the Allfather. I must confess, Henry, I was frustrated not to have my revenge on you, but I feel lucky now. I can take my time and kill the whole family. The father, the grandmother, the irritating sisters..." Her gaze fell on Trinity, and the smile sharpened. "And the young one."

Jayne sprang forward, but Vivienne was faster. The tigress hit her mother full in the shoulders. Gina's expression gave way to shock, and a moment later the lioness was back, flinging Vivienne away. Vivienne changed midair into a fly and disappeared.

Gina was human again in a flash. "Rogues. Hear me! You are making a mistake," she called to the empty air around them. "You are throwing away your lives, agreeing to serve a lesser people. Odin has offered us land, freedom, and your Masters as our slaves instead. We will own humans the way humans owned us, for so long."

Alastor's great maw opened. "Freedom," he rumbled through sharp and broken teeth.

"Nah, mate. I've seen your freedom." Cillian squeezed Sofia's shoulder. A moment later he was the wolf, and he attacked. He slammed into Alastor and fastened his teeth around the Wraith's throat. Alastor snarled and clawed at him. Sofia swept forward and pulled her knives from the air.

Jayne moved to help with Gina, but Amanda's voice rang sharp in her ear. "Odin, Jayne! We must draw out Odin."

Odin. Jayne ran her hand over the patch of scaly skin on her arm, and felt Hayden stir again in her mind. She braced herself for the pain of him pulling free. He spun into the air and materialized into a dragon that rivaled Alastor for size.

She clambered on his back and they took off. Below her, the battle shifted. Alastor twisted and caught Cillian by the scruff of his neck, then howled as Sofia plunged a dagger into his side.

"Viv?" Jayne panted. "Need help?"

I think this is a family matter, Vivienne said. She was back in

251

tigress form, she and Gina circling each other, both spitting and snarling.

"Don't you remember what I said?" Jayne breathed deep and put her finger down on the imaginary map of time. The moment stopped, with Gina coiled and ready to spring. "We're sisters. Your mother never did what was best for you. Now I'm going to help you do what's best for you."

Jayne swooped low on Hayden and used her staff to tag Gina on the side. The Knockback spell in the staff tossed the lioness like she was a stuffed toy. A moment later, time was back on track again, and Gina lay on the ground ten feet away and confused.

Vivienne leapt.

She slammed her mother's head into the ground. *I am no one's servant,* she hissed in Jayne's mind. *I finally know what it is to be equal, Mother. And it is nothing you have ever given me. You are the ghost of my past, and I do not want you.*

She brought her claws down across Gina's belly, and the skin ripped with a sickening sound and an even more sickening smell. Jayne wheeled up, trying her best to lend her Rogue strength.

She didn't need it. Gina Labelle was no more. She hoped Vivienne didn't regret being the one to destroy her.

It was as though Gina's death was the signal Odin needed. Jayne felt the earth shift and shake. She looked out over the field. A shadow was growing behind the pocket, larger and larger until a great horned head emerged.

The Allfather stood before them, enormous. His head was the size of a boulder. Each of his arms looked as long as Jayne's entire body. And when he opened his wings, they were at least as wide as Hayden's.

His one black eye fixed on her, and a thrill of adrenaline shot through her.

That's right. Come get me.

The monster's wings pumped once and took him into the air.

Jayne's familiar flew for their life.

Hayden sped over the moss-covered land, casting a dark shadow. An instant later a second shadow appeared right behind her, and the dragon curled into an upward barrel roll, narrowly missing a swipe from Odin's claws. Odin was *fast,* faster than anything she'd ever fought before.

Pain seared in her as Odin caught the tip of Hayden's tail and sliced it neatly off. *Keep him locked on you,* Hayden told her, gasping in pain that she felt deep in her own body. *Don't let him think about Alexandra or Trinity.*

Right. He had to think that Jayne was the biggest threat. "That the best you can do?" she gasped and aimed a Freeze spell at him. She missed.

The totems, Hayden shouted. Jayne called up a whipping wind, reminding Odin what she had—and what he wanted. The wind slammed against Odin, putting him a fraction of a degree off course—enough to throw off his aim when he swiped for her.

"All this power," he snarled in a voice that made her head pound. She squeezed Hayden with her knees tightly and clapped her hands over her ears. "You have all this power, and you conjure a little breeze? You run away? The world has truly become a pitiful place if you are the greatest Master in it." A spell whizzed over her head, and Hayden flipped over so she could spin a Block. Odin's next attack bounced neatly off it. "I will build a world full of Masters. Of Wraiths and Rogues and Adepts who understand that power is power, and whoever has it makes the rules."

Jayne risked a glance at the volcano. Still a good two miles away. *Any way we could go faster?* she thought, even though

Hayden didn't need the prompt. They sped up. Behind her she felt Vivienne's rage and triumph. Alastor was dead.

Odin roared in anger, and spells whipped past them. Hayden jerked back and forth in the air in evasive maneuvers, trying to present a difficult target. The mountain sped closer and closer—

And Hayden was hit with a spell Jayne couldn't even name as they came upon the slope. He simply disintegrated from beneath her, and she tumbled though the empty air. Luckily he'd been angling them in for landing, and she hit the ground with less force than she might have otherwise.

She screamed his name, wrenched up her sleeve, but felt nothing. It was as if he had simply ceased to exist.

Rage helped her scramble to her feet just as Odin slammed into the ground with enough force to shake the whole mountain. She barely had time to summon a Block before his first attack hit it, hard. The next attack was close on its heels, and she threw herself to the side to avoid it.

She took a step farther up the mountain. The closer Odin was to the top, to the eruption, the better.

Odin's eye narrowed. "You're nothing," Jayne gasped. "Imagine being as old as you are and sacrificing anything that might have made you a decent being, just so you can get your ass kicked by a librarian." She swung the staff with all her power.

He knocked it from her hands like it was a toothpick, and she a child. Then his anger smoothed over into a laugh, a deep rumbling thing that sounded like a rockslide. "Nothing, am I? I will be the master of your children and your children's children. I will be your destruction, and I will be your eternal sorrow."

Keep talking, Jayne thought, stumbling back. She felt a growing heat within her—the heat of the volcano, latent but ready to answer her call.

"I do not think I will kill you, impudent Master. Not yet. I will tuck you away in a rotting pocket, allow you to go mad on your own. I will tell your father to find a way to pull those wretched totems from your head, and he will do it, because he will think you can be saved. And when we have removed the totems, I will kill you in front of him. But not before you see everything that you have wrought."

He spun his hands. Between them sprang a golden cage, the same sort of cage that had held the Norns.

"Been there, destroyed that," Jayne told him.

She closed her eyes. *It's now,* she begged the goddesses and reached within.

She dug her feet deep into the soil, calling for Medb. She reached for the scorching fire of the volcano, calling on Vesta. She reached for the power of the storm and the power of spirit. *You were bright and angry once,* she thought at the volcano. *You were the mouth of hell.* She felt the ground shake.

There was no plume of ash. There was no warning. The fire spewed everywhere, and in that moment Jayne realized that while she might hit Odin, she herself had no way out.

Time began to crawl. Odin's eye followed the curve of the magma in agonizingly slow awe, mouth opening in a roar. Hayden would not stir in Jayne's mind. She needed to get out of here on foot, which meant she had to be faster than the lava—

Two talons fastened around her shoulders, and Vivienne snatched her right off the side of the mountain, pumping her wings.

"I didn't know eagles could get this large," Jayne gasped, looking at the expanse of wing above her. It glowed golden and auburn.

"It is a roc," Vivienne replied. "If Cillian can turn into a mythological creature, so can I."

"No argument from me." Especially not when it saved her life.

They sped over the land. Jayne watched the original battle unfold beneath them. The Rogues hadn't yet been called to the pocket. The crack team had a few Wraiths to deal with, but Isra and Ruger seemed to be handling it. Everyone else's eyes took in Vivienne as she set Jayne down gently.

Jayne grinned. "I'm back—"

A roar of rage drew their attention. They all looked past her, toward the mountain. Alexandra murmured, "I would not celebrate yet."

Jayne turned. The entire mountain was covered in lava, a shimmering glow of orange and red.

Except for one horned shadow that stood tall on the mountainside. Odin was untouched.

"Impossible," she breathed.

He raised a fist. She saw the glint and flicker of spells as he cast them, one after the other, and fire began to flow as fast as a flooding river down the mountain toward them.

"We need to run," said Amanda.

"To where?" Ruger asked. The portals back home were closer to the lava than they were. Adepts were beginning to notice; they started screaming.

"The pocket. Retreat!" Alexandra shouted and took off with a speed that belied her age. Trinity ran after her without question, which left Jayne no choice but to follow. Fire began to fall like rain; Jayne called on her Wind totem to blow it away. Red-hot pebbles spattered the grass, hissing and cracking as they hit earth. Bursts of fire leaped around them.

The pocket of Rogues flared and sealed just as Alexandra got to the base of Kirkjufell Mountain. Amanda bent and put her hands on her knees. "Now what?" she gasped.

"We must go inside," Alexandra said. "There, Jayne will unfold time, and the pocket will be empty."

"How do we pull that off?" Amanda asked. "The pocket's sealed, and Odin's the Guardian."

Alexandra lifted her head. "That monster's no Guardian. He can't control this pocket." Golden magic glowed at the tips of her fingers, and the mouth of the pocket began to split again in a slice of light. "*I* am the Guardian of the Kirkjufell pocket."

Amanda, Jayne, and Ruger looked at one another. "If we go in there and unfold time, he's won," Jayne said. "He'll have had control of the world from this moment."

"He's won anyway, Jayne." Amanda looked back toward the volcano. Fire was pouring into the sky in one gigantic spout. "You couldn't kill him. We have no other option. And if we stay here, he won't spare us."

Jayne took a deep breath. Trinity moved to clamber through, but she put a stern hand on her daughter's shoulder. "Me first," she said.

"All of us together. As quickly as possible," Isra suggested. Jayne nodded.

They went one after the other, leaping through the pocket into the snarling chaos of Rogues. Alexandra was last, closing the pocket behind her with a sort of Sewing spell. "*Now,* Jayne," she cried, just as the first few wild eyes of the Rogues turned on them.

Jayne unfolded.

And they stepped into a void.

CHAPTER

THIRTY-FIVE

Suddenly, they were alone.

The Torrent had calmed to a gently flowing river that came up to their calves. Nothing at all like the rock-laden, black stream that Jayne had created. The pocket seemed at once tiny and vast, consisting of the river and only the river, flowing from eternity to eternity. It was much like the primeval mound myths from ancient cultures from around the world. Water, then earth, then life.

Except they were living in the opposite of the beginning of all life. They were at the end of all life. They were lost in this vast empty space, the whole team, and if they ventured out of their pocket, Odin was sure to destroy them. If they went back in time to defeat him, they'd start creating Time Wraiths and destroying the fabric of reality.

They were screwed.

Jayne felt her energy shut off like a switch. She sat down heavily in the Torrent, feeling the magic flow around her back and ribs. She barely felt Tristan's hand on her shoulder and closed her eyes against the tears. "What happened?" she whispered.

"You tell *us*."

Jayne opened her eyes again, half out of surprise. Amanda's and Ruger's eyebrows were raised, while Tristan's hand tightened on her shoulder. Vivienne snarled. Henry found something of sudden and all-encompassing interest in his bag. Trinity said, *"Grandmama."*

Alexandra stood, arms crossed, refusing to even look embarrassed that she'd said it. "Well?"

Jayne didn't have enough energy to be rankled by her stern expression. As Tristan opened his mouth to tell Alexandra off, she squeezed his hand in warning. She didn't think her grandmother was asking her out of anger. "Hayden was vaporized. But just before he was killed, he told me to call on the totems. I did. I...called the fire. Just as Vesta instructed. I called for the wind and the storm. I asked them all to help me."

"And did they?" Alexandra asked, just as Jayne realized it herself.

"No. Not all of them. And without all of them at once...I couldn't do it."

Queen Medb hadn't responded to her call. Medb never responded. And when Jayne spoke of having all the totems, she lied, didn't she? Because there was one goddess who had never lent Jayne her power, not truly.

"Medb," she breathed. "I need to talk to Medb."

"Why?" Vivienne asked, still in her Rogue form. *"She is the goddess of the earth, not flame. Why is she so important?"*

"Maybe because volcanoes are both earth and fire. Maybe because I just need her power. Whatever the answer, she has to be the key." Because if she wasn't, Jayne had no idea what else to do.

"So you must talk to Medb. How are you going to do it?" Alexandra asked.

"I..." Jayne closed her eyes, dug her fingers into what passed for the ground in this pocket. Called to Medb.

No response. As usual. "I don't know. She has always been reluctant to chitchat. I thought, though, that in a moment of great duress she would show up. She has her own problems to deal with, you know. We aren't her priority."

Alexandra stared at her long and hard for a moment. She sighed through her nose and sat on a rock. "Then we will all die here."

~

SOFIA GLARED AT ALEXANDRA, but a warning pat from Cillian told her not to interfere. How could anyone place all this blame on Jayne? Her sister was the only reason they'd gotten as far as they did. Jayne had offered up everything, over and over again, and the only thanks she got was a dismissal for not being good enough?

"It'll sort itself out, love," Cillian told her softly. She sighed and leaned her head on his shoulder. Out of the corner of her eye she saw Trinity creep forward. Tristan sat and stuck out his arm, and the girl folded into it with a practiced ease. He stroked her hair almost absent-mindedly, putting his other arm around Jayne and pulling her close. Sofia was struck with an odd feeling, and it took her a moment to sort everything out.

She was jealous.

She'd never sit like this with her own children, comforting them in times of anxiety. She got pregnant first and she didn't even know if she'd meet the baby. She didn't even know what it would do to the baby, to spend time in this pocket. It wasn't a Time Catch in the same way as Aegis, but what did that mean, exactly? And did it even matter?

"Surely we can get out of here another way," Amanda said

after a few awkward moments. "Don't you have an entrance and an exit for the pocket? Or is it one way only?"

"Only one, and Odin is keeping the pocket sealed from his side," Alexandra replied. "He cannot get in, for I have been called to be the Guardian of this pocket, but he can do much to keep us here. It is taking most of my power to keep him out."

"What sort of portal could we put together?" Amanda asked.

"To what purpose? No matter where we go, Odin's forces will be lying in wait," Isra said. Amanda shot her a disgusted look, and Sofia half expected her to go on about needing solutions and not more problems.

"Well, resident genius." Amanda spun on Henry, who cringed. "What can you give me?"

"I...I don't have anything from the lab with me," he admitted.

Amanda began to pace. "I refuse to believe that this is how I die," she said, clenching her fist and running the other hand through her hair. "Stuck in a pocket with the smartest person I know and the most powerful Master I know. There must be something the two of you can cook up! Jayne, you can control the elements."

"She won't come," Jayne murmured, sounding dazed.

"Make her," Amanda snarled.

"I'm not her boss. I can't just give her orders," Jayne snapped back.

Sofia deflated against Cillian while her sister and her boss bickered. This was not how she'd imagined spending her last moments. Her fingers slid between Cillian's thick, rough ones. "I'm glad we got to be together again," she murmured.

"Me too." He turned and kissed her ear, then tucked a bit of her blonde-silver hair behind it. "I'm glad we got to see each other for who we really are. I'm glad we got to anticipate that"

—he gestured to Tristan and Trinity—"even if we won't experience it." Sofia felt a fresh wave of longing and envy. "And we did amazing things in our day, didn't we, Sof?"

They had. Their legacy would be one of learning and nurturing, and Sofia couldn't think of anything that would have made her prouder. Aegis would stand tall because of them. "Life could have been worse," she whispered. "Even if I'm not glad it's over, I don't regret anything."

"That totem was given to you for a reason," Amanda was shouting. "You can and you *will* get it in line."

"She entrusted it to me. That doesn't mean she's suddenly my servant." Jayne sounded close to tears. "It's a two-way street. She has to be willing."

"I've had enough of this. You control every other element. You control *time*. Surely you can summon one dead hag—" At Jayne's horrified look, she tried again "—I mean warrior queen to you."

"Well, I can't."

Trinity sat up. She had an odd gleam in her eye.

"I've spent every waking moment since I learned of magic trying to save the world." Jayne palmed furiously at her face. "I've pushed myself to the limit. I've faced death and defied it. Time and time again. I can't go any further now."

"So what?" Amanda threw up her hands. "Is that anything Ruger and I haven't done? The rest of the TCO? We've all been to the abyss, Jayne."

"Mama," said Trinity. No one was listening. No one but Sofia.

"You're talking to a pocket full of people who have sacrificed everything for the greater good. Don't wail like you're some martyr. I offered you a job, and I told you what it might take from you. And you said yes."

"You never told me that you expected me to solve every single problem at the TCO!" Jayne shouted.

"Children," said Sofia in her most severe headmistress voice.

They stopped. Jayne's lips were pressed together so hard that all blood had left them. Amanda looked shocked to be addressed in such a way. Her anger would probably come later if Sofia let it.

Sofia wouldn't let it. "Trinity has something to say," she said.

Trinity darted a quick, nervous glance her way, then swallowed. "Well, Mama can travel in time," she said. "And Medb lived once, didn't she? So maybe the best thing to do is go back in time to find her."

THIRTY-SIX

Everyone in the pocket was silent for a long moment. Jayne felt her breath catch somewhere in her throat. Of *course* she should go back in time to confront Medb. But—

"Your hypothesis needs expanding." Alexandra stood and began to pace, summoning her walking stick to help her. "What is your fold point?"

"Um." Trinity darted a quick glance at Jayne, who nodded, smiling with encouragement. "The Bronze Age?"

"The Bronze Age is a very broad point for a very large fold. The sort of power that would require is beyond even your mother's goddess-enhanced capabilities," Alexandra said.

"I mean, we haven't tested the spell to see how far back I can go..." Jayne started.

Alexandra shot her a look. "Trust me." Jayne narrowed her eyes. Why did she get the feeling her grandmother was keeping something from her? "In any case, the time for such tests is long past. We must get this right the first time."

Jayne closed her eyes and brought up the invisible map of time. The second she did, she realized Alexandra was right: The days around them were clear, mapped out in branches upon branches, easy to select like she was picking through a box of chocolates. Going back a few weeks made things fuzzier, and a few years even worse. "But I time-traveled with Dad to Colonial Virginia without any trouble at all," she said, opening her eyes.

"And where were you aiming to go?" Alexandra asked.

Jayne furrowed her brow. "Nowhere," she confessed. "Or rather, anywhere. I was taking Dad away from some...issues."

"So." The staff tapped. "We must find the correct fixed point for Medb, and we must ensure Jayne has enough power to get there."

Henry bit his lip. He glanced at Isra, Amanda, and Ruger. Then he reached into his bag. "I think this might help," he said.

Jayne sighed when she recognized the Time Reverse, version one. "We talked about this, Dad," she said.

"We can modify it to amplify your Fold spell," Henry argued. "That should only take a few spell adjustments."

"It will not be enough. Human power will need to supplement and support Jayne," Alexandra declared.

Tristan squeezed her shoulder. "I will give everything," he said.

Everything? Was this going to kill him? Jayne opened her mouth to object, but Alexandra got there first. "You will not, young man. You will ward off Odin's attack while *I* supply the power." She turned to face the entrance of the pocket. The line of her magic still dotted it, like a line of mending done with the wrong color of thread. "The moment he feels any sort of weakness, he will come for us. You *must* hold him off."

"Surely if you can keep Odin from invading the pocket, you should remain focused on that," Tristan said.

"Jayne will need a lot of power," Alexandra replied. "More than you can give. Trust me, Tristan Labelle, I am a far more powerful Master than you. This is what must be."

I think arrogance runs in the Thorne family, Vivienne snorted.

"Hey!" Jayne replied without thinking, before realizing Vivienne was still in Rogue form. No one else had heard the insult. The tigress chuffed at her paws.

"So...we have power. But we need to know where Jayne's going. And when, exactly. Right?" Amanda said. She looked at Sofia, Cillian, and Jayne. "Between the native Irishman and the two history nerds, surely you must have some idea."

"Don't look at me." Cillian leaned back. "History was never my thing at school."

Sofia puffed up her cheeks and blew out a long stream of air. "Jayne, you told me once the Táin Bó Cúailnge is set in the first century. We do know that Queen Medb wasn't just a legend,, because she gave Jayne her totem. But when did she exist? She could have lived in the first century, or before, or after, and any number of events could have been pushed together for narrative cohesion. Since the epic was first written down in the Middle Ages, it's hard to know how far back the oral tradition goes, so it's impossible to nail down her exact dates."

Jayne blinked. It wasn't often her sister had the chance to pull out all the professorial stops.

"She sounds just like your father." Tristan sounded trepidatious. "But with books."

"Is a hundred-year gap enough?" Jayne asked Alexandra.

She chewed on the inside of her cheek. "It's not ideal," she allowed. "If you overshoot you will have to fold time again, which means I must lend you power for a second trip. I am not sure I have it in me, Jayne. We need to be more precise."

"Grandmama. Mama." Small fingers slipped through Jayne's. Trinity squeezed her fingers lightly and smiled at her great-grandmother. "I know how to find her."

"You do? How?" Jayne asked, then saw the look in Alexandra's eyes. The old woman already knew this fact, and she'd been keeping it from them. Which meant Jayne probably wouldn't like it.

"Trinity takes after her mother and aunt," Alexandra began.

"Impulsive?" Ruger muttered.

"Disobedient toward her superiors?" Amanda suggested.

"Destructively creative with her spell work?" Tristan said.

"Or creatively destructive," Cillian put in. Then he said, "Ow," very softly. Sofia had punched him on the arm.

"All of these things, yes. But she studies—will study—the magically arcane at Aegis. She has a better understanding of slipping through time than perhaps anyone, and that is most likely related to you, Jayne. Trinity has..." Alexandra grimaced. "...located people previously lost to time. It is her specialty. A power unknown to Masters and Adepts alike."

"Are you saying our daughter is some sort of magical bloodhound?"

"Nothing so crude as that, Jayne. She has the power of *Temporum Vestigium*—timefinding. It is rare, a lost magic from the beginnings of time itself. The Norns are the only ones who've ever witnessed a timefinder before, and even they cannot completely explain the power. It's something you won't even find in your books, Jayne, a talent known only to those who are of the Torrent."

Jayne looked at her daughter with new eyes. If she squinted, she could see a liminal green glow around her body. An aura of the Torrent. Of time itself.

"I can lead you to Medb," Trinity explained with a shy smile. "I don't have to know exactly *when* she is, but I can find her."

Jayne met Tristan's eyes. They were brilliantly blue, like he was trying not to cry. He shook his head minutely. "Is this dangerous?" she asked.

"As dangerous as your traveling there is," Alexandra said. "If you are lost to time, you are lost forever."

"But with me there, Mama won't get lost. That's the point. And we're not traveling back to some horrible time to get killed. We're going to talk to a queen in her palace," Trinity argued. She turned to Jayne. "Mama, please? This is why I'm here. This is how I help."

"But I can't put you on a dangerous mission." Jayne tried to pitch her voice soft. "You're a kid. My kid."

"Not if we don't save the world." Trinity threw her arms wide. "We have to get out of here, don't we? Otherwise you'll never have me, and this is the only timeline in which I'll exist anymore."

Tristan put a hand on Jayne's shoulder, and a hand on Trinity's. "What if I lose both of you?" he whispered. His eyes were so liquid they made Jayne want to cry.

"You won't." Trinity looked up at both of them, her face serious, and in that expression Jayne saw not just the twelve-year-old daughter she'd never known, but the young woman Trinity would grow up to be. Thoughtful, adult. Probably still mischievous. "You don't know me yet, but I know you. I know your story. I know how much you sacrificed for this world." She turned back to Jayne. "You taught me what was right. It's what we have to do. So now I want to do what Mama and Père have taught me."

Jayne fought with the lump in her throat and lost. Today was just a crying sort of day. At least she was crying with pride now, and not despair. Trinity looked awkward for a moment, then added, "Besides, Grandmama would never let me go on a mission where my life was actually in peril. She's a very strict teacher."

Tristan opened his arms, and Trinity came into them. He squeezed her tight and bent to murmur something in her ear. Jayne turned to Alexandra to give them some privacy. "What's your take on this?"

"I cannot think of another way to ensure that you find Medb," Alexandra admitted. "And Trinity is right: You can avoid battle, and you won't be there long enough to get sick without recourse to medicine. But it will require more power if we are to send two people."

"I believe that's where I come in," said Henry. He held up the Time Reverse. "Between the machine and me, we ought to take care of it." Alexandra shot him an appraising look. "The Norns did tell me I would do this," he said quietly.

A cold fist formed in Jayne's stomach. "Dad? What are you talking about?"

He put his hands on her arms. "I asked them how I could help save you. This was their answer. Jayne..." He blinked rapidly. She recognized the expression—he had a lot to say and little time. "Be careful," he said.

Sofia and Cillian hugged her next. Amanda shook her hand. "I don't mean to be a bitch, Jayne, but—don't come back without that totem in working order."

"To be fair, getting stuck in the past would probably be preferable to the present with Odin," Jayne tried to joke. At least she'd have her daughter there. Even if her partner would be lost to her forever.

Ruger stuck out his hand. Then he used it to pull her into a hug. "Don't listen to her," he muttered. "We want you back."

Jayne felt a flush of warmth. A fresh spate of tears trickled from her eyes.

She turned to Tristan. He lay a hand on her cheek and kissed her softly. "Come back to me," he whispered against her lips.

"I promise." She met his blue gaze and willed for him to see it in her eyes, in her slight nod, in every line of her body—she *would* return. And she'd take care of their daughter, too.

"The moment Odin realizes you are gone, he will make his

move," Alexandra told her. "You must endeavor to return in the same instant you left. We...we will all need your power."

Alexandra and Henry met each other's eyes and nodded. Again, there was something they weren't telling Jayne. "What are you two planning?" she said.

"Nothing." Henry blinked and leaned away. Classic guilty move.

"We will tell you when you return," said Alexandra in her most regal voice. "Begone, granddaughter."

"I didn't realize anyone said stuff like that anymore," Jayne muttered, squeezing Trinity's hand.

"Yeah," Trinity said. "Grandmama's real old-school."

Jayne closed her eyes.

And folded.

THIRTY-SEVEN

The Allfather stood atop his volcano, watching lava chase the pitiful Adepts who would dare defy him. Beautiful. Everything was beautiful. The slate sky roiled with energy, the shrieks and cries of death rose to his ears like a symphony. His bones sang with power, so much power that no one could possibly sense the vulnerability within him. Ice and snow and fire, the battlefield red with the blood of his enemies, and the fiery warmth of the magma coursing around him. His Wraiths, and his Rogues, and the world at his feet.

He was invincible.

The little time-traveling team had been easily dispatched, shoved into a pocket where they could starve to death or return to the field to face death by Wraith. They were no longer a danger to him. The rest of the forces assembled against him were scattered, and those who didn't succumb to him now were faced with the inevitability of his might. He had waited long for this moment; he could wait a little longer.

An energy signature seemed to surge from the pocket. Curious. He probed at it with his magic; the pocket opened. Curiouser.

They were relentless, he could admit that.

But he was Odin, all-knowing, all-powerful, the Allfather, and he would not be thwarted.

Well, then. He'd like to eliminate the pesky Jayne Thorne and her friends once and for all. And, it seemed, there was no time like the present.

He chuckled at his joke and strode across the field.

THIRTY-EIGHT

P ower spun around Jayne and Trinity as they sank into the spell, launching them back in time at a rate that left Jayne feeling quite like she'd left her stomach behind. Almost as if a roller coaster was swooping her body through the air, though she hadn't moved her feet from the ground. She didn't actually know *when* she was going, so she began the fold at around the first-century mark, pulling the spell along behind her, ready to press down at any moment. The world around her and Trinity dissolved into mist. For the first time, she got a sense of movement, maybe because she had no end destination; she merely moved and would keep moving until she jumped out of the spell or hit the end of time itself. A bubbling sound uncurled on the air—Trinity laughing.

Events flashed before her, vague things she knew from Ancient History classes. The Vikings, the Romans. The world turned wilder and greener. The spell began to pull at her, urging her to stop, to pull over in some time or another. "Not yet," she heard Trinity call, and she absolutely had to trust her daughter on this. Trinity held tight to her hand, and Jayne pushed them past time after time, epoch after epoch.

The sense of rushing backward began to drag on her. She was running out of spell, and she quickly tried to fold again so that they hopped through one time and out into another, but the spell seemed to hate that and resisted, forcing them back into the flow. They paused for a long moment on a green field, and Jayne stumbled, almost losing her focus and rooting them in whatever time this was.

"Come on!" Trinity pulled hard, and for the first time in their little adventure, Jayne saw fear on her daughter's face. She forced herself to follow. She couldn't do this much longer, even with the added power of Henry and Alexandra—but she couldn't fail, either.

"Here! Now. Now, Mama!" Trinity yanked on her hand, and they stumbled into a verdant world together.

Jayne collapsed on a hilltop covered in dew. She took in a great lungful of air, then another, before she allowed herself to open her eyes.

It was dark, but the air was alive. At first she thought she was still in the pocket, because the Torrent sparkled all around them. Magic caressed her skin in welcome, and the power within her grew. She looked up at a sky of unfamiliar stars and gasped. She couldn't remember ever having seen the Milky Way so clearly. The stars were so thick they were a blanket across the sky. An aurora borealis glowed pink and green, waving at her from the horizon. She heard the sea, the water singing as it splashed against the rocks. She felt peace from the Earth, vivid and tangible.

This is what the world had been like before magic had been throttled. Before Odin placed his curse on the Torrent.

She sat up. The historian in her had suspicions about the little mound of earth they'd landed on, and she nearly groaned. "Don't tell me this is Medb's tomb," she said. They couldn't have come all this way just to attend the queen's funeral.

Trinity rolled her eyes, though she was smiling. "Give me some credit, Mama." She hopped to her feet and extended a hand to Jayne, who took it. "She's definitely alive. And she's around here somewhere."

Trinity closed her eyes and turned, swinging her face one way, then the other. Jayne took the opportunity to look around. This was clearly tended land: There were tilled fields on one side, and the trees had been tidied into little copses. Night birds sang and squawked to each other, and the chirping of the grasshoppers was riotous. The world was both emptier and fuller than Jayne's: She knew there were far fewer people on the Emerald Isle during this time period, but the crack of branches and the sound of rustling leaves told her there were far more animals here.

But the real difference was the Torrent. It lapped gently over the ground like a transparent sea, a flow of magic that answered to Jayne's call with a cluster of sparkling lights that rose and formed a ruffling Wind spell when she waved her hand through the air. She suddenly understood why the Kingdom had wanted this. What her mother had been seeking. A world unmade and untamed. It felt so right.

"Mama." Trinity jerked her head. "Don't call attention to us."

Jayne stopped playing.

Trinity led her toward a copse of trees, and Jayne was glad for the combat boots that kept the moisture from soaking into her socks. "We're going to look more than a little out of place," she realized aloud.

"That might work to our advantage," Trinity replied. "We did come out of time in the era of the Táin. Lots of people fighting around here. Our odd clothing choice might make them think twice."

"Think twice about what, stabbing us?" Jayne laughed. Trinity didn't answer. Which meant they *might* be stabbed.

As Trinity led them through the trees, Jayne caught sight of the golden lick of campfires between the trunks. The sounds of men laughing and speaking in rough brogue reached their ears, and as they drew closer Jayne saw they had their swords out, sharpening and polishing. Some of them had taken off their boots. They passed around a jug of something, stopping in their work to take a swig.

Jayne sucked a breath through her teeth. "Shoot. It occurs to me that I don't speak ancient Gaelic," she said.

Trinity's smile was smug and mischievous in the way that only twelve-year-olds could manage. "Good thing you've got me, then, isn't it?" she said, and strode through the trees, hailing the men in lilting tones.

Jayne was quick to follow, reaching for her staff. It grew from the Torrent and solidified comfortably in her hand before she'd finished visualizing it. If this was magic back in Medb's time, no wonder she'd been considered a goddess.

The men had all leapt to their feet at the sight of a girl in camouflage pants and a Kevlar vest. Trinity had evidently asked them a question. She looked from man to man, and when none of them answered, she repeated herself, putting her hands on her hips.

One of the men reached for his sword. He asked her a question in return, which she answered easily. He gestured at Jayne and asked another question. Trinity paused, then said something that Jayne could only surmise was unpopular, for the next moment every man was up, swords pointed at them.

Jayne stepped in front of Trinity and brought up her staff. "What'd you say to them?" she asked out of the side of her mouth.

"I said we wanted to talk to Medb. I'm pretty sure this is her army." Trinity was frowning, chewing on a fingernail.

"*Pretty sure?* Trinity, we're going to have to talk about planning if we get out of this one alive, honey."

"Come on, where do you think I learned my mad skills?"

Jayne didn't dignify that with a reply. Instead she swung up her staff to block the first dart of a sword. She swept her hand in a Repel spell at the same time, so when her staff hit the sword the man who held it stumbled back twenty feet.

The rest of the men froze. They stared at her staff, which was glowing with the residual of the spell. "That's right," said Jayne, sounding a lot more confident than she felt. "And there's more where it came from."

The man who'd attacked righted himself with a frown. He made a quick beckoning motion with his hand and let out a stream of words.

"He says we have to come with him," Trinity translated.

"I'm not going anywhere until I know what they're going to do with us." Jayne planted her feet and spun a Shield spell for good measure. Unlike in their own time, the spell had a luminosity, visibly warping the air. Jayne couldn't help but admire it for a moment. So cool.

Trinity asked. At his reply, she grinned. "He's taking us to see the queen. He says she'll want to see another witch."

Jayne rose from her battle stance but kept the staff out and ready. "Who're you calling witch?" she asked the man who'd spoken.

He turned and led the way without reply.

They'd come out on the outskirts of the army encampment. As they moved toward the center, the grass became mud, and tents began to spring up like fluttering ghosts in the night.

The men brought Trinity and Jayne to a tent almost as large as Jayne's apartment, so green it was nearly black in the night, and spoke to one of the guards there. The guard ducked beneath the tent flap and spoke to someone else. Then he beckoned to Jayne and Trinity.

The tent was lit by a small brazier, upon which sat two clay cups. The air was thick with the smell of honey and sweat. A long cloth lay over the ground, and pillows stuffed with what looked like feathers and hay dotted the space. In one corner of the tent stood a table, and at that table stood a queen.

Queen Medb was taller than Jayne had remembered, and her dark red curls had been pulled back into a haphazard circular braid that was falling off her head. She looked up as they entered and asked a question. The guard answered, and she dismissed him with a few curt words.

"What are they saying?" Jayne asked.

"She wants to know who we are." Trinity began to speak, then, in a halting voice. She gestured to Jayne.

Queen Medb looked at them both for a long moment.

"You don't speak Latin by any chance, do you?" Jayne asked in Latin. She hadn't been able to resist getting her hands on an ancient Latin dictionary in some of her rare downtime at the TCO. She'd assumed she'd use it to read old manuscripts, but this was much better.

"You speak the Roman tongue." Medb arched an eyebrow. "Are you Roman spies?"

"Definitely not." Jayne glanced at Trinity. She wasn't sure what to say. "We..."

"Then you are spies for Ulster," Medb decided. "Though poor spies, to wander lost as you did."

She stretched, twisting in her red wool dress. Then her hand flicked a complicated symbol into the air, and a spell Jayne didn't recognize flew toward her. In panic, she flung up all her defenses, feeling the swell of the totems as they reacted to the Torrent. The wind howled and tore through the open flap of the tent. The fire in the brazier flared high. Medb's spell swung awry and singed a hole in the side of her tent. A bright light flared, like the sun, making the queen put a hand over her eyes.

When she lowered her hand again, she was staring at Jayne with something that was not quite hostility, not quite awe. "What are you?" she said.

Jayne took a deep breath. *"Tempus viator."* At Medb's gasp, she nodded. "My name is Jayne Thorne, and I am a time traveler from the future. A future where the whole world is threatened, where you've helped me before, so the only thing I could think to do was to come here for your help again."

She explained their complicated relationship, ending with their problems with Odin Allfather. How they'd planned the perfect battle by uniting all the totems, only to fail. Medb did not snort, or snicker, or seem disbelieving: she listened carefully to everything, taking in the way Jayne spoke and the clothes they wore.

"I have never heard of this Allfather," she said.

"I think he's a little bit after your time," Jayne confessed. "He has not been created yet."

"And far away," Trinity added. Of *course* she could speak ancient Latin. Jayne barely kept herself from ruffling her daughter's hair proudly.

"But if we can't stop him, he'll destroy everything. And I think I'm the best chance we have...except I need the power you gave me. The totem you gifted me doesn't seem to work like all of the others. I can't connect with you in times of need."

Medb's mouth formed a small O. Her eyes blazed grass-green by the light of the fire. She came forward slowly and touched a slim, pale finger to Jayne's forehead. Jayne felt heat blaze from her. Medb gasped. Then she brought her hand up to her own forehead. For a moment the Earth totem flared and Jayne was knocked off her feet by a jolt in the earth, a ripple and a rumble as though the ground were a bit of fabric and someone was shaking it out. Her palms pressed down, and from beneath them she felt the wriggling of roots, the struggle of grass to grow beneath the tent.

"You hold the symbol of my power," Medb said in awe. Somehow, she was still standing.

Jayne climbed to her feet. "We call them totems. In the future, you are a goddess, and you granted it to me."

Medb arched an eyebrow and smiled, a coy twist of red lips on her pale face. "In the future? I am a goddess now, or as good as. I am the most powerful witch my people have seen, and I control the very Earth. I have opened it and bid it swallow my great enemies, and it gladly obeys me."

"Maybe that's what I need." It wasn't what Alexandra had said, but what if she didn't have the whole picture? "To create an earthquake, to break the crust of the Earth open and send Odin so far down he can't possibly get back up again."

"Earthquake?" Medb shook her mane of russet hair. "I did not say earthquake. At my command, the Earth itself opens, and the Underworld takes those souls I commit to it."

Underworld. Fire from beneath. Jayne felt a thrill run through her body. Could that be the solution? Bits of mythology drifted to her mind—Hades, Persephone, the five rivers, including Styx, Acheron, and Phlegethon, the river of fire...and Hephaestus, the god of fire, who made the weapons for the gods and goddesses of Olympus. Maybe they needed the fire power of Hephaestus' forge to kill Odin. Only one way to make that happen...

That must be why they had failed. If Jayne had been able to use her Earth totem to drag Odin into the Underworld, he wouldn't have been able to harness the power of the volcano. She was surprised Vesta hadn't told her this. She'd query the goddess later, assuming she got back to her own time unscathed.

"Mama?" Trinity interrupted her train of thought. "What is it?"

Jayne gave her daughter a brilliant smile and turned to Queen Medb. "So here's the situation," she said, feeling the heady rush of a plan take over. "I need you to teach me how to open the gate to the Underworld."

Medb regarded her for a long moment, steepling her forefingers. Her eyes held an age to them that spoke of many more years on this Earth than did her full cheeks and the slight lines around her mouth and eyes. "Let us say that you open the gate to the Underworld, Jayne Thorne," she said. "How will you close it again?"

"Well, how do *you* close it?" Jayne asked.

"I do my best to never open it, now. The longer the portal to the Underworld stays open, the harder it is to close. And there are things in that place...things I sent to perish, long ago. They wait for their chance to escape the Underworld again, and if you open the door, they will fight to get out. Or the Underworld itself might try to pull everything in—you, your child, the very things you fought to save." Medb sighed and sagged. "I am *tired,* Jayne. I have borne this totem, as you call it, for many years, and when I was young I too thought it was the solution to all of my problems. Now I have sworn: No more. I have committed my soul to guarding the gate."

"So that's why you stopped responding to me when I called," Jayne realized. "You were guarding the gate...you didn't want it to open!"

She looked to Medb for confirmation. The woman raised one shoulder in a shrug. "It is your past, but it is my future," she said simply.

Jayne opened her hands and held them out, willing for Medb to take them. "You put your trust in me and gave me what you could of your power. You can see that. But I need to use it all now. Otherwise the Underworld will probably be preferable to what's happening on Earth."

Medb looked between Jayne and Trinity. Then she came forward, and took Jayne's hands in her own, and closed her eyes. The Torrent swirled around their legs in a sudden frenzy. Jayne felt the pull of power, and something else, something like a cold shard piercing her center with a suddenness that made her gasp.

Medb opened her eyes. "You are a warrior. You have the heart of a warrior, and a good soul. I will choose well when I choose you. For you have been bestowed with power none have seen before, and this means your heart is pure, and your intentions honorable."

Good to know, Jayne thought, but didn't dare make a joke. Medb never did seem to have a sense of humor.

"I am already proud of myself." Medb smiled, and Jayne reassessed that no-humor thought. "And I think I will be proud of you."

Jayne felt a sudden prickle of heat behind her eyes. Why was she close to tears? Was it because she'd never heard those words from her own mother?

"We both have battles to win, Jayne Thorne. Go back to your own time and call upon me. This time I will answer. I will help you open the last gate. But remember, this will not guarantee your success. You cannot ask me what I would do, when you are the queen commander of your own battle. You will have to be quick and decide for yourself. Perhaps you will have to be brutal, even. Sacrifice is a strategy. And you must remember: The longer the gate to the Underworld is open, the harder it will be to close. Do you understand?"

"I understand," Jayne whispered.

"Go, then," Medb said, and released Jayne's hands.

Jayne bowed and pulled Trinity close. "Good luck in your battle," her daughter said to the queen before them.

Medb smiled. It was a dangerous smile, a confident smile, a smile that seemed to have sharper teeth than she really had. "I do not need luck. And neither should you."

"We'd better go," whispered Trinity. The longer they stayed, the more power they ate up. Jayne took her hand. She raised the other in farewell, then drew the Fold spell in the air.

Returning to her own time was so much easier than coming backward. For one thing, she knew exactly where she was going. And it felt as though the Torrent *wanted* her back there: An invisible hook seemed to latch around her belly, hauling her forward as the world dissolved to mist around them. She focused on landing precisely where she'd been, remembering Alexandra's words.

The world shuddered beneath their feet, and the mist turned to the dull gray-and-black pocket in which they'd hidden. The crack of golden light at the front of the pocket flared, making Jayne put her hands up to her eyes. Odin had already started pushing through.

Catching sight of the huddled people on the edge of the Torrent, she cried, "We did it! We found Medb. I know what to do."

Her jubilation crumbled when they turned toward her. Two bodies lay still and ashen on the ground. Between them, the Time Reverse was melted and scorched through the force of the magic.

Alexandra Thorne barely breathed. Next to her, as Jayne watched, her father burst into flames and became nothing—no body, no wire-framed glasses, nothing but a pile of ash gently flaking away.

THIRTY-NINE

Jayne dropped Trinity's hand and sprinted over to the space where her father had once been. "No," she whimpered. "Dad, *no...*"

"We couldn't stop him." Sofia's face was streaked with tears and dirt. "He wouldn't let us near, and then he was burning..."

"*Why?*" Jayne said. She couldn't breathe.

An arm slid around her. Tristan. "He did it because he knew it was the only way to save us," he said. "We tried to tell him there had to be another way—"

A great *crack* interrupted him. They all looked up. The golden cleft in the pocket was growing, and a huge midnight eye stared into the slit.

And Trinity was standing closest to it.

She saw Odin's massive figure and screamed. Tristan let go of Jayne and lunged for her, but Cillian got there first. He scooped up Trinity as Vivienne leaped forward in tigress form, bolstering the first line of their defense.

"Jayne, I know it's a bad time, but you said you had answers?" Amanda was pale, one hand on Alexandra's wrist, monitoring the old woman's pulse.

Jayne's thoughts were scattered like seeds to the wind. Medb, Earth, calling, the Underworld—

The Underworld.

She was supposed to open the gate to the Underworld. And who knew? Maybe, just *maybe,* her father would be there in some way on the other side.

She took one more great shuddering gulp of breath. Then she reached within herself, pausing only slightly for a touch of calm from Amaterasu before calling on Medb. *You promised.*

And I have waited a very long time for this moment, Medb replied. From within the pocket, another, greener line began to split the edges of the world.

The realm beneath it was gray, too, and had the feeling of endlessness. Jayne felt the pull like a void, like the airlessness of space, sucking at the pocket around them as though the Underworld could swallow the whole thing. Now she started to understand what Medb had meant. The pull was getting stronger, and would continue to get stronger, until she managed to close it—or fall to it.

"We're going to lure Odin in there," Jayne said, just as a huge gray hand reached from the real world into their pocket.

Using the Earth totem, she quickly spun a ledge together at the edge of the Underworld. While she worked, she saw a sliver of something light float past her. A spirit? She forced herself to focus. *There will be time for that,* she promised herself. But only once everyone else was safe.

"You're going to have to be bait," Jayne said. "Be careful."

Trinity and Cillian moved onto the ledge first, with Cillian between Trinity and the vast nothingness. Ruger came next, Alexandra bent in half over his shoulder. Then Sofia and Tristan and Isra. Finally, Amanda stepped backward onto the ledge, holding what looked like a pitiful Shield spell between her fingers. Jayne supposed it was better than nothing.

"Jayne," whispered a voice from behind her. "Sofia."

Jayne turned. There stood Henry Thorne—and yet not Henry Thorne. He looked...bland, really, without color, lacking the spark in his eyes that she'd never really noticed until it had gone out. Even when they were settled on her they seemed slightly out of focus. His touch seemed solid enough when he reached out to stroke her hand, but the fingers there weren't his. They were more the approximation of fingers, like he'd put a body back together from memory and clay. A ghost.

"Dad." She swallowed hard. She didn't have much time.

"I know. You don't understand. But the important thing, Jayne, is that you made *me* understand. When you failed, I realized I stood at the fork of a road. I could let my life go with dignity to save my children, or I could enter into a series of time-travel experiments that would make me regret everything."

"You didn't have to die, Dad. There's always another way," Sofia said. She let her tears flow freely, falling from her chin over the ledge and into nothing.

"There was no other way for me." He smiled, and it did not seem sad to Jayne. "The Norns told me that I would be faced with this choice, to die honorably for my daughters or to live dishonorably with secrets I didn't have the right to know. I made the right choice. I never set out to save the world, girls, because you are my world, and saving you is what I'm meant to do." He leaned forward, and his cheek felt like a cool breeze against hers, smelling of tea and old paper. "I'm glad I got to say goodbye."

"Goodbye, Dad," Jayne whispered. Next to her, Sofia said it, too.

"That's quite enough of that," said a no-nonsense voice from off to the side. Jayne looked over in surprise to see

Alexandra smack Ruger around the ear with the flat of her hand. He lowered her carefully to the ledge.

When Jayne turned back to Henry, he was gone.

Alexandra smoothed out the front of her dress and looked around. "So I am dead," she declared, fixing a sleeve.

"Not yet," Jayne replied quickly.

Alexandra flicked her hand dismissively. "More or less. I cannot leave this place without collapsing, I know that much. My heart will not allow it. No matter, child. Do you have what you need? Can you defeat him, once and for all?"

"I—" Jayne looked one last time to the space where she'd last seen her father. His sacrifice wouldn't be in vain. "Yes," she said.

"Then go out there. I will remain here. I am the Guardian of this pocket, after all. It is my place." She smiled. "I'm simply on, one might say, the wrong side of things."

"Jayne, take this," Amanda said, wrenching the necklace from around her neck. "You might need it. It has Guardian magic."

"I don't know how to use it."

The older woman caressed Jayne's arm, the spot now so empty without her familiar's weight.

"Nor do I. But there will be a moment when you might need something extra. It will not fail you. I know this in my very soul."

"Thank you, Amanda." Jayne shoved the pendant in her pocket. Then she said, "All right. Odin's going to come for me, so keep out of his way. Don't let the Wraiths get me."

"That's all, huh?" muttered Amanda. "She have any idea how many Wraiths there are?"

Jayne smiled at her grandmother. There were so many things she wanted to say. She wanted to ask Alexandra about everything she'd experienced, about her time at the World Tree, about Trinity. About Henry, and what he'd been like before.

She simply didn't have time.

"We're proud of you, Jayne," Alexandra said with a smile, and pulled back the edge of the pocket.

FORTY

The field in front of Kirkjufell had hardened to volcanic rock, but it was still hot enough to soften the rubber soles of Jayne's combat boots when she ran out onto the land. She could feel the pull of the Underworld behind her, growing stronger. She needed to end this, and soon.

A shadow fell over her. A moment later, she heard the *twang* of a bow and arrow, and a Wraith twisted away, howling. Black blood spattered over the ground. Vivienne turned into a harpy eagle and took to the air. *The ground will melt your boots and burn you,* she warned.

"Good to know." It wasn't like they didn't already have a ticking clock. Jayne drew on her totems and released a blast of cold air and a spatter of rain to cool the earth. She pulled on the storm, drawing clouds in over their position.

But as they drew closer, she felt them tug away from her, as though they were obeying a different master. A gust of heat buffeted her, and she stumbled forward. She was already too tired.

The earth rumbled. And Odin was there.

He was somehow taller than she'd remembered. And the

hand that swung toward her was at least as large as her entire torso. Jayne threw herself to the ground, remembering too late how hot it was, and creating a cushion of air to stop her fall. She rolled and got to her feet, summoning a flash of sun that made the Allfather recoil.

"You," he rumbled in a voice like thunder. "You are a tasty morsel. I look forward to your destruction." He came forward. "I have been looking forward to it for a long time, in fact. You gave me a good challenge in our last meeting."

Jayne bared her teeth. "I can do better now."

Odin smiled. He reached his hand toward the sky—

Jayne felt the charge of electricity with just a moment to spare. She threw up a Shield spell, pouring all her power into it as a lancing bolt of lightning slammed toward her body. It shattered against the Shield. Staggering, Jayne called upon the power of Vesta, and fire spun out of the lightning, turning into fire spouts that danced over the ground. A fire spout scooped up a Wraith and spit it out wreathed in flame; the Wraith howled as it flapped aimlessly and plowed into one of its compatriots. Both fell to the ground, burning.

"Not a bad trick." Odin laughed. "Let's see how my work compares." He raised his hands, and the clouds above them began to spin down into tornadoes of their own. One touched the ground and began to speed toward Tristan, who faced off against a four-hooved Wraith that didn't seem to mind the heat of the ground. Jayne gasped and threw a mighty gust of storm at it, tearing the tornado off course right before it could bear down on Tristan. Then, she had to turn the storm the other way to keep a second tornado from enveloping Sofia and Cillian from where they flew. Trinity, where was Trinity—

Odin laughed. "You may have the love of the goddesses, puny Adept, but I *am* a god. I have devoured gods. Your abilities are nothing compared to mine."

"That doesn't mean I have to give up," Jayne snarled, shoving on the earth. It buckled and knocked him off his feet. He stumbled back up with a wordless growl. "That's the thing about us humans. We don't really know when to quit."

She sort of wished she had the Time Reverse now. She could use a few seconds' head start in battle. Stopping to fold time would leave her too vulnerable, so she had to rely on the rest of the totems, and the staff she now called into her hands and layered with a few Piercing spells. She used it to jab at Odin's stomach.

He grabbed the end of the staff and, seemingly unaffected by the spells that activated at its end, pulled it from her hands and threw it away. "Now, now, dear." He smirked. "Let's not get into battles of brawn. I wanted to test real skill. Show me your magic."

Glowing balls of light appeared in the air. They were a bit like fireflies, almost beautiful—until one zoomed toward Jayne and she realized what it truly was. A fireball.

She summoned a Throw spell and hurled it to intercept. The fireball bounced off her spell and hit another Wraith. She stepped back and began to reroute her fire spouts, sending them across the field to scoop up Odin's fireballs and chase Wraiths. The air was choked with the smell of burning leather and skin and hair, the screams of Wraiths that hadn't been able to avoid her onslaught. More than one body lay charred on the field. *You must be brutal,* she thought, remembering Medb's words. And she had to be quick. The Underworld pulled at her like a magnet; she fought it at every step.

Odin swept out his hands, and behind him she saw a rising wave of water from the sea. *Oh—* "Behind me," she yelled. "Vivienne, Cillian, fly up, fly away—" She brought her fire spouts together into a wall of flame and called upon Vesta, Freya, Amaterasu. *I need everything. I need the heat of the sun and the pull of the oceans and the power of the wind and the stamina of a warrior.* She braced herself as magic flowed from her very being.

The fire and the water met in a crash that nearly sent Jayne tumbling. She felt her eyebrows singe and the skin of her palms peel off. She gritted her teeth and held in her scream, bracing her legs as water crashed through her defenses. The world filled with a hot mist that scorched the inside of her nose and lungs.

Everything was obscured, the fog hot and thick. Jayne reached up, forming the misty clouds into hands that could close around the ankles of the low-flying Wraiths and bring them to the ground. She heard the crunch of bodies all around her.

A cold wind blew the mist away, and she stood on the volcanic plain again.

She'd moved back in the battle. Farther back than she should have. Jayne glanced at the pocket behind her. The Underworld was still trying to drag her in. She needed to get Odin down and through the portal. "Your allies look like they could use a little help," she taunted.

Odin looked around the field. It was scattered with bodies. Tristan was covered in black blood, swinging his sword, breathing hard. Amanda held her bow with quiet competence, one arrow nocked and shining with golden spells all along its shaft. Ruger stood with her, swinging a massive mace, ready to withstand any Wraith that tried to come at them in close quarters.

"You know, I think you're right." Odin sounded anything but upset. He smiled, revealing sharp, crooked teeth. Then his chest inflated with an enormous breath. He pulled the eye patch away from his face.

What was beneath was utter blackness. And somehow, it was *moving*.

Tendrils of shadow shot from the eye socket, zipping across

the field to wriggle into the vulnerable forms of the Wraiths. Their bodies twitched.

Then they began to rise.

Odin laughed. Jayne gasped, taking another step back that slid as the icy fingers of the Underworld grabbed hold of her. The Wraiths stumbled to their feet, limbs rotating and returning to their proper alignments in sickening crunches. The Wraith with four hooves like a bull, shed scraps of its skin that had crisped on the hot surface of the magma plain.

"How am I supposed to get rid of these things?" she muttered.

You are not, said Vivienne's voice in her head. She looked up. The harpy eagle soared on the wind. *We are. Trust us, Jayne. Do what you were meant to do.*

"I don't know if I can," Jayne confessed.

If you do not try, we are doomed for certain. You've never backed away from a challenge before.

She'd never pulled out all the stops before, either. She'd never tried so hard, and it felt as though she'd never been so tired. And she'd certainly never contended with zombies. Maybe she was the one doomed to fall into the Underworld...

"As long as I take you with me," she breathed, resolve filling her. She braced herself again and stopped trying to hurl spells. She focused on the Underworld pull and resisting it.

Odin watched her from across the field. "What goes through your mind, little Adept?" he asked.

"It's Master to you, you stupid beast," Jayne said.

That seemed to rankle him. He rushed her, raging, and was on her in a second. He picked her up by the waist and squeezed. Jayne was pretty sure she felt a rib crack.

"You're nothing," he crooned. "And all your efforts amount to nothing. I'm going to reach into that skull of yours and pull the totems out myself."

Jayne smiled and stopped trying to resist. "Yeah, I don't think so."

She really wished she'd come up with a better comeback. It might well be her last.

With an inward sigh, she dissolved the ledge he was standing on. She tightened her arms around Odin's neck, squeezing until he choked, and the world began to slip away from them.

"Wha—" Too late Odin realized they were falling. The opening of the pocket zipped past, her grandmother's face white with shock, then the world turned cold and bottomless.

CHAPTER

FORTY-ONE

They fell.

Odin's mouth opened in a roar of fury, so wide Jayne thought he would fasten his teeth around her throat and rip. She dug her nails into his Adam's apple, aiming for the vocal cords. Too late, she saw his open hand. It hit her on the side of the head so hard she felt her jaw crack, and she let go of him. She was free-falling.

He brought up his legs. His feet now ended in wicked talons, and the first slash shredded the skin on her forearms. She screamed and felt a ripple of alarm...from Hayden.

I thought you were dead, she cried with unfathomable relief. *Pull free,* she thought desperately. *Help me.*

She grabbed onto an ankle as Odin pumped his wings. "Get off," he snapped. Jayne tried to summon a staff, a knife, anything from the Torrent that might help her—

There was nothing. For there was no Torrent.

She could feel it now, or rather the lack of it. The magic was far above her head, in the land of the living. Here, she had nothing but her fists and her wits. And Hayden, if he could wake up. *Please,* she thought. She could feel him straining at her arm; it burned nearly as much as the claw marks.

Odin slashed wildly for her face. She ducked his arm and punched him once, twice in the solar plexus. He made a satisfying *oof* sound. Even gods had to abide by some rules of biology.

"You pathetic worm," he growled. "You think you've defeated me? You've only defeated yourself. We'll be falling forever, and you can't even reach the top of the portal to close it." His laugh shook Jayne down to her bones. "You've doomed your world out of spite. They will be sucked in here with us. We can all fall together." He brought his face close enough to hers that she could smell the rankness of his breath, feel it hot and moist on her face. "You'll never be free of me."

Jayne didn't know what else to do. She looked straight into that abyss where his eye should have been and shoved her fist in the socket.

Odin howled. Shadows streamed around them. She pulled on his face and brought her forehead down on his nose, hearing a satisfying crunch. "Are you sure it's not the other way around?" she grunted, chopping at his body with the sides of her hands as though they were blades. She drove her palm into his elbow, hearing the same satisfactory crack as when she hit his nose. Blood flowed black over his face, and his one remaining eye swirled with hate.

The bastard laughed.

One huge hand closed around each wrist. "Just you and me now, Jayne Thorne," Odin said. "How long do you think you can keep me from disemboweling you? How long do you think it will take you to die, here in the land of the dead?"

Hayden pulled free with a feeling like someone was ripping Jayne's arm out of its socket. Amanda's necklace glittered on his neck. He grew, and grew, and grew more. He was gold as a phoenix, Guardian magic flowing through his body. A massive golden dragon, impressive enough that even Odin caught his breath.

Fly, Jayne, Hayden commanded in reverberating tones, emerging between them, placing his claws on Odin's chest, his head gnashing with strong jaws toward Odin's. He continued to grow, and Jayne slipped from the Allfather's grasp and slid down Hayden's back. He was becoming larger than he ever had been, one last act of complete desperation. *Let go of him now,* she thought desperately. *Fly us out of here.*

This is my purpose, Jayne. I will always be with you, Hayden promised. And then she was at the end of his tail, and it flicked her high up. She soared through the air, passing more tumbling shapes—Wraiths, following their master, howled and thrashed below. She made her body as small as it could be, like a missile being shot into the sky.

She hit one Wraith full-on in the chest. It pulled up short, wings pumping, giving her a few extra feet of lift even as it snarled and lifted a clawed hand to rip her head off. And Jayne had nothing, not even Hayden, to protect her now.

Something screeched, very much like an eagle, and very much nearby. The Wraith and Jayne looked up.

A shadow fell upon them, raking talons across the Wraith's face before gripping Jayne by the back of her shirt. *Got you!* Vivienne seemed out of breath.

Jayne delivered one final kick to the face of the Wraith and watched it fall. "We'd better get out of here—"

On it. Vivienne swung her and released. Jayne's scream was swallowed up by the air. She rushed toward the entrance of the pocket and the renewed ledge that now held no one but her grandmother.

She was certain she wouldn't make it. The pocket, and the world beyond, were just out of reach of her straining fingertips.

She was going to fall again, among the debris, and now she was going to fall forever. Then Vivienne grabbed her by the belt, claws puncturing her shirt and digging into her skin, and threw her again. The eagle and the woman tumbled beyond, onto a battlefield cooled by seawater and wind, scattered with the bodies of Wraiths and jumbled debris. Jayne hit the ground hard.

"I can't believe you did that." Jayne rolled over, staring at the storm-green clouds above her. They meant something bad, she knew, but she could barely piece together what.

"I cannot believe it, either." Vivienne sprawled next to her. She was in her girl form again, pale and panting. "I did not think I could."

"Then why did you?" Jayne asked. "You shouldn't risk yourself like that."

"Why not?" Vivienne smiled at her. "Isn't it what we do for our sisters?"

A strange noise filled the air, and Vivienne started to slide backward.

Jayne grabbed her hand and held on for dear life. "We have to close the gate," she said.

"But Hayden..."

A spike of golden sorrow coursed through her, but Jayne nodded grimly. "Hayden is doing what he was meant to. And we must, as well."

She looked around. Ruger and Amanda had spun some sort of protection circle, and Isra, Tristan, and Trinity stood within it. Sofia and Cillian were a dot on the high wind, fighting more Wraiths and trying not to get blown into oblivion.

Jayne dug into the earth. *I need you,* she called to Medb. But the goddess' reply seemed far away and crackling with interference. The earth itself mounded around the pocket as if to make a physical wall, but it kept crumbling away. Jayne called on her

Fire totem, then her Spirit totem. Nothing. "I think the Underworld's interfering with my connection," she shouted to Vivienne.

Dark hair whipped across Vivienne's face. "I cannot reach Vesta," she shouted. Jayne could barely hear her as the wind began to howl.

They had to close the gate somehow. Could they Sew up the pocket, the way Alexandra had done?

Probably, but Jayne wasn't sure she'd survive that.

She stood. You never got anywhere if you didn't try. She started limping for the pocket.

"What are you doing?" Vivienne shouted.

"We've got to make sure it closes," Jayne called back. "Tell the others to hold it shut from the outside while I Sew it together."

"But you'll be stuck!" Vivienne grabbed her arm. "Jayne, no. There has to be another way. There always is."

Jayne smiled sadly at her. Yes, there were always options. Like time travel, some of them were simply bad, and you had to take the fork that helped the most people. No matter how it hurt.

Vivienne must have seen the look on her face, for she gripped Jayne's arm tighter. "You cannot leave," she said. "You promised we would do the things that sisters do. We had a deal."

Jayne cupped a hand around her face and summoned a Sleep spell from the Torrent. "Sorry, little sister," she whispered as Vivienne's eyes rolled back in her head. From across the magma plain, Tristan and Trinity were running toward her, hand in hand. *Take care of her, Tristan,* Jayne thought. *She's the only daughter we'll ever have, in any time.*

Jayne yanked her staff from the Torrent. Around her, patches of earth and moss were ripping from the ground and tumbling past her into the vacuum of the Underworld. Jayne's own feet kept trying to lift up, too, to carry her away. She drew spell after spell from the Torrent without thinking, a Rooting spell and a Binding spell and even a Sticking spell in an attempt to keep herself grounded. A Wraith tumbled past her, one talon nicking her shoulder and tearing at her vest. A chip of rock slashed across her cheek. The edges of the entrance were turning blurry, and the world outside of them stretched and fuzzed. Vivienne's prone body slipped toward Jayne. She was out of time. She threw all of her power into it and summoned the last spell she would ever use.

She couldn't rush this, even as her heart pounded and her fingers shook and Vivienne seemed to be getting closer and closer. She had to be thorough, and careful. She gathered the edge of the portal and honed her staff into a point as sharp as a needle, then slid it through the fabric of reality. She threaded it with all of her magic and pulled tight.

The portal didn't want to close. It strained against her; she bared her teeth and pulled harder. Her arms groaned with the effort. She pulled one corner tight and threaded the staff through the other edge. The edge curled back. She felt a growing prickling at her spine, as though the Underworld could see what she was doing and took umbrage at it. The boundaries of the portal pulled against the thread, resisting. Jayne propped a foot on the side of the portal as though it were a wall and hauled back, pulling her makeshift magical needle with her.

Her Binding and Rooting spell broke the second she lifted her foot. The Underworld vacuum hauled on her viciously, and her feet slipped away. She screamed. She held her staff tight, the magical thread she was weaving catching her. If she let go to conjure a spell, she'd fall away.

I guess I'm just stuck here forever then, she thought stubbornly, and closed her eyes. Surely it was no worse than what the Norns had endured, stuck in cages for millennia. But if she could just finish what she started—

A warmth grew behind her eyes. The warmth of the fire, the warmth of the sun. The warmth of good mead drunk before battle, the warmth of blood singing in the storm. Her body buzzed. Magic slipped out of her as though she were one of her father's devices, and this time it took shape. She felt her body growing, building strength with the magic of the totems. She could see the stitches in time in her mind and knew she was the only hope they had left.

I submit, she whispered to the roaring winds. Her body burned in the light of the sun, great gouts of water filled her lungs. The ground below her feet subsumed her legs, her chest, her head.

Jayne became the magic she sought to control. The swirling green Torrent moved through every pore, every cell of her being, swirling her into its flow. Its sentience was her own; there had never been anything so beautiful or perfect in the world.

She opened her eyes. Ghostly figures clasped the edges of the portal and drew it inward. They hauled with all their might, gritting their teeth, opening their mouths in a wild howl that was whipped away by the pull of the Underworld. They forced the edges closer and closer, even as the pull on Jayne's back became almost unbearable. Her hands, slick with sweat, slipped down to the end of her staff. In her mind, the weft and warp of time wove into an unbearably bright fabric.

The weaving pulled tight, and the edges closed. Golden light ran the length of the seam. A deep and terrible scream came from within, one of fury and failure, and she was seized with triumph. Odin was gone.

She knew Hayden was gone with him, and grief filled her. His second death was almost worse than the first. But she would be with him again soon.

She heard the chorus of goddesses growing louder and was relieved by their presence. She didn't want to die alone.

Now, Jayne Thorne. Now.

Jayne's fingers spasmed and released the magical needle. And with one last thought of joy and safety for all of those glorious people she loved, she splintered into a million pieces and tumbled away.

FORTY-TWO

J ayne came to lying on the ground.

She opened her eyes. This was not the Underworld, where she was falling forever—or else the fall was a lot shorter than advertised, and she'd already reached the bottom. But it was heartening to know that what she'd suspected for so long was true: Matter could not be destroyed. She was in another plane of existence. Purgatory, or Heaven, she would surely soon find out.

The ground looked a lot like an Icelandic field, but rivers of green stars spread in every direction, from the springy emerald grass beneath her body to the deep sage shadows between the trees at the edge of the field, to the gold-touched olive of a hill beyond. Jayne sat up. Memory twinged in her. She recognized the placement of that hill. The field was no longer churned to mud or dotted with tents, but it was the theater where Medb had met her enemies in the Táin. The site of the Battle of Ulster.

At the top of the hill, under a huge branching willow tree, stood eight figures. Jayne got to her feet, putting a hand to her spinning head, and started off over the field. At some point, she realized she was breathing. That had to be a good sign, right? Or did the Underworld just let you pretend you were breathing? The grass crunched beneath her feet, letting out a sweet, fresh scent that cleared her headache.

Well, if this was the Underworld, things could be a lot worse, she decided. The air was clear and it seemed to be free of Wraiths and would-be world dictators and other things that wanted to kill her. A distinct lack of books, and an equal lack of hobbits, porgs, or other things she'd come to expect from such a landscape due to her media consumption habits, but she'd expected a lot worse. And at least, it seemed, she had an excellent sisterhood for company.

The goddesses stood together at the top of the hill, hands clasped. They were waiting for Jayne.

Vesta wore a vibrant red tunic and two bands that looked as though they'd been woven from gold over her forehead. Her mantle fluttered delicately in the wind. As Jayne came to the top of the hill, the goddess of the hearth reached out and stroked her cheek. Her eyes sparkled as though lit by candles from within.

Freya was next. She wore a rich blue dress belted with gold at the waist, and a heavy gold necklace that seemed to crackle with lightning. Her golden hair shone softly by whatever sunlight filtered down here. She pressed Jayne with hands rough from driving a war chariot and wielding a sword.

Amaterasu wore a bright kimono of shifting yellow and white and gold. Her long dark hair lifted away in the wind, and she bowed to Jayne. She was too bright to look at for long, and Jayne's eyes began to tear up. Amaterasu smiled gently and her brilliance dimmed, shimmering away over her skin.

The Norns waited calmly. Jayne approached them as a set: First Skuld, the Maiden, embraced her in a fleeting and easy hug that nevertheless held strength and resolve. Verdandi, the Mother, put a hand over Jayne's heart for a moment, closing her eyes and smiling. Urd, the Crone, leaned on Jayne's staff and put a hand on Jayne's shoulder. Her normally hard eyes were softer now. She looked—proud.

A woman she'd never seen before but recognized immediately from her close reading of the *Poetic Edda* as Rán, a Norse goddess of water and the original owner of the Water totem before it was stolen by Ruth Thorne, smiled benevolently. "You've freed me as well, Jayne Thorne, and allowed me to return to my sisters. I will not forget this."

Medb was last. She stood with her back to Jayne, clad in bronze armor, with her helmet tucked upside-down under her arm, just as she must have looked during the Battle of Ulster. When she turned, the sun caught on her fiery hair. Her helmet had been filled with earth and sprouted with wildflowers.

She smiled at Jayne, and came forward to press their foreheads together.

"We chose well," Medb said when she broke away. She looked to the other goddesses. They all nodded. Vesta's smile was the most maternal; their relationship had been the closest.

"You are strong, and you think on your feet," Vesta added.

"You are timeless." Urd cackled at that. "You act without thought toward the future—and sometimes without thought toward the past."

"Utterly in the moment," Verdandi sounded approving.

"You shine like the sun," Amaterasu said. "You bring others into your orbit."

"You fight to the last, and you are fearless," Freya said.

Rán's voice was as melodic as a summer stream. "You never took for your own gain, unlike so many we know."

"And you are selfless," Vesta finished for them. "We chose well, indeed."

Jayne looked from goddess to goddess. She saw proud looks, impressed looks, satisfied looks. But she did not see the answer to her most important question. "Is the world safe?" she said. "Did we do it?"

"It is," said Verdandi with a gentle smile.

"It will be forevermore." Skuld's eyes shone. "Because of you."

"Because of *us*," Jayne said. They were all in this together, weren't they?

So that was that. She was trapped in the Underworld, away from her family, unable to see the world she had saved. And she was okay with that. She swallowed and nodded. "Then I'm ready."

"Ready for what?" Medb sounded amused.

"Ready to die." For this had to be some kind of astral projection, right? Not truly the Underworld. "Can't have a living soul tethering our Underworld to the land of the living, can we? I'm ready."

"Ready," snorted an entirely new voice behind her. Jayne turned and her jaw went slack. There stood Alexandra, tall and proud, still in her fine linen dress but looking younger than she had on Earth—in her forties or fifties, with silver just beginning to thread through her dark hair. She walked without the aid of a cane or staff, and the wrinkles at her eyes and mouth were less pronounced, seeming less prone to frowning. "You are so young, Jayne. None of us is truly ready for death and what comes next."

"I don't have much of a choice, Grandmama," Jayne said, using Trinity's word for the lady. "This is the price. I can try to be ready, or I can face it kicking and screaming." And she'd already decided to accept it.

"*You* can accept it," Alexandra allowed with an incline of her head. "We do not have to."

Her eyes flicked behind Jayne. Jayne turned back to find that the goddesses had formed a circle and linked hands. Their eyes were closed. Urd swayed a bit. Vesta began to sing in a high, clear voice, threads of Latin and an older language, perhaps Etruscan, or perhaps something even older than that, a language that united all the goddesses and spoke to them on a deeper level.

They began to shine.

The light collected in the space between them, like a sun in miniature, a light it hurt to look at directly. Little tendrils of it whipped out like solar flares, leaving sooty marks behind as they lashed against the goddesses and their clothes. Jayne took a step forward without conscious knowledge of what she was doing; she only realized when Alexandra put a strong hand on her wrist. "This is not for you, Jayne," she said firmly.

Then a tendril came straight for her.

It touched her forehead with a motion as soft as a kiss, a brush against her skin that left it tingling. A moment later Jayne felt something within her start to pull out, and a long thread of power emerged from between her eyes and snaked toward the ball of light. It was the brownish green of the earth. As it punctured the ball of light, Medb's eyes flew open. They were the purest, brightest green, devoid of pupils.

Jayne gasped. She felt lighter, somehow, emptier...as though her feet stood less solidly on the ground.

Her Earth totem was gone.

A tendril struck out again. This time it drew back and took a red thread of magic with it. Vesta's eyes opened, blazing as the hearth. The third tendril drew out a pink thread that made Freya shudder and convulse. The fourth, a golden thread for Amaterasu. Then three in quick succession: White, gray, black. Past, present, future. Urd let out an ululation of triumph as power flowed into the glowing ball, and Jayne's mental map of time rolled up inside her head.

Alexandra herself removed the Water totem, the aquamarine thread pulling away from Jayne's body toward the woman who'd help create her. Alexandra passed it to Rán, who accepted the totem with a happy sigh.

Jayne felt lighter than she could remember feeling in a long time. Emptier. The goddesses raised their linked hands, and the ball of light rose with them. Then, with a shout, they let the link —and the power—go.

Jayne's entire world went white. She blinked until her vision turned spotted. She could see Alexandra's hand clasped tight around her own. And beneath their feet, the Torrent flowed like water. It swirled around them, twinkling with little lights like trapped stars, flowing thick and fast past the feet of the goddesses, up their bodies, and into the air that surrounded them.

Jayne couldn't feel it at all.

The eight goddesses turned. They glowed with their newly recovered power, the power that Jayne had once held on their behalf. They were all smiling.

"Thank you, Jayne," said Medb, and made a twisting motion with her hand.

The Torrent rushed up, sweeping her off her feet just like a real river, and suddenly she couldn't swim with it, couldn't fight it, couldn't do anything but cling to Alexandra and watch the goddesses and the battlefield and the sunshine all disappear. The Torrent roared, rising like a flood through the gray in which she'd fallen. Bits of debris swirled around her: rocks, sticks, Wraith wings. The World Tree appeared, its branches growing, pushing them to the top of the great cleft.

Jayne couldn't even breathe. Now, perhaps, was her moment. Her death.

They washed up to the ledge she'd hastily constructed to protect the strike team what felt like an age ago. The Torrent deposited them as gently as though they were mice in a hand, then receded as quickly as it had come, leaving Jayne and Alexandra alone. Jayne realized she was shaking. She felt so tired. She felt so weak.

Alexandra stood, working with deft hands at the sealed portal. "I wish we had more time to say goodbye," she told Jayne, her fingers flashing with magic. "But without the goddesses to protect you, you only have a minute in here, two at most, before you die. And the goddesses would not have you die today, Jayne."

Jayne lifted her head. A foggy confusion had descended upon it, and she was having trouble thinking of anything. "Huh?"

"I am so proud of you, even if I seemed exacting and uncompromising in life. You are a credit to the Thorne name and a worthy Master, and the mother of more worthy Masters. Your daughter was my great solace after the many mistakes I made in my own life. So go out there, and make sure she exists for me, Jayne."

Heavy resolution reared its head. *No man left behind.* "Not without you, Grandmama," she murmured.

"Me? Ha!" Alexandra actually did sound amused. "I'm already dead. Humans don't last long in the Underworld, remember? Besides, I'm the Guardian of this pocket, and it might just be the most important pocket of all." She sounded rather satisfied with herself at that. Then she bent down and hauled on Jayne's arm with a lot more strength than Jayne would have expected from a grandmother who'd been trapped out of time for goddesses knew how long. "Don't worry about me, Jayne. I have rather good company." She smiled and wrenched another bit of reality open with a sound like cloth tearing. Then she heaved Jayne over into the real world.

Jayne landed on her back and all the breath went out of her. She gasped like a fish and saw the blue-gray sky of Iceland as it readied itself for a storm, and one aged hand, fingers spread in a last goodbye, before the portal closed up forever.

Someone was screaming, but Jayne couldn't figure out who. A human, or a Wraith. Someone coming to kill her, or someone coming to save her. She certainly couldn't save herself.

She let her head fall back. On reflex, she reached for the Torrent.

It was gone.

Jayne passed out.

FORTY-THREE

Henry Thorne's funeral was held on a Saturday, back in Jayne's own time. She'd gotten two days of leave to try to shower the ash out of her hair and remember what life was like with two other people in her apartment.

To try and find out what life was like without any parents.

The day was sunny, which Jayne rather appreciated. Rainy funerals were so cliché; she might have had to take a black umbrella and veil her face and stare mysteriously at her father's tombstone just for some sort of narrative satisfaction. The ashy bits of Henry's earthly remains they'd recovered were removed for preservation in the TCO mausoleum. "Off-limits to experimentation," Amanda had intoned.

The service was in the TCO chapel. Instead of a priest, it was officiated by Amanda herself, and for the first time since Jayne had met her, she looked misty-eyed in her crisp black suit.

"I'd like to offer you the official condolences of President Eisner," she said, giving Jayne a rare hug. She patted Jayne on the back like she thought the woman would break.

"The president knows my dad died?" Jayne said. She'd meant for it to sound like a joke; it fell flat.

"I mentioned it to her in our weekly call. The TCO has been removed from beneath the purview of Director Fitzgerald, and we answer personally to her now." Amanda offered her a tight smile that in no way reflected how she obviously wanted to pump her fist in the air.

"Go on, do a victory lap," Jayne urged.

The smile widened and turned much more genuine. "Thank you, Jayne. But I'll keep things somber. Good comes with the bad, and we're all grateful, but let's take a moment to celebrate the life that got us here." They were silent for a moment. Then Amanda tried, in a rusty voice, to speak. "Henry was…" She seemed at a loss for words. She blinked rapidly, then slid a finger under her eye to catch a tear. "We'll never see anyone like him. I am truly sorry, Jayne."

Me too, Jayne wanted to say. *He made his choice,* she also wanted to say. And perhaps most of all: *I'm so proud of him.*

"Thanks," she said instead. "You know, you saved me in the Underworld. Your necklace resurrected Hayden, and he was able to fight off Odin long enough to fly me out of the Underworld to Vivienne's depth."

"My husband would be thrilled to hear that. He would have liked you very much, Jayne Thorne."

It was high praise, and Jayne swallowed back the lump in her throat. "I'm sorry you lost him."

"We never truly lose the ones we love. They're always with us." She tapped her heart. "And on that note, we should get started."

Jayne gave Ruger a much more normal-feeling hug and held on to Tristan's arm as they found a seat for the service.

The entire Torrent Control Organization had turned out for the memorial. Many of her father's fellow Guardians had sent flowers and remembrances. Jayne was touched to see at least twenty Disciples of Gaia there as well, many of whom told her that her father's inventions had saved their lives at the Battle of Kirkjufell. During the service, Sofia told a funny story about Henry trying to fix a remote-control Barbie car, before they'd become functional orphans, and Katie related anecdotes of their Oxford years. Quimby spoke of his genius in the lab, with tears shaking her voice.

Jayne didn't say anything. For once in her life, she wasn't sure *what* she had to say.

Everyone else seemed to have such stories. Her sister knew Henry better, because she'd been older when he disappeared. Katie had known him before the girls were born, and Quimby worked with him ten to twelve hours a day, speaking a language that no one else really knew. Jayne didn't have any of that. She just had the private moments between them, pie and tea and small reassurances that life could be better, would be better, because of the work they did. And when she thought of those moments now, she felt part of herself curl around them selfishly, as if to hoard them from the outside world. These moments with her father were the only things she really had. And they were *hers,* and she didn't want to share.

She stood numbly in the receiving line after the service and shook hand after hand. A few people hugged her—Isra, Katie, Ruger. "You know what's funny?" Sofia muttered after what must have been the hundredth hand. "If Dad were here, he'd have already snuck off to experiment on something."

Jayne snorted with laughter, earning an odd look from a TCO agent down the line.

Her laugh died a moment later as a short, brown woman with silver braids stopped in front of them. Xiomara stood as straight as ever, her mouth drawn down, her dark eyes sharp and bright.

Jayne half expected to feel the sharp, prickly anger she'd felt the last time Xiomara had confronted them. But one look in the

Guardian's eye told her that Xiomara was grieving, in her own way, as Jayne was.

"I was sorry to hear of your father's death," she said to them. "I regret that we parted on difficult terms and never had the chance to forgive one another."

Jayne swallowed a lump in her throat. So many arguments, discussions, questions that Henry would never be able to answer. "I know he regretted it, too," Sofia replied softly.

"He valued you," Jayne said.

"He'd have been a fool not to," said Xiomara, looking faintly proud. "Of course, your father was a fool about many things—but not about people. Not usually."

She stopped there. Jayne wasn't sure what to do next. But Sofia did. She slipped her arm through Xiomara's and said, "I'm tired of standing around. Would you like to go for a walk with us?"

Xiomara's hard mouth softened, just a little. "Yes. Get an old woman's stiff joints moving."

They headed outside into the sunshine. The CIA campus moved as usual, people coming and going, unaware of their somber occasion. There was a long lawn of springy green grass, and tulips had been planted all along the edges in pale spring colors; they headed there.

"The old guard dies, and an era ends," Xiomara said as they walked. "I hardly know what to do with myself now that Odin is gone. And Labelle. And—well, Ruth. And all the pockets."

There were no more pockets, except for the pocket containing the Underworld that was guarded from the inside by Alexandra. There was no need for any other entrances. The spell had been broken, and the Torrent flowed freely, wisping over the ground, blending into the earth, barely detectible to Jayne out of the corner of her eye. She could feel it, though, in her very bones. Not that it mattered. Jayne no longer had access to magic.

"At least the sacrifice Dad made did what he meant it to do," Sofia was saying. "His life wasn't wasted."

Xiomara laughed. "No, indeed. Your father knew how to make the most of things."

They walked around the Kryptos sculpture and stood, looking at the carvings. The sun flashed against the bronze edges, and Xiomara read the ciphertext riddles, and smiled.

"You know the final answer?" Jayne asked. Three of the four riddles had been solved, and Jayne shivered at the phrasings, especially the one that spoke of the absence of light. It reminded her too much of the Underworld and the battle they had just won.

"Of course I do," the old woman replied. "You do as well; you just don't know it yet."

They walked a bit more before Xiomara complained of sore legs and old joints and they took her inside. As Sofia fussed with a cup of tea and a chair, Jayne looked at the wall of stars that celebrated the fallen heroes of the Torrent Control Organization. A cluster of them had been newly affixed, gleaming fresh bronze. They'd been cast after the memorial for those who had died at the first Battle of Kirkjufell. Henry's name hadn't yet been finished, nor put up. Jayne tried to imagine it at the end of the wall. Alexandra's wouldn't be up there, she realized suddenly. Alexandra had never, to her knowledge, been an agent with the TCO. And Hayden? Did her familiar warrant a star? Her arm ached sometimes, but the skin there was smooth and pale like the rest of her. Whenever she looked at it she felt a corresponding ache in her heart. Hayden had been a part of her spirit in many ways, but he'd also been something different. Something more. A way for her to talk things through, not to mention a direct path to the Torrent. He'd had a name, a being, and now he was gone, and she didn't even know if she could access their kind of connection again, much less what to call it and how to treat it.

Cillian had turned up, and found a chair for Sofia, and was fussing at her at least as much as she'd fussed over Xiomara. The pair of them would be impossible with kids, Jayne thought with a little smile. *Impossibly wonderful.*

He brought them a plate of cookies from the canteen, and Jayne went over to sit with them again. "We should probably be back in the line, shaking hands," Cillian said without enthusiasm.

Sofia sighed and put her head back. She was starting to be obviously pregnant, her belly rounding out in that special way. "I'm just...finished."

"I think we deserve to be finished," Jayne told her, patting her leg.

Xiomara arched an eyebrow consideringly. "Finished with the TCO? The CIA?" she said. She sounded intrigued.

"Maybe," said Jayne. She couldn't really fathom being finished with the TCO. It had swooped into her life, given her unimaginable power, made all her dreams come true, and sent her on the adventure of a lifetime.

And now she was washed up on what felt like sandy, foreign shores, and expected to act like everything was normal. Soon she'd have to confess to Amanda that she had less magical access than Quimby. She could talk to Vivienne when the other woman was in her Rogue form, and she could summon a few sparks from her fingers. That was the full extent of the magic she possessed. She was less impressive than a Fourth of July sparkler.

And maybe that was for the best.

The Thorne family had been torn apart in their quests for power: Henry's thirst for knowledge, Alexandra's thirst for control, and Ruth's thirst for domination. Now they were all gone, and when they should have been forces for good, they'd often left Jayne and Sofia to carve their own paths. Jayne wouldn't be that way for her own daughter. Jayne would do better. Jayne would *be* better.

So maybe it was for the best that her totems were gone. That the goddesses were free, released from their grimoires, and had power over themselves and their fates again, rather than working through a human agent.

It was better, and eventually she'd even believe it.

Next to her Sofia heaved a sigh and reached for another cookie. "I've just got a whole school of new recruits to manage," she said with a smile. "We'll be busier than ever. I can't really see myself resigning from the TCO, not when I have young minds to shape for the good of the world."

"And I suppose it is better that they are shaped by you than by some CIA die-hard," Xiomara admitted. She groaned and got to her feet. "I, however, will not be returning. Ever. I appreciate that things went...better than I foretold. I am glad of it. And I am glad that you are no longer the sort of threat I feel we must protect ourselves from, if you will forgive me, Jayne." Jayne tried to smile through the sting of that. "But my fate has been dictated by others for as long as I can remember. By the powers that selected me as a Guardian, and by the people who sought to use those powers in their battles. I am finished with fighting. It is late in my life to decide who I am, but it is not *too* late."

She nodded to Jayne, who rolled her eyes and threw her arms around Xiomara. The old lady stiffened for a moment, then chuckled, relaxing into the embrace.

"Sorry, you don't get to avoid Thorne hugs so easily," Jayne said.

Sofia hugged her, too. "Come by for dinner sometime," she said softly. "Please."

"I'll think about it," Xiomara said. But the old woman was fighting a losing battle with a smile when she headed out of the TCO and into the sunshine.

Jayne was emotionally and physically exhausted when they returned to their Nashville apartment. Vivienne went straight into her room and shut the door; Jayne couldn't blame her. Tristan took a shower and ordered a variety box from the bakery, then forced Jayne to have some soup from the cupboard.

They hadn't solved the Trinity puzzle yet, so she and Jayne sat on the sofa together. Trinity put her head on Jayne's shoulder, and Jayne was amazed at how natural it felt, how easy it was to slip her arm around her daughter's thin shoulder.

She felt a tremor, then another. Trinity was crying.

Jayne tightened her grip and felt her own battle with tears slip into defeat. Trinity took a great, shuddering sob and said into her blouse, "It's just—Grandmama had all these stories about him from when he was a kid, and—"

And Trinity's Grandmama was gone, too, and Jayne didn't know whether there would be a funeral for her at all.

She hugged her girl, and cried with her, and even though they were mostly crying about different people, they were crying about the same thing, and that helped. At some point Vivienne slipped out of her room and made them both a pot of herbal tea, and came to sit with them quietly, because that was what sisters did for each other.

And Jayne felt that knot of selfishness loosen in her, just a little. Her moments with her father were rare and they were *hers*, but that didn't mean sharing would diminish them. Especially here, where she was with family instead of a room of strangers.

She handed out the cups and stroked Trinity's hair while she took comforting sips, then passed everyone a brownie. Chocolate and tea—there wasn't much of a better balm for heartache anywhere.

"Now," she said, when they'd all had the chance to stop hiccupping and get a few fluids back into them. "Would you like to hear a story about your grandfather?"

FORTY-FOUR

A few days later, Tristan and Jayne were married. It seemed like the only natural thing, now that he'd moved in and they'd met their child. Life was anything but certain, and life was meant to be lived. Jayne finally felt that she could live it, now. She was no longer trying to save the world on a regular basis, and even if she wanted to, she couldn't.

She wore a long, pale lilac dress she found in her closet. Vivienne had opened her mouth to object—then smiled sweetly and said, "Allow me to do your hair." Sofia was the maid of honor in a blue summer dress, and Vivienne, a bridesmaid in a stunning dove gray. Vivienne curled and pinned her hair. Sofia found a bouquet of lavender and lily-of-the-valley.

"It's funny. I always thought that you would get married first," Jayne said to Sofia, plopping down on her Nashville couch. In a few hours, it would be undisputably *their* apartment. She wondered if it would feel different. Tristan fit so well here already.

Sofia's mouth turned up at one end. "We've talked about it, of course," she said. "Especially after we knew I was pregnant. Cillian's not a big one for marriage, though. It didn't work out well for his parents. Come to think of it, it didn't work out so well for ours, either."

"Nor mine," Vivienne added softly. Then she turned red. "Not that, er—"

"Your marriage is going to be fantastic, Jayne," Sofia said quickly.

Jayne smiled. "I know."

"I already told them," Trinity said, coming out of the bathroom. Sofia had taken her shopping for a new dress, and now she looked coltish and nervous in a dark purple that complemented Jayne's light. Vivienne had curled her hair, too, in adorable ringlets that were already starting to pull out despite the liberal use of spray.

"Trinity Thorne, you didn't," said Sofia in her most severe schoolmarm voice. Trinity shrugged and smiled, a mischievous glint in her eye. "We're not supposed to go into detail about the future," Sofia half-wailed.

"I thought it was a great idea," Jayne said. Trinity grinned, and Sofia shot her an irritated look, saying, "Anyway, we're going to be fashionably late, so let's get there before the groom thinks you've stood him up."

Jayne laughed. She collected the bouquet from its pitcher on the table. Tristan would never have to be afraid of that.

They traveled by portal to the TCO grounds. Amanda had the power to marry them, and she'd even had the desire once she'd stopped grumbling about all the extra work she had and how she didn't need more. They met Tristan, Ruger, and Cillian on the lawn. Ruger and Cillian wore dapper suits with a sprig of lavender pinned to their lapels. Tristan wore a suit the same dove gray as Vivienne's dress, with a shirt the same color as Jayne's dress. Vivienne had obviously told him the color scheme, such as they had one.

Tristan's eyes were a piercing blue as they lit on Jayne, and a smile so big split his face that Jayne felt her heart falling to pieces. *It's all right,* she thought. *He is here to pick them all up.*

She hugged Cillian first, making a small "oof!" sound at the squeeze from his bear-like arms. "Don't ruin her makeup," Vivienne scolded him, and he let her go, laughing. Ruger was next, as Tristan's best man. His hug was careful, but warm. When he pulled away Jayne caught the glint of something gold on his finger.

"Ruger. *Ruge.*" She grabbed his hand and, grimacing, he let her. "Are you..."

His smile turned shy, and a blush darkened his cheeks. "Right before the battle. We figured that we might not have the chance after, so..."

Jayne smacked him with her bouquet, ignoring Sofia's clucks of protest. "And you didn't tell me? I wasn't invited?"

"No one who calls me Ruge is invited to my wedding, *Agnes,*" he countered, and she couldn't help laughing. Only she could call Ruger Ruge, and only he could call her by her first name. It was TCO law.

Jayne took a closer look at the ring. It was delicately inscribed with Māori symbols. She blinked away sudden tears and met his eyes. "I'm happy for you," she said quietly. She knew it hadn't been easy for Ruger to let down his guard and open his heart.

Were his eyes just a little brighter than usual, too? "I'm happy for *you,* Jayne," he replied.

"Come." Tristan offered his arm to Jayne. "*Mon amour. Mon couer. Let us be married.*"

"Let us," Jayne replied, warmth filling her chest.

Amanda had directed a couple of underlings to set up a small table with all the legal documents ready to be signed and stamped. She would be the officiant, and she'd even put on one of her nicest suits for the occasion, with a deep gray silk blouse. She cleared her throat.

"Thank you all for coming. Tristan Labelle, Jayne Thorne, we are gathered today to witness your legal marriage in the state of Virginia. If anyone had told me, when you two first met, that I would be officiating your wedding, I would have laughed them out of the building. Then I probably would have needed to go lie down. Your rivalry at the TCO was nearly as infamous as the power you both had, and we're all proud—and a little worried for what comes next." She smiled at Trinity. Then she coughed and looked down, and it was with a much softer, more serious voice that she said, "Real love comes from within. It is a willing choice, once the storm fades, to face everything together. You have shown a commitment to each other that withstood the end of the world, and I can think of no stronger test to your bond. I wholeheartedly look forward to watching the next steps you take together. And not least because Trinity promises to be an exceptional student. Now, I understand you have your own vows?"

Tristan squeezed Jayne's hand. *You first.* She smiled. His eyes were so dazzling, she wasn't sure she could remember anything she'd rehearsed. "Tristan...when we first met, even in my fury at you, my enemy, I was so in awe of your command of the Torrent, and your power, and your knowledge...I think I was in love with you already, and I just didn't know it. You always have the answers. Even when things look at their worst, you have a way forward. And seeing our child, meeting her...it confirmed what we already knew. I no longer have my magic, but with you, Tristan Labelle, life will never be ordinary."

Tristan blinked three times in succession. His voice was a little hoarse when he said, "Jayne, I never met anyone like you. Perhaps because no one else had goddesses living inside their

heads"—he paused as their family chuckled around them—"
and perhaps because no one else has your unflinching heart,
your absolute certainty of right and wrong, and your willing-
ness to *do* right, no matter the personal consequences. I grew
up with a strong woman for a mother, and she taught me that
strong women were as selfish and power-hungry as strong
men. You taught me that strong women were made even
stronger through their utter selflessness. You taught me that
families can be healed and added to. You made me know that
love is worth it. I love you, Jayne."

Jayne couldn't resist. "I know."

"You and your references." He laughed.

They exchanged rings, and some of the more formal
language required to turn them into husband and wife. Finally,
and too soon, Amanda said, "You may kiss the bride."

Tristan leaned forward and his vanilla-and-soap scent filled
Jayne's nose, and his mouth was gentle on hers, and promising.
And it didn't matter that their whole family cheered around
them, or that Trinity said loudly, *"Ew,"* or that Amanda's phone
went off right after, because Tristan was kissing her and she
was utterly ordinary and extraordinary at the same time.

Amanda heaved a sigh. "I have to take this, if you don't
mind." She stepped away and Jayne heard her mutter into the
phone, "Madame President?"

It wasn't the life Jayne had pictured when she'd started out
in history and library sciences studies. Having a boss who
answered to the president. Having a husband who could cast
spells. Having a daughter who was some sort of magical time
bloodhound, and a telepathic connection with a shapeshifter.
Having a sister whose magical powers rivaled the most
powerful magicians.

Being so loved, by so many.

They got another round of congratulatory hugs. Everyone

had obviously been lugging their presents in a Carry spell, for when Jayne was finished signing the papers for the state of Virginia, the pile sat pristine and wrapped on the table. Sofia and Cillian had gotten them a classic set of crockery, while Vivienne had found a cookbook devoted to pies, both savory and sweet. Tristan groaned when he opened it. "You torture me," he said. "Now I will have to cook Jayne pie all the time."

Jayne snuggled up against him. "Can't wait," she murmured.

Ruger and Danilo had gifted them a set of books on the history of the Torrent and magical practice in different parts of the world. She ran her fingers over the fine, gold-embossed covers and felt an odd stab of emotion. She couldn't be a part of this world anymore, except in its liminal spaces. Like Quimby. Well, Quimby managed to make everything work, didn't she? Jayne could probably help Katie in the library if she wanted.

But do you want that life anymore?

"It's beautiful," she said after a moment. "Thank you so much."

A wide cream envelope lay on the table. Tristan picked it up with a frown. "From Amanda?" Jayne wondered.

Tristan held the envelope to the light. When he turned it over, Jayne saw *To Monsieur and Madame Labelle* in spiky ink on the front. Vivienne watched them with an odd, waiting expression.

"Just so we're clear, you're taking my last name," Jayne said as Tristan brought out his pocketknife.

"I will happily hyphenate, my dear," he said with a twitch of his lips, and cut the letter open neatly.

A single sheet fell out, and a brass skeleton key.

To my good friend Tristan Labelle and his fortunate wife. I hope that fate will bring us together again someday. I hope that some of the pain I have caused can be undone by this gift. It is ready for you and yours. We in France await your command.

Tristan was very still. "What is it?" Jayne asked.

He picked up the key, turned it over in his hand. Drew a complicated spell, layered it with another, and draped it over the key. The key shone briefly, then went back to its dull, speckled brass color.

"It is the key to the manor at Domdaniel," he murmured.

Domdaniel. The Time Catch headquarters of La Liberté and Gina Labelle. Only Gina was no more, and La Liberté had either disbanded or declared for Tristan.

"It's from Pierre, isn't it?" Jayne said. She was looking at Vivienne. The other woman nodded slightly. "Do we trust him?"

"Enough to be intrigued. Enough to check it out. Not enough to check it out without backup." He smiled and tucked the key into his pocket. "But that is a matter for another time, *mon coeur*. Shall we move onward to our celebratory lunch?"

They turned to go. Amanda was still twenty feet away or so, talking in a low voice. She'd insisted on arranging the lunch; her gift to the happy couple, she'd said.

Trinity tugged on Jayne's skirt. "Mama," she said quietly.

Jayne followed her gaze down to the end of the grass. Against the massive glass-and-concrete façade of the TCO stood three figures: one young and fluttering in a white dress, one matronly in a morning suit, one hunched and leaning on her staff. Jayne's eyes grew wide. *Impossible.*

But of course, for Masters of Time, nothing was impossible.

The Norns walked slowly up the path. Jayne knew better than to try and rush them. She felt something curl beneath her heart, something very much like fear, for if they were here, what was wrong? What world needed saving now?

When they were close enough, Skuld wagged a finger at her. "You are trying to see the future. That is my job."

"I just—" Jayne felt Tristan squeeze her arm in support. "I just wonder to what we owe the pleasure, that's all."

"We wished to offer you felicitations," said Verdandi, tucking a loose strand of gray-black hair behind her ear.

"And condolences," rasped Urd.

"You lost loved ones," Verdandi continued. "It is difficult. But Henry and Alexandra Thorne both accepted their fates. Bargained for them, even, to save you. And your familiar Hayden made the ultimate sacrifice out of pure love."

"You are in an unusual position," Skuld said, fiddling with the edge of her dress. "You fulfilled your destiny and successfully saved the world." Jayne felt herself sag. That was a relief. She hadn't realized that she'd been half-expecting Odin to come roaring back, more powerful than ever. "And yet, despite the odds, you lived through the experience. This means you have created a new fate for yourself, a new ending."

They leaned forward as one, three voices reverberating. "Would you like to see it?"

It was as though the world held its breath. Jayne glanced around the assembled group: Ruger and Cillian were wide-eyed. Trinity's mouth was half open and she bounced on her toes, eager to soak up more knowledge, more magic. Sofia looked slightly panicked. There was a misty fuzz in the background that looked shockingly like an astral version of her father and grandmother, beaming down at her. And Tristan... Tristan just smiled gently at her, like he knew what she would do.

"No, thank you," Jayne said, without breaking his gaze. "I'm perfectly content with being my ordinary self again now. I'll do what everyone else does and meet my fate without knowing what it's going to be."

JOSS WALKER

Tristan quirked a quick smile. "You will never be ordinary, my love."

"No, never ordinary, Jayne Thorne," sighed Skuld, fluttering the lacy white edge of her gown. She had a crown of sunflowers in her hair. Any bystander to this party would assume she was the bride.

Verdandi smacked her lightly on the arm. "You are wise," she told Jayne. "We approve. And we do not take offense that you refuse the gift we have given you. Rather, we offer you your second gift."

She reached into a pocket that Jayne couldn't quite see, couldn't quite suss out. And she brought out—

"*Hayden,*" Jayne breathed.

He was the size of a small cat, blinking his fiery eyes sleepily as Verdande held him out to her. His wings shifted on his back, and he scrambled eagerly up Jayne's arm before wrapping himself around her shoulders and breathing a deep sigh of happiness. *You're back!* Jayne thought to him. *I missed you so much.*

She felt his thrum of contentment through her whole body.

"Just as you have given up most of your power, Hayden has given up most of his," Urd told her. "He will not shift size, nor retreat into your arm. He is, in essence, a pet. But we found him, scraped and bleeding in the Underworld after his fight with the Allfather, and we figured that we might as well return him to his rightful place."

Jayne lay her head on Hayden's warm haunch, let her tears slide off the leather there. *"Are you there?"*

He licked her thumb. *"Do not weep. I am."*

Jayne's heart exploded with joy. "Thank you. I could not treasure a gift more."

"And for you, groom. We have information on your family as well. If you use the key in your hand and open the bottom

328

drawer of your mother's desk in the Domdaniel, you will find papers. Beneath the papers is a false drawer bottom, spelled to look and feel and sound like a real one. Break the spell and you will find the deed to your father's house and the secret of his fate."

Tristan's jaw dropped.

Before he could compose himself, Urd tapped her staff on the ground three times. It made an odd ringing sound. "We are pulled, constantly pulled. We must go back or risk opening the Underworld gate again. But you." She jabbed the staff at Trinity. "It is time, now. You have played in your past, and now you must face your future. We will send you back to your own time."

Trinity's face broke into a big smile. "They are *never* going to believe the time I've had." She turned. "Mama? Père? Looking forward to it. See you in a minute."

A minute for you, twelve years for us. Jayne knelt in front of her daughter. "I look forward to giving you a kiss when we all get there," she said. "Trinity...you saved the world, too. Maybe we never would have done this if not for you."

"She is twelve, do not give her an inflated sense of her own importance," Vivienne said. Trinity stuck her tongue out. "I remember being twelve. I know what I am talking about." Vivienne stuck her tongue out right back.

"We'll miss you every day until we see you again," Tristan said, sweeping Trinity into a fierce hug.

"You'll be way too busy with the baby." Trinity flapped her hand, then danced around the circle—Sofia, Cillian, Ruger. She waved to Amanda, in the distance. Amanda didn't see it.

"Baby? A different baby than you?" Jayne asked.

Trinity grinned and took Urd's outstretched hand. A moment later she and the Norns were gone.

They stood in silence for a moment. "Well," said Ruger at last. "She's got her mother's sense of drama."

Tristan laughed. Jayne barely heard him. "How many children are we supposed to have, exactly?"

He leaned in and touched her lips with his, catching her when her knees gave out. Her heart stuttered but held. He'd always keep its pieces together. When he broke the kiss he nuzzled her ear, making her flush from her cheeks all the way down to beneath the collar of her dress.

"Enough," he murmured. "And we will enjoy the making of them."

"Sorry about that," Amanda said, trudging over the grass toward them. "Ruger, we'd better finish celebrations and get Danilo. Eisner's got intel on the last of Gina's faction. We act fast, we can quash what's left of La Liberté."

"Are you telling me I have to leave the Queen of Dessert's wedding without getting any dessert?" Ruger said.

Amanda snorted. "Of course not. Jayne, Tristan. I hope you're hungry. Follow me."

She led them to—the canteen. Jayne heard Vivienne's little sigh of disappointment behind them and swallowed a laugh. No good coffee for her little sister today.

Or...maybe there would be. As the canteen doors opened, at least a hundred voices shouted, *"SURPRISE!"*

The entire TCO was here. And they'd brought an enormous wedding cake.

They cut the cake as caterers pushed out cart after cart of food from all of Jayne's travels: lamb stew, bouillabaisse, meat pies, Icelandic lobster, Japanese pancakes. She squeezed Tristan's hand. "I can't believe it."

"Not a bad gift from the boss, is it?" He leaned in. "Nor the year's sabbatical. Which I intend to make good use of, by the way."

Jayne giggled. She couldn't remember the last time she'd *giggled*. She turned to Sofia, trying to scrub the blush from her face before she gave up.

Sofia was rubbing her belly. "And when are you going to have that baby?" she said. "I can already tell, mine needs her playmate."

"Enough with the babies," Jayne said with a laugh. But she was too happy to mean it.

EPILOGUE

ONE YEAR LATER

J ayne sat in her chair with her swollen feet up, reading and drinking a glass of ice water. The music of insects droned outside the window. The French summer wasn't as sweltering as the Nashville one, and the old house Tristan had inherited from his father was far enough out in the countryside that they'd escaped much of the city heat. It was glorious. When her belly prevented her from a good night's sleep she could always head out onto the back porch and look up at stars she could never see in the city. It was almost like being back in Late Antiquity Ireland.

Though the reduced mortality rate for pregnant women and running water are two big pluses, she thought.

She was halfway through one of the history books Ruger and Danilo had given her for their wedding, but she'd put that aside in recent days to do a little re-reading. Soon she'd be finished with the works of Terry Pratchett. As long as the baby wasn't early, she could read them all before going into labor.

She heard the familiar buzz of a portal in operation, and a moment later her sister's voice sounded from the kitchen, herding little Morrigan Astraea. Morrigan was just ten months old, an early walker, and insistent on showing off her new superpower.

"Right." Sofia sighed and Jayne heard the sound of groceries thumping on the counter. Sofia insisted on bringing food every time she came to visit them—which was every day, at the moment. She was a terrible mother hen, clucking over her own child and Jayne and Jayne's child in equal measure. "Cillian, did you remember the eggs? And the fresh fish? Tristan was very specific about what kind—"

"Stop, Sof." Cillian laughed. "I remembered it all. Here. I'll put this away, you go say hello to your sister."

Sofia swept into the living room a moment later with Morrigan in her arms. She took one look at Jayne and scowled. "You're laughing at me, too."

"Never." Jayne put her book down and stretched, then rubbed her hands over her belly. The baby was turning, restless. She always turned at the sound of her aunt Sofia's voice. Hayden, who was curled up next to her, looked up, blinking. He seemed supremely annoyed to have been woken from his nap. She rubbed the spot between his eyes and he sank back into a blissful sleep.

"How's the portal?"

"It's finally been approved." Sofia rolled her eyes. "I only had to threaten to quit three times to get it. But honestly, what's a signature on a few pieces of paper?"

It was far more delicate than that. Both the TCO and its French counterpart had to sign off on the approval of a portal for personal use, especially one that wasn't really overseen by any officials aside from the Adepts who were using it. Sofia had become very forceful in persuading authorities that the portal was necessary to transport Jayne to her own doctor and her own hospital the moment she started feeling contractions. It hadn't hurt that Ruger had been promoted to head of the TCO when Amanda had moved to the White House as the official Secretary of Torrent Affairs. His soft spot for Jayne had won them his grudging support and pushed the French into submission, too.

"Uh, Sof?" That was Cillian's sheepish *uh-oh* voice.

Sofia's scowl only grew deeper. "What?"

"I think we forgot the cream."

Sofia opened her mouth, then closed it again. And sighed. "He means *I* forgot the cream," she said. "I did. I don't know, Jayne. How is it so hard to make chowder?"

"We should have just ordered takeout," Jayne said.

"Takeout has too much salt. Too much salt is—"

"Bad for the baby," Jayne finished with her. Sofia had a list of things that were bad for the baby. Jayne was honestly astonished that she'd found any fish at all that fit her exacting standards.

Morrigan reached for Jayne, and Jayne reached back. "I'll just pop back for the cream," Cillian said. He smiled at the sight of Morrigan, drumming her chubby palms on Jayne's watermelon belly.

"I'll do it. I'm faster." Sofia gave him a quick peck.

"American grocery stores," he grumbled by way of explanation.

He took up a seat in a wicker chair next to Jayne and stretched out his feet. Morrigan cooed at him; he laughed and cooed back.

"Ten months and already walking! Can you believe it?" he boasted. He smiled wider than Jayne had ever seen him smile, even before the baby. Fatherhood suited him. His big arms screamed protection and his face was always set in a gentle-giant expression, softened permanently by Sofia and Morrigan.

"I can't believe it." Jayne took a sip of water and arched her eyebrow. "Tell me again. In fact, I'm pretty sure there are some lost souls in the wilderness of New Zealand that haven't heard it—"

Cillian laughed, and she broke off, laughing, too. "There's the girl I used to know and love," he said.

They were silent for a few moments. Jayne ran her thumb over the top of Hayden's head. *Used to know.* True enough; Cillian had years on her now, working hard in the Aegis Time Catch. Learning more about who and what he was. And Jayne had learned more about herself, too. Someone who'd seen the cost of saving the world and paid it.

She'd never imagined how lucky she could be.

His thoughts seemed to be running parallel. "I never thanked you for saving my life," he said quietly.

"You must have saved mine at least as many times," Jayne replied.

"I'm not talking about battles, Jayne." Cillian reached out and stroked Morrigan's cheek. She turned and gnawed on his finger with great enthusiasm. "Before you, I had nothing. No power, no sense of right and wrong, no love, no family. If I hadn't met you, I'd have died young doing something stupid. Or become a Rogue slave to the Kingdom. But instead, I'm here. With Sofia and Morrigan, with all the Aegis kids... The young me couldn't have imagined what I'd become." He chuckled. "Not sure he'd have liked it, either. But we live and we wise up, don't we?"

"We do." Jayne knew what he meant. Before learning of the Torrent, she would have done anything to be a Master of it. She would have wondered if life was worth living, for one who'd been so strong to then have such magic taken away from her. But now, life was...beautiful. It was just the way she wanted it.

Tristan's rickety bicycle rattled up the gravel drive just as Sofia came back, crowing triumphantly with cream in hand. Jayne watched him from the window. He dismounted and pulled a box out of the basket on the front of the bike. He caught her eye and grinned rakishly, waggling the box. Jayne felt the baby kick. She liked sweets just as much as her mother, it seemed.

"I'm going to make some tea," Sofia called, and Jayne groaned. No caffeine for the pregnant lady, and everyone was intent on making her follow that rule. "Stop whining. I lived through the experience, and you will, too."

Morrigan squealed when Tristan unlocked the front door. He bent down to kiss the top of her head, then opened the cardboard box in his arms. Twelve perfect eclairs nestled in frilly paper wrappings. Cillian retrieved Morrigan before she could smash her fingers into them, snagging one deftly as he passed.

"No pie?" Jayne joked. She asked that question at least once a day, whenever Tristan returned from the little village nearby.

Tristan pressed his forehead to hers and caught her lower lip in a quick, fierce kiss. "You are too sweet for pie." Then he dipped his head and pressed his cheek against her belly. The baby kicked again and he laughed. "She loves me," he declared.

"Of course she loves you." Jayne tried to lean in to kiss him at the top of his ear, but her belly got in the way. Hayden put his tiny gray claws on Tristan's head and licked at his hair with a forked tongue. Then he made a face, scrambled up to Jayne's shoulder, and settled in, purring.

Sofia came in with the tea and some water for Jayne and took an éclair. She sighed blissfully at the first bite, then accepted the latter half of Cillian's when he'd had enough. In the silence, she nodded at the history book next to Jayne. "Any insights?" she said.

"Tons," said Jayne. "Nothing about Masters being busted back down to Adepts, though. Or non-Adept, either."

"You heard what Urd said, though. You gave up *most* of your powers. Not *all*. I just can't understand why you can't do any magic anymore."

"Maybe it just needed a break?"

Sofia wrinkled her nose. "Maybe you used so much at once, you needed a little healing period. Have you tried anything recently?"

Jayne rolled her eyes, but only in her mind. Sofia was always clucking about Jayne's loss of powers, as though Jayne had lost all reason to live along with them. She'd even confessed, once, that she'd wished it were her instead. Even with her own kid to look after, she had to make sure she was looking after Jayne.

Jayne lifted her hand and closed her eyes and reached for the Torrent. She could see it, if she concentrated, flowing near her. Her fingers moved in a simple Grow spell. She opened her eyes and thrust—

A handful of green sparks shot from her hand in a sound like a defunct Christmas cracker. Sofia jumped. Jayne laughed.

"Alas. No power for me yet. I'm fine, Sof," she said, and patted her belly. "I'm saving up the magic for the baby."

Sofia looked like she was trying not to cry on Jayne's behalf. "It just...it did used to be everything to you. You can talk to us, you know?"

"I know." Jayne smiled. "I have a new everything now." She took Tristan's hand and placed it over her belly. At his touch, a tingle shot through her, like a live wire, growing stronger by the second. She tasted starlight, and her eyes swam for a moment. With her next breath, she was surrounded by glowing green stars. It was so much like the first time she'd accessed the Torrent that she gasped aloud. It was everywhere. Even Hayden's head rose to take in the sight.

As quick as it came, it was gone. The living room went back to normal. No river of stars, or glowing green air. But unlike that first day in the Vanderbilt archives, she knew she wasn't imagining things.

"*Is our magic coming back?*" she asked her familiar.

"*It is indeed,*" Hayden replied, settling back in with a purr. "*But do not rush. You have time.*"

Tristan lifted his hand to her cheek. "Jayne? What's wrong? You just tuned out on me."

"Did you feel that?" she asked.

"The static electricity? Yes, but I didn't mean to shock you. I'm sorry."

She grinned at her husband. "Do it again."

From that moment, Jayne knew the Torrent was never far away. Sofia was right, whatever strange organ of magic she'd burnt out while saving the world was healing, rebuilding. She saw more of the Torrent every day, especially out of the corner of her eye. And when she dreamed, she felt formidable indeed, racing across the Earth and sometimes even matching powers, momentarily, with the goddesses. And every time it happened, she awoke filled with anticipation. The Torrent was out there, and it was waiting. Soon enough, it would call her home again.

And until then, life was perfect.

THE END

Dearest Reader,

Thank you for going on this incredible journey with me. Jayne Thorne and her magical world—friends, family, coworkers, even enemies—have become a part of my very soul, and I hate to be parted from them.

Alas, as was foretold many years ago by the Norns, this story marks the end of the Jayne Thorne, CIA Librarian series.

At least... for now. As we all know, magic works in mysterious ways and sometimes, we can change our fate.

Until we meet again, may the road rise up to meet you.

Blessed Be,
Joss 🤍

ACKNOWLEDGMENTS

First, to Claire Bartlett, who stepped in to help me get the series to the finish line. I know how hard it is to take someone else's vision and create a world, and I am so glad we were able to have such an excellent collaboration! I couldn't have created this story without your ability to interpret my ideas. Two brains make one whole.

Alisha Klapheke—thank you for helping me dream up the Torrent all those years ago!

Thank yous to the usual suspects: my agents, Laura Blake Peterson and James Farrell; Erin Moon and the fine folks at Tantor Audio; Kim Killion; Phyllis DeBlanche; and notably, Jennifer Jakes—who vehemently opposed the planned ending of this book and made such a great case I had to reconsider and rewrite the whole thing. I am SO glad you argued for magic!

Thanks to the fine folks at Ingram and Amazon, for all the help over the years getting these books into your hands. And my friends at Poisoned Pen, Murder by the Book, and Parnassus Books have supported this series from the get-go. You're the best! And thanks to you sweet librarians who help get Jayne into the world, too.

Laura Benedict, Ariel Lawhon, Lisa Patton, Patti Callahan Henry, Paige Crutcher, Jayne Ann Krentz, and Barbara Peters— incredible supporters, all. Sherrie, Joan, Erin, Sara, Brandee, Chad, and Carol: thank you for loving Jayne as much as I do.

Deepest thanks to my parents for their incessant support and my dad for his love of the uncanny.

My darling husband, without whom magic would not exist. *Je t'adore!*

And lastly—the most important thanks go to you, my dearest reader. You glorious creature. You have cheered me on for years and rooted for Jayne and crew, and I will forever be in your debt for your kindness and support for this entire series.

About Joss Walker

Photo credit: KidTee Hello Photography

Joss Walker is an award-winning fantasy author and the alter ego of *New York Times* bestselling thriller author J.T. Ellison. Through her fantasy works, Joss delves into her passion for the genre and crafts stories of extraordinary women discovering their power in the world.

With the creation of Jayne Thorne, CIA Librarian, Joss has developed a captivating contemporary fantasy series that appeals to lovers of books, libraries, romance, and, of course, magic.

For more, visit josswalker.com or follow her online.

ABOUT TWO TALES PRESS

Two Tales Press is an independent publishing house featuring crime fiction, suspense, and fantasy novels, novellas, and anthologies written and edited by *New York Times* bestselling author J.T. Ellison, including the Jayne Thorne, CIA Librarian series under J.T.'s fantasy pen name, Joss Walker.

To view all of our titles, please visit

www.twotalespress.com

www.ingramcontent.com/pod-product-compliance
Lightning Source LLC
Chambersburg PA
CBHW021241190726
48289CB00005B/1433